HAVILAH'S GOLD

The Genesine Chronicles

JAMIE SEWELL RODRIGUEZ MA

By Him, through Him, for Him

S.D.G.

LUCIDBOOKS

For Efrain
You are the music to my words.

Contents

Acknowledgments

With many thanks . . .

To Efrain, the love of my life and my soul's companion. You never doubted this day would come—not once. You made this project possible from start to finish. I love you forever.

To Grace, my loyal friend through thick and thin. You have put up with me all these years. You deserve a medal, but you'll have to settle for sharing a birthday with Corrie.

To Anneka, Conner, and Liam. You grew up with a sibling you never knew. Mom is finally finished. I love you all more than life itself. This book is for you, Stefanie, and Hannah. Special thanks to Anneka for always being my first (and favorite) editor.

To Mom. You prayed for me from the time I was born and all through this project. I love you to the moon and back.

To Janet and Sofia, the sisters of my heart. Where would I be without you? Thank you for your unending love and support. I love you both so much.

To the Rodriguezes, Piedras, Greens, and Blackmons. You are my joy in good times and tough times. You show me every day that family is quite a beautiful thing. I love you all.

To Jimmy (you will always be my Jimmy). This certainly would not have happened without you. There is not a better big brother on the planet. I love you.

To the Sanchezes. Thank you for your love and prayers through all that life brings our way. So thankful God brought us all together.

To Kellie, Sonjia, and Jenny for your help, prayers, encouragement, and sweet friendship.

To Nathan, my super editor. You gave your time, effort, and expertise, and taught me the value of the Oxford comma. I sincerely hope you are *finally* satisfied. You are the best.

To Chris because you were the first person outside my family to make me believe this thing could be a real story. You and Joleen have loved and supported our family beyond what I could ever dream possible. Thank you from the bottom of my heart.

To Margaret, my friend, colleague, sister in Jesus, artist extraordinaire, and fellow warrior who will likely do jail time with me some day (haha). I will always be grateful beyond words.

To Lawrence for your wise counsel and endless support on this journey. I am so grateful to call you my friend.

To Mike for bringing the artistic vision to life. I am truly the grateful and undeserving recipient of your amazing talents and sacrificial effort.

To Janette who brings a smile of joy to my soul. I can always hear your laugh in my head. You have prayed for me on a depth that few have known to go. With love always from your introverted hermit neighbor.

To Aunt Jan, my favorite aunt because you are the best. I will always cherish your "Go for it!" spirit on my behalf.

To Leianna for your patience and skill. I can't wait to see what God does with your amazing talent.

To the incredible Lucid team. I so appreciate your commitment to excellence and your astounding patience with all my questions and concerns. Let's do it all again!

To all my family and friends, the JAMS, the staff and family of Benchmark Bible Church, the amazing Benchmark Media Group team—thank you for your love prayers, help, and support.

Guide to the Realms

Seventh Heaven
Holy Throne Room of God

Paradise
Heavenly home of the saints, state of eternal bliss

The Meridiem
The Courts of Justice, the outer limit where demons and unredeemed
souls may pass

The Shamayim (the Air)
The unseen realm surrounding the inhabitants of Earth and
spiritual battleground of angels and demons

Erets
Earth, the habitation and physical realm of man and beast

Sheol
Dwelling place of the dead

The Abyss
Bottomless pit of eternal torment

Prologue

The wind whistled through the cracks in the old shed, rattling the metal roof. It was cold. John Tobias didn't care. He bent over the plywood board in front of him and gripped a block of wood wrapped in a sheet of sandpaper. Sweat dripped off his chin and onto a pile of sawdust collecting on the floor around his boots. Small puffs of steam rose in the night air toward the lantern hanging on a nail above him as he sanded every inch of the board to smooth perfection.

John worked quickly, stopping every now and then to blow clouds of dust away and feel the sanded surface beneath his leathered hands. He ignored the ache in his back and the blister on his thumb. John had surrendered himself to the rhythmic swishing of sandpaper moving across the board so fully that he did not hear the footsteps coming toward him in the dark.

The shed door swung open and slammed against the outside wall. Though John never looked up from his work, he already knew that the figure in front of him stood with her hands on her hips. She had appeared in the doorway just like that for nearly 50 years, and it was always the same question. "What in the Sam Hill are you doing out here at this time of night?"

Usually, the sound of John's Manhattan-born wife speaking Southern idioms made him smile. "They're on their way," she said briskly as she turned on her heel and marched back through the yard toward the house. She had left the shed door open, clearly expecting John to follow her.

Setting down his sanding block, he watched her go, wringing her hands in her apron all the way.

John waited until Rose had disappeared into the house. Then he reached under a stack of boards and pulled out a package wrapped in brown paper. He glanced one last time toward the door and then unwrapped the small, black, leather book. He held it for a moment, feeling its weight between his hands. There sure had been a lot of fuss about such a small thing. *Against policies of public safety,* John muttered to himself, quoting the letter they had received from the office of the newly appointed governor. *Hmph.* He didn't know what was so dangerous about a book, but something compelled him to keep it. This book would not be destroyed with everything else the state decided was against policies of public safety. Enough was enough. He would build something to hide it in plain sight.

Safety officers had already searched John and Rose's property earlier that year. John had watched them ransack the house and then search the barn as if they—John and Rose Tobias, law-abiding citizens of this town for decades—were common criminals. The officers hunted for extra rations like hungry wolves. They looked for eggs, cheese, meat—anything beyond the allotted amount per household that would result in either a hefty fine or jail time, depending on the weather and the officers' moods on any given day. They tore up floorboards and searched closets, hunting for hidden guns and ammunition. John wondered what he would have told Rose if he'd been dragged away and thrown in jail, all for a book.

John measured the thickness of the book between his thumb and forefinger and then laid it down on the perfectly sanded board in front of him. Taking a pencil from his shirt pocket, he traced around the four sides of the cover. The board was only a quarter inch thicker than the book. If he was going to construct a secret compartment, every cut of the saw would have to be precise or he would cut right through the wood.

John stared at the book sitting right out in the open for anyone to see. He reminded himself that walls don't have eyes. No one else was there. He drew in a breath and blew it out slowly as he dropped his shoulders. The cricket that had been chirping in the corner of the shed was suddenly still. John sat in the eerie silence, listening. The night the officers came, he had slipped the book under the stack of boards so quickly that they could have easily found it if they had looked. They walked right past the dilapidated old shed as if it wasn't even there. Maybe they never suspected people would hide anything valuable in an old tool shed, or maybe something else had happened, something John still could not explain.

He stared into the silence until the October wind tickled the back of his neck and sent a cold shiver down his spine. He would wait to make the cuts in the wood until after he had a chance to sharpen the blade. He tucked the book safely back under the boards just as the screen door squeaked open and the frantic shouts of his wife pierced the crisp night air.

"They're here, John! They're here!"

Sure enough, John heard the unmistakable crunch of gravel on the front driveway. The car skidded to a sudden stop. *One, two, three, four,* he counted. Four car doors opened, but only three slammed shut. He bolted the shed door, snapped the padlock in place, and then quickened his pace toward the house. Taking a deep breath, he squared his shoulders and stepped inside.

Chapter 1

The Live Oak Tree

On the 15th day of June at precisely 10:59 in the morning, it was already 90 degrees in the shade without the slightest hint of a breeze. But the old live oak on the banks of Miller's Pond clearly and unmistakably *shivered*. There was not a cat stuck in the tree disturbing the leaves, and there were no squirrels leaping among the branches to cause such a stir. There were no birds nesting in its boughs. Even the cicadas, normally buzzing their serenades of summer, were unusually silent. Then, as if one occurrence were not odd enough, the leaves trembled a second time and again were still. The third time, the whole tree quivered and quaked as though a gust of wind had blown through the meadow, and yet there was no wind. Anyone observing the scene would have agreed that the tree moved of its own accord, though such a thing was not possible, not even for a live oak tree. Seeing is believing unless the two are worlds apart. What caused the tree to shiver on its own had nothing to do with the tree or even the natural world it resided in. On that hot summer morning, three visitors arrived at the live oak tree by Miller's Pond and perched on the topmost branch.

To anyone able to see them, they might have been mistaken for three large birds sitting among the leaves, but they were distinctly human. They were dressed in fine clothing suitable for a holiday party. The lady sitting closest to the trunk of the tree wore a fine linen tunic of royal blue that was tailored to her lean, angular frame. Her slippers were simple and unadorned, nearly matching the color of her olive skin. Her dark hair was swept up into a neat fold on the back of her head. She was elegant and graceful, and her lean figure suggested the build of a dancer. She sat perfectly straight on the tree branch as if she did so often and was quite comfortable there.

The gentleman beside her wore a navy pinstripe suit with gold buttons and a smart, white, linen shirt, impeccably clean and perfectly ironed. His tie was a beautiful red and gold brocade. A matching handkerchief peeked out from the left pocket. His hair, combed neatly back, had a touch of gray at the temples, as well as scattered throughout his bushy eyebrows, giving him a distinguished look. He sat with his arms folded and his jaw set. The latest arrival, seated on the far end of the tree branch, was a woman dressed in a vivid purple evening gown and matching pumps. A colorful hat in shades of fuchsia and lime green with a generous spray of purple feathers adorned her mop of blonde curls. This one looked the most like a large, tropical bird roosting among the leaves. She shifted herself on the branch to adjust her dress, causing the tree to shake all over again.

"Evangeline, could you please sit still?" said the woman in blue.

"I'm sorry, Prudence. I've just never been on a mission before," Evangeline replied. She folded her hands in her lap for a moment but soon began swinging her legs wildly. Her companions bobbed up and down with the bouncing branch.

"I understand, but you are going to kick your shoes off," Prudence said. Prudence had been sitting quietly with her chin slightly raised in the air as if sniffing the breeze or listening to something in the distance. Then she turned toward the gentleman sitting between them.

"Have you received the mission directive yet, Horatius?"

Horatius, who had been studying the landscape and the skies around them, reached into his pocket and took out a small scroll that was about the length of his hand. He unrolled it carefully, his eyes scanning the ivory parchment.

"Yes, just now it seems," he said, as gold letters shimmered on the open scroll. He cleared his throat and read it aloud.

> *I, Gamalieus, Archangel of the Seventh Command, do hereby commission Horatius Simon Portuno, Prudence Ophelia Jane Helfgott, and Evangeline Esther Bloom to the live oak tree beside Miller's Pond, Seventh Region, Fourth Quadrant, 183rd Sector for the following tasks:*
>
> *Horatius Simon Portuno: Prepare the Way*
>
> *Prudence Ophelia Jane Helfgott: Close the Gate*
>
> *Evangeline Esther Bloom: Hold the Line*

"Any questions?" Horatius asked, rolling up the scroll and tucking it back in his pocket.

"Oh! That is delightful," Evangeline said cheerfully. All right, then. I will hold the line. Yes, that will be just fine." Evangeline had stopped swinging her feet. Her eyebrows were furrowed. Prudence and Horatius both turned to face her.

"What exactly does that mean? Exactly?" Evangeline asked.

"Discovering the meaning of your task is inherent to the mission, Evangeline," Horatius explained, showing the slightest hint of a smile though his eyes were intense. Prudence nodded in agreement.

"Oh," Evangeline replied quietly, biting her lip. "Well, when do we begin?"

"That shall also be made apparent when the time has come," Horatius answered and resumed his study of the land and skies with a scowl of concentration. Prudence folded her arms and closed her eyes as if in repose.

"Oh, all right then," Evangeline said with a loud sigh, resuming her leg swinging. Her silence was short-lived, however. A moment later she burst out, "If we are just waiting, then why did we need to be here *now*?

There is nothing happening," Evangeline pleaded, gesticulating with both hands outstretched.

"Evangeline, dear," Prudence began. "We are not merely waiting. We are watching and listening. This is part of our mission as witnesses here as well, so it is my recommendation that you act accordingly. And do stop swinging your legs because you are going to kick off your shoes."

"Well, I see trees, a pond, some grass, a few cows, nothing more," Evangeline observed, her frown wrinkling her nose. "And where is the color? Why is everything so gray?"

"It only looks gray because our eyes are used to far more brilliant colors and more colors that don't exist here anymore," Prudence explained. "But what else? Look closer, listen more deeply," she added, watching Evangeline with expectant scrutiny.

Evangeline glanced all around. She pursed her lips and squinted her eyes. She turned herself completely around on the tree branch and back again. She frowned and sighed, fussed and fumed a bit more, and then drew a breath to speak again when suddenly her eyes flew wide open.

"Is that—?" she gasped.

"Yes," Prudence answered, nodding solemnly. "The groan. Creation is weary," she said, patting the branch of the old live oak. "This old tree has known some secrets. They all have."

"I had heard about the groaning of Earth but had not until now—." Evangeline's voice drifted into silence. Her shoulders slumped. Her feet remained still.

"A lot has changed since we were citizens here," Horatius added after a few moments had passed, though his eyes had never stopped roaming.

"And yet the strangest thing about this century is that it looks quite a bit like ours. Have you noticed?" asked Prudence.

"Not completely," Horatius said, motioning toward the towers nearby with tall spires jutting upward into the skyline. "They use them for communication, information exchange, and such, or at least they used to."

"True, but the people, the gardens, the rations!" Prudence exclaimed.

"Yes," Horatius agreed. "And things are only slightly better here than in much of the world. There are places where the droughts are continuing without any sign of reprieve. Famine, disease, war—." His voice trailed off. "It won't be much longer," he said at last.

"I agree," Prudence affirmed. "There seems to be another level of excitement at every feast. It cannot be too much longer now indeed."

"What a day that'll be," Evangeline sighed in agreement.

"Circumstances will get worse before they get better," Horatius reminded them.

"Marvelous opportunity for the churches, I imagine," Evangeline offered.

Prudence shook her head silently.

Horatius explained, "The churches are no more, at least the church buildings. They've been either burned in the riots or converted into community centers. All public readings of the Scriptures were banned several years ago. In fact, the only legal form of Bible readings is from what they call *The Inspiration Series*, a compilation of acceptable texts from all religions."

"Acceptable?" Evangeline scoffed. "Whatever does that mean?"

"It means whatever does not create sides," Horatius replied. "The Scriptures are not known for promoting world peace, you know, at least not the way the world wants it."

"And what of the remnant?" Evangeline asked.

"It was the Remnant who caused the wars," said Horatius, and Evangeline nearly fell off the branch. "Or so they say," he added.

"What he means," said Prudence, glancing at Horatius with a stern frown, "is the political group of zealots who call themselves the Remnant, not the remnant of the faithful."

"True," said Horatius. "As it turns out, the political zealots resemble nothing of the faithful, although they have committed atrocities of violence, claiming to be the same. Oh, it has been quite a debacle. I'm sure you can imagine who is behind all this, while the true remnant has gone underground—those who were not imprisoned, that is."

They lapsed into silence again, contemplating the current nature of life on Earth, except for Evangeline. She sat with one hand gripping the branch and the other covering her eyes as she muttered to herself about what the world had become. That went on for several minutes when suddenly she hollered, "Why is it so bloomin' *hot*?" She sat up and began swinging her legs again and fanning herself with her hat.

"Because this is Texas, Evangeline," Horatius answered, and the slightest smile wrinkled the corners of his eyes. "We are close enough to the veil to experience the climate of this region."

Prudence turned to Evangeline, whose legs and arms were now pumping wildly, and opened her mouth to speak. But at that moment, a bright, purple object went sailing through the air and landed in the pond below with a splash. Evangeline gasped as her shoe floated on the surface momentarily and then sank into the brown water. The turtle that had been sunning itself on the rock turned around and disappeared in the murky depths as well. Evangeline's eyes widened, her mouth agape as she turned slowly toward Horatius and Prudence.

"I suppose I should have stopped swinging my legs," Evangeline said sheepishly. Then she chuckled to herself as she wiggled her toes, now free of their confinement.

"Will they see it, Horatius?" Prudence asked.

"We are still outside the veil of the third realm. No one here *should* be able to see it unless—." Horatius was suddenly quiet, for they were interrupted by a rustling in the bushes near the barbed wire fence.

"A bicycle. Right over there," Prudence said, pointing to a space in the bushes on the other side of the fence.

"I see it," Horatius nodded.

"Oh, how exciting!" Evangeline squealed.

They watched intently as a child wriggled out from the bushes. She was a little girl who looked to be about 10 or 11 years old. She glanced in both directions and then sprinted across the meadow. Her chestnut brown hair, pulled loosely back into a ponytail, whipped in the breeze as she ran toward the pond—and toward *them*. She had a small bundle in her hand that she dropped into a hollow at the base of the live oak tree. Then she sat on the bank, pulled off her socks and shoes, and dipped her feet in the water. She lay back on the grassy bank, fingers laced behind her head, and stared up into the branches of the great old tree with a contented smile.

"Isn't she just precious?" Evangeline cooed. "Is she the reason we are here? What's her name?"

"Right on time," Horatius answered, glancing at his pocket watch. "Her name is Corrie—Cornelia Rose Callahan, to be precise. She is 12 years old as of June 5th, just 10 days ago."

"You knew?" Prudence asked, her eyebrows raised almost imperceptibly.

"Yes, but I was not permitted to speak the details of it until she actually appeared," Horatius replied.

"Twelve? Tiny little sparrow, isn't she?" Evangeline said, still staring down at Corrie.

"What else do you know about her, Horatius?" Prudence queried.

"According to the pre-mission briefing, she is the youngest of three, with two older brothers. They live with their grandmother, having been brought there by their mother after their father died. It . . . it hasn't been easy for Corrie," Horatius said.

"And yet she smiles," said Evangeline, looking down at her tenderly.

The three of them sat in the tree, watching as Corrie stared up into the branches, singing quietly to herself. Suddenly, however, Corrie stopped singing and seemed to stare straight at them.

"Horatius, are you *sure* she can't see us?" Prudence whispered from the side of her mouth.

"She sure looks like she does, doesn't she, Pru?" Evangeline didn't bother to lower her voice.

Horatius didn't respond but stared down at Corrie with a puzzled expression on his face.

"Evangeline, drop your other shoe," Horatius whispered. His eyes were still fixed on Corrie.

Evangeline nodded vigorously and pulled off her other shoe. She held it over Corrie and let it slip from her fingers, but Prudence snatched it mid-air with one hand and held her finger to her lips with the other. Below them, Corrie stood, still staring up into the branches. The trio sat motionless, waiting to see if there was any sign of her having seen them. Corrie finally looked away when a butterfly brushed past her.

"If for some reason she can, indeed, see us—even our shadows—what would she make of a shoe falling down on her face?" Prudence wondered aloud. "That would not be the way to introduce her to the next realm, now, would it?"

"My curiosity got the better of me," Horatius admitted. "I've been noticing some strange things on missions lately, you see. But nevertheless, good thinking, Prudence. Good thinking indeed."

"But what if she really did see us? What does that *mean*?" Evangeline asked, gesticulating wildly with her purple shoe in one hand, for Prudence had passed it back to her.

Horatius did not respond but sat quietly, massaging his forehead. Whether Corrie had seen or heard even the slightest hint of their presence was a question that would remain unanswered for the time being; she had slipped quietly off the bank for a swim in the pond.

"It would mean that this will be a mission like no other," Horatius replied at last.

Chapter 2
The Treasure

Corrie slipped through the warm, shimmering surface of the pond into the cooler depths below. This was her solace, her kingdom. She flipped her feet behind her like a mermaid's tail and plunged downward. She glided along the bottom, stirring the wet earth with her fingertips. An old tire lodged into the muddy floor of her castle made the perfect throne. Exhaling deliberately, Corrie waved her arms upward and seated herself in a flurry of bubbles. She was queen of the mermaids, and no one could tell her otherwise. In her watery palace with the sky above and the earth beneath, time held its breath in reverent pause. Corrie closed her eyes, enveloped in the comforting cushion of silence.

When her lungs burned for air, Corrie kicked up from the bottom and broke the surface with a loud gasp. She drew a breath and plunged back down. This time, she flipped under water, planted her feet in the mud, and pushed off hard, swimming straight for the surface like a dolphin launching into the air. She clapped her arms over her head and dived down again, flipping and turning through imaginary hoops and obstacles. There was no better place in the summertime than Miller's Pond—no better place in the world.

The only problem with Miller's Pond was simply that it belonged to the Millers. Like most families in Bellam, they had lived there for several generations. Bellam was originally a farming community, established in the late 1800s. While the town had weathered the years of hardship with the rest of the country, it had never really changed that much. It was still a small town where everyone knew everyone else's business. The pond used to be a great fishing hole, but it had been emptied of fish long ago. When the Miller kids still lived at home, they brought their friends there to fish or swim and toast marshmallows over a campfire. But they were gone long before Corrie and her brothers arrived in Bellam four years ago to live with Gran and Papaw. Corrie often wondered what would happen if Mr. or Mrs. Miller caught her swimming in their pond, but she did not worry about it that much. The Millers had been friends with the Tobias family years ago, or at least Corrie thought that was true based on the way Gran talked about them. Gran had never had the Millers over for dinner or anything, but she didn't socialize much outside of her knitting circle. Besides, it wasn't like Corrie broke anything or stole something from them. No, the biggest worry was not the Millers; it was Gran.

Rose Tobias was an anxious soul. She would get something stuck in her craw and yammer for days about it to anyone within earshot. Corrie and her two brothers tried their best to stay upwind of her at all times. The old Tobias house where their mother grew up had bars on all the windows and doors. Many houses did these days, but Gran went above and beyond and had bars put on the upstairs windows too. She had rules about getting up in the morning and going to bed at night. There was a rule about opening the oven door when the biscuits were rising and about closing the bathroom door when it rained. There were rules about chores too. On laundry day the kids had to fold their underwear and iron their socks. If they missed wash day when their neighborhood had electricity, they had to hang all their clothes on the line, beat them to soften them up, and then bring them in to fold and iron them. The most important rule, however, was to never leave the house without permission. The kids all knew what that really meant. You didn't leave the house ever, for any reason except to go to school, because Gran never gave permission. So summers for the Callahan children were an extended prison sentence.

There are ways around anything, however. Corrie and her brother Collin were the masters of escape. For them, every rule was just an opportunity to find a way to break it without getting caught. Each game was a delicious challenge worthy of the most careful plotting, which they did without a hint of remorse. "If there is a Collin, there's a way," Corrie always said of her second-oldest brother. Will, the oldest, was useless in that regard. He never did anything wrong. If he wanted to spend his whole summer cooped up in the house with Gran, they figured it was his business, but Collin had worked out a little insurance for his and Corrie's secret adventures. He threatened to destroy Will's entire rare coin collection if he told on them. That had worked without a hitch up to this point.

Corrie's trips to the pond were brilliant and elaborate schemes timed to perfection. Just after lunch, Gran would sit down in her favorite chair by the window that overlooked the garden. She would read a little while or start a few stitches of needlepoint, and then slowly her head would start to bob. Her chin would droop to her chest and then suddenly bounce back up like a yo-yo. Corrie counted each time her head drooped. By about the fifth time, Gran would be snoring, which meant about an hour of glorious freedom. Corrie would tip-toe quietly up the stairs, carefully skipping the creaky fourth step, and make her way to the small attic room at the end of the carpeted hallway. The door was smaller than the others and had an antique glass doorknob. The kids were not allowed in that room (rule number 998 that she and Collin had been pleased to break), probably because Gran kept all kinds of old things in there— clothes, boxes of shoes, an antique sewing machine, and beautifully crafted pieces of wood furniture that Papaw had made—things that were special to Gran and no one else. Most interesting to Corrie were the boxes of photos Gran kept of their mother, framed photos of her as a child and as a teen. Corrie had pored over each of them in minute detail. She knew every pose, each pair of shoes her mother had worn, and every stray curl. There were stacks of these framed photos, even several of their entire family throughout the years, just collecting dust. Corrie wanted so much to ask why none were hung on the walls, but her fear of being discovered sneaking into the attic outweighed her curiosity. The door remained locked with a world of history and memories ensconced within.

The key was somewhere in Gran's dresser. That much Corrie knew from sneaking behind her one day as she came out of the attic room and put the key away. But it didn't matter. Corrie didn't need a key. She had Collin who had a unique skill. He could pick any lock ever made, and he had taught Corrie his ways.

The attic room was the ideal escape route for two reasons. First, it had a small window that opened to a giant elm tree that was older than Gran herself, so the branches were thick and sturdy. Collin had taught Corrie to crawl out the window, grab hold of the closest branch, and shinny down the trunk. Corrie kept her bike hidden behind a bush just under Collin's bedroom window for easy access. Gran never noticed the bike, but she also never had any reason to walk around to that side of the house. The attic room was also perfect for another reason. Its small window was the only one in the whole house without bars. Gran had tried years before to have bars installed over it, but there was something about the construction of the house around that small, oddly shaped window that would have required specially ordered parts, and Gran could not afford it. So she simply locked the door, which confirmed to all the Callahan children what they had suspected all along—the bars were not to keep bad people out but to keep grandchildren in.

Corrie, Collin, and Will had climbed out that window many times over the past few years to go on numerous adventures. Corrie owed Collin so much. Besides swimming at the pond, they caught minnows or frogs at the creek. Sometimes at night after Gran went to bed, they snuck out and caught lightning bugs. Or they would just lie in the grass and stare up at the stars—anything to get out of the house.

At first, it was just the three siblings in the house with Gran and Papaw. They didn't have any friends when they first moved to Bellam, but they had one another, and that was enough. They were close friends as much as they were siblings. Then things changed. Will didn't want to make up games anymore. He stopped catching lightning bugs with them. He said it was because he was too big to crawl through the window. Corrie knew that was a lie because even back then, Collin was bigger than Will. But Will became interested in other things. He studied a lot, even in the summer. He brought home page after page of perfect this and A+ that, which Gran hung proudly on the fridge. One day a letter arrived saying Will had won a scholarship to the university. Corrie understood then that Will had never stopped trying to escape; he just did it in a different way. The coming school year would be his last with them. Soon he would be on the other side of those bars for good.

Collin had become sullen. Corrie didn't know if he was just mad at Will, if he was mad at the world, or if this was what growing up looked like on him. It was a sudden change, one she hadn't expected. He didn't stop his nightly adventures; they just weren't with her anymore. Corrie followed him one night all the way into town. She had crept through the darkness, well behind him and four of his friends. And there was also a girl. She was all giggly, walking really close to Collin and laughing about stupid things. Then she took Collin's jacket right off of him, and he let her. It was disgusting. Corrie never brought it up to Collin. He would never forgive her for spying on him.

Collin had a need for independence. He had always been that way. But those friends of his didn't know Collin like Corrie did, which brought her a measure of comfort through his recent moods. She kept these thoughts to herself like a splinter that she figured would work its own way out. She would be patient. The Callahans had been through a lot and had always stuck together. They were close in their own way, she reminded herself often. Their adventures together were some of Corrie's favorite memories, the best she had since coming to live with Gran 1,460 days ago.

It had seemed like a very large number when Corrie scrawled it that morning in her journal, an old spiral notebook she kept hidden in the small space between her dresser and bookcase. Each morning, she wrote a new number for a new day on the page. Every evening she wrote at least a couple of sentences about what happened that day—just the highlights. She had begun writing when she was only eight. Most days it was something like this:

Day 45   I had sinnaman tost. It wuz good.
Day #285   Randee Jinnings sat on my sience project.
            he smells like beens.

There were some days she preferred to not write in her journal at all, like the day Stacy said loud enough for the whole class to hear that Corrie got her clothes from the dumpster. And there was the day that Ahmad pushed Corrie down the stairs, and the teacher blamed her for tripping. The neighbor's cat, Checkers, had wandered into her yard on Day #347 and pooped in her favorite flower bed. Corrie had been waiting and waiting for the lilies to bloom, and when she went out to check on them one morning after breakfast, there was Checkers in her flower bed, taking care of business with no shame whatsoever. She snuck up behind him and shoved him hard with the toe of her boot. "Go on! Git!" Corrie yelled. Checkers let out such an awful screech that Corrie was afraid she'd hurt him, but the poor thing just scrambled to his feet and ran off. She felt so bad about it later that she set a bowl of milk out by the garage, but Checkers never came back.

The hardest day to write down more than any other, however, was Day #445. She could hardly bear to scratch out the words on the page, but she had made a promise that she would record the important things every day. So she wrote.

Day #445 Papaw died today. I miss him already.

That day had started like any other, which is the whole trick of it all. That day she was out picking vegetables with Papaw like she always did when he stopped and quietly knelt down between the rows of corn and okra. "Go get your grandmother," he said weakly in almost a whisper. Corrie tried to run into the house, scream for help, or do something, but her feet were planted on the ground, frozen in place. Papaw grabbed at his chest and gasped for air, and then he lay down like he just decided to take a nap in the dirt right then and there. The sunshine, the blue sky, all those rows of corn and okra that Papaw had planted just days ago all tricked her into thinking nothing had changed. It seemed as if any second now he would sit up and say, "How 'bout we go in the house and get us a cold drink?" It was not the first time she had witnessed her whole life turning on a dime and did nothing to stop it. But it was the first time she had looked at death square in the face and understood just how thin the line is between living and dying. She understood it so deep inside that it rattled her very bones.

That was the first day she wondered about it all—how people were born and how people died, how the corn began as a tiny seed and then grew to a tall stalk producing food for them. But somebody had to plant the seeds. Was there anyone or anything that planted people, let them grow, and then gathered their souls in harvest? Was there a God? If there was a God, Corrie had a whole lot of questions for Him.

Corrie's mama and daddy believed there was a God. Corrie remembered the day it happened. They started talking to God one day when they all sat down for dinner and also before bedtime. Mama called it "praying" and said they had to bow their heads and close their eyes. Her daddy would thank God for their blessings and thank Him for giving them life. Then Daddy said the word *amen* at the end of the conversation. Nobody ever answered, or at least Corrie never heard anybody say anything back. It wasn't long after her mama and daddy found God that they lost him—because Daddy died. He walked right out in the street and got run over by a car. One minute they were buying ice cream, and the next minute he was lying in the street, covered in his own blood. Later, Corrie was told that he died on the way to the hospital. Either God was looking the other way that day or God was never there in the first place, Corrie decided.

They'd been tricked—Gran said it herself. Only crazy people believed things like that anymore, people who couldn't see real life right in front of their faces. Corrie assumed "things like that" meant things like God. Corrie didn't know any of the crazy people anymore. There was nobody like that in Bellam. Those people called themselves the Remnant. They were the last to hold onto the things that were destroying the world, and everybody hated them for it, or at least that's what Gran said. They said those people were responsible for the riots and the wars. Collin and Will believed the Remnant people were responsible for their father's death, but what did they know? Only she had been there with Daddy that day, a day that was supposed to be a good day but definitely was not.

This was a new day, though, and the only way to avoid those trick days was to get a jump on them and make them what you want them to be. When Corrie wrote out today's number in her journal earlier that morning, she had a feeling it was going to be a good day. She had brought something with her to the pond—a small can of corn—to add to her rations pile. Gran wouldn't miss it, she had decided, and corn would be a good source of energy and nutrition. She had learned that in health class last spring. Corrie had already collected a few coins, a pocketknife, a canteen, an old blanket, and a bar of soap. Now it was time to start collecting food rations, and she was off to a great start. She would need enough for at least a week, more if she could convince Collin or Will to come with her, though that was highly unlikely. It was June 15. If she could gather enough food, she would be able to leave by the beginning of July. There was only one thing she was missing, and that was a map. If she was going on a trip, she had to have a map unless, of course, this might be the day. *No.* She chided herself for thinking such things. There had been 1,459 other days it had not happened. She wasn't a child anymore. She wasn't going to waste another summer waiting and hoping that their mother would come back for them. Her brothers had stopped believing months ago that she would come back. For Will it was probably years. It was time for Corrie to grow up. She had accepted that. Corrie was going to go find *her.*

Corrie had a clue where their mother might have gone. She remembered the conversation clearly. It was the day after Daddy's funeral, and they were in his car. Corrie found a half-eaten bag of potato chips her daddy had thrown in the back seat, as well as the suit coat he kept in the car for court. It seemed right then that perhaps they were borrowing his car while he was at work and would see him in a little while. It was another one of those trick days.

They had left in his car at night in a hurry. Corrie barely had any time to pack her small suitcase. She remembered sitting in the back seat with Collin and watching the light wash over them with each passing car. Her mother sat low in her seat, with both hands gripping the steering wheel. All she said was that she was taking them to Gran and Papaw's. Will's voice broke when he asked where she was going. *She?* Weren't they all going together? Corrie had not even thought about the possibility that their mother wasn't staying with them. She watched Will's silhouette as he stared at their mother. "East" was all she said. When the next car passed, Corrie could see that her mother was crying. Her tears glistened in the pale wash of light.

Corrie was so confused that she only remembered bits and pieces after that. There was something said about them being safe and their mother needing answers. Then they were standing on Gran and Papaw's front porch. Their mother didn't even go inside with them. Gran opened the door, and Papaw reached for their bags. Their mother kissed them all goodbye. She held Corrie's face between her hands. Her hazel eyes were spilling over with fresh tears. Her voice sounded like syrup was in her throat, which made Corrie's stomach turn over a million times. Her mother said, "Be brave, Corrie. Find the truth." Then they watched as the red taillights of their daddy's car disappeared in the darkness.

Corrie didn't know at that moment why she needed to find the truth. They had never been allowed to tell a lie, so she wasn't sure why the truth needed finding. She knew why she needed to be brave, though, because she wasn't brave at all.

"East," Mama had said. The only other time her parents had ever talked about going east was to visit Aunt Sarah. She was Papaw's only sibling and her mother's favorite aunt. As she got older, Corrie realized that of course there were many possible reasons her mother would have traveled east. It was her eight-year-old self that had made such a simple conclusion based on the only information she had at the time. However, as simple as it was, there was a very real possibility that Aunt Sarah, who lived in Georgia, would have had contact with her mother at some point. It was not much of a clue, but it was all she had. It was enough.

Corrie once tried mailing Aunt Sarah a Christmas card, but it was returned. Then she tried calling the number Gran had in her little book. It was the wrong number. Oh, how she wished Papaw were still alive so she could ask him about his sister. Gran had not kept in touch with her since Papaw died. Corrie had decided that a wrong address was better than no address because her neighbors at least might know where she could have moved.

Corrie had the perfect plan. She would use the money she had won from the Young Scholars essay competition. That should be enough for bus fare from Bellam to Atlanta. Once there, she would use her school's passcode to search data files for a local map. Even though the passcode was for a school in Texas, she figured it would work since all passcodes were linked to the Global Union office in D.C. Educational research was a legal search, so she did not anticipate any problems. She had it all figured out. She could picture herself sitting in her aunt's living room, sipping lemonade and mapping out a plan to find Mama even now.

She imagined that her mother was stuck somewhere because she ran out of money and could not get back home. Or maybe travel restrictions between states had changed where she was and she couldn't leave. Maybe she was in jail, wrongfully accused, though some would disagree with what Gran had called her "political affiliations." Gran often reminded Corrie and her brothers that the Callahan name had earned a reputation for trouble. A "legacy of dissension" was one of Gran's favorite phrases, and it was clear to Corrie that it was the primary vocation of Rose Tobias's life to rid her grandchildren of any remaining trace of that legacy. Corrie knew that her parents were good citizens, regardless of what anyone else said, and that was all that mattered. When kids at school teased her, she just told them to "kiss my grits." She would have said much worse, but it didn't seem right to defend her parents' honor with bad words they never allowed her to say. She couldn't even say it in her imaginary conversations with people while in the mermaid kingdom of Miller's Pond.

Corrie swam up to catch her breath and look around. She checked for anyone who might be watching. She looked for Mr. Miller's truck to drive up into the yard by the house about 50 yards from the pond. Every Saturday, he came back from the feed store by 1:15 for his afternoon meal. If her timing was right, that meant she had about five minutes more to swim and then sit on the bank to dry off in the sun before Mrs. Miller came out to feed the chickens and take her laundry off the clothesline. As long as she left before Mrs. Miller came outside, she would make it home before Gran woke up. The trip back up the tree and back through the attic window had also been faster since Collin nailed a small chunk of wood about halfway up the trunk for a foothold. So far, Gran had never noticed it.

Corrie dived down and brushed the earthen floor of the pond again with her fingertips, grazing every rock and piece of debris left behind from swimmers past. She had collected a few treasures here and there, but she was always careful to not dig up broken bottles buried in the mud. She could never tell if glass had a sharp or jagged edge. As she passed her hands over the pond floor, she heard the muffled tumble of rocks over one another before finding the softer soil again. Then she heard something different. It was not the sound of a rock but more like the muted tap of metal, ever so slight. It was so slight, in fact, that she thought she might have been mistaken. Her heart fluttered slightly with anticipation nonetheless, and she passed back over the place where she had heard it. If only she could see! It was too dark. The sunlight didn't filter down to this depth.

There it was again. She heard it as her hand waved over the ground. Her lungs were starting to burn. She would have to resurface in a few seconds. She closed her eyes and focused her attention on her fingertips, searching for the source of the sound. She traced over something that felt like tiny ridges just barely sticking out of the mud. She followed it quickly with her fingers. It was a chain. She pulled on it gently. It was so small that she feared she would break it before she could free it from the mud. Her body started to inhale on its own, hungry for air. She had to surface, *right now*. She quickly grabbed a bigger rock, set it on top of the chain so she could find it again, and then swam to the top. She gasped desperately as soon as her face broke the surface. She took a few gulps of air and then dived straight down again.

She found the rock that marked her place, traced the length of the chain again, and began digging and clawing with her fingertips all around it. She worked part of it loose, but something was still holding it down. She decided it was worth the risk to give it a good tug. When she did, the whole chain came up out of the mud. She fingered the length of it. Amazingly, it was still intact.

Corrie swam up as quickly as she could, anxious to examine this rare treasure. As soon as her head popped up out of the water, she held the chain up in the bright sunshine and gasped in disbelief. There in her hand was a gold chain with a gold medallion about the size of a 50-cent piece dangling from it. She laughed out loud at her good fortune. "I knew today was a good day," she said, still laughing in pure surprise and joy. She swam over to the bank and pulled herself up to examine it more closely.

The medallion sparkled in the sunshine. It had strange markings in a circle surrounding an empty space in the middle. At first, the markings just looked like scratches, but they were similar and orderly. They seemed to have a pattern. No, they weren't just random scratches at all. Someone had engraved something on it. Corrie had never seen anything like it. Stranger still, the medallion was not hanging on the chain with a loop or anything like that. It was part of the chain itself, which was completely intact, every single loop.

And the gold—it sparkled as if it had just been shined. It didn't look like something that had been stuck in pond mud for who knows how long. It looked as if it had just been forged and polished. It was amazing. And now it was hers, opening up a whole world of possibilities. She could sell it to buy bus tickets or anything else she needed for the trip. It had to be worth hundreds of dollars, maybe thousands. Maybe she would keep it instead as her very own treasure. Corrie was still admiring its beauty when she heard the chickens squawking and Mrs. Miller talking to them as she threw seed out on the ground. She gasped as she spotted Mr. Miller's truck already parked in front of the house.

Corrie scrambled to her feet and shoved the gold chain and medallion into her pocket. She had taken too long getting the chain out of the pond and had lost track of time. Gran was probably already awake. If Gran discovered Corrie had left the house, summer was over before it had hardly begun. There was not a minute to spare. Corrie raced over to the barbed wire fence, ducked underneath, jumped on her bike, and sped away.

Chapter 3
Category: World Events

From their perch in the old live oak tree, the trio watched as Corrie disappeared from sight. Evangeline spoke first. "Well, shouldn't we go after her?" Evangeline looked toward the fence and then back at Prudence and Horatius. "I don't understand why we aren't doing anything," she said. "We sit and we watch, she comes and she goes while we sit on a branch. I'm supposed to 'hold the line.' Now I'm not all that sure just what that means, but I know good and well it doesn't mean a fishing line right here at this pond. Now, why don't we go?" Evangeline gesticulated with such passion that she almost fell over backward.

"We were told to come to these exact coordinates," Horatius explained patiently. "If you have received further instructions, then please, dear sister, follow them. In every mission I have had, it has been very clear when we were to move."

"I am sorry, Horatius. I forgot you hold the mission instructions," Evangeline replied apologetically.

"That is quite all right," Horatius answered. "We all have had to learn protocol for these missions. Your zeal is always welcome."

"Horatius," Prudence said, tapping on his elbow. "Horatius, *look.*" Prudence pointed at the skies behind them. Something was racing toward them from the west. Horatius shifted himself on the branch to see what Prudence was referring to.

"Prepare yourselves," Horatius said sternly. No sooner had he spoken than a low rumbling in the clouds and the thunderous pound of hoofbeats swelled like a mighty wave tumbling toward them, growing louder by the second. The sight was ghastly. Dark, billowy clouds rolled and boiled toward them and eventually materialized in the shapes of creatures. They were similar to horses but had faces of dragons and black, leathery wings like giant bats. They flew like a swarm through the skies, pounding the air.

Flames leapt from between sharp fangs in their gaping mouths, leaving trails of black smoke behind them. Mounted atop the creatures were demons clothed in black armor studded with hundreds of sharpened barbs of Imperial Jade that flashed green in the red fires of the beasts' mouths. The demons each held a sword in one hand and a whip in the other. The whips swirled in the air with bands of leathery cords ending in forked tongues of fire. Every crack of the whip caused the creatures to roar with fury as they bounded forward. The whole formation dipped toward the pond and rose back up again, charging like a massive freight train. Then another cloud of them came from the south and followed suit until they had caught up with the first group.

"Horsemen," Horatius said in a whisper.

"I have never seen them before," Prudence replied as the creatures passed.

Horatius shook his head vigorously. "No. Nor have I. I have only heard tales. The Horsemen are a specialized unit, vicious and vile like rabid dogs without any loyalty to their master. They are subdued and controlled by force alone."

"What could be the reason for such a violent demonstration?" Prudence wondered. "There are only a few hundred guardians in the area, and I see no angel warriors. This seems like such a sleepy town."

"It's a sleepy town because it is clearly in the grasp of darkness already. It is the sleep of Death. The ruler over this quadrant has had little resistance. I can't imagine what has changed in the last few moments," Horatius said, his voice trailing off.

"What are you thinking? That it has something to do with Corrie? Surely not," Prudence replied, shaking her head.

"Did you see the gold she collected from the bottom of the pond? There was something unusual about it," Horatius answered.

"I noticed that, too, but a piece of gold jewelry bringing the horsemen? That would be preposterous. That has never happened before, has it?" Prudence asked.

"Very rare indeed," Horatius agreed, nodding. "Could it be the jewelry or the girl?" he mused.

"Or both," Prudence answered.

Horatius suddenly dug into his pocket and took out the small scroll that had originally given them instructions. He studied it carefully again, humming in a low groan. Then he unrolled it all the way to the very last edge of the parchment.

"How could I have missed this?" Horatius sighed.

Prudence eyed him curiously and leaned over to see the scroll herself. There at the very bottom of the scroll were these words shimmering in gold letters:

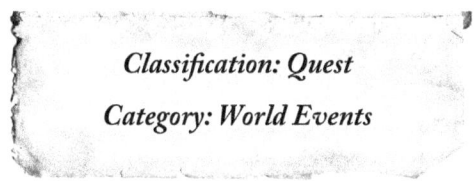

Classification: Quest

Category: World Events

"World Events?" Prudence exhaled, drumming her fingers on her chin. "I had thought maybe Search and Rescue or maybe even Celebrations. She seems like such a happy child, but World Events? My goodness, Horatius, that means—"

"Yes," Horatius interrupted. "She has a very important job to do."

"She is quite young for World Events, quite young indeed. Are you *sure*, Horatius?" Prudence queried.

"It would not be the first time the Almighty changed the world through a young girl, would it?" Horatius said, smiling gently. "Evangeline? Any thoughts?" Horatius asked, glancing at Evangeline who simply shook her head. For the first time since they had arrived, Evangeline had nothing to say. She clung to the tree branch, wide-eyed and tight-lipped.

"Companions," Horatius said, speaking now to both of them. "We have all our instructions now and have thus been given license to engage. Are we all of one accord then?"

"Yes," Prudence answered.

They both glanced over at Evangeline who was still clinging to the branch.

"Evangeline, dear," Prudence prodded gently. "Mission protocol states that we must all agree before continuing. All missions are voluntary. You do have a choice."

Prudence had been sitting with her back straight and arms folded, but now she reached toward Evangeline and patted her gently on the knee. Her action seemed to startle Evangeline, who blinked her eyes and slightly loosened her grip on the branch. Then she shook her curls like she was shaking off a bad dream and sat up straight.

"Where exactly do you think the Horsemen were heading?" Evangeline asked, staring intently at Horatius and then Prudence.

Prudence lifted her arm and pointed past the hole in the fence toward the dirt road where the dust still hung in the air over fresh bicycle tracks. The clouds were gathering, and the darkness was deepening. Evangeline stared for a moment at the clouds that were writhing and undulating like fat snakes in the sky over Bellam—and right over Corrie. When Evangeline looked back at Prudence and Horatius, her blue eyes were blazing.

"Then *yes*, I'm in."

Chapter 4

The Face of Evil

As Corrie raced home, the wind licked the droplets off her damp skin and mussed the top of her hair into wild ringlets. What remained of her ponytail was still a wet clump, and her clothes were sticking to her. She would worry about all of this later. Right now she had to hope she could manage to slip back through the attic window before Gran woke up and noticed she was gone. The medallion in her pocket pressed a circular outline through the wet denim clinging to her thigh. She hoped her treasure would be worth the risk she faced now.

There was no time to go back the way she had come. That would have taken her down Browder Road all the way to Route 9 and then Hilltop Road, which was her street. That was the safer route because there were no houses along the way, no nosy neighbors telling Gran that they saw her granddaughter out riding her bike, but it was slower. The faster route was to cut through High Street, a small stretch that took her directly to Hilltop, but it was by far the more treacherous. She always avoided that street, and for more than one reason.

The crunch of gravel under her tires became a low hum as she angled her bike onto the paved surface of High Street. The noisy squeak of her pedals might as well have been a siren coming down the tree-lined street where many of Bellam's well-to-do lived. Gran always called it "Old Money Street." Only recently had Corrie understood why. The houses were neat with well-manicured lawns. It was Saturday, the day people sat outside on their porches to gossip with their neighbors and sip tall glasses of sweet tea or lemonade for hours because somehow, they had sugar to spare. Corrie kept her head down but snuck sideways glances at the houses as she passed. Surprisingly, she didn't see anyone.

It was probably the gathering clouds that kept them inside. It had been sunny not even an hour ago. There was only a cat lounging on the porch, flicking its tail indifferently as she passed. Maybe she had avoided this route for nothing since there was nobody around.

Her pedals squeaked in rhythm. It was an old bike, one of the many things that had belonged to her mother. She had begged Gran to let her keep it. She didn't have to beg Papaw. He was standing in the garage door with his tools ready the moment she discovered it. That was over three years ago. It needed some paint and a new seat, but she loved that old bike because it was hers. She hadn't even noticed the pedals squeaking until now. She was almost to the end of the street when the second reason she avoided High Street came into view.

The end of High Street was very different from the beginning. There was only one house at the far corner—an old, dilapidated dwelling with broken down cars and greasy auto parts strewn about the yard. It stood apart from the other houses like a toad at a tea party. Weeds and red top grass poked out from the bushes surrounding the front porch. Broken bottles and beer cans littered the gravel driveway. This was the home of Emory Goodson and his four good-for-nothing sons.

The stately columns and elegant masonry on the old house left clues of happier times for the Goodson family in earlier years. Marian Taylor Goodson had come from a wealthy family in the city. Her father had made his fortune in real estate decades before. Emory had charmed his way into her heart and the family fortune when Marian was just 19. Little did she know the sorrow that awaited her not long after she pledged her life and her love to a man who was to become not only the town drunk but the progenitor of her deepest grief. Surely there is no greater sorrow for a mother than to pour out her life on her beloved children only to discover that she had effectively raised a litter of pigs.

Marian Goodson had disappeared from all public view a few years ago, leaving the town to their own assumptions regarding her whereabouts. Rumors had swirled around the remains of her family's reputation like buzzards around roadkill. The most gruesome tale claimed that Emory killed her and buried her somewhere on the land behind their house. Other stories said she had died of a broken heart brought on by her sons' disreputable behavior. Probably the most outlandish rumor that circulated through town was that she was still alive but was trapped in an upstairs bedroom. People said she was too large to fit through the bedroom door, so they kept her up there and brought her meals and daily accoutrements as the years rolled on.

Corrie knew the youngest Goodson, Mark. He had sat in front of her in math class this past year. She didn't actually talk to him but had once loaned him a pencil. She noticed that he always seemed sad. Every day she wished she could think of something to say to him, something nice, because he seemed like he needed a friend. She knew a little about sadness, but she never talked to him. Instead, she just stared at the back of his head and wondered what it was like to be the youngest in his family instead of her own. Whenever she felt sorry for herself, she thought of poor Mark Goodson and always felt a little better about her life.

The oldest sons had moved away a few years ago or were in prison; nobody knew. Only Joe and Mark were left at home with their dad. Of all the brothers, the third-born, Joe, was the cruelest. Last year, Mark came to school with a black eye. Corrie remembered that their teacher, Miss Byers, who was new to the school and new to Bellam, questioned Mark after class about what happened to him. Everyone knew Joe was responsible, but most people knew it was not only useless but dangerous to speak up about a Goodson. You did not confront Emory Goodson or his sons about anything. They and their old money, sunk deep in the pockets of the mayor and the sheriff, held Bellam in a vise. Mark Goodson had come back to school the next day with his black eye turning new shades of color. Miss Byers was never seen again.

Joe was the same grade as Collin. Everyone knew that Joe had probably been held back a year or two. He had been the only eighth grader with a full mustache. Corrie could never forget his face, the look in his eyes. Her daddy had always said you could see a person's soul by looking in their eyes. Anger was a frightening thing to see in someone's eyes, but she had seen something far worse in Joe's. She had looked into Joe Goodson's gray eyes and was instantly terrified because there had been no anger or even hatred. There was absolutely nothing.

Joe stared at people when he'd chosen them. Corrie had wracked her brain to figure out why she had been the one chosen of all her classmates. She had tried to be invisible and fade into the crowd when they passed in the hallway at school, and then she'd tried to be strong and confident with her head held high. Nothing worked. Joe always managed to find her and call attention to the way her hair curled funny in the back, or how she walked like a penguin, or the fact that she wore the same shirt three days in a row. It was always something, and the "punishment," as he called it, was always waiting for her when she least suspected it. He would push her into a locker and say it was an accident, or he'd trip her when she was walking in the cafeteria with a full tray of food. Joe Goodson was a problem that never went away. She wished so badly she could just be invisible, but that would have been a miracle, and miracles never happened.

Collin tried to protect her, but that only meant that both of them got the punishment. Collin couldn't be around her all the time anyway. Corrie had to learn to fend for herself. She had kept a record in her diary of everything Joe Good-for-Nothing had done to them. One day she would get even. She had made that secret and solemn pledge.

Corrie's bike pedals squeaked at a faster tempo. She was nearly to the end of the street, nearly past the Goodsons' house, when something caught her eye—movement near the back of the house. The backyard was fenced, but it was just a chain-link fence, easy to see through. As her bike glided past, she turned and saw a large, wooden crate next to a hole in the ground. The crate was as big as a casket, and puffs of dirt flew up in the air around it. Somebody was burying something—or *someone.*

Corrie forgot all manner of haste and the threat of punishment from Gran. Curiosity drew her like a cat to a cockroach. She had to see what was in that box. She circled back, angled her bike into the soft grass behind a clump of azaleas growing wild at the corner of the Goodsons' front yard, and slipped off the seat without a sound.

She hid behind the bushes, peering out between the leaves as she saw first the handle of a shovel and then someone emerging from the hole, caked in dirt up to his eyebrows. The guy looked like Joe's lackey, Jed Muncy, but it was hard to tell. Corrie squinted, wishing for a better view. She had to see what they were up to. This could be big news that even Collin would want to know. If she could just get a little closer.

Corrie crawled on her belly toward the corner of the house. She kept her eyes on Jed, but his back was still turned. She made it across the yard to the front porch, staying low to the ground and peeking around the corner of the concrete porch.

Jed bent over the wooden box and opened the lid. Then he reached in with both arms. Her heart pounding, Corrie watched as Jed heaved a large bundle out of the crate. She could see one end of what looked like black metal poles. They clattered in his arms as he lowered the bundle down into the hole he had crawled out of. Then another set of arms reached up from the ground to take them. Jed reached into the crate again, but this time he pulled out just one of the black metal things. He looked it over real good and then turned and brought it up to his shoulder. *Guns*. Corrie's stomach jumped up in her throat. She should have suspected it sooner. Guns may be illegal, but of course the Goodsons would have a whole crate of them. They had probably confiscated them from everyone else. Most people still kept a few hunting rifles hidden, but nobody had that many, and these didn't look like the hunting rifles she and her brothers used to hunt deer with. It wasn't even dove season yet, and they sure wouldn't need that many unless . . .

Corrie's stomach dropped around her ankles as she watched Jed unload armload after armload to the person waiting in the hole. She assumed the person packing them in the ground was Joe. She didn't see the figure standing under the tree in the back corner of the yard. She was too preoccupied with her own thoughts to see him leave his post and walk along the back fence until he was out of view.

A clap of thunder startled Corrie. She wanted to stay, to see what else was in the crate, but the coming storm startled her into common sense. She crawled back to the bushes and mounted her bike, pushing off toward home again. She glanced back just to make sure no one had noticed her, and only then did she see Joe rounding the corner on the far side of the house. He was lifting black steel to his shoulder.

Corrie's heart was pounding in her ears. Her bike pedals squeaked frantically. A sharp ping rang out as a bullet ricocheted off the street sign mere feet from her. She was almost to the turn onto Hilltop Road when she heard a loud pop from her front tire. The bike suddenly jolted, sending her tumbling over her handlebars. She landed hard on her right shoulder, but the momentum made her skid across the pavement into the grass. Instinctively, she tried to scramble to her feet and run, but a moment later a heavy weight crashed into her back, knocking her headlong into the ditch beside the road.

Corrie had no air to scream or even breathe, and even as she struggled to pull air back into her lungs, a hand clamped tight against her face. With the taste of earth in her mouth, she was turned over roughly, her injured shoulder jammed hard into the dirt. Joe kept one hand on her mouth while the other hand pinned her hands above her head.

"You think you saw something interesting, huh?" Joe said in a low, guttural voice.

Corrie shook her head. *No, I didn't see anything*, she tried to say, but she could not speak. She could hardly breathe. She looked up through tangled hair into the lifeless, gray eyes of Joe Goodson. A torrent of words flew out of his mouth, words she could never say and words she had never heard.

"You're a Remnant dog, just like your mother," he whispered gruffly near her ear. His breath smelled like rotten meat and alcohol. "You know you are."

He removed his hand from her mouth to reach for his back pocket.

"No I'm *not*," she said hoarsely and tried to wrestle free, but his grip was too strong. She tried to kick him, but he slammed her small body into the ground, knocking the wind out of her again. She struggled to catch her breath, but suddenly she felt the sharp point of his knife at her throat.

"Make another sound, and I will gut you clean right here and now. You're going to do whatever I want you to, whenever I want you to, or your whole family dies," Joe growled into her ear.

A scream welled up in Corrie's chest, burning her throat. She couldn't move, and she couldn't run. There was no escape. Corrie fixed her gaze on the branches of the trees that reached high into the sky. She was floating in the trees. Higher and higher she climbed, lighter than air over treetops and across the meadow, back to the great live oak tree beside the pond. Then down, down, down into the depths she sank, down to the very bottom. She could see nothing. She could hear nothing.

After a while she heard the clamor of voices, an engine sputtering, and a dog barking, but they were all so far away like a whisper in the wind. She was still hidden away within the watery fortress of her mermaid kingdom. It was safe here. She wanted to stay.

Little by little, however, the cool of the deep became solid beneath her. If she wanted, she could reach with her fingertips and touch the warm soil. But not yet. She flew up to the treetops again and looked down. There was a girl lying in the mud, her body pressed into the soil with a quiet rain falling on her face. She looked familiar. Was she dead?

Something tickled her face and snuffled in the girl's ear. "Lucy," said a deep voice. Was it Joe? No, this was someone else. The voice was gentle. Someone knelt beside her. The depths of the pond enveloped her once again, slipping soft arms around her, filling her ears, and blocking the light from her eyes. A sad whimper broke through the stillness again, and soft velvet passed over her face. She gradually felt the weight of her body lodged in the mud, aching and throbbing. Her throat felt tight and sore. Her eyes were still closed.

"Lucy, come now. That's a good girl."

The man was still there, but why?

"Wait in the truck now," he said. Corrie heard the shuffling of paws in the grass, followed by silence. All was still except for the soft patter of rain and the mournful sigh of a dove in a nearby tree. Her eyelids parted in a tiny slit, just enough to see that the man was still there. Then the rain suddenly stopped. Though the clouds remained, the man's face was swathed in bright sunlight, making it impossible to distinguish his features.

A whimper came from the truck. The man gave no response but laid his hand on Corrie's foot. She felt a rush of energy pulsating through her. He rubbed his hands together and nudged closer to her. His hands passed near her face, and the air was filled with the fragrance of flowers and sweet cedar. He gently pressed his fingers to her forehead, her face, and her neck. As he did so, he began to sing soft and low.

Corrie listened. Her heart ached, rising as if from a memory so deep she could not hold it in her conscious mind. She felt his hand behind her back, pressing into her aching shoulder. She winced, but a moment later all tension and ache were gone. Strength seeped into her body and mind like a gentle stream trickling through her veins, gradually filling every empty space.

The man slipped something around her neck and whispered softly. "Wake up, Corrie. It is time for you to find what you're looking for." Then she felt a gentle breeze over her face and smelled the same sweet aroma. She inhaled deeply and opened her eyes.

No one was there. Corrie sat up and looked for the truck, the man, and Lucy the dog. Not only were they gone, but they left no trace of ever having been there. Her mind was playing tricks on her, or maybe she had merely passed out and what she remembered so clearly had only been a dream. There was only one thing she could not explain. The gold medallion now adorned her neck. It was the jewelry she had found and stuffed in her pocket. She knew she had not put it on. She had been unable to, and yet there it was. She fingered the circle of gold and the delicate chain. How?

Suddenly remembering Joe's words to her, she searched for evidence of his knife, her fingers tracing the slope of her neck where she had felt the sharp point. Not even the tiniest scratch remained. Her hands passed across her face and the other side of her neck, and then her shoulders, arms, and legs. Nothing. No clothing was torn. She sat up and checked herself again in disbelief, but there was no wound, no injury whatsoever. She was perfectly fine. Still marveling in confusion, she heard a voice.

Get up, Corrie. Go now. Corrie heard it as plain as day. It was *his* voice, the voice of the kind stranger. She whipped her head around looking for him, but she was alone in the ditch. His voice was gentle but insistent. Her bike was gone. She stared down at her legs. They would have to get her home. She took one last look down the road, thinking perhaps she would see the kind stranger again or his dog, but the street was empty. The mourning dove, now sitting silently in the tree overhead, was her only witness. She was alone. Her mind worked feverishly to put pieces of this bizarre puzzle together. *Get up, Corrie,* she heard again as she found her legs under her and started home. As she rounded the corner, the realization hit her like a bolt of lightning. The stranger knew her name.

Corrie started walking but soon broke into a run. She ran and she ran, all the way home and straight to the elm tree outside the attic window. Her foot found the chunk of wood nailed to the trunk, and she climbed with practiced agility. She climbed without thinking and slid through the small window, landing on the floor with barely a thump.

All she wanted to do was get to her room unnoticed. She slipped down the hallway with the stealth of a jungle cat. She could hear the sounds of the television downstairs. She was almost to her room when a lone marble appeared out of nowhere and rolled past her feet. She turned around to see her brother Collin standing at the top of the stairs holding a half-eaten apple.

"Where have you been?" he said coolly, taking a bite and then walking in front of Corrie to retrieve the marble. He pocketed it and then stood in the doorframe of her room, partially blocking her way. He was 14, just two years older than Corrie, but he was big enough to nearly fill the doorway. He looked down at her, glowering.

"It's nearly suppertime. Where have you been?" he asked again.

"Nowhere," Corrie said and pushed past him into her room. Her hair and clothes were damp and dirty. There was no point in argument or denial. "I just want to be left alone," she said and tried her best to ignore him as she gathered some dry clothes.

"I covered for you," Collin muttered.

"Where's Gran?" Corrie whispered.

"Knitting Circle," Collin answered, taking another bite. "I told her you were catching up on your summer reading and didn't want to be disturbed. The least you could do is tell me the truth," Collin said, glaring at her.

"Not now." Corrie stared right back at him but found that she couldn't hold his gaze. As soon as she dropped her eyes, she knew she shouldn't have.

"You might as well say it," Collin persisted. "Your bike is gone, isn't it? Corrie? I told you not to ride it to the pond anymore."

"Collin, I just —"

Corrie tried to close the door, but Collin wouldn't move, and she didn't want a fight. The bike was the last thing Papaw had given her before he died. Collin knew she wouldn't just leave it somewhere or let someone take it if she could help it. Why couldn't he just let it go? Her eyes burned. She shoved him out of the doorway and shut the door just as hot tears spilled down her face. She brushed them aside and sat down on the bed. She pressed her palms into her knees to try to steady her legs, but the trembling spread from her knees to her whole body. The door creaked open. She refused to look over where Collin had stood. She could feel his eyes boring into her, sizing up the situation.

"What's up?" Will said, poking his head in behind Collin's shoulder.

"Nothing!" Corrie shouted, feeling the heat rising in her face and ears.

"Somebody stole her bike. One guess who," Collin said to Will.

"I never said that," Corrie said flatly, staring at the floor and willing her body to be still. They had no idea what she had been through and what would happen if she told the truth about it all, about anything. She had seen a side of Joe Goodson today that her brothers would never understand and probably never believe. He wasn't just a school bully anymore. This was different. This was pure evil.

"Fine," Collin said. "But if you don't want to get in trouble, you better go get your bike from wherever you left it." It was bait to make her mad. She knew it, but she took it anyway.

"I didn't leave it anywhere! Somebody took it, okay? Just leave me alone. Just go away!" Corrie shouted.

"See?" Collin muttered to Will, just loud enough for Corrie to hear.

"Well, you better not do anything about it, or you know what will happen," Will said to Collin. "Some things are better left alone," he said dismissively.

That was it. Those were Gran's words, and Will said it just like her. Bile rose in Corrie's throat, and she suddenly wanted to punch Will in the neck. Gran said that same thing when Mr. Goodson stole from them and nobody did anything about it. She said it when Collin came home from school with a bloody nose. She said it when Corrie asked Gran why their mother left them.

"Get out!" Corrie bellowed as she pushed them both out of her room, slamming the door behind them. Collin muttered something, but she didn't hear it. She didn't care. She didn't care if Gran knew she went to the pond. She didn't care if her bike was gone. She didn't care if the whole world blew up.

Corrie buried herself under her covers, the same red and yellow bedspread that had been her mother's, and folded her knees up to her chest. She was still shaking. She sobbed silently into her pillow until her tears slowed to ragged breathing. Past the twilled edge of her bedspread, the sun shone through a break in the clouds. The leaves outside her window danced in the breeze, their shadows shaking and bobbing like drunken phantoms on the wall. She watched, drifting into their rhythm, riding the wind, fluttering and bouncing like a fairy, a wood nymph without a name. She drifted until the dance gave way to the soft patter of rain on the roof, and the heaviness of sleep numbed her body to all but the weight of the gold medallion resting just above her heart.

Chapter 5
Day 1,460

The aroma of coffee and pancakes wafted up the stairs. Corrie pulled the covers over her head, trying to hang on to the last wisp of slumber as it drifted away. It had been a fitful night's sleep filled with strange nightmares of a bicycle accident, Joe Goodson's leering face, and his cold, steel knife. As the darkness pressed toward dawn, there were other sensations and images in her dreams—the wet muzzle of a dog, the sweet fragrance of cedar and roses, and the faceless stranger whose lullaby enveloped and soothed her as if in a soft, warm blanket.

Corrie's stomach growled. She couldn't remember the last time she had eaten. She threw back the covers and swung her legs over the edge of the bed. Something was very strange. She was not wearing pajamas. She had slept in cut-off denim shorts and a dirty T-shirt. The sheets were stained in a halo of muddy residue where she had slept, and her whole bed reeked of dirt and pond water. Her ribs twinged sharply when she took a deep breath. Suddenly, memories of the day before rushed back in vivid detail like a freight train colliding with her senses, jarring and violent. It had not been a dream; it was real.

She stared numbly at the reflection in the dresser mirror, not recognizing herself at first. The person in the mirror looked tired and disheveled. Her hair was a mess, matted and tangled. Slowly, Corrie stood up and fumbled through the dresser drawers. She changed into clean clothes, brushed her hair carefully, wincing with every tangle, and pulled it up into a neat ponytail as she did every morning. She stuffed her dirty clothes under the bed.

Sunlight streamed in through the bedroom window and caught the glimmer of gold around her neck. She held the medallion, feeling its weight in her palm. Then she traced the chain with her fingertips, trying to find the catch to take it off, but there was no catch. She tugged on it, hoping to loosen its hold, but it only dug into her neck. She tried pulling it over her head, but it would not fit.

Corrie glared at the girl in the mirror, but the image only stared back, looking stupid and guilty with someone else's treasure around her neck. Hot tears stung Corrie's eyes. She was no longer excited by the medallion's supposed value or thrilled that she had found it. It was this stupid jewelry that had caused her trouble in the first place. She had stayed too long at the pond because of *this*. She didn't have a bike anymore because of *this*. She yanked as hard as she could to break the chain, but it didn't budge. She looked at the red line forming on her neck. *That's what you get for picking it up in the first place. You should have left it at the bottom of the pond. You should have left yourself at the bottom of the pond!* Pure rage, wild and hot, flowed through her like liquid fire. Blood rushed to her cheeks, burning away any hint of self pity she may have held onto until it was completely gone. Corrie seethed, daring the girl in the mirror to show any sign of weakness.

The clang of pots and pans echoed up the stairs, startling Corrie from her spiral of self-condemnation.

"Breakfast!" Gran shouted from the kitchen.

Gran did not like to be kept waiting. The last person to the table always had the worst kitchen chores such as scraping the fat from the skillet into the jar or taking the scraps out. That was usually Corrie. She didn't care about chores today and had no desire to explain why she was late to the table this time. Quickly, she found another T-shirt with a higher neck in hopes of hiding the jewelry. She fussed with the shirt, pulling it this way and that. It did not hide the jewelry completely, but it would have to do until she could find a way to remove the chain. She would get a chainsaw if she had to.

"Coming!" Corrie shouted.

Corrie started for the door but remembered one last thing. She knelt on the floor beside the dresser. A corner of blue peeked out from the small space between the dresser and the bookcase. Her hands trembled as she turned to the last unfinished page of her journal. Beside yesterday's number was a blank space staring back at her. This was the first and only time she had neglected to finish her journal entry. Fresh anger boiled up inside her. She had broken her own promise. She pulled the small nub of a pencil out of the spiral coil where she kept it and started to write.

Day 1,460

Corrie paused. The pencil hovered over the paper. The space beside yesterday's number seemed at once infinite and yet impossibly small. She stared at the paper for a while and then slid the pencil back into the coil, stood up, and tossed the journal in the trash. Yesterday, today—it didn't matter. They were just days. She left her room and shut the door behind her.

Chapter 6

Gran and the Gold

G ran stood at the kitchen sink scrubbing a large cast iron skillet. She faced the window overlooking the garden in the backyard. She would often stare out that window while she washed dishes, dipping her arms in bubbles up to her elbows as white clouds of steam billowed around her. She seemed to enjoy the ritual—dirty plates submerged, clean plates made new again by the simple elements of soap and warm water. Dishwashing was the one chore Gran did not delegate to her grandchildren. She would methodically scrub and rinse, stare out the window, and whisper to herself with a far-off look in her eyes. She did that even more after Papaw died. As Corrie got older, she gradually understood what Gran had seen over the years—her only daughter digging in the sandbox and making mud pies, her farmer husband tilling the soil in their garden or trudging up to the house from the barn after a long day's work, and the changing of seasons and stages of the moon over decades of memories past.

Beyond the backyard were miles of woods filled with pin oak, pecan, and cottonwood trees. Settler's Creek wound its way among the trees with a few tributaries reaching as far as the Mississippi. Spring rains brought sand bass enough to feed the county at the first blush of the redbud trees. Papaw had taught Corrie and her brothers how to fish there. Their mother,

Rachel, had grown up picking pecans by the bushel and hunting rabbit, deer, and squirrel in those woods.

Beyond the woods was the rest of Texas, it seemed. They had watched the courthouse explode into flames and even felt the windows rattle from the initial blast of the bomb. When the riots spreading throughout the country reached the outskirts of Bellam, they heard the gunshots and grenade blasts from their living room. Corrie remembered watching the flashlights streaming out from town and into the woods as rioters escaped the remains of what had been the local police. To Corrie, their flashlights looked like lightning bugs flickering in the dark. Gran said the rioters wouldn't climb the hill to their house, but she stayed at the kitchen sink, watching long after she told the children they all had better go on to bed.

This morning, Gran wore a pale blue housecoat, a white apron tied around her waist, and slippers that came to a point. Corrie called them her elf shoes. Gran—Rose Tobias—was a petite lady, but she handled the heavy skillet like it was made of paper. Years of cooking and cleaning had made her strong. Years of living had made her formidable.

"Did you wash your hands?" Gran called over her shoulder as she put the last of the dishes on the drying rack.

"Yes, Ma'am," Corrie answered flatly, sitting down in front of a plate piled high with scrambled eggs and buttermilk pancakes. The butter had already melted and mingled with the syrup, pooling in a rich amber moat around the edge of the plate. What they called "syrup" was a little brown sugar, water, and whatever honey they could get from Mr. Zikstra's bees. When the syrup wasn't too watery, it was very, very good. A pool of it formed on the table beside Corrie's dripping plate.

"There's no bacon this week. Maybe next week," Gran said absentmindedly, drying her hands on her apron.

Meat of any kind was becoming more of a delicacy. Rations for those living outside the boundaries of Bellam proper were always smaller than rations for those who lived or owned property in town. Luxuries like meat, cheese, nuts, and fresh fruits that were not grown locally were typically bought up by those who could afford them, those who had a higher status for reasons that everyone knew but no one discussed openly. The city limits of Bellam began one street over on High Street. Hilltop Road, Corrie's street, was considered to be "out in the country." At least they had their own chickens. Eggs had been an important source of protein for the family, and they were lucky to have enough almost every day.

Corrie didn't care about bacon. That was Will's favorite. What Corrie missed were the hams with sweet honey glaze and pineapples studded with cloves. They used to have ham at least once a month with enough left over for breakfast the next day with eggs and hot biscuits slathered in butter and strawberry jam. This morning, however, she hardly cared about breakfast at all. Though she had been starving when she woke up, her stomach was now in a knot.

"Don't worry about the bacon, Gran," Will said quietly.

Will had been first to the breakfast table, as usual. His plate was empty except for a thin coating of syrup. He watched Corrie as she seated herself at the table, as if he was waiting for her. Corrie eyed him curiously. The expression on his face when he met her gaze sent a little shiver down her spine. *Where is Collin?* she mouthed. But as soon as she said it, she knew. Will nodded silently, almost imperceptibly. Corrie also knew Will hated keeping things from Gran. His days of loyalty to the sacred oath of secrecy among the siblings were numbered. She could see it in his eyes.

"Where is your brother?" Gran asked, setting the clean skillet back on the burner, ready for use the next time. Corrie shot daggers at Will, but he didn't look up from his plate of syrup.

"Oh, you know he likes to sleep in on Sundays, Gran," Will said. Corrie breathed a sigh of relief and noted that he did not lie. Will never lied, especially not to Gran. It would kill him for her to be disappointed in him.

"Well, you better wake him up before I finish here or there will be nothing left but the scraps," Gran said, putting away the milk, juice, and butter. The scraps were the bits of food, eggshells, and coffee grounds that went out into the composter. The rich, fertile compost would then be added to the soil for the garden. Better soil meant better vegetables, not only in taste but in nutrition.

"Yes, Ma'am. I will," said Will. He rose slowly from his chair and picked up his plate to take to the sink. Before he reached the sink, however, he stopped and turned around. Corrie looked up at Will whose back was turned to Gran. He stood there with his glass in one hand and his plate in the other. He looked like he wanted to say something. A glimmer of light moved across his shirt, something that had caught the sunlight streaming in through the window. The gold chain had slipped out a little from Corrie's T-shirt and was shining there for all to see. The moment she realized it, she tucked it back under her shirt. Surprisingly, Will didn't seem to notice. Corrie was not prepared in the least for what happened next.

A terrifying wail filled the small kitchen. Will jumped back, looking around and trying to find the reason for the horrifying noise. The dishes in his hands clattered back down onto the table. Gran stood facing Corrie with her hands over her mouth, showing only her eyes that were wide with horror.

"Gran, what's wrong? What happened?" Will shouted.

Will was immediately at her side, easing her into his chair. Corrie had been too terrified to move. Gran was staring at *her*. Corrie wanted to stand up, move, or leave the kitchen, but her legs wouldn't work. It seemed as though one movement might cause the earth to crumble beneath her.

"Where did you get *that*?" Gran said accusingly, pointing to the space just above Corrie's heart. Corrie had tucked the chain and medallion away mere seconds before, but it had been too late. Corrie felt the blood drain from her face, right down to her toes.

"F-Found it," Corrie replied, barely above a whisper. She could see the scene clearly in her mind, but she could not form the words to describe what had happened, much less tell the story in such a way that concealed important, non-incriminating details.

Collin would have known what to say. He always did, and he always spoke for Corrie. Oh, how she wished he were here! She looked from Gran to Will. She hoped Will would make an excuse for her as they were both doing for Collin. *Just once more, Will*, she begged with her eyes. Maybe they were too far gone for that and their secrets were all unraveling right here, right now. The strangest thing of it all was the expression on Will's face. His eyes were searching, unsure. Then he said something in a voice so quiet that if she hadn't been looking at him right then, she wouldn't have heard it.

"What are you talking about?" he said, his eyes searching. *He doesn't see it*, Corrie thought to herself, but she couldn't be sure.

"You found it? No. No, that isn't possible. Who gave this to you?" Gran demanded.

Gran's face flushed beet red, and her eyes bore into Corrie like knives into a Christmas ham. Gran was no longer distraught. Her fear was quickly replaced by haughty disdain. A familiar knot twisted in Corrie's stomach. The small kitchen was becoming unbearably hot. The heat prickled the back of Corrie's neck, and sweat dripped down between her shoulder blades.

"I did. I f-found it, but then there was a man," Corrie blurted and felt herself falling into a hole. Before she could find her footing, scrambling for a way to justify herself, she fell deeper even as her own mouth betrayed her.

"On the road," she rasped. Her mouth was as dry as a flour sack.

"A man just gave something to you? For no reason?" Will said, puzzled. He stood beside Gran with his hands gripping her shoulders tightly, protectively. Derision crept into his eyes.

Corrie felt the rising anger and confusion cloud her thinking. Only a moment ago Will didn't even know what was going on. Now he was siding with Gran against her. The jewelry was *her* problem. Why did it matter so much to them anyway? They acted like she had robbed a bank. She was no thief. Corrie's head was spinning. The jewelry was only a shiny piece of junk from the bottom of a pond after all—thrown away, unwanted. Corrie had broken about 50 rules by even going to the pond, and yet Gran only focused on this one small thing. It was like ignoring the snake, the bear, and the skunk in the kitchen and going after the gnat in the applesauce. Gran persisted.

"Who was it? What did he look like? Was he a wandering vagrant out on the road? *Who?* Tell me, child," Gran demanded, but she didn't wait for an answer before continuing.

"Here I try to raise you and your brothers right and protect you from all the hogswallop your daddy got all of you into, and you go and get yourself into more trouble. You ought not to have anything to do with this necklace. Now you listen to me, young lady. That is not something for you to have!" Gran was yelling and waving her arms at this point. "Now you take that thing off right this instant! Why, I am of a mind to—"

Gran leaned toward her with her hand outstretched toward the necklace. Corrie jumped up and fled from the room, away from her grasp. Gran's shrill screams were ringing in Corrie's ears as she bounded up the steps. Before she was halfway up the stairs, the doorbell rang, interrupting the chaos with a sudden and perfunctory pause. Corrie hid behind the wall in the turn of the stairs, watching the shadows shifting on the front porch through the colored glass on either side of the door.

Will's bare feet shuffled across the wood floor, making dull thumps and creaks with every step. The front door squeaked open, sending a hot breeze up to where Corrie was waiting and listening. She didn't know why just yet, but fear and foreboding washed over her. Suddenly, her heart skipped a beat. She knew what was wrong, even before she heard the next words out of Will's mouth.

"Collin?" Will gasped. The tone of his voice sounded like someone had punched him in the gut. "Gran, I think you need to come here," he said somberly.

Chapter 7

Trespasser

Will opened the door wider as Gran came up beside him, hands on her hips. She looked small next to Will and even smaller across from Collin and the tall, lanky police officer standing next to him. They faced one another through the row of iron bars between them. Will reached for the key to unlock the security gate, but Gran pushed his hand away.

"Good morning, ma'am," the officer said politely. His eyes met Gran's for a second as he shuffled nervously. "Do you, *um*, know this boy?" he asked apologetically. Collin's head was down, and his hands were handcuffed behind his back. Gran's shoulders rose and fell.

"Nathan Grimes, you know this is my grandson. I have known you since you were only a twinkle in your daddy's eye," Gran said politely. She delivered condescension with such finesse that it was hardly detectable. Corrie didn't have to see Gran's face to know that she was staring him down.

The young officer shifted awkwardly in place and cleared his throat. "It's Officer Grimes now, actually, ma'am, *um*, Mrs. Tobias." He cleared his throat repeatedly as though he had swallowed a June bug.

Collin looked up at Gran. His eyes were pleading, but his jaw was set. Corrie knew his expression well. He believed he was absolutely justified in his actions, even if no one else did. His conviction was unwavering. Corrie had always admired that about him, but she also knew what that meant. A wave of panic swept over her. She was about to be pulled into an even bigger mess.

"Well, *Officer* Grimes, thank you for bringing my grandson home," Gran said, as though he were doing her a favor. She then snatched the key out of Will's hand and flipped the lock open to let Collin in, but of course that would have been too simple.

"Your grandson trespassed on my land and cut through my fence. He's a thief!" a man shouted from behind Collin and Officer Grimes. From her angle on the stairs, Corrie had not seen him there, but she knew the gravelly voice of Emory Goodson anywhere. She peeked around the wall just enough to get a better view without being seen.

"I will press charges, and I will see to it that this incident goes on his perm'nent record," Emory drawled, glaring at Gran with an evil smirk on his lips. He looked like he had just won a prize. He had a sickening gleam in his eyes, eyes that bulged from his alcohol-and-pork-rind-bloated face like a swollen bullfrog's. His head was too big for his body, as though somebody was squeezing his neck too hard. Corrie could usually find something nice to say about most people, but good grief, this man was ugly, and his meanness put a fresh coat of ugly on him every time he opened his mouth.

Everyone who knew Emory Goodson despised him, not only because he had fathered the most worthless offspring in the county but because he was a cheat who got away with everything. The only reason Goodson had not been flogged and dragged behind somebody's pickup years ago was that he owned half the town. Legally, his wife's family owned most of the town property and would eventually pass the holdings down to the four Goodson boys. Emory naturally assumed some of the entitled power that was bequeathed to his sons, and he wore it like a crown on his shiny, fat head.

Gran straightened like somebody was pulling her spine up through the top of her head. When she spoke, her voice was silky smooth but with an edge as sharp as a razor that left you bleeding before you knew you'd been cut.

"Emory Goodson, the only person trespassing is you," Gran spewed. "I own this house and the land it's set on. The only possessions you have to your name are the evil spite in your eye and the load of manure you dump everywhere you go. I am not intimidated by you."

"Well maybe you *should* be *imitated*," Emory growled under his breath. Officer Grimes opened his mouth like he was about to correct Mr. Goodson's grammar but cleared his throat again instead.

Corrie's insides wobbled like Jell-o. She had been standing motionless, trying to stay out of everyone's view. No one had noticed her due to the shadows cast on the landing of the stairs where she hid. She had stood at an awkward angle for too long, however, and could hold the position no longer. She sat down as discreetly as she could.

Collin had been staring at a spot on the porch floor through most of this. When Corrie sat down, however, his eyes flicked over to where she was. Her heart jumped to her throat.

"Do you, *um*, have anything to say for yourself, Collin?" Officer Grimes asked. "Do you admit to, *um*, trespassing on the Goodson's, *um*, private property?"

"Don't answer that, Collin," Will said quietly.

Collin barely and almost imperceptibly nodded his head. Corrie's heart fell. *No. Oh Collin.* She stared into his eyes.

"And did you, *um*, attempt to cut through their fence?"

"He done it. There wasn't no attemp. He cut the fence. You saw it for yerself. Now I have a big hole I hafta fix. And that you're paying for," Emory said, pointing a fat finger at Gran and then spitting a long arc of tobacco juice in the grass.

Officer Grimes mopped his forehead with his sleeve and shifted his weight.

"I cut the fence," Collin said quietly.

Emory Goodson let out a satisfied grunt.

"To get my sister's bike that Joe stole from her!" Collin shouted. "That was the only reason I went over there," he said, and a hush fell over the front porch.

No one had noticed the figure lurking behind Mr. Goodson. He had just been standing there watching the scene through his greasy bangs, arms crossed under his armpits. He wore a white T-shirt spattered with motor oil, coffee, and who knows what. A sneer spread over his face, just enough to show one of his yellow teeth. Joe Goodson laughed at the mention of his name. Corrie's blood froze, and all the hairs on the back of her neck stood up. His voice seeped into the darkest corners of her mind. Her stomach clenched violently, threatening to empty her breakfast onto the stairs right then and there.

"You gonna believe this liar?" Joe retorted, standing beside his father now.

"Ask her," Collin said, staring right at Corrie.

"Silence!" The low hiss came, not from the officer who stood with his hand raised but from Gran, who then turned toward Corrie.

"Did this boy take your bicycle, Corrie?" Gran asked calmly, but there was no comfort in her piercing gaze. All eyes were on Corrie now. She could feel herself receding into the wall. She opened her mouth to speak, but no sound came out. She could not utter a word.

There was a voice speaking, however, a little voice from somewhere in the far corner of her mind that was trying to get her attention. It was begging, entreating her, but she could not hear its message. She could only focus on the faces in front of her. Like the second hand of a clock, her glance ticked from face to face until it fell on Joe's leering glare. *Don't look at him! Don't look at him!* The voice pleaded from inside her thoughts, but it was too late. Her eyes fixed on Joe's. She was trapped in his gaze and could not escape.

Since everyone focused on Corrie, no one noticed Joe silently mouthing threats to her. She could only make out one word—*mine.* The message from his lifeless gray eyes, however, was perfectly clear in its directive to her—silence. Only she knew that there was much more to this than a stolen bike. She knew there were enough guns in his backyard to murder everyone in Bellam County, and he would not hesitate to do it. Corrie knew that the only reason she was still alive was that a stranger showed up with his dog. She also knew that the only way to *stay* alive and keep her family safe was to erase any memory of it from her mind. She looked at the officer and shook her head resolutely, denying all knowledge of his crime.

"What?" Collin said, distraught. "Corrie, tell them!" he shouted, his anger rising. "You know he took your bike!"

"So, your bike was not stolen?" Officer Grimes asked.

Corrie shook her head a second time. She searched again for her voice, but it was caught somewhere behind the lump in her throat. Her face burned hot.

"I want this boy held responsible to the full *extenation* of the law!" Goodson bellowed triumphantly, jabbing Collin in the shoulder.

"Mrs. Tobias, *um*, I will have to, *um*, take him on down to the, *um*, station," Officer Grimes said apologetically.

"It wasn't a felony," Will said, quite unexpectedly from beside the open door. "Trespassing and vandalism of private property is a misdemeanor. And he is a minor. He cannot be charged."

Mr. Goodson looked like he'd been slapped.

"How old are you, Collin?" Officer Grimes asked.

"Fourteen," Collin mumbled. At nearly six feet, he was as tall as any adult.

A look of relief passed over Officer Grimes' face. He shook his head slightly and straightened his shoulders. "Mrs. Tobias, you will be held, *um*, responsible for your grandson's actions, resulting in a, *um*, a probationary period of 30 days in which he must not be away from your supervision for any reason, and, *um*, arrangements must be made for the repair of the Goodsons' fence. After the 30 days have been, *um*, completed successfully, the charges will be dropped and, *um*, his record, *um*, expunged," he recited, taking the keys from his belt and releasing Collin from his handcuffs. Gran opened the barred gate and pulled Collin into the house.

"How dare you!" Emory Goodson exclaimed, reaching out toward Officer Grimes, who stepped back to elude his grasp.

"You don't want to do that, sir," Officer Grimes replied, reaching for the nightstick hanging at his waist.

"Have you forgotten how the law was changed in Bellam, Emory?" Gran said icily, locking the gate again. "I know Joe does. All your boys do. No one under the age of 18 can be held guilty for any crime without a felony indictment."

Emory Goodson looked like his head might blow clean off his shoulders at any moment. He glared at Gran, then Officer Grimes, and then Gran again. "You'll regret this. Mark my word," he said, shoving his index finger toward her nose. Gran did not even flinch. "These bars can't keep the world out forever, Rose," he growled. Gran waited until he had stepped off the porch and was walking away before responding.

"I might be willing to deduct the cost of the fence repair from any unsettled debts," she intoned coolly.

Emory stopped mid-stride, fists balled up at his sides.

"There is something else you have forgotten, Emory. Truth. Your wife, Marian, always wanted to know the truth," Gran said stolidly.

Emory Goodson glared at her. He opened his mouth as if to speak, but instead he spat in Gran's flower bed and stormed off.

"Say hello to your mother for me, Nathan," Gran called cheerily after Officer Grimes as if they were parting after a nice picnic. With a brief, tight-lipped smile, he tipped his hat in her direction and walked briskly toward his car. Joe, however, stood riveted to the ground. He had not taken his eyes off Corrie since he had discovered her hiding place on the stairs. Gran shut the door, finally separating them, but the grim reminder of the danger Corrie would bring to herself and her family if she ever spoke a word against Joe Goodson was stamped indelibly on her mind.

The three of them—Will, Collin, and Corrie—stood there dumbly as Gran pivoted to face them. Before she could speak, Collin pushed past Corrie and stomped up the stairs.

"Collin, wait!" Corrie shouted. She wanted to apologize, to explain, to tell him the horrors she had endured. She wanted to reverse time and start yesterday over completely. Corrie started to follow him, but Gran clamped onto her arm.

"I will ask you one more time, and you had better answer me," Gran said, speaking only to Corrie. "Use your words. Where did you get this jewelry?"

"What? I . . . I . . ." Corrie stepped back as if she'd been slapped. Why this again? Both she and Collin had snuck out of the house. He had even gotten himself arrested, and yet Gran was only focused on her, on a piece of jewelry. Corrie could not use her words. She had none.

Gran's patience ran out. She grabbed the medallion around Corrie's neck and yanked on it, hard. It didn't budge. Corrie cried out in pain. Gran pulled again even harder, nearly sending Corrie to her knees, but the medallion and chain remained intact.

"Take *this* out of my house immediately," Gran said, jabbing the medallion with her finger. "I never want to see it again. And if you don't get rid of it, don't even bother coming back," she screamed.

Don't even bother coming back. Corrie's head was spinning. She staggered as if the earth had moved beneath her feet.

"Gran," Will said. "But . . . you don't mean—" His voice trailed off.

"You have broken my rules and have brought trouble on this house," Gran continued. Her words were clipped and precise, but Corrie heard it through a haze. Gran continued ranting, her voice rising in pitch and volume until finally she screamed, "You are just like your mother!"

The blade had found its mark. The room was swirling. Corrie heard the roar of blood rushing in her ears. The questions in her head were spinning too quickly to sort through. She bolted for the back door with the echoes of Gran's words still ringing in her ears.

Corrie tore out across the backyard, through the garden, and down the hill. She ran as fast as she could, her feet beating out a frantic rhythm in the dirt. The ground leveled off onto an open field surrounded by tall trees at the edge of the clearing. Weeds and tall grass clipped at her bare legs. A concrete drainage pipe jutted out from the hill in the clearing. She followed the foot path leading away from the drainage pipe across the meadow. Her lungs were burning, hungry for air. Her legs moved on their own, churning relentlessly.

The rhythm of her feet pounding the ground cleansed her. The heat of the sun melted the tension in her body and freed her mind. She would not stop. She would not go back home. Collin hated her, Will had betrayed her, and she had no way of removing the gold chain around her neck— Gran's latest condition for her to live there. She had no home.

A plan began to materialize. She had been scheming to leave town, and this would be the day. She angled right and turned onto Route 9 toward the pond, and this time it wasn't for a quick swim. She would gather her supplies from the oak tree, leave Bellam immediately, and never come back.

As Corrie neared Miller's farm and the adrenaline began to wear off, she slowed to a walk, kicking up rocks and sticks along the way. Her mind began to wander. What was it like to live on the nice end of High Street? What did normal kids have to do to get kicked out of their families? She used to believe things like that happened if you murdered someone or went to prison, but for her, all it took was finding something buried in the mud.

Corrie swallowed hard against the lump in her throat. *Everything is going to be fine*, she reminded herself. She had a plan. She could still go to Aunt Sarah's. Her great-aunt was family, and if she was anything like her brother, Corrie's beloved Papaw, Corrie would love her dearly. Maybe Aunt Sarah would love her too. And if she didn't take her in? Well, she would figure that out later.

Corrie scrambled under the barbed wire fence surrounding Miller's farm and ran across the meadow to the old oak tree. After a quick inventory, Corrie gathered her supplies and set out for the highway leading out of town. She stepped into the future with the clothes on her back, worn-out shoes, an old backpack halfway filled, and a medallion of pure gold still resting over her heart.

Approximately 30 years before Corrie was born.

The package had arrived soon after Rose and John Tobias finished breakfast and put their infant daughter down for a nap. It was a small, unassuming box about the size of a slice of bread, wrapped in brown paper and addressed to Rose. It was her father's handwriting on the package that caused her heartbeat to race at first. Her mother had always handled such things of the household. Rose could count on one hand the number of phone calls or messages she had received from her father. He was a good father, but communication was not his most admirable quality.

Things were different now. Mother was gone. The package in Rose's trembling hands meant that it was important enough for her father to wrap it and find Rose's address in Texas where she had moved with her young husband, leaving the East Coast and all family connections behind. Her father would have had to drive to the post office, which was no small feat for him since he rarely left his chair by the TV. There was only one item of such importance that would merit his supreme effort. Rose set the package aside until John left the house.

Alone at last, Rose opened the package and held the jewelry in the palm of her hand. It was heavy for such a small thing that was no bigger than a 50-cent piece, and yet for Rose, it carried the weight of the world and a memory she had tried in vain to forget.

It had been a simple game of hide-and-seek, something she and her brother Jacob had played often in their Manhattan apartment. Rose was eight at the time; Jacob was four. They were not allowed to walk to the playground alone, and there was seldom an adult available to take them, so they spent hours creating games indoors. Hide-and-seek was one of their favorites. On rare occasions, their cousin Moshe spent afternoons with them when his mother came to help in the family restaurant. On this particular day, 10-year-old Moshe was playing hide-and-seek with them. He always seemed to find them no matter where they *hid. Rose had felt especially bad for Jacob since Moshe always found him in the first few seconds of the game. This time, as Moshe began to count, Rose took Jacob by the hand, and they snuck into their parents' bedroom. Their parents and their Aunt Talia were working in the restaurant and would be gone for hours. They would never know.*

At the foot of the bed was a large cedar chest filled with treasures. Rose knew this because her mother had let her peek into it from time to time, but only when she was with her. The items in the chest "are not playthings," her mother used to say. Rose and Jacob tiptoed quietly across the wood floor dotted with prisms of sunlight filtering in through the windows. Every floor in their home shined. Meticulous housekeeping was a necessity due to Jacob's extreme allergy to dust. He would sometimes have such bad coughing fits that they would have to take him to the hospital three blocks away from their apartment building.

Rose knew not to take any books from the shelf, fluff the pillows, or open the drapes too quickly—anything that may stir up dust. She knew right where Jacob's inhaler was kept and how to administer it. She was in charge of Jacob's care when their parents had to work, and she was a dutiful and devoted big sister. Jacob was the love of her life. Nothing made her happier than seeing his smiles of joy and hearing his laughter when she told silly stories or pretended to be a chicken, clucking and pecking for invisible worms. Jacob would laugh uproariously.

The cedar chest was the perfect hiding place for Jacob. It was away from any books, pillows, or curtains, and Moshe would never think of it. Jacob would win this game for once. Rose's plan was to help Jacob hide and then sneak out to another spot behind the vacuum cleaner in the coat closet near the front door. She closed the lid of the chest and made it to her own hiding place by the time Moshe called out, "Ready or not, here I come!"

Rose giggled silently, barely able to contain her excitement. Moshe would never find them, especially not Jacob. She heard the quiet patter of Moshe's footsteps as he trotted to various places in the large apartment. There were three bedrooms. Rose listened as Moshe opened and closed doors and scooted furniture and small objects across the floors as he searched. She waited, hoping she did not hear Moshe's excited "I found you!" coming from Mama and Papa's bedroom.

She sighed with relief as she heard footsteps approaching her hiding place. She held her breath. Suddenly the door opened, and Moshe shouted, "Ha! I found you!" Rose giggled. "But you didn't find Jacob!" She followed Moshe around the whole apartment, triumphant when he finally declared that he had given up and Jacob had won.

"Come out, come out, wherever you are!" Rose shouted, aware that if she did not divulge his most excellent hiding place, he would be able to hide there again. They waited. Jacob was making the most of his victory. "Jacob, you won! Come out!" Moshe shouted. "I'll close my eyes. I won't see where your perfect hiding place was." They waited in the living room, but still Jacob did not come out. All was quiet.

"Close your eyes. I'll go get him," Rose said, making sure Moshe's eyes were shut tight before she left the room and walked down the hallway to her parents' room. "Jacob," Rose whispered. "Come on, Jacob. You can come out now. You won!" she said again, assuming he did not hear them when they said it before while he was tucked away in his perfect hiding place. Still there was no sound from the trunk. Rose lifted the cedar chest's heavy lid. Jacob was curled up in a ball, holding a jewelry box in one hand. He always liked opening and closing hinged boxes—the way they squeaked open and then snapped shut like a snapping turtle. The box was open, but there was nothing in it. The jewelry had probably slipped out and fallen into the clothes and afghans that were stored in the bottom of the cedar chest.

"Jacob," Rose said, supposing that he had gotten so comfortable that he decided to take a nap. Rose poked him in the ribs. "Jacob," she said again, only louder. Jacob did not stir. "Jacob!" Rose shouted and shook him by the shoulders. He did not respond. "Jacob! Jacob! Wake up!" Rose screamed, shaking his limp body over and over. She began to sob. Moshe ran into the room, startled by Rose's screams.

"Let's get him out of there," Moshe said, and they hoisted him out of the cedar chest. Jacob tumbled to the floor, lifeless. His face was ashen in the sunlight, his lips a dull gray. He didn't look like himself. Rose ran to retrieve Jacob's inhaler from the medicine cabinet.

"Wake up, Jacob!" Moshe yelled. "Wake up! Jacob!" Moshe shouted his name as Rose held the inhaler to Jacob's lips, trying desperately to gather enough *strength in her trembling hands to administer the life-saving medicine. Moshe grabbed it, squeezing quickly, but the liquid trickled from Jacob's mouth.*

"Breathe, Jacob! Breathe in your medicine! Please!" Rose begged through her sobs.

Over and over, they screamed his name, shaking him and even slapping his pale face, but Jacob never opened his eyes. Had he even tried to push open the heavy lid? Had he cried out for help but she didn't hear him? Rose crushed his small, limp body to her as she wept into his soft curls. She heard a dull thud on the floor as something rolled from Jacob's unclenched fist. It was a gold medallion. It hadn't fallen to the bottom of the chest after all. She knew Jacob had wanted to keep it. Rose picked up the small disc, still warm from her brother's hand. He had been alive just moments ago. Alive! Would he have escaped somehow if he had only let go of his treasure and used both hands to push the heavy lid open? If only she had come to him sooner!

"Oh, Jacob. Jacob, I'm so sorry. I'm so sorry," Rose sobbed in anguish, her grief inconsolable. Rose trembled from head to toe as the memories of that day engulfed her in sorrow as if no time at all had passed. She took slow, shuddering breaths to steady herself, in through her nose and then blowing out through her mouth as though clearing poison from her lungs. She had since fled far from New York, far from her memories. As a young woman of 18, her chance came, and she took it. Her ticket from despair arrived in the form of a young rancher named John Tobias.

Rose had noticed him immediately when he sauntered into their family restaurant with a group of rowdy guys she had never seen before. John was the one who sat quietly at their table, just stirring his coffee. He looked up briefly when Rose approached the table. He had the softest brown eyes, and Rose thought she might just melt right into them. She suddenly couldn't remember her own name or why she had come to their table. She dropped the menus and ran back to the kitchen. The other guys laughed at her, but not John Tobias.

He was headed to Texas, he said. He had inherited a piece of land and intended to begin ranching. He had everything he needed and was leaving next week, bound for a new life. New life—that was exactly what Rose was looking for. Within 36 hours, John Tobias proposed. They said their vows before the Justice of the Peace and were on their way to Texas before the ink had dried on the marriage license. That was six years ago.

Rose fell into the chair nearest her. The gold medallion clattered to the kitchen table, so loudly that she feared it would wake her sleeping daughter. A note inside the package read simply this: "Your mother wanted you to have this."

Quickly, Rose lit a fire in the fireplace. As the smoke in the kindling finally gave way to roaring flames, she tossed the whole package—envelope, box, gold, all of it—into the fire. She sat for a while, mesmerized by the flames, dulling her mind back to a place of stolid forgetfulness. She had not thought of Jacob in years and did not want to. It was her fault that he died.

She stoked the fire, certain that everything had been consumed. There was nothing left of the envelope or the note. One thing did remain, however—the gold. It glowed in the firelight, completely impervious to the flames.

Horrified, Rose drew it from the fire with the poker and carried it to the sink. She dropped it in a pan of water where it sizzled and produced a cloud of steam over the sink. She checked on baby Rachel. Seeing that she was still sleeping peacefully, Rose fetched the shovel from the shed and dug a hole in the yard beyond the garden where it could not be seen from the garden or the house. She threw the gold necklace in the hole and covered it quickly. Then she returned the shovel to the shed and went back inside to prepare supper.

Seven days later, after taking the scraps out after supper, she was walking to the back door when she saw it. There on the stoop rested the gold medallion and chain. Rose shrieked involuntarily.

"What is it, Rose?" John called from inside the house.

"It's nothing. J-Just a spider," Rose answered quickly, fearing that he would come out to see what she had found. She shoved it into her coat pocket as a foreboding swept over her that nothing could shake. It would stay with her until the following afternoon.

The next day, Rose bundled up baby Rachel after lunch and left for a stroll with the medallion still in her pocket. She would carry it far from her house and the people she loved most. Rose eventually found herself standing at a neighbor's fence, staring at a pond not more than 10 yards away. The pond was deep, based on the color of the water, deep enough to swallow a pocketful of memories at least. Rose hurriedly retrieved the cursed gold and hurled it over the fence toward the pond. One small splash and it was gone, out of her life forever, or so she thought.

Chapter 8

The Runaway

The trees on Route 9 arched over the road on either side, forming a tunnel of deep green that stretched for nearly a mile. It was Corrie's favorite part of the road, or at least it used to be. Today the trees towered over her, watching her every move and whispering their judgments. A distinct loneliness, familiar and foreboding, settled in her chest. She tried to shake it off and instead set her mind on the task at hand.

At the far end of this road was the highway, which would take her out of town. The highway also intersected the railroad tracks. If she were lucky, she could hitch a ride on the Southern Express. Saturdays at noon were when the hopper cars, filled with bushels of golden corn or light amber kernels of wheat, passed through Bellam. The train always slowed as it approached the county line and then crawled through town before speeding eastward with its bounty.

A few coins jingled in Corrie's backpack, not even enough for bus fare to the other side of the county. She hadn't had time to find the check from the Young Scholars essay competition. That would have helped a lot, but she realized that Gran wouldn't have let her cash it anyway. If she could only get the gold chain unlatched, she could sell it for enough to get her all the way to Georgia. She was sure of it. Corrie was invigorated with the possibilities. She would make it there, no matter what.

Water. That was one thing she had forgotten. Her mouth was already dry, and her canteen was empty. She debated whether or not to make her way to Settler's Creek before leaving town. She would risk missing the train and delaying her way out, but she wouldn't last long without water. Everybody knew that. Settler's Creek was fed by a spring, so the water was always fresh and cool. The thought of it made her even thirstier, making the decision obvious. She had not gone too far yet, and besides, she knew a shortcut. Things were looking up.

Corrie was just starting to feel better about her plans when she remembered she still needed a map of the states and government checkpoints between Bellam and Atlanta. She had not been able to access any map files, not since school had let out for the summer. Using her student passcode at home had not been an option either since Gran would not have let her access them anyway. It was too expensive these days to search for a map from home, given the rising cost of government-approved Internet searches, let alone download and print one on real paper. She was still okay, though, she reasoned. Papaw had taught her to read the position of the sun and stars, and she had a compass—or did she forget that too? *Ugh.* Corrie sighed audibly. She had left in such a hurry. If only she had thought things through a little more before leaving. A pang of regret burrowed into her heart. There was deeper regret as well, more profound than a missing compass or even water.

How had she gotten into such a predicament? That was one problem she couldn't reason through. One tiny necklace had caused so much trouble from the moment she found it. It was strange as if there were something evil about it. No, that wasn't possible. She pushed the thought out of her head immediately. There were no such things as evil curses, and jewelry *sure* didn't cause bad things to happen. She didn't have it when Papaw died or when her mother left. Her father's death had been so long ago that there was absolutely no connection. But why was Gran so upset by it? There was that. *Wait a minute*, she thought. How did Gran know about it in the first place? She recognized it, and yet her brothers didn't even see it. Nothing about it made any sense, nothing whatsoever.

As Corrie walked along the hot, dusty road pondering the events of the last 24 hours, she was not alone, although she did not know it. Flanked on either side of her were two enormous beings of light with wings of brilliant white tipped with gold—angels. They each wore white tunics emblazoned with glittering gemstones and a diamond-studded belt with swords fastened on each side. Their complexion was that of polished bronze shining in the afternoon sun. They each had strong, sturdy legs and wore gold sandals that bound their feet and crisscrossed up their solid calves. They walked along the road, but their feet kicked up no dust. They were as tall as most of the trees lining the road, their bodies the same circumference as the largest of the tree trunks.

Two more angels hovered over Corrie's head, one on each side, while two more covered the air space before and behind her. Those four that hovered in the air had their swords already drawn. The blades burned with a light as brilliant as the sun, swallowing up any hint of shadow from any angle.

Immediately behind Corrie were Horatius and Prudence, so close they could have each rested a hand on Corrie's shoulders. Bringing up the rear and a few steps behind them was Evangeline, hobbling with one shoe on, one shoe off.

"You've already lost one shoe, Evangeline. Why don't you just leave the other one behind? Just toss it," Prudence called over her shoulder to Evangeline who was falling farther behind with every step. "You would walk much easier without it."

"Well, it's just that Lois in the Mission Wardrobe Department worked so hard to make these. They are so beautifully crafted and fit so perfectly. You know what I mean, Pru?" Evangeline yelled. Then she stopped completely and slid the purple shoe off her foot. "But I guess you're right" she called, yelling louder now since she was trailing several feet behind them. "I'll just throw it over here in the grass."

"Very well, dear. They can't see it anyway," Prudence answered.

Evangeline shrugged her shoulders and tossed the shoe over her shoulder into the air. It bounced off the tip of the guardian's wing and landed beside the road.

"There now. Problem solved," Prudence said, smiling slightly at Evangeline who was trotting up beside her. "Perhaps we should have chosen a more suitable ensemble for walking."

"I couldn't agree more, Pru," Evangeline chuckled, hiking up her dress in order to walk. Her bare feet padded along without a sound.

"And perhaps we should turn our attention back to the mission," Horatius said. As usual, his expression was serious, and he was looking about, sizing up the situation. "Do you see now why we did not immediately leave the premises of the pond?" he asked, glancing at Evangeline who was walking right behind him now.

"Oh yes. Yes, I do. The little cub came back," Evangeline said. "I understand now that we follow the instructions on the scroll to a tee," she said, nodding exuberantly.

"Prepare the way, close the gate, hold the line," Horatius muttered to himself. "Prepare the way, close the gate, hold—"

"Any further clues as to what that means yet, Horatius, or what it is she needs to find?" Prudence asked, pointing at Corrie.

"No," he answered. "No clues. We must remain on the alert for the mission to manifest. In every instance, it has always been clear when the timing is right."

"I see the guardians are armed and ready," Prudence observed, looking upward left and right. "Wherever it is that she is going." She sighed heavily, and they walked quietly on.

"She looks different than when we first saw her at the pond," Evangeline said, moving closer to Corrie until she was in step with her. She studied Corrie's face for a moment. "She looks like she carries the weight of the world in her backpack. Oh, little lamb, what happened?" Evangeline cooed, patting Corrie gently on the shoulder. "You are not alone," she said as they all turned off Route 9 and followed Corrie down a little hill onto an unmarked dirt road.

"She can't hear you, dear," Prudence said softly.

"Not unless special permission is granted for a specific purpose, but I have not been informed of such permission in this case. Not yet anyway," Horatius said.

"I understand, really I do," Evangeline nodded, her curls bobbing in unison. "I just . . . I mean . . . it's just that . . . there is no *light*," she said, motioning toward Corrie.

"You're right," said Prudence sadly.

"I-It's like, there's no . . . what's missing is—"

"Life," Prudence answered quietly.

Evangeline nodded, understanding filling her eyes.

"You walked among them before, Evangeline. You just didn't know it," Horatius said.

After a few more steps, Horatius checked his pocket watch and then the mission manifest. "Let's keep up," he said, hurrying their pace so they stayed within the perimeter the angels had created around Corrie.

"Did you have children of your own? Before?" Prudence asked. She seemed to glide more than walk, with her head held high. Evangeline trotted alongside her.

"Oh, yes. Certainly did. All of them precious. I attended the First Feast of the last one to arrive Home just recently. Not one lost lamb, not one," Evangeline beamed.

"What are their names? Perhaps I have met one or two of them," Prudence said.

"Martha, Mickey, Shorty, Petey, Patty, Louie, Ricky, Hunter, Gunther . . ." Evangeline continued without stopping for breath, " . . . and Mack," she said at last.

"How many is that?" Prudence gasped.

"All total, 39."

"You gave birth to 39 children?" Horatius chimed in.

"Oh, for heaven's sake, no," Evangeline chuckled. "Ernest—he was my husband—and I managed a home for children in the 1930s. Some said it couldn't be done with so little supplies and so many mouths to feed, but the Lord always provided. It wasn't easy, but none of our children ever went hungry, not even one day. Beloved lambs all of them. And you know, we could always tell the moment they stopped being an orphan and became one of our own. You can always tell," she said thoughtfully, watching Corrie as she walked. "This one believes she is an orphan."

"How do you know?" Prudence asked.

"I can see it in her eyes. She's wandering, searching. She's lost her way," Evangeline said sadly.

"I would have to agree with Evangeline on more than one count. She is truly lost. The creek is that way," Horatius said, pointing in the direction opposite the way they were going. "I saw it when we surveyed the area."

"That's it, Horatius!" Evangeline exclaimed. "This could be your mission. *Prepare the way*. It makes perfect sense," she said cheerfully.

"Hmm. I don't know," Horatius replied. "Although I can understand your excitement at possibly cracking the code so early in the assignment, I'm not sure it is right. I can see no specific way to accomplish that, and furthermore, I—"

Horatius was interrupted by the sight of a car turning onto the road ahead of them.

"I do believe that is a 1995 Ford Mustang. I would recognize it anywhere," Horatius remarked dreamily.

"1995? Horatius, that is well after your time. How do you know that car?" Prudence asked.

"I recognize it because of a mission I was on back in 2000. There was a young man who owned one of these cars, and oh, it was a beauty," Horatius continued. "Sapphire blue, leather interior, chrome detailing and with a carbon rear spoiler."

"I'm surprised a car that old would still be in existence," Prudence interrupted.

"True, true," Horatius agreed. "Most of the cars they have now are older models or relics that have been maintained. Owning a new car in these smaller towns would be almost unheard of. No more new cars, no more intelligent phones, no more free Internet access, and absolutely no unmonitored airnet access. Much simpler times now, much more than even 50 years ago. And in any case, whoever owns a Mustang has both skill for repair and access to resources for its upkeep. It is a fine machine."

Horatius and Prudence were enjoying their conversation with a momentary exclusion of their surroundings when Evangeline interrupted and asked, "So, a Mustang is indeed a car, then. Not a horse, yes?"

"Yes, dear," Prudence answered. "This whole conversation began by talking about a car. You really need to—"

"Because I think we have a problem," Evangeline interrupted again. "It looks like that Mustang is picking up speed and heading straight for us."

"Oh, heavens to Murgatroyd!" Prudence exclaimed as the left flanking guardian's wings exploded into full extension, shielding Corrie from the left bumper as the car passed beside them. The driver was none other than Joe Goodson.

"He's not alone," Horatius noted. "I count three other humans and 40 to 50 demons with them."

"Demons?" Evangeline cried. "Is that what the dark cloud is around them? It flew by so fast that I . . . my goodness gracious, I never—"

"Yes, Evangeline," Horatius blurted. "I understand that this is your first mission, and you have not yet ventured outside the sixth realm until today, so you must understand that you will see demons in this realm. Oh, yes. They are aggressive and becoming more emboldened every day. This province is nearly overrun with them, Horatius spoke hurriedly, his words tumbling out as they all watched the car skid to a stop in a cloud of dust and turn completely around. The engine revved. Corrie stood frozen in fear as she saw the metal tip of a rifle peeking out from the back seat window. It was aimed at her.

There was no time. There was little more than 50 feet between Corrie and the speeding car. In the blink of an eye, two guardians faced the vehicle, and with one stroke of their wings, the car was instantly farther behind as the gun fired off three rounds. The bullets fell to the ground as if they had hit an invisible wall.

"To the field, *Sa'ana*," said the guardian who had been in the lead ahead of Corrie. He and the fourth guardian who was stationed behind her beat their wings toward the field. Strength returned to Corrie's legs, and although Horatius, Prudence, and Evangeline all knew very well that Corrie could not hear them, each one of them shouted in unison as the car hurtled toward her, "*Run!*"

*   *   *

Corrie ran as fast as her legs would carry her. Adrenaline surged through her body like lightning, pushing her faster than she had ever run before. She felt a tailwind behind her as she broke from the dirt road and took off through the field. Her only hope was that Joe would not follow her. As she cut through the tall grass, she saw a cornfield ahead with tall, green stalks already ripening. She could disappear within them if only she reached the field in time.

She heard the rumble of the engine. She glanced behind her to see a flash of blue careening through the field in a haze of dust. She reached the edge of the cornfield and ducked into the safety of the tall stalks, but that wouldn't last. There were four of them and just one of her. A farmhouse stood about 50 yards away. She could probably make it there before Joe ran her over, but what if the people weren't home and the door was locked? She would be an open target. A pickup truck was parked in the yard. She could hide there or maybe even start it. Having grown up around farm equipment, Corrie could drive, and Collin had taught her how to hotwire a car to get it started. Her options flew through her mind, but she was running out of time. She had to make her move.

She peeked out from the rows of corn, looking for any flashes of blue and listening for the sound of an engine idling. Every sense she had was piqued. Though she knew Joe would not give up the hunt so easily, she also knew the best way to survive was to keep moving and head toward home. *You have no home*, a little voice said. She swallowed the lump in her throat. She had to try. She had nowhere else to go.

Corrie counted three seconds more. When there was still no sign of Joe, she sprinted for the truck. The door was unlocked. She squeezed the door handle and slipped into the front seat, keeping her head low. She searched the floorboard for a key. Nothing. She reached under the steering column and felt for the wires, but her hands were shaking. Sweat beaded on her forehead and dripped down her face. Finally, she found the wires and mashed them together. Nothing. She tried one more time, but the truck was dead as a hammer. Her heart fell, and raw panic rose up in her throat. She would have to make it home on foot. She hadn't even made it out of Bellam, but she suddenly felt like she was already a whole continent away.

Quickly scanning the yard, Corrie slid out of the truck and ran toward the back of the house, trying to stay low. She crouched beside a bush. She could cut across the chicken yard to the field. If she could make it through that last field, she was home free. Corrie still saw nothing of Joe and his friends. Maybe—just maybe—they had given up and left.

The bush Corrie hid beside concealed a small spigot. It was old and rusty and likely did not work. She reached between the leaves and twisted the round handle with all her might. At first, only hot liquid spluttered out with copious amounts of reddish-brown mud. Then, to Corrie's delight, clear water gushed in a cool, refreshing stream. She gulped eagerly and then splashed her face and arms.

Corrie took a few deep breaths, steeling herself for the distance she had to travel—at least half a mile. She had to run like the wind and look for cover where she could. *Three, two, one*, she counted to herself. Leaving her backpack behind, she dashed toward the chicken coop, causing a flurry of feathers and squawking loud enough to alert anyone nearby of her presence. If Joe were still stalking her, he would surely know her whereabouts now. Her feet pounded the earth in rapid drumbeats.

The field seemed bigger the longer she ran. Fresh-plowed soil kicked up and caked on her shoes, slowing her pace. Her calf muscles tightened into knots. She winced in pain but pushed herself forward. She had no choice. The edge of the field was in view now. She was close to home. She had only to cross Browder Road and she would be in the small field not far from her own backyard. She was going to make it. A flood of relief washed over her as she stepped onto the pavement, but she had let her guard down too soon.

The engine revved. Corrie had seen the flash of blue even before she heard the sound. They were waiting for her. Joe knew where she lived. They knew exactly where she would go and were just waiting for their prey who was now winded and tired. Corrie could see the back of her house at the top of the hill in the distance. With every last ounce of strength left in her she began to run. One more time. One little rabbit racing against a sports car. The blue mustang roared off the road behind her, kicking up dirt and dust in a torrent around it. She sprinted with all she had. Just a little farther.

The car was so close on her heels that she could feel the heat of the engine. If she slowed down at all she would be run over in a second. Raucous laughter, jeers, and curses rang out over the roar of the open throttle. She didn't look back. She was gasping for air, desperate to stop, but she was almost to the hill.

The ground sloped downward before it angled sharply up again. It was riddled with bumps and ridges. The bottom of the slope leveled off into a shallow ditch. If she could make it to the ditch, she might have a chance.

Corrie willed her feet forward. It felt like knives were in her chest. She glanced behind her. The car had stopped in a cloud of dust. Bodies were piling out of the car amid renewed choruses of whooping and hollering.

Corrie nearly fell into the ditch, barely managing to keep her feet under her. The voices grew louder. She was almost to the drainage pipe she had seen earlier, but she did not have the strength to climb the hill. She felt a sting on the back of her leg. Then a hard object slammed into her back. *Rocks.* The hunters were closing in on their prey.

Corrie tried to zigzag to miss their blows, but her legs were useless on the uneven ground. She stumbled again and fell. She was not going to make it up the hill. The tunnel—she was only a few feet away from the drainage pipe. She could squeeze in there. There was nothing else to do, and she was seconds away from having no options at all.

She picked herself up again and strained with every last ounce of strength to reach the opening of the tunnel. Suddenly, a rock slammed into the back of her head, and she lost her vision. She lurched forward with arms outstretched, trying to stay upright, but the earth rose beneath her feet. She could not steady herself. With voices surrounding her and her legs crumbling, her vision came back in a blip. She reached the opening of the tunnel and dragged herself in, heaving, clawing at the concrete, and scrambling deep into the protective womb of the tunnel and the earth around it until all was swallowed up in darkness.

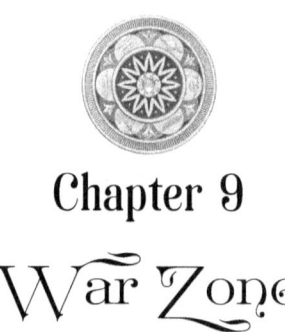

Chapter 9

War Zone

"Nooo!" The sound broke through the heavens like the blast of a cannon, lingering in the air before blowing through the trees in a visible and sudden gust of wind. Horatius and Prudence turned toward Evangeline, the source of the outburst, who was holding her head in her hands.

"Evangeline! You must, you absolutely must contain yourself," Prudence began.

"Contain myself?" Evangeline sobbed. "This is not the time to . . . how could I possibly . . . they chased her into a hole like a hunted animal!" Evangeline shuddered. "They are like, l-like wolves!" Evangeline wailed inconsolably. Her body shook with her weeping. Prudence and Horatius exchanged glances as Evangeline continued to sob. "Oh! The evil in this place!" she wailed again.

"It is truly sorrowful. Truly," Horatius whispered quietly and with a long sigh.

Prudence patted Evangeline gently while Horatius scanned the premises. They were standing on a hill overlooking the scene below. They had seen and heard all of it—the chase, the barrage of insults, and the blow to Corrie's head. Behind them were thousands, possibly more, of faces young and old. All were watching and waiting intently and prayerfully. These were the saints, a gathering of witnesses called to observe and record the events of human history that continue on beyond their time on Earth.

Some stood on Earth itself just behind the veil separating the third realm from the fourth, rendering them present though unseen. Others stood on the canopy, the invisible shelf separating the Earth from the Air, causing them to look as if they hovered like a cloud. Surrounding them were angels of various rank, size, and appearance.

Guardians stood silently with gleaming swords drawn. Their eyes roamed the heavens and the Earth. Their great silver wings captured the sunlight and reflected it back with a light so bright that no one could gaze long upon them. They formed the perimeter while demon warriors and mongers—those vile spirits who thrive on torturing humans and multiplying their miseries by feeding off of negativity and then depositing their own foul poison as filthy parasites do—tried to push their way past. They were testing the boundary to see how far they could press into the forbidden space before the angel's sword, with just one shift of the blade, sent them tumbling into the skies.

The couriers were slightly smaller and faster than lightning with two sets of wings that shone pure white, tipped with gold. They beat their wings so rapidly that a haze of gold glowed in the space around them.

Angel warriors were dreadfully large creatures with legs like iron pillars and a wingspan of nearly 20 feet. They carried swords of diamonds, swords of fire, and arrows of lightning. They rode upon the wind, some leading in chariots, some on horseback, and some by the power of Heaven itself pulsing through their bodies in rushing currents.

A ripple of energy had passed through the crowd at the sound of Evangeline's cry, like echoes of a resounding gong. Horatius recognized one of the guardians who glanced his direction, and their eyes met briefly. Horatius nodded. The wind in the trees died down, and the crowd stilled to barely a murmur. Horatius turned back to Evangeline and Prudence who were whispering softly. Evangeline's sobs had quieted to ragged breathing by now. He caught Prudence's eye. Although Horatius was the mission director for this assignment and the senior ambassador among them after several field operations, Prudence had been assigned the task of mentor. She had the primary duty of supervising the first field experience of this new ambassador.

"Evangeline," Prudence said gently, but Evangeline did not respond. "Evangeline," she tried again. A third time she persisted. "Evangeline, you must understand. You—you cannot," she hesitated. "Well, to participate in a mission of this magnitude you must understand that—"

"Oh for goodness' sake, Pru. I *know* I have to keep quiet or I'll sabotage the mission and possibly more than that. I know," Evangeline said, her face still wet with tears. "I just was not prepared to witness such things. And this place. This place! I do not know how we lived in the third realm, how they continue—" Her voice trailed off. She looked around as if suddenly aware that everyone was watching them, distracted from their tasks as witnesses on the scene. "Is the canopy still intact?" she asked, her eyes wide.

"All is well," Horatius said calmly. "There was a small ripple in the atmosphere, but all is contained. The canopy is secure."

"Yes, but you must understand that our actions have great impact, Evangeline," Prudence persisted. "Direct your outburst heavenward rather than earthward. Up, not down. The heavens can absorb it, but the Earth cannot. They have so much to deal with already. I declare, Evangeline, this place is affecting you."

"Well, of course it is affecting me, Pru!" Evangeline sniffed loudly.

"I believe Evangeline just expresses her emotions more exuberantly, Prudence," Horatius said.

"You understand now that you must have, well, a bit more restraint, don't you, dear?" Prudence asked Evangeline.

Evangeline stood quietly by, nodding in agreement. She was thinking, considering their words. She bit the corner of her lip. When at last she spoke, she lifted her chin and looked first at Horatius and then at Prudence, smiling warmly at each of them. Her blue eyes shone like burning sapphires.

"I do understand the importance of the mission," Evangeline said resolutely. "And I do understand that my words impact the very molecules of air they breathe. But as the Lord lives, I cannot be silent. I won't be unless there is a command issued against it. The darkness has had its way far too long, and I can tolerate it no more. I may not have a sword, but I do have a voice, and my voice will join ranks with the warriors against the evil invading this place or I will be dragged under the hooves of the dark horses of old Lucifer himself. Now I must attend to my mission. I don't know how I will hold the line or even where the blooming line is, but I will find it, and I will hold it with God as my strength."

They had never seen her so determined. Both stood speechless beside her. The next thing they knew she was marching down the hill directly into the skirmish.

"Evangeline!" Prudence gasped. "You mustn't get involved in this way. Evangeline, wait!" Prudence called after her, but Evangeline was already out of hearing range.

Horatius smiled slightly. "Let her go, Prudence. Ultimately, she will give a report on her own behalf. Technically, she has made no mistake. She is completely free to engage according to the revelation she has been given. Just as some of us prefer the left hand to the right, she expresses first from the heart, not the head. All is well."

Prudence sighed deeply. "I know. But she is likely to get caught in the crossfire. And there are too many things she still needs to understand. Perhaps she wasn't ready to volunteer so soon."

"But she was approved for missions and chosen for this one. If you don't mind my saying, Prudence, try to simply care a little less," Horatius said with a wink. "And as they say—"

"I know. She's already dead. What could happen?" Prudence sighed. It was the running joke among the ambassadors. "Then there must be a reason," Prudence said, still watching as Evangeline marched right past the guardians and warriors.

"There always is," Horatius agreed.

As the saints and angels witnessed the events on Earth, something was happening deep within the planet. The core—that hidden, secret place about which poets have mused and scientists have conjectured, that place that is obscured from human view—trembled for one brief moment in the fabric of time. It was not enough to disturb the delicate balance of crust over mantle but enough to reach through layers of history, sagas, and the blood-soaked soil encasing the bones and dreams of souls long dead, disturbing their rest. For one millisecond, the whole Earth shook, and the soil uttered an unmistakable groan from its depths. It was so brief that it could have been dismissed as fantasy, but the creatures of Earth, still tuned to the frequency of their Maker, heard it. The air twisted upon itself, uttering its call in a whisper while the trees offered a low, mournful response.

"Did you feel something?" Prudence said, nudging Horatius. The gathering of saints had obviously noticed it as well, for a murmuring circulated among them and then fell to a hushed silence. Horatius stood, listening and observing.

"Something is happening, something that only happened in a past so distant that only creation itself can recognize it," he answered quietly.

"What is it? Do you know?" asked Prudence.

"I cannot say for sure. We are expected to experience a rare convergence in the heavens, five of the planets. However—" Horatius's voice trailed off.

"Horatius, what is it? What?" Prudence implored.

Horatius had taken out the small scroll again. He traced the gold inscription with his finger, muttering to himself. He already knew what was written there, and yet it seemed there was something missing. He looked all around, noting the positioning of the guardians and posture of the warriors. He counted the number of demons, a number that was increasing exponentially with every passing second.

"What is happening, Horatius?" Prudence asked again, this time more emphatically.

"I am not sure. I am not purposefully being ambiguous, you understand. I can only say that the demons are behaving extraordinarily strange. They are like rabid wolves that have just caught the scent of their prey. Look," he said, pointing toward a pod of mongers flanked by demon warriors beside them. Some were attempting to push past the line of guardians to reach the entrance to the tunnel where Corrie had burrowed moments before. Others were gathering at every point along the perimeter above Earth and within it.

"It is rare to see mongers and warriors side by side," Horatius continued. "Each detests the other. They would only both be joined together in any kind of unified purpose if there were a greater cause to unite them, with greater spoils of war involved. This is not the typical attack formation. No, they are after something," he said, watching the scene while rolling the parchment and securing it again in his vest pocket.

"That could explain the horsemen," Prudence said. "There are enough demons here for a whole army," Prudence marveled, her mouth agape.

"Agreed. I have never seen such a gathering," Horatius noted. There may be war, but we need prayer against it. This is not the time," he said, stroking the side of his face and murmuring more to himself than anyone else. "Prepare the way. Guard the gate. Hold the line," he mumbled.

A wave of voices rose and fell on the wind. A courier hummed past them and signaled to several other couriers who then suddenly took flight.

"Why are they leaving at such a time?" Prudence wondered aloud, her eyes following the exit of the couriers as they fled the scene. Still more demon warriors and a fresh influx of mongers arrived. The demon warriors formed ranks between the angel brigade and the humans while the mongers closed in, surrounding the scene and hovering around Joe and each of his comrades.

"They are not fleeing the scene, Prudence," Horatius replied. They are mobilizing the saints to pray, wherever they can find them."

Prudence nodded. A moment later, however, she gasped, for a band of mongers had broken off from the group and were hurtling toward the tunnel. They moved like large, undulating bodies of black ink, though neither solid, liquid, nor gaseous. They were chaotic and uncoordinated while detached from a human host. A murmur rose among the witnesses, but suddenly there came a loud *whoosh* past them. Scion, the leader of the angel battalion, sped toward the entrance and deflected the mongers with one deft motion of his sword. A roar went up among the demon warriors who responded in kind by brandishing their swords of fire.

Prudence gasped yet again, for making her way through the tumult was Evangeline, and it was obvious by now that she was heading straight for the entrance of the tunnel. Evangeline pushed past the mongers who hissed and growled as she passed and squeezed past the guardians who formed the perimeter. Undaunted by the mounting tension among the ranks, she marched right up to Scion, said a few words, and proceeded to climb into the tunnel head first, which of course left her purple-clad rear end protruding from the tunnel.

"Oh dear," Prudence whispered.

"Oh dear is right," said Horatius, "for they bluffed, and we called it."

"I was referring to Evangeline. She's forgotten how to fit into tight spaces. She can't get her large—well, I think she may be stuck." Prudence took a step toward her, but Horatius held her back.

"Wait," he said.

Evangeline's legs kicked and wiggled until her bare feet finally disappeared into the shadows.

"She's in," Prudence said with a sigh, exhaling into almost a chuckle.

Horatius was not smiling. He surveyed the scene with concern. The moment was unbearably tense. Warriors were appearing from everywhere. Then there was Evangeline. She was temporarily in his charge. Although each of them would report individually for the completion of their missions, Horatius felt responsible as the senior ambassador of the mission for not only the success of their efforts but for the care of those he led.

He reminded himself of his own mission. First and foremost, that was what he was responsible for. *Prepare the way.* He didn't have to be here. It was a choice. He had already experienced the wondrous *paneem'akavode.* He had finished his journey on Earth and entered the unspeakable glories of Heaven. No one in their right mind would leave such perfect bliss, having felt not only the most sublime joy that anyone could experience but also the wondrous freedom from the darkness of your own faults and the pain of a world so broken.

Service to the King was a privilege, an act of pure gratitude. After the reunions, the first feasts, the ceremonies, the celebrations, as well as the dances, festivals, architectural meetings, and second feasts, newcomers were apprised of service options. Many chose the choir because there is nothing on Earth like the music of Heaven. Those who sing in the choir have been able to transport directly to the very Throne Room of the Almighty. Within the glory of worship, they have been able to see not only the cherubim but the very light and glory of God the Father undimmed.

Horatius would never forget the first time. As the music swelled, he felt that his spirit could go no higher, but it continued to rise until at last he was surrounded with light as dazzling as a thousand blazing suns. He would forever remember the sound. Oh, the sound that filled his ears caused him to weep, for it was the melody and the harmony of not only the heavenly host and the saints but the powerful and delicate, thunderous and lilting melody, as well as the harmony of God Himself that shook the heavens and whispered quietly to his spirit all at once. And then He *laughed*. The God of the universe uttered a sound of joy so pure that it was like diamonds filling the air, casting rainbows as far as the eye could see. No one passed up the opportunity to sing in the choir, and Horatius had returned many times. Each time was more magnificent than the last.

That was the aspect of Heaven that was one of the most amazing delights to Horatius. On Earth, there were limits to your joy. All earthly ecstasy dimmed after a time. Even the greatest pleasures, once experienced the first time, never had the same effect of surprise and delight. In Heaven, there were no such limits. There was joy leading to joy leading to joy forevermore, as high and as deep as the limitless resources of God Himself. Every activity and every task was more gratifying than the last. All was worship, and worship was in all.

Some accompanied angels, both in fight and in flight. These were adventurous souls who trained in sword and shield and either fought alongside the warriors or participated in the protective work of the guardians. Some chose to participate in the works of nature—painting the sunrise, scattering wildflowers, or arranging the migratory patterns of the animals and care of their young. Most everyone participated in the ministry of hospitality at one time or another. These were especially joyful assignments. When it was time for one of the redeemed to come Home, if they had few friends or family ready to welcome them, a whole gathering of saints met in the penumbra, the space just outside the veil, in preparation to receive the soul into glory.

The strangest welcoming party Horatius had ever witnessed was when one gentleman entered the welcoming corridor and was suddenly pelted with grapes. Horatius later learned that the fellow had come from a place where the tradition in his village was to give fruits to young married couples as a blessing on their wedding day. A young child who had been in attendance at the wedding had misunderstood and grabbed a handful of grapes in order to "bless" the couple. The boy had thrown them at the bride and groom all the way down the path. He had launched a whole basketful before someone in the crowd was finally able to catch him. It had become a well-known tale shared for generations. The boy grew up and married a bride of his own, raised a family, and lived a full life. When his time on Earth ended and he was made ready for his own glorious *paneem'akavode*, he had a surprise waiting for him on the other side. The grapes came sailing through the air and pelted him, followed by gales of laughter. That same bride and groom, along with several others from their village had been waiting to welcome him Home. It was quite a celebration.

There was an infinite number of service opportunities that reflected the rainbow of personalities God has made. The missions, however, were probably the most unique of them all. The reason for this was most obviously due to participation in the third realm, which is the dimension of life on Earth that rests within the parameters of the material world, perceived only through the basic five senses. It is a most curious thing to have experienced the peaceful and perfect rule of God in Heaven and then return to a land that has long forgotten the meaning of peace, much more the pursuit of it.

Why did the ambassadors participate in missions when there was no promise of success or satisfaction? Horatius had asked himself the question many times. And yet even with several missions having seemed like failures with no visible results, every single soul he knew who had once walked on Earth had volunteered for at least one mission. Horatius had participated in more than 80 missions. He could recount in vivid detail the encounter that propelled his heart to sign up for missions time after time.

It had been the second feasting. Horatius's heart had only begun to understand the wonder of eternity, the layers and depths of joy unfolding endlessly and never running out when he looked into the Savior's eyes. His Savior was holding a pitcher in one hand, pausing mid-sentence with the laughter still in His eyes, and then held the other hand out to Horatius. For the first time ever, Horatius dared to really look at His hand, and saw something he would never forget. Horatius had left all memories of pain and sorrow behind. He had gratefully shed every last reminder of the suffering he had endured on Earth, and it was wiped away—all of it. When he looked at the hand of Christ, however, he was baffled, for there in the glorified flesh of His unblemished Lord was a crude, unsightly scar. He had understood at once that Jesus, who held the power to create every living thing, also had the power to heal His own hand of all scars, and yet He had not. He chose instead to *remember*. So too would Horatius choose to enter into the deepest heart of the One who loved the world, and also remember.

So here he stood with over a thousand witnesses equally eager to enter into service in this place, equally willing to enter the fray with a burning desire to succeed for the sheer delight of true and faithful service to the King, completely free from selfish motive. What joy! But would he succeed? That remained to be seen. By reentering this realm, even just beyond the veil—the thinnest of membranes between them—he embraced once again the likelihood of pain, the necessities of faith and hope, and the possibility of apparent failure.

Horatius waited for the flutter of wings beside him, a courier to tell him to report back to the Meridiem to await further instructions because someone else would be taking his place on this mission. He looked behind him at the sea of faces, the witnesses. Some he recognized; some he did not. As his eyes scanned the crowd, he felt a quickening in his spirit and the words clearly spoken in his thoughts. "Prepare the way," came the command. *Yes, yes I will. With Your grace and Your strength, I will,* he answered in his spirit, joyful for the new affirmation of his continued assignment. *Please guide me.* He breathed the prayer, knowing the answer would come, and yet he was also keenly aware of the memories returning to him from this realm. They were like an echo from a distance, but undeniable nonetheless. He could remember a time when he asked for guidance while still a pilgrim on Earth. That experience was much different. It had been a cry for help in a time when there was no hope in circumstances too dark, and only the blind faith of a desperate young man.

It was roll call in the middle of the night, hours before dawn. Horatius's assigned barracks was at the far end. It was the longest walk to the open yard. His shoes scraped over the rocks that were peeking through the thin layer of snow still on the ground. The cold seeped in through the holes in his borrowed shoes, spreading a dull ache to his feet and ankles. He had no socks. He made his way among the steady stream of bodies pouring from the rows of wooden buildings, hardly inhabitable by cattle, much less humans. The shouts of the guards stabbed through the frigid air in short staccatos of rage against those whose crimes consisted of simply being alive. Skeletons moved in the shadows like phantoms under a full moon and a roving searchlight. Feet shuffled in the dirt. The other boys were passing him. In a few seconds it would be too late to be counted, too late to live, if that were living. He walked faster but clung to the fringes of the darkness. A woman cried out into the night, calling out a name. Over and over she called. She was desperate, searching. Guards rushed into the huddle of bodies seeking the source of the disturbance. A loud crack pierced the night, followed by a dull thud. Then there was silence, so deep and so dark that it hollowed out the soul.

It was then that Horatius saw her hiding in the eaves of the women's barracks. She was a child so small that she could fit in a flour sack. Horatius was 12, among the oldest of the children, though he had left childhood far behind the moment he stepped onto the train that brought him here. He was soon to make a decision that would either save the child or cost them both their lives. "Please guide me," he whispered. "Please guide me."

"Horatius? Horatius," Prudence said, tapping him on the shoulder. "Horatius!"

Horatius jumped, startled out of his reverie.

"Horatius, the canopy is filling up, and a large majority of them are demons. Warriors, Horatius! This is not looking good, not at all." Prudence clucked her tongue, looking this way and that.

"Indeed," Horatius said gravely. "Look there," he said, pointing to another pod of mongers in the gap between Joe Goodson and Azarel, the angel guardian standing behind Joe and attempting to hold the perimeter. The mongers were undulating wildly, hungry to feed. Their numbers were growing as more arrived from the southern territories. They billowed like formless orbs but with talons and rows of sharp blades protruding from their spines that rolled and curled with every wave of their bodies.

"Detestable creatures," Horatius said, grimacing. "They can fill any space—any energy pocket whatsoever—suck the very life out, and inject their poison before any human even detects their presence."

"What is the most a human host can carry? Have you seen more than 20 at once?" Prudence asked.

"One of my earliest assignments was to a man in prison who was host to more than 300 of them," Horatius said grimly. My task was to stand in front of the guard as the man's grandmother prayed over him, right in his cell. She was not supposed to be allowed in, but that's another story entirely."

"Three hundred?" Prudence gasped. "How can a soul even survive?"

"He nearly didn't," Horatius replied.

Below them the guardians were arrayed in full wingspan with swords in both hands. Demon warriors were pouring in from every quadrant. The lines began to shift. The perimeter that had been formed by the guardians was becoming a wide band. Demon warriors arrived and circled around the scene like massive bats careening through the air. The mongers, now too great in number to be held behind the perimeter, began to surround Joe and his gang while the demon warriors squared off from the line of guardians. Angel warriors appeared in flashes of light, filling the spaces between them.

"Battle formation," Horatius said tersely. "The mongers are swarming, trying to distract."

"They're going to try to draw away some of our warriors, aren't they?" Prudence asked.

"I think so," Horatius responded. "Watch the one in the middle. I think that will be the one. They will try to create a diversion while the demon warriors press their battle line forward."

No sooner had he spoken the words that the monger broke from the pack and hurtled toward the tunnel entrance. The rest of the pod followed, creating a swirling black cloud certain to create a vortex of despair and destruction.

"They are not backing down. The next move will have to be a counterattack," Horatius stated.

"And then?" Prudence asked, wide-eyed.

"War," Horatius answered solemnly.

The sky was filled with the noxious odor of charred sulfur. Horatius, Prudence, and more than a thousand witnesses watched as one by one demon warriors dropped from the sky like black meteors and lined up against the angel battalion, swords drawn. The demon warriors beat their weapons against their shields. A low growl was mounting among their ranks. The angels' swords were blazing with white, hot fire.

"But Horatius, there cannot be a battle here," Prudence persisted.

"Agreed. It would be extremely detrimental to this region and very costly indeed. There is but one hope of change in our present circumstances," Horatius replied.

"Yes? What is it?" Prudence asked.

"That Corrie leaves this place," Horatius answered soberly. Wolves do not simply let a cornered rabbit go free, and there was nowhere for Corrie to go.

Circa 1942

    Miriam stood at the window overlooking the streets below. Genova was bustling at a faster pace, it seemed, or at least that was true in the ghetto. Men and women alike walked briskly with their heads down, darting from doorway to doorway. No children played in the street. Even Golda, a widow who lived two floors above Miriam and Samuel's apartment, usually had friendly conversation or advice to offer as she hung her laundry out on her balcony. But lately, she worked quickly and then retreated inside.

    Samuel would be home for lunch soon, sweaty and smelling of fish from the docks. Miriam hoped he would bring home a small tuna or a couple of sardines to add to their noon meal. A glint of gold shone in the window from the medallion around Miriam's neck, a family heirloom she never parted with. It had been given to her by her mother on her 18th birthday. She was told to always guard it. Her mother had warned her, threatened her even, to keep it and never sell it, or harm would come to them. It had been passed down for several generations. It represented the "hope for the peace of Jerusalem."

    That was what Miriam had explained to Samuel when he pressed her to sell it to some merchants at the port. It would have bought food for weeks or even a new dress or two, but Miriam had insisted they could not sell it.

    "I have to agree that the hope for the peace of Jerusalem is much too valuable to sell," Samuel had finally relented, and Miriam loved him all the more for it.

    Samuel was a kind man with a gentle smile. In some ways he reminded Miriam of her father, another hard-working man who now spent his days bouncing grandchildren on his knee and telling stories of King David, Moses, and Elijah. Miriam wondered how her father and mother were doing, swallowing the lump that suddenly formed in her throat.

    Miriam pulled herself away from the window, troubled in heart though she was not sure exactly why. She busied herself with preparations in the kitchen, focusing her mind on the task in front of her. She had a few small potatoes and a turnip to peel and slice for soup. Samuel would walk in the door at any moment, ravenously hungry.

Working in the kitchen was also a way for Miriam to keep her hands active when her mind needed to figure something out. She did her best thinking that way. Sometimes she pondered how to trim or adorn an old dress to make it look newer. Sometimes she thought about the readings from the Torah or what the rabbi had taught at the temple. Today she thought about what her sister Chaya had written from Rome. The Germans were demanding that the Jews in their community pay them exorbitant fees. For what? Chaya was thinking of leaving. Miriam could tell, though her words were cryptic. Miriam had sent a telegram to Chaya immediately, encouraging her to come to Genova. They would make room for their family of four. Samuel was in complete agreement. Miriam hadn't heard back from Chaya yet. She didn't even know if she had received the telegram. Phone service had been cut off in the Jewish ghetto weeks before. Still, Miriam couldn't help watching the door, expecting a knock at any moment. She longed to hear it and throw her arms around her older sister.

The front door creaked open. It was Samuel. He was not smiling.

"What is it, my love? Why are you so troubled?" Miriam asked, dropping the paring knife and turning down the fire on the stove. She walked to the small living room where Samuel sat down with his head in his hands. He was quiet for a while. When he looked up, he took Miriam's hands in his own and spoke softly.

"They are cutting my pay. By half," Samuel said soberly. His face suddenly aged 10 years right before her eyes.

Miriam stifled the urge to cry or lash out. It wasn't Samuel's fault, and it would only add to the burden he carried already. They barely survived on what he made in a month. She could not imagine how they would eat or how they would live. Miriam kissed Samuel's cheek tenderly and walked back to the kitchen. She removed two of the potatoes from the soup pot and turned up the fire. Samuel could have the soup, and she would have a cup of milk for lunch. Hunger pangs soon became the norm.

The scourge was coming. Miriam had seen it through the window even before the soldiers' boots would be heard on the streets. Neighbors and friends she had known for years who once held their heads high now walked hurriedly down the street, hardly speaking to one another. She could feel the evil that would soon be at their doorstep. From the morning their supply of flour ran out she had begun to prepare, to conserve their rations, because as she was told by the shopkeeper that day, "There is no flour available for Jews."

One morning after Samuel left for the docks, Miriam opened the cupboard and selected two mugs from her small collection of broken, chipped, stained dishes. She took one of them and carefully chiseled through the side of it using a small nail. She chiseled and broke all the way around the cup until she had separated the bottom of the cup from the rest of it. She sanded and smoothed around the edges of the severed piece until it was a flat disc. Satisfied with her work, she unlatched the gold chain around her neck and placed the medallion, her most prized possession, in the bottom of the second cup that was still intact. Then she fit the disc neatly inside the cup, perfectly covering the medallion ensconced in the bottom of the cup. Spreading a thin ribbon of resin around the sides of the disc, she fit the disc snugly, sealing the family treasure in the humble hollow of an old cup remade. Miriam tucked the cup back in the cupboard with the other cups, bowls, and other common household items that no one would take a second glance at. It was the one earthly treasure she knew she must protect at all costs.

On the day that Evil arrived, Samuel and Miriam heard shouts of "Schnell!" from the hallway. Soldiers were busting down doors and ordering everyone out, herding them like cattle into the streets. Samuel and Miriam joined their neighbors, all with glazed expressions of horrified shock. Miriam searched frantically for her parents and brother who lived in the next quarter. She scoured faces in the crowds, but she could not see them. She never saw them or her beloved sister ever again. She would catch a glimpse of Samuel after the train was unloaded, but then the men were separated from the women and children, and shuttled away. She would never see her dear Samuel again. She would never tell him the miraculous secret that she had discovered even on that most horrible of mornings, that she carried their child. She wondered if she would ever return to their home, if she would one day pass to her child the gold medallion, the most treasured family heirloom and the hope for the peace of Jerusalem.

Chapter 10
Through the Tunnel

Darkness. Corrie opened her eyes, but all around her it was pitch black like the middle of the night. The surface beneath her was cold, hard, and damp. The side of her face was wet. A foul odor filled her nostrils, like something rotten or dead. She jerked her head up. A wall of dark nothingness stretched endlessly in front of her. Her sudden fit of coughing ricocheted off the concrete walls surrounding her.

Voices drifted in from outside. The memory of why she had burrowed into the drainage pipe drew her body up into a tight ball. A rock careened into the tunnel, bounced off the walls, and landed with a dull thud just inches from her foot. She pulled her knees in tighter, listening to every sound coming from the small patch of light at the opening of the tunnel. The tunnel was only big enough for her, which was the only thing in her favor.

"Come out, come out wherever you are!" Joe called mockingly. His raspy voice penetrated the hollow space and wrapped around Corrie's neck, choking the breath out of her. He whistled as if calling a dog. Then he called her a name that not even the meanest kids at school would repeat.

Her heart thrummed in her chest. The medallion slipped out from the neckline of her shirt and tapped the concrete with a soft clink, reminding her of its presence and the fact that she could not take it off. Her eyes stung with fresh anger, revulsion at what she had gotten herself into. Her head throbbed. She wanted to scream, but there was no one to help her. No one could even find her except her enemies. Her throat tightened against a groan in her chest too deep for words. Amid the whirlwind of her own thoughts, an idea slipped through, just a simple suggestion. *Time to go*, it said, though there was no audible voice.

Go? There was nowhere to go. Toward one end was certain death, and toward the other was darkness with all the rats, snakes, spiders, and everything else that hid in the dark. Corrie shivered, hugging her knees. She tried to imagine herself back at the pond, but try as she might, she could not escape the darkness, the cold, or the foul smell where she lay. She was trapped, and both her imagination and her soul were broken.

Another rock came hurtling through the tunnel, hitting Corrie in the leg. Then another bounced and landed inches from her face. Raucous laughter echoed through the concrete pipe. Suddenly the patch of light disappeared, followed by the sound of Joe's gravelly voice inching closer.

"No one's gonna save you. You're mine," said Joe. The patch of light returned as Joe stepped back. The boys were talking, and Corrie strained to hear what they were saying. It was something about what Joe had found in his pocket. She caught the word *round*, and then Joe said, "Get my pistol under the seat."

Corrie snapped her body forward, scraping over the mud and moldy leaves. She uncurled her limbs frantically and started crawling, dragging herself on her elbows through the muck and mire, away from Joe and into the deeper darkness.

The stench was unbearable. Her body retched involuntarily if she forgot to breathe through her mouth. Her hand brushed against something solid that skittered away from her in the blackness. She stifled a scream and recoiled momentarily, but there was no going back. She balled up her fists and kept going, dragging herself through the oozing slime, keeping her hands in front of her in hopes that the first thing a snake encountered would not be her face.

Corrie kept her eyes closed but looked from time to time to see if she might see another light in the distance, if she might find the other end of the tunnel, but there was only darkness. The patch of light behind her was a tiny dot now, but there was no time to slow down. *I can't do this*, she sobbed. She felt her body swathed in complete darkness, pressing and squeezing all the air out of her lungs. A wave of panic urged her forward. She had to make it. There had to be another end to this somewhere. She crawled faster and faster in desperation until she suddenly smacked face first into a solid wall of concrete. The shock threw her head backward. Tears stung her eyes from the blow to her nose. She traced the edges of a fresh bump on her head that was tender and throbbing. Then it dawned on her that this was a dead end. *No!* She cried, but her voice was swallowed up. She was panting; it was getting harder to breathe. Both light and oxygen were being devoured by the dark.

Click.

The sound came from the tiniest dot of light. If she was still close enough to hear the click of the pistol, she was still close enough for a bullet to reach her. Their voices drifted into the pipe, echoing off the concrete. They were arguing about whether it would hit her directly or bounce off the walls first.

Desperately, her hands searched. She discovered open space toward the right. She felt along the left side and discovered that it, too, was another opening. The tunnels formed a T, and she was at the top. *But which way to go?* One could lead to an opening, while the other could be a dead end. She couldn't breathe or think. She was going to die here, alone and invisible like a sewer rat, never to be found.

Where was the voice telling her what to do? Suddenly, the distinct fragrance of fresh flowers drifted through the tunnel. It was the sweetest aroma she had ever smelled. It was gardenias or roses, she wasn't sure, or maybe honeysuckle. It came from the right. That was the direction she should go. By now her knees were aching and her elbows were burning, but hope had awakened. She was dragging her body away from the junction of the two pipes when the gun fired with a deafening crack. The bullet slammed against the wall of the pipe where she had been just seconds before. The bullet couldn't reach her now. She was safe.

Her hope was short-lived, however. The fragrance drifted away, and tiny blips of light flashed against the darkness. The lights shimmered in circles. She was about to pass out.

Then the smallest spot of light suddenly began to grow bigger and brighter than the others. A current of air tickled the wisps of hair around her face. She inhaled again, filling her lungs with fresh air. The circle of light remained solid. The crushing darkness was unfolding around her, releasing her from its grip. Relief washed over her.

The tunnel had grown larger at this end. Corrie could feel the space widening all around her as she began to crawl with renewed vigor. As her eyes adjusted to the light streaming in from the opening in front of her, she soon realized that she could possibly even stand up.

Slowly, Corrie sat back on her heels and placed her feet under her. She carefully lifted herself halfway up to a crouching position. Her back was still bent over. Not trusting her own perception of the space around her, she stretched her arms upward over her head and then slowly uncurled her spine bit by bit until she was standing to her full height.

She stood and watched the circle of light at the end of the tunnel. There was something strange about it. It reminded her of the end of a kaleidoscope, glistening and moving. It was not a clear, steady patch of light. She blinked a few times and could see more clearly now, though she was still a fair distance from it. She also noticed that the sounds in the tunnel were changing. The stifling silence of an enclosed tunnel were growing into the roar of rushing water. But how could this be? There were no waterfalls in Bellam or even hills big enough for water to tumble down. Maybe she didn't know Bellam as well as she thought, she reasoned, for this was clearly a waterfall.

Corrie walked cautiously toward the edge of the tunnel, distracted momentarily from her purpose of finding a safe exit by the fascination of a natural wonder she had never seen up close. The smooth concrete of the drainage pipe was solid rock here. A cave! There was no mistaking it. The sewer pipe ended in a cave at this end. She looked back, trying to see where concrete transitioned to rock, but there was only darkness behind her. Her fingers explored the smooth edges of the stones near the entrance. She was close enough to the water that tiny droplets of the cool mist dotted her face. There was no more foul odor of rotten leaves. It was fresh and clean.

The water danced before her eyes in a shimmering curtain. It fell in streams and foaming rivulets. In one part nearest the edge of the cave, the water passed before her in a sheer, liquid veil separating the shadows of the cave from the bright sunlight beyond. It rushed past her, racing to reach the depths below. She reached out, pressing just the tips of her fingers into the watery curtain.

"Oh!" she cried. She felt a burst of adrenaline with heat in her face and chest. It was so very strange and exhilarating. She reached out again, feeling the force of the water's flow against her fingers. It happened again, a rush of sensation, but it was also something very different, even surreal and distinctly unpleasant that surged through her. It was emotion, raw and unfiltered. She withdrew her hand immediately. Did every waterfall do that to a person? She wasn't sure since it was her first encounter with one. Corrie decided she did not want to experience that again, a decision that was problematic because if she wasn't going to crawl back through the tunnel, she would have to pass through the waterfall or simply stay in the cave forever.

Corrie peered out over the edge as best she could without touching the water. There was a cloud of foam and mist at the bottom. It was impossible to see the depth of the water below or determine if there were rocks she would fall onto if she jumped. She could tell it would be a steep fall. It was much higher than the high dive at the public swimming pool she had gone to when she was little. She reached around the outer edges of the cave as far as she could. The rock was so smooth that even if she could climb out past the rushing water, she would have no handhold or foothold to scale down the face of the mountain. *Well, that's just great*, Corrie thought to herself and sat down to figure out what in the world she was going to do. She would not have long to ponder, however, for a low, rumbling growl had begun in the heart of the mountain and was growing louder. The floor of the cave began to tremble.

Chapter 11

Beyond the Veil

Horatius spun around to see Thrael, the mighty angel warrior with his battalion dispatched to the zone only moments ago. Thrael was now standing on the canopy observing the scene while the angels under his command took their positions in bursts and flashes of light. Thrael's sword was sheathed, but the energy pulsing from it was still powerful enough to cause the hairs on the back of Horatius's neck to stand up. Horatius had grown accustomed to seeing angels, even the massive angel warriors, but he still stared. The sheer power and glory compelled him. Thrael was joined by Tabbach, a guardian who maintained his watch at all times, eyes roving in every direction as the two consulted. They spoke in Malakýin, the common tongue of angels outside of the Throne Room. The conversation between Thrael and Tabbach was brief, as is often the case with angels on active watch. Thrael then shot straight up into the air without even a flutter of his wings.

The moment had come. Tabbach returned to the post just as a band of demon warriors stormed past Scion who had been standing guard, and entered the tunnel. Mongers rained down upon the hillside in torrents, uninhibited by earthen walls or concrete boundaries. The demon forces had made their move. The next sequence of events was critical. Would the angels simply defend human life, or would they engage in a counterstrike, a bold offensive move that would challenge the terms of treaties and established powers in this quadrant? The demons began to roar and beat their wings in a slow, rhythmic hum. The air was thick with smoke, illuminated only by the fire and light of swords that were now unsheathed and held at the ready.

"The gate. *Close the gate*. I think perhaps I should have been at the tunnel entrance. Is it too late?" Prudence asked, nearly shouting into Horatius's ear with all the noise surrounding them.

"I don't think that is correct, Prudence," Horatius answered. "To guard the tunnel right now would involve either engaging in battle or shutting Corrie inside, and Evangeline may not know how to escape the earthen walls. No, there is another meaning or another time. I am sure of it," Horatius insisted. Prudence nodded. There was nothing else to do in any case. The lines were clearly drawn, and this would soon be a battleground.

Angels with flaming swords drawn dropped down from the heavens while an additional battalion established another wider perimeter around the area to prevent further infiltration. Horatius knew they still would try to prevent war if at all possible until the time was right. In the meantime, angels descended into the tunnel, and demons were hurled out, end over end past the perimeter almost simultaneously. It seemed that as soon as two were thrown out, four more joined the scuffle. The demons were not giving up easily. The activity near the mouth of the tunnel was beginning to resemble a swarm.

"There is a problem, isn't there?" Prudence queried. "What is it, Horatius? Why does it seem that the demons are beginning to outnumber the angels?"

"Because they are," Horatius answered simply, his gaze scanning both the ground and the skies. "We do have a problem, and I think I know what it is." His gaze fell on Joe Goodson. Prudence followed his eyes to where Joe was standing with his four friends. There were mongers surrounding them like large overcoats on every side, digging their claws into them. There was something different about the mongers surrounding Joe, however. At first, Horatius hadn't seen it, but as he looked more closely, he realized the more sinister presence attached to Joe was not an ordinary monger.

"I was afraid of that. It is a sentinel," Horatius said, frowning as he studied the scene in the center of the tumult. "Heinous creatures. They keep the human host open to demonic forces. They are difficult to identify, but if you look, you can see the additional claws. Two are for attaching to the host, while the additional two—and this is unique only to sentinels—are for creating new openings in the energy field for the attack and infiltration of others as needed."

Prudence listened attentively. She had seen a number of encounters with demons but never a sentinel. The sheer number of missions Horatius had participated in made him somewhat of an expert in such matters.

Horatius continued. "They aren't limited by physical space, either. Any number of these vile, ethereal creatures can inhabit a human energy field or, even worse, completely possess the soul." Horatius shook his head, partially in disgust and partially with a look of true sadness on his face.

"A stronghold," Prudence replied.

"Precisely," Horatius said grimly. "Perhaps even full possession. We will need extra reinforcements or else even the smallest progress is unlikely."

"But Horatius, how? Is there no fortress in this place? There does not seem to be any strength on our side here at all," Prudence said, gesturing toward the darkness that was encroaching and would soon envelop the entire region.

Horatius thought for a moment, massaging the crease between his eyebrows. The memory of fatigue and weariness was coming back to him. He sighed deeply. "We may not witness the mighty or the wonderful today in this place. It may only be the necessary. The messengers have been dispatched. Now we wait."

Horatius and Prudence stood and watched the scene continuing below them. Demons, mongers, guardians and warriors rolled and boiled, vying for position and control over the area. The tension was mounting to the point where the slightest clash of blade against blade would have erupted into a full-scale war. Where Joe and the other boys stood, the growing shield of darkness grew so dense that no angel could penetrate it. The mongers were feasting on the boys relentlessly. Soon they would have complete dominion over all the boys. It was a truly grisly scene. Prudence looked away, unable to continue watching.

"There may be a reason we are so close to war," Horatius said gravely. "If there is no fortress here, then this could very well be the last remaining sector in the quadrant that they have yet to rule entirely. If this sector falls, the demons will have full control, unhindered and unimpeded."

"Or could it be—" Prudence began with her hand holding her chin.

"Yes, Prudence? What is it?" Horatius asked.

"Could it be that the angels don't want to engage in battle because this province has been zoned?"

"I hadn't thought of that, but now that you say it, it could very well be zoned," Horatius reasoned. "The angels are allowing such a large influx of demons that it just might be the perfect opportunity to make a spectacle of them. That would be one for the books, wouldn't it now?" Horatius chuckled for the first time since their arrival, but it was a mirthless laugh.

Scion still stood at the entrance of the tunnel with a sword in each hand, wings fully extended, guarding the way and striking down any attempts to penetrate the surrounding space, though he was sorely outnumbered. Both angels and demons flew in and out from Earth surrounding the tunnel and airspace around it, swarming in a blur of fire, smoke, and oppressive darkness so that even the light emanating from the angels was gradually dimming. Suddenly, however impossible it may have been, there was a loud noise like a clap of thunder and the crash of a wave over the rocks, and then everything stood still.

A moment later, out from the earth surrounding the tunnel, a massive angel warrior burst into the sky, his sword still flaming. As he flew upward toward the heavens, all eyes fastened on him. His face was gleaming so brightly that the cloud of darkness was instantly dispelled. It was Gamaliel, commanding officer of the 707th Brigade in active duty since the days of Daniel the prophet. He flew straight up through the canopy separating the third and fourth realms and stood directly in the Meridiem, the space in the fifth realm separating the Air from the Celestial Heavens. He shouted with a booming voice that echoed throughout the realms the words of Holy Scripture.

"Yehovah malak 'owlam 'ad!" "The Lord shall reign forever and ever!" The battle had been decided; the angels had claimed the victory with hardly a fight.

Cheers and shouts of joy rose to the heavens from the 1,000 witnesses. Angel warriors and guardians alike lifted their swords to the skies in unison as beams of light emanated from the tips of their blades. They formed an unbroken circle that hovered overhead, widened, and then began to descend. Before it could touch the earth, however, there was a loud rumble that shook the ground, the canopy, and the firmament around them. Suddenly before them stood a large demon as tall as a house and with huge, leathery wings. He was clothed in black horsehide studded with onyx stones and beryl. He had the face of a man and long, flowing hair the color of pale smoke. Demons, warriors, and mongers who had begun to flee the scene returned and dispersed across the area, bowing to their demon lord.

Whispers from the witnesses floated on the wind, followed by murmurs of displeasure when the demon squared himself off across from the mighty warrior who had now descended to the canopy, sword in hand. The heavens and the Earth fell silent.

"Malphas, overlord of this province," Horatius whispered to Prudence.

Demon and angel stood directly facing each other. They were speaking loudly, one in Malakýin and the other in a similar cadence but guttural and harsh. Their voices sounded like wind and waves, percussion and woodwinds in an eerie strain of unearthly music that rose and fell in such a way that both Horatius and Prudence quivered inside at the sound of it.

"My guess is that they are discussing terms," Horatius surmised. "The whole dark realm is so concerned with territory, power, possession, and domination, you see. There are treaties agreed upon while time is still passing. There are rights and regulations. I would assume that Malphas is accusing him of breaking a treaty agreement."

"Well, that is absurd. They don't have any rights to speak of," Prudence huffed.

"While that is true, they claim certain freedoms that have been allowed them for the time being. Those freedoms are what *they* consider rights, and they will fight for them until Earth itself goes up in flames," Horatius replied. "Oh, that is interesting," he added as he observed the angel tracing a mark in the air with his sword. "Oh yes, that is very interesting. I cannot possibly understand the number system of the heavenly realms, of course, but a few numbers I do know, and that is one of them. Gamaliel has written the number one." Flames hung in the air in the pattern of lines before dissipating into smoke.

"The number one? What does it mean?" Prudence asked.

"I'm not sure," Horatius answered.

"Malphas does not look pleased," added Prudence.

"They never are," Horatius said. Malphas suddenly roared and disappeared in a whirlwind. All but a few demons in the perimeter followed suit and departed the scene in every direction. They left only the mongers surrounding the boys and the sentinel attached to Joe, which burrowed even deeper.

Everyone in the crowd of witnesses was rejoicing and talking excitedly all at once. What had nearly been a full-scale battle was suddenly a victory, and everyone was celebrating—everyone except Horatius and Prudence. They stood on the hill overlooking the scene with the remaining guardians, who, Horatius noted, still had their swords drawn.

"Something isn't right," Horatius said, his voice barely above a whisper. "War was averted in the air, and yet nothing has changed on Earth. The mission is still continuing. And where is Corrie?" He spoke slowly and deliberately as if weighing each word in the balance of everything he knew in the universe.

"If she hasn't come out of hiding here, then she must have found another way out," Prudence presumed. "It is a drainpipe, after all, so it must lead to other pipes to carry the excess rainwater. Wouldn't you agree, Horatius? She must have crawled through who knows where."

Horatius dug into his coat pocket once again to retrieve the scroll. "Coordinates. We may have new coordinates now if—" Horatius stopped mid-sentence for there on the mission assignment scroll underneath the lines of gold writing where the coordinates *should* have been was now a blank space. "We have no coordinates," he continued. "Our mission is still active, but we have no coordinates." Horatius stewed, turning over the facts and observations in his mind. "We still have a mission but no location in which to work. Our charge has disappeared in a tunnel, and we don't even know where she is." Horatius continued discussing the matter with himself as Prudence looked on. Her dark eyes darted from Horatius to the remaining witnesses, to the tunnel below them.

"I have never been without coordinates on a mission before. It is as if she is—" Horatius stopped abruptly, his eyes wandering, unseeing, and searching for recollection.

"What is it, Horatius?"

"It's as if she is in no man's land," he said, turning to Prudence. "Where is a place that you know of with no coordinates?"

Prudence gasped silently. "No, Horatius. It can't be. You have surely made a mistake."

"Think about it," Horatius corrected. "The number of demons, even the horsemen. The classification of 'World Event.' My goodness, even Earth itself trembled. This mission is most unusual. I do not yet know why, but I do know where. I'm telling you that is the location. It has to be."

"It can't be. No, I won't believe it," Prudence whispered to herself. "Horatius, is that even *possible*? That land has been closed to humans for centuries, millennia even. It is in the fourth realm. How could she—" Prudence's thoughts faded.

Horatius was silent, still holding the scroll in his hands. His lips moved silently as he stared at the words glowing from the parchment. When he did not respond, Prudence continued.

"But Horatius, the stories. If it is even possible that she could pass through, it's a wilderness. You know what is there," she protested.

"Yes, and if I am correct, our girl is also there. Alone," he said soberly, his eyes suddenly tender.

Prudence nodded silently.

"I must consult briefly with the Council in the Meridiem," Horatius continued. "I won't be long. You know where to go. Meet me there." Horatius adjusted his suit coat and slipped through the veil. "And bring

Evangeline with you," he added, his voice echoing behind him as he disappeared from sight.

It was true that Horatius had been on more missions than Prudence, and it was also true that most of the time he was right about things. But the wilderness in the fourth realm? Could Corrie really be there? No ambassador ever crossed into that God-forsaken land, much less attended missions there. Citizens of Earth certainly did not. Doubts notwithstanding, Horatius had been given the scroll and was therefore commissioned to determine their location on this assignment. He had also assumed that Prudence knew exactly where to go to meet him. The trouble was that she didn't. At the moment, however, she had other concerns of a more temporal nature. Evangeline had yet to be accounted for.

Prudence did not have long to wonder, however, for at that very moment, two pudgy feet were slowly edging out from the mouth of the tunnel. A second later, a blob of purple filled the entrance and stopped. Prudence didn't wait. She ran down to the tunnel, grabbed both feet and tugged. She tugged again. Then suddenly out popped Evangeline, and they both tumbled onto the ground in a heap. Evangeline looked at Prudence with an expression of flustered surprise.

"I can walk through walls with this body, but I can't fit into a concrete pipe. I don't understand," Evangeline fumed, wide-eyed and covered in a layer of fine silt. Prudence looked at her as a cloud of dust rose up between them, and they both burst out laughing at the sight of themselves.

"Well, did anyone see if she made it home?" Evangeline huffed, hoisting herself up to her knees. "Corrie crawled on through the tunnel, the brave lamb. I would have stayed with her but—"

"But you couldn't have squeezed through. I know, dear," comforted Prudence.

"Well, no, that was not what I was going to say, Pru. Anyway, so the angel there—oh, he was massive, Pru. Definitely a warrior. I could see him hovering there beside me but not beside me in the tunnel, if you know what I mean. But anyway—"

"What did he *say*, Evangeline?"

"Right, well he said that I was dismissed. My job was done, and I was dismissed to join my team. So did she make it home?" Evangeline asked again, mopping her face with her sleeve.

"We . . . we are not certain where she is," Prudence said, being truthful but not sure how much to share with Evangeline about what had transpired while she was in the tunnel. She didn't even know how to explain Horatius's theory of where Corrie might be now.

"Well, if no one sees her here, then she is probably home by now, surely," Evangeline guessed. "The angel assured me—"

"You are sure the angel said 'dismissed'?" Prudence interrupted, furrowing her brow.

"Yes, he did," Evangeline affirmed, nodding enthusiastically. "I'm not exactly sure how I 'held the line' as I was supposed to, but maybe I did and didn't know it."

"Or maybe that was not an angel who spoke to you," Prudence said abruptly as Evangeline's eyes grew wider than saucers. "Angels do not have the mission manifest; they do not know when our mission is complete, Evangeline."

"You know, I did not even think of that, Pru. Oh no! I forgot that they can disguise themselves. Ooh, those tricky devils!" Evangeline wailed.

"Literally," Prudence replied solemnly. "We must find Horatius immediately," Prudence stood and dusted herself off hurriedly. Then she and Evangeline slipped silently through the veil toward the wilderness of the fourth realm.

Chapter 12

Safe

The trembling quickly grew into a thunderous roar as a cloud of dust came billowing out of the darkness. Corrie sprang to her feet, turning to see what was happening behind her. Something was moving within the mountain, moving toward her. Suddenly, she realized in horror that it was the mountain itself. The cavern behind her was transforming into a solid mass of rock and inching toward her. In a few moments there would be nothing left of the cave. Corrie scrambled backward toward the advancing wall of rock and then bolted toward the only remaining opening as fast as she could. As her back foot left the edge of the cave, the yawning mouth of stone slammed shut with a force that propelled her straight through the waterfall and into the open air.

Corrie screamed as her limbs flailed in the wind. She sailed through the air like a stone from a sling, gathering speed as she hurtled toward the water below. The remaining air in her lungs pushed past her vocal cords in an involuntary groan. She pinched her nose and closed her eyes, not knowing if she were plunging into a deep river or falling to her death in a shallow pool.

Her toes broke the surface, slicing through the water. She braced herself to pound into the river bottom, but instead, she kept sinking. Deeper and deeper she sank. She waved her arms and kicked desperately, but the surface of the water still drifted farther and farther away. Her lungs were already burning. A wave of panic washed over her.

Images passed before her eyes, some of them flashing like a momentary blip and others rolling like a freight train passing on its tracks, pulling her into its wake. These were her memories. She knew that, and yet in another sense it was as if the water itself held those memories, presenting them to her scene by dreadful scene.

Joe's leering face bore down on her. The raw terror was as real as if she were his victim even now. And just as before, she could not scream. As soon as the images of Joe passed, she saw her father lying in a coffin and her mother bent over him, sobbing. She felt her own despair more intensely than she had even felt it that day. Any remaining shroud of defense had now been stripped away. The garden rows holding the lifeless body of her grandfather appeared next, filling her with agony and the culmination of grief unexpressed. Were there no happy memories? Was this how everyone spent their last moments, remembering everything horrible in life? Despair wrapped its cold fingers around her and began to squeeze.

Corrie's diaphragm clenched involuntarily. She was desperate to breathe. Her descent through the water had slowed, but she was still sinking. She looked up toward the surface. In what she knew were her last moments, all she wanted was a glimpse of light. She strained to see beyond her grief and the painful memories that enveloped her, but she could not. As one single bubble floated up from her lips, something moved swiftly toward her from the surface.

She thought it was a snake at first. Although the water was clear, her mind imagined new danger approaching. As it neared her face, she saw that it was a long tree branch or a vine of some kind. She reached for it, grabbing onto it with both hands. She felt herself being pulled upward. Before she could break the surface, however, her body reached its limit. Her chest burned hot, and all her muscles contracted in one last attempt to breathe.

*   *   *

At the surface, water gushed from every orifice above her neck. She vomited, retched, and vomited again until what remained of the river inside her completely emptied out. A fit of coughing triggered a fresh wave of nausea from the sharp throbbing in her head. She swallowed hard against the heat in her throat that burned raw from bile and stomach acid. Finally, she lay down slowly, exhausted and limp as a wrung-out dishrag.

The grass along the riverbank was coarse and dry as though the sun had scorched it long ago and it remained a dull gray-green, alive but barely so. Corrie propped herself up on her elbows, watching as the river flowed swiftly along about 20 feet down the bank. Her eyes followed the waterfall up to where the cave should be. There was no trace of it having ever been there. She heard a low murmur of voices above the din of the roaring waterfall, like overhearing the conversation of people speaking in low voices in the next room. Corrie shivered even though the afternoon sun shone warm on her face.

Someone rescued me, she remembered, looking around for any sign of her rescuer. But she was alone. As the pounding of her head settled to a dull ache, she could feel someone watching her. She scanned the riverbank left and right. Behind her was a forest of trees so dense that it seemed to absorb all light around it. Still, she saw no one.

Corrie winced, and her head began to throb again. She traced the bump on her forehead. It was oozing fresh blood, staining her fingertips bright red. She lowered her arm to swipe her hand through the grass since she had nothing to clean off the blood. But before she could do so, her arm was arrested in mid-air. A hand held tight to her wrist.

"You don't want to do that," said a deep voice.

Startled, Corrie looked up to see who was speaking to her. The young man looked taller than Collin and older than Will. She could not tell where he had been hiding since he had appeared so quickly. Her pulse was still racing, but his appearance was immediately calming. In a sense, he seemed familiar to her.

"Do what?" Corrie asked, as he still held onto her and lifted her to her feet. Oh, he *was* tall. His skin was tanned like he had spent all summer at the beach. His hair was tousled in loose curls of light brown with the slightest hint of golden blond. Her heart fluttered.

"Do not let your blood touch the ground here," he said as she stole a glance into his eyes. His *eyes*—oh, they were like pools of chocolate, dark brown with a circle of caramel sugar around the edges.

"Okay," Corrie said shyly, supposing that he just wanted to keep the riverbank clean or whatever. She didn't care. He looked like Jesse Palacios, a guy in the eighth grade that everyone wanted to know, especially all the girls, except this was no boy. He was at least 19 or 20, a mature *man*, and he was still holding her hand. It was her wrist, but that was the same thing, wasn't it?

"Thank you for saving me," Corrie said, breathless and certain that her cheeks and ears were a rosy pink by now. "I'm Corrie," she continued, remembering her manners. He let go of her hand but remained standing close to her. She shifted uncomfortably. This was the second time a stranger had rescued her that day. The first one had put the gold medallion on her, a fact she had forgotten as she crawled through the dark tunnel, jumped off a cliff, and nearly drowned in the river. Her fingers found the small circle at her neck. It was still there. She felt him watching her. When their eyes met, her heart jumped a second time.

"What's your name?" Corrie asked, trying to shift the focus off herself. He didn't answer immediately. His gaze had shifted to the medallion. He stared intently at it.

"You have Havilah's Gold," he said with a hint of incredulity in his voice and expression.

"Oh! So do you know who this belongs to?" Corrie asked, but quickly continued before he could answer. "Well, she must have lost it in Miller's Pond because that's where I found it. But I don't know how she could have lost it… I mean, I can't even take it off," she explained. "I didn't steal it," she added, for Corrie was no thief. "Boy, this has been a weird day in so many ways, she prattled on, more to herself than to the stranger. "You have no idea how…" she continued, but then stopped herself, feeling even more self-conscious than before.

"I'm sorry. What did you say your name was?" Corrie asked again.

"Vincentiel," he answered.

"Well, thank you again for saving my life, Vincent," Corrie said, calling him by a name more familiar to her, as people often do. "If you know how to unlatch this chain, I can give Havilah back her necklace. I'd be happy to get rid of it." She fingered the chain, still hoping to find the missing catch. She was familiar with the name Havilah because it was the name of one of her classmate's older sisters. She assumed that she was the one Vincent was referring to since they looked to be about the same age.

"Havilah is a place, or it once was, where gold was as plentiful as the dew on the grass. You could pluck it right off the ground," said Vincent. "I know this medallion from long ago. How the time has passed," he said wistfully. He wasn't asking a question. He was remembering. Corrie could see it in his eyes. They were no longer the eyes of a young man. He was neither young nor old; he was timeless. Suddenly, he roused from his daydream and took her hand again.

"The gold belongs to you now, Corrie. It cannot be removed," he said. "It has come to you, and it has brought you to this land. It is your destiny. You must trust me. I will take you somewhere safe."

Safe. The word hung in the air. It was an odd thing to say having just been rescued from the river and with no one else in sight. Was she not already safe? Had Joe and his friends found their way over here too? Her stomach tightened. She tried to withdraw her hand, but Vincent did not let go. He held tight to her wrist and started walking toward the dark forest, pulling her along with him.

Chapter 13

Gerushah

Horatius arrived at the Eastern Gate, a narrow pass between two towering stone columns. He studied the massive rocks looming in front of him. Gerushah was a land hidden in plain sight through the ages. If someone did not know there was another realm within the circle of rugged peaks, Gerushah would have been dismissed as a mountain range like any other. Therein was the significance. It was a world juxtaposed on another. If anyone residing on Earth passed through the stone gate, there would only be more of the same topographical features of that region to see. Gerushah was in the fourth realm, the unseen realm of the spirit, torn long ago from the third realm where all Earth-bound souls reside. It was not always so.

Gerushah—expulsion, violence. The name itself betrayed the sorrow for which it was named. The land had once been overflowing with every kind of flowering plant and tree for food, shelter, and beauty. Eden, it had once been called. Paradise. Rivers teemed with life, flowing outward toward civilizations, progress, and a hopeful future. Gold and precious stones could be plucked from the earth in the surrounding land of Havilah like ripened fruit ready for harvest. It was beautiful and perfect. However, before the ink had dried in the story of humanity, man and woman seized the quill to write for themselves. Sorrow befell them, and grief never known before. Eden perished in their wake.

Eden, oh Eden! How lovely once you were.

Adam's womb, become his tomb

How long thy plight endure.

Horatius whispered the familiar stanza of the old poem, "The Great Sadness," as it was called, for indeed it was. Once living in the Sacred Alcove, the *Shabbathon Qôdesh*, in the very heart of holy rest and peace, the first children of her womb became aliens to her.

They fled with the flames of the sword licking at their heels. At first, they lived within sight, remembering, longing to retrace their steps to hear the incomparable voice of their Creator rolling like the mist over the ground once again. They had been the first and would be the last for many long years.

As generations crawled from creation's cradle and spread throughout Earth, the longing to hear the Creator's voice faded. Humanity stopped peering through the gate to see the path to the *Shabbathon Qôdesh* with the flames of holy fire guarding its rest. They forged their own paths through the wilderness, seeking their own ways until the way to the garden was slowly, deliberately, and then completely forgotten. They eventually forgot that there had ever been a path. There is none more destitute than one who knows not that he is lost. Slowly but surely, year after year the way faded from the material world itself, retreating into the fourth realm, the unseen realm, until at last the physical boundary was dissolved in the Great Flood, never to be found by creatures of Earth again.

Though the cherubim had long been removed, the flaming sword remained, a silent warning to any who would dare enter and be consumed. Even so, memory left fingerprints of the Creator's hand through lingering traces of promise, emerging once again in what was called *faith* and *hope*. These were words, ideas, mere thoughts in the third realm, yet it was only in that realm that they were anything but tangible. What is mysterious to the blind is plain to those who see. Faith and hope would endure for all who seek them.

The Eastern Gate where Horatius stood was heavily guarded by enemy soldiers. He hid within the foliage just outside the stone wall, watching as demons with fiery swords patrolled the area in crisscrossed patterns just beyond the threshold into this land. They were warriors—hell's warriors. They mirrored angels in size and appearance. Though they lacked the radiance and glory of their former brothers, it was evident that they had once been angels of light. What Horatius observed before him now was surely the manifestation of that hideous revolt that turned beautiful creations of God into creatures warped and twisted by evil.

Every now and then they would halt their pacing, unfurl their wings, and beat the air. Then they would pause, as if listening to something afar off or detecting a scent in the breeze. Horatius had seen them do this numerous times when they were on the hunt. They could sense their prey from a distance like evil bloodhounds able to detect the slightest fluctuation in temperature, energy field, and blood—even to the most unique aspects of its scent, that of the genetic particles within the bloodlines of those on Earth. It was a supernatural ability unlike any on Earth, a trait likely due to the fact that unlike their former angelic brethren who have a keen sense of vision with abilities to see well beyond the spectrum of light and colors known to humankind, they could not see any shade of any color whatsoever. The handicap led to an overdeveloped sense of smell, especially with regard to blood. Blood reading was the natural evolution of such an acquired propensity. Their master taught them this abhorrent skill. His unnatural preoccupation with human blood had so evolved over time that it left the realm of obsession far behind. It wholly consumed him.

While the presence of demons created a problem for Horatius, it was also reassuring. If Corrie was their main concern in being there, then the fact that they were still guarding the gate could mean that Corrie had somehow slipped in undetected. She had possibly gotten in before the gate had been heavily guarded and had not yet been apprehended. There was no other entrance that Horatius was aware of. The question remained. Where was Corrie? Horatius checked the scroll again. There were still no coordinates. In every mission Horatius had participated in, he had operated at least within close proximity of the person or people for whom the mission was conducted. He always had precise coordinates of where they were to be. He expected the same of this mission, although given its unique category of World Events, he supposed it could be completely different than the norm.

Then there was also the matter of his fellow ambassadors on this mission. He was still expecting Prudence and Evangeline. He thought perhaps he should wait for them, and then together they could find their way. Certainly, they would have better success finding Corrie if they stayed together. However, three were also harder to hide than one. That was another problem. Stealth would likely be necessary in order to help Corrie in this quest unimpeded. There were now too many variables to contend with and no time to waste. Horatius had to act now. Prudence and Evangeline would have to find their way the best they could. Someone had to reach Corrie.

Farther north but still outside the boundary, a river flowed out from the mountains, too swift to even consider fording it upstream to gain access across the border. Horatius scanned the face of the mountain, searching for any way to climb over it rather than entering through the gate. That, too, was folly to even consider, even with the best of tools. The only entry was designed to be this gate and no other way. The demons knew that, which is why it was impossible to get past them. Horatius did not know what to do, so he inclined his heart toward Home.

Just as the words of petition took shape in his mind, the blast of a horn sounded from the distance. Its low, resonant call carried on the wind toward the Eastern Gate. Immediately, the demon guards began leaving the premises and moving westward toward it, thundering away in clouds of dust. Horatius's heart fell since there could only be one reason they would be recalled—Corrie had been found.

Quickly, Horatius dashed through the gate and followed them, intending to keep a distance between them and him so he would not be detected. Soon, however, he lagged behind too far to keep up with them. Although their prince demanded that wings not be used within the border of Gerushah, they were still much too swift. Their legs alone were nearly the length of Horatius's entire body. It was impossible to keep pace. He resorted to following their tracks.

Demon footprints were more than double the size of his own, so they weren't hard to see. The path angled away from the river and toward the woods. Soon, Horatius was climbing over large rocks the demons had easily leapt over in one bound. He waded through weeds and ferns that came up to his waist. Progress was dreadfully slow. He wished they had taken the path around the woods rather than through it. He had heard tales about this forest, the Wood of Pa'laam.

Some said the presence of evil resided among the trees like a skin that forms over milk left too long on the table. Horatius could feel its skulking presence. It seeped into his bones in a wearying fatigue he was not accustomed to experiencing. It was different than the darkness of Earth in the third realm. These woods held the withered longing of Earth's malnourished twin, abandoned and forgotten.

Horatius trudged up a slight hill. As the downward slope leveled off through a patch of clover, he followed the tracks until he came right up to a cedar tree with a trunk so large he could have parked a school bus inside of it. *Well, this is odd*, Horatius thought to himself. The footprints did not move around the tree as you would expect. They followed their established pattern and then were interrupted by the cedar. There were even partial footprints abutting the tree trunk as if the tree appeared and cut the foot right in half. *How can this be?* Horatius wondered.

He considered whether to go around the tree toward the right, a path rife with thorn bushes and some brightly colored mushrooms that could have been edible or poisonous. He didn't know. The path to the left was not much better with a dense thicket of brambles laden with berries of some kind. He wished Prudence were here at this moment since she had a much wider knowledge of plants, even the more obscure species and aberrant varieties of edible weeds. He leaned against the great cedar tree, unsure of what he should do.

Horatius had lost his charge and his companions and had completely lost any sense of clarity or unction on this mission. What was he to do, really? "Show me," he said, but he was careful to not let the sound escape his lips beyond a whisper. He dared not forget where he was and who or what might be listening.

A tendril of green emerged from a nearby thicket and crept along the ground in his direction. He watched it curiously as it began to slowly climb the cedar tree. It wound itself around the vines that covered the large trunk of the tree, inching closer to him. Just as it stretched toward his nose, he instinctively brushed it aside, saying, "Go away. Be gone," and the vine suddenly withered and slipped back into the thicket.

Curious, he thought. He shifted his weight and leaned with his backside against the tree. He had intended to take off his shoe to remove a small pebble. As soon as he rested his full weight against the tree, however, the vines began to move beneath him. Suddenly, he slipped right through the middle of them and into the tree trunk, falling on his back with his feet up in the air. He was startled but unhurt, as he had landed in a cushion of cedar needles that were still soft and green. The tree was so large that he found himself in a spacious yet cozy room. As Horatius took in his surroundings, his eyes caught movement in the shadows. He was not alone.

Chapter 14

Lost

"I really need to be getting home. I didn't mean to come this far," Corrie blurted. She tried again to pull her hand back, but Vincent would not let go. She steadied herself inside, trying to remain calm. What would her mother have said to do?

"Corrie, did you not hear the blast of the horn?" Vincent asked. "At this moment, a battalion of warriors is gathered to receive orders, and some of those orders most assuredly pertain to you."

"Warriors? You mean soldiers? Are we on government land? And what do I have to do with anything?" Corrie asked, confused at what she might have done wrong without even knowing it. There were no fences or warnings to trespassers.

"They want *this*," said Vincent, pointing to the medallion.

Corrie's mind was spinning fast. "This? I'll take it off. Really. They can have it. I can just get a tool. At my house. That way," she said, pointing back toward the waterfall, back toward home.

"You do not know what you are saying," Vincent snapped. His eyes narrowed under his furrowed brow. "You have no understanding of its value," he said sternly.

Corrie was taken aback and confused by the sudden intensity of his anger. "I'm sorry," she said. "I . . . I didn't mean to insult you. It's beautiful work, really, it's—"

Vincent ignored her apology, instead reaching into the leather satchel he wore. He pulled out a small nub of a root and held it out for her.

"Chew this. It will help your thirst until I can find something for you to drink," he said.

Corrie hesitated.

"Would I have saved your life if I had intended to harm you?" he reminded her.

Corrie stared into his eyes, trying to read his expression. What a strange sensation she had, gnawing fear mixed with a sickening, twisted guilt. She did not want to make him angry again. What might he do then? She took the root and chewed slowly. The flavor was slightly bland, like a raw potato but with the sharp zest of a plum picked too early. Perhaps she had judged him wrongly, she reasoned. She was always reacting too strongly to situations. Her brothers were always telling her so. He *did* save her. He had a point. Why would someone help her only to hurt her later? She had no such category for people.

Sometimes the smallest decisions can alter a trajectory completely. The slightest bend in the road can set the wheels of a car spinning out of control. Corrie was about to once again thank Vincent for helping her, but when she looked up at him, he was staring hungrily at the medallion. She glimpsed for a millisecond something she recognized immediately as greed. It was too late. She had made a decision and set a course that would now be impossible to correct.

"The root will also calm your nerves. It is a mild sedative," he added.

Corrie spat the root on the ground when he turned away, but she had already swallowed some of the juice. She looked one last time toward the waterfall, toward home, as Vincent pulled her into the dense forest, cutting through the underbrush like a knife through warm butter. The trail closed behind them as if no one had passed through it at all. The waterfall was growing smaller in the distance, the sound of it steadily fading.

Corrie's mind was working feverishly against the gnawing in her gut. She had already broken the cardinal rule her mother always taught her— *Never let a stranger take you anywhere. You scream, and you fight. It is better to be dead than to be taken someplace where no one can find you.* Her mother never told her he might look like Jesse Palacios or that he would save her life first.

Corrie focused on remembering landmarks along the way and the direction they were going so she could escape and find her way back. When she looked behind her again, she discovered that not only had the footpath disappeared but the trees had also changed. They looked taller and darker, like looming silhouettes against an unending canvas. There seemed to be no beginning or end. The forest was swallowing her up.

"Where are you taking me?" Corrie asked. Already her head was starting to feel fuzzy. Her feet plodded on mechanically behind Vincent.

"To the center of the woods. There is something you must do for me," Vincent replied.

"Do?" Corrie asked. Even though she had much more to say, the words seemed scrambled in her drowsiness. She was also feeling a bit dizzy. She held onto his arm to keep from falling. Vincent never slowed his pace.

"You have come here for a purpose, Corrie, to fulfill the prophecy," said Vincent. The bushes, weeds, and underbrush swished around them as they passed. "When the talyth stone meets the gold, the end of the age will unfold," Vincent continued. "The enemy doesn't want the prophecy to be fulfilled. What they don't know is that it already has. I have seen the great halls of justice. I know where the volumes of the ages and epochs are held. I formed the gold you are wearing with my own hands. You are the talyth stone, Corrie. I plucked you out from the river as I have harvested pearls for the celestial city for millennia. The stone has met the gold, and the gold has come home—to me."

Corrie had tried to follow what he said, but her thoughts were fuzzy. Vincent picked up the pace; Corrie could hardly keep up. Her limbs were heavy as lead, and she felt so very strange. She had the sensation that her head was floating a few inches above her neck. Vincent was practically dragging her through the forest.

"I don't know what you're talking about," Corrie said. Her own voice sounded strange. Her tongue was thick.

"You do not need to know," Vincent replied. "You only need to do what I tell you."

"What if I don't do what you say?" Corrie wanted to know. Even from the haze of her root-impeded mind, she knew she had to resist.

"Then you will die," Vincent answered flatly.

"I'll fight. Or run," she said thickly, tripping over an exposed tree root.

"I did not say I would kill you, Corrie," said Vincent.

Corrie didn't know what to say to this. She was having a hard enough time just staying on her feet. She was also becoming consumed with another problem at the moment.

"I'm thirsty," she said. It had been quite a while since she had had any water. Though chewing on the root had helped her thirst for a time, it did not take it away entirely.

"It is not much farther," said Vincent. As soon as he said this, a light began to pierce the darkness ahead of them. At first it was steady, shining like a beacon over the sea of forest green. As they continued toward it, however, Corrie saw that it twinkled in the blackness. It was the North Star of the woods, and they were on a direct course to intercept it. Corrie began to feel a distinct surge of strength grow inside of her.

The drowsiness began to subside. Corrie could think more clearly now. Vincent still held her hand as they walked, but they were also walking toward the light. That had to be a good thing, she reasoned. Yet her thirst consumed her. Her mouth was parched. She had never been so thirsty.

"Are we almost there?" Corrie asked breathlessly. As they neared the outer perimeter of light emanating from the center, Corrie saw that the vegetation differed from the rest of the forest they had trudged through. There were fewer weeds and more flowers. The trees were taller, lush with bright green leaves and draped with vines. There were fruit trees as well as bushes laden with berries. Corrie tried to pluck a blackberry from a bush as they passed, but Vincent would not slow down enough for her to grasp it.

"Yes, we are almost there, and you will have fruit that is better than you have ever tasted," he said.

"What is that?" Corrie marveled, for she could see now that the light streaming through the woods was coming from a very large sword stuck in the ground and surrounded by flames of blue, purple, orange, and yellow.

The very center of the fire was pure white. The flames flickered and danced around the gleaming sword, itself a white-hot blade of luminescent fire.

"The Sword of Lemuel," Vincent answered. "And that," he said, pointing to a massive wall of thorn bushes across from the flaming sword, "is the Sacred Alcove." He spoke in a voice barely above a whisper.

High above and draping over the top of the thorn bushes was a tree branch laden with large, round fruit that looked to be painted in swirls of pink, red, and pale yellow. Vincent let go of Corrie's hand and pulled out a folded length of thin rope from his leather bag. He hurled the end of the rope over the branch and pulled on both ends. The branch bowed down toward them. Beneath the main branch was a long, slender branch that was just low enough for Corrie to nearly touch it.

"Pick some fruit, Corrie," Vincent said, waiting for her to choose whichever one she liked.

For a moment, she questioned taking the fruit. It was obviously in a place that was off limits to everyone, but she was so thirsty and hungry that she didn't care. She jumped as high as she could and grabbed the largest of the fruits on the lower branch. Not waiting to ask whether the peel was edible, she sank her teeth into the juiciest, sweetest, most delectable fruit she had ever tasted. Pale pink juice dribbled down her chin. Vincent had told her the truth. The fruit was better than good. It was amazing.

"In a moment, we won't need to pick fruit from the outside of the garden," he said. "We will enter the gate, eat from the trees, and drink from fresh springs of water that never run dry, if you do as I say."

Corrie swallowed and watched him closely. The knot in her stomach returned. He walked toward her. All hints of a smile on his face had vanished. Corrie started to back up, but in a flash, he was by her side and had grabbed her by the arm once again.

"I will not harm you, Corrie. All I require is a small measure of your blood," he said calmly.

"My blood?" Corrie whispered, feeling the color drain from her face. "And h-how will you get it?" she asked, trembling.

"One small cut. Just one. I only need seven drops of your blood," he answered.

"Why? Why my blood? I swear, my blood is nothing special," Corrie wailed.

"You are the long awaited *talyth*. You *are* special. Your blood will allow me to grasp the sword," he said, pulling her toward the flames.

"But you s-said my blood must not touch the ground here," she stammered, desperate to find a way to stall.

"That is correct. Blood carelessly spilled on the ground will leave traces of your presence for the enemy to find. You are too special to be spoiled by such hideous beings. Too special indeed," he said quietly, almost to himself more than to her.

They were within a few feet of the sword. The heat emanating from it burned Corrie's eyes; she had to look away.

"Once I am able to wield the sword, we will both be able to enter the garden inside the gate, and there you will be safe until morning," he said.

There was that word again. *Safe*. It had lost all meaning to her.

Vincent held her arm up in the air with one hand, and with the other he pulled a small knife from his bag. His countenance had transformed. He was no longer handsome. His face seemed chiseled from granite, hardened and cold. His eyes no longer sparkled from his tanned face. They were dead orbs of blackened stone.

"I have served the King for millennia, faithfully waited, and yet I have been treated as nothing but a gardener. I have tamed the land, preserved it, tended it, and harvested the bounty of land and water. Who else should govern this territory, this forgotten territory? I have been forgotten. Who should rule if not me? I have earned it. I am now Vincentius Esus Vidar al-Malik."

And with that, Vincent gouged the knife into Corrie's hand and watched as the blood pooled in her palm. Corrie shrieked at the shock of sudden searing pain. Vincent ignored her. He dropped the knife and manipulated her hand, staring greedily as the blood dripped onto his own palm.

"Your blood is rich. You bear the lineage of mighty men—royalty—and yet you have suffered. This bodes well, Talyth," he intoned. His voice had lowered, almost to a growl. He let go of her hand and rubbed his palms together. Then he stepped toward the sword. He reached for the hilt through the flames, but before his hands could touch the sword, the flames roared to life, leaping from the sword and engulfing Vincent.

Corrie screamed and jumped back. Vincent disappeared without so much as a wisp of smoke remaining. The fire surrounding the sword began to swirl around it in a circle that was steadily expanding as the ground trembled. Corrie took off running as fast as her legs would carry her. She didn't know where she was or where she was going. For the first time in Corrie's life, she was in every possible way completely *lost*.

*   *   *

"Who's there? I am here on assignment for the Most High God. Show yourself, and be gone from here," Horatius demanded, speaking directly into the shadows of the great cedar and standing quickly as he spoke.

"Pipe down, Horatius. It's only us," said a familiar voice as Prudence and Evangeline emerged from the shadows.

"We were wondering who *you* were, crashing in here like that," said Evangeline.

"In any case, what took you so long?" Prudence asked as she tried to brush away the layer of dust on her formerly sapphire-blue dress.

"And I might ask, how did the two of you arrive here so quickly?" Horatius asked. "The Eastern Gate was crawling with demons when I arrived, and you left after me."

"We bypassed the gate," Prudence said. "You see, we ran across Phanuel as he was returning from the Meridiem just beyond the veil, and—"

"Oh, he is a fierce angel, Horatius. His hair shines like burning copper," Evangeline interrupted.

"Anyway," Prudence continued, "he gave us the coordinates, and we came straight here."

"It really does pay to ask for directions, Horatius," chimed Evangeline.

"But there were no coordinates. I never thought they existed," Horatius replied.

"I explained to Phanuel that we were on a mission and that our charge was in Gerushah, of all places, but that we—Evangeline and I—did not know precisely how to reach the gate," Prudence explained.

"The fourth realm is really such a complicated network, Horatius. I had no idea!" Evangeline interjected.

Nodding in agreement, Prudence continued. "He told us that there was a refuge here, and that this was the very best place to establish a presence rather than enter through the gate and then wander through the wilderness. His coordinates were based on a pre-Davidian angelic numeral code, which would explain why the coordinates aren't in the mission navigational system. He even escorted us directly to the intersect point of the tree," she said, folding her arms contentedly.

"So this old tree is a refuge," Horatius mused, rubbing his chin. "That would explain how the demon's footprints came right to the trunk of the tree as if it wasn't here. To them, it isn't."

"Could this be Ezerel—you know, the old tree painted on the mural facing the southern courtyard back Home? It sure looks like it," said Evangeline.

"You may be right, Evangeline," said Horatius thoughtfully. "You just might be. I had supposed that the tree in the painting was simply part of Garden lore, especially given its extraordinary size, and yet here we are," he said, taking in the wide expanse of the ancient trunk.

"It's really quite lovely," said Evangeline, "and it seems that someone has lived here before," she added, indicating a simple cot against the smooth bark wall, a low table, and some cushions on the floor. Pots and bowls made from clay and hollow gourds were arranged neatly on shelves carved into the great cedar trunk, and dried herbs hung on a cord from a knot in the bark.

"Indeed, it is rudimentary but perfectly adequate," Prudence agreed.

"It must be thousands of years old," Horatius marveled.

The massive tree was completely hollow at the base yet had walls thick enough to support its massive circumference. The ground dipped into a shallow basin under the trunk just as someone entered the natural doorway formed by a large knothole. The entry was hidden by thick ropes of Estruscan ivy. Natural light filtered into the cozy room by a small window facing east, as well as by the light shining down through the partially hollow trunk. There were a few large moonstones—smooth stones made entirely of rare calcite that absorb light in the day and produce a soft glow at night. The moonstones were set directly in the beams of sunlight streaming in. The floor was generously cushioned with layers of moss and cedar needles. The whole space held the calming aroma of fresh cedar, pine, and all things living and green.

"It will make a fine shelter for Corrie," Evangeline said, clasping her hands together. "And by the way, where is our little lamb? Do we know where to find her?"

Horatius's typically placid face clouded with concern as he remembered the sound of the horn. "I'm not sure where she is, unfortunately. However, this may tell us something," he said as he dug in his vest pocket to retrieve the small scroll once again. He unrolled it quickly and scanned the page. The gold letters still shimmered from the parchment as they should have, unchanged. "It still does not reveal our coordinates. However, the mission is still active, which is good news. There is still time to act," he said, checking his pocket watch.

"That's a relief," Evangeline sighed.

"So what did you learn from the Council? You met with them before coming here, did you not?" Prudence queried.

"Ah, yes. The Council," Horatius began. "They allowed me to peruse the Book of Days, Volume 737, which, I noted, was the very last book. The angel guarding the book instructed me to open it to Chapter 12, which I did. The title of it was 'The Ages of Man.' It was written in High Malakyín, so there were only a few words I was able to read. But then the angel touched my forehead, and I was able to understand the words written before me."

"Yes? Go on! What did it say?" Evangeline said excitedly, her blue eyes wide.

"I read several pages about the Ages long past, of the dispensations of grace that exceeded even what I was aware of," Horatius explained. "I was so captivated by the story that for a moment I quite forgot my purpose in being there; that is, until my eyes fell upon a painting in the book that reminded me of the tapestry in the Great Hall. You remember the first feasts, don't you? The tapestry that hung behind the empty gold laver in the foyer, yes?"

"The child with the long ribbon in her hand, and she's running," Prudence added.

"Running, yes, oh I do! And under one of her little feet is a pathway of stone and under the other a path of gold," Evangeline chimed in.

"Yes, exactly," continued Horatius. "So as I continued reading, I learned that according to the Book of Days, a child will usher in the final age of man, *if* she finds what she is meant to find."

"Which is what?" Prudence asked.

"A precious stone. The *Yahalom Shalom*, the diamond of peace, the most valuable stone in all the realms," he replied.

"Oh, how lovely!" Evangeline exclaimed.

"Lovely, yes," Horatius said, and there was caution in his eyes. "But very, very costly," he added.

"Hmm," Prudence said thoughtfully. Her dark eyes were pensive beneath the stern arch of her brow.

"A question?" Horatius asked.

"Yes, Horatius," Prudence replied. "Did the book say whether she finds it or where it might be?"

"No. Alas, it did not," Horatius answered.

"And if she fails?" Prudence voiced the question that was in all their thoughts.

"She must not fail," he said pointedly. "If she can overcome, she will succeed, and the timeline will continue in its current course. If not, well, who can say what the end of the age will hold or to what end each soul shall come. So, my friends, we sit upon the edge of a single leaf of paper, waiting to see if the page shall indeed turn. Only God knows," Horatius concluded.

"Amen," they agreed in unison.

Horatius stood quietly for a moment, pondering. Though he did not know what would happen in terms of World Events if Corrie did not succeed, he did know what would become of Corrie. He chose, however, not to discuss it with his companions. He did not want to cause them distress. He would focus all his energy on doing everything he could to help Corrie succeed and help them all complete their tasks. To do anything else was futility, he reasoned. The Lord would accomplish His own sovereign will. That fact Horatius knew deep in his soul, and there was no point in discussing other temporary outcomes unless and until it was necessary to do so.

"All right then," Horatius said suddenly, straightening to his full height and glancing at his pocket watch. "Our objective is to find Corrie before nightfall and bring her here. I'm beginning to think that she entered through another means, possibly in the West, given the recall of the demons in that direction."

"Since when is there another passage than the Eastern Gate? That's unheard of," Prudence remarked.

"Oh?" Evangeline chimed in curiously, though she had only recently learned of the existence of Gerushah.

"I understand your doubt, Prudence," Horatius replied. "Even I did not think of that possibility at first. However, is it not also possible that Gerushah is seeking union with Earth again in preparation for the Last Days? The veil between physical and spiritual, between Earth and Air, seems to be growing thinner. It's even opening in places, much like fabric begins to grow thin over time," Horatius explained.

"Apparently," Prudence agreed. "At many of the welcoming feasts lately, new arrivals are claiming to have seen visions of the fourth realm, even of the fifth and sixth realms while still on Earth, though the higher realms are seen only rarely. So I do agree that the thinning of the veil is a real possibility."

"And if that is the case," Horatius replied, nodding in consideration, "then Corrie would be the first to actually pass through the veil without experiencing death since Elijah."

"Don't forget Stephen who looked straight up into the seventh realm," Prudence added. "And John. They had at least been able to see beyond the veil, even if not passing through it."

"True," Horatius said. "The veil has never been completely impermeable, and yet we should expect an increase in such activity in these final days, for thus it was written."

"Oh, it does sound exciting!" Evangeline exclaimed, her eyes twinkling.

"Well, in any case, I believe we will cover more ground if we each search individually for Corrie," Horatius replied, abruptly returning the conversation back to the task at hand. "Look for the smallest footprints, the slightest snap of a twig. Evangeline, you will head southwest. Prudence, you go northwest. I'll head directly westward. We will meet back here when the last colors of the sunset have faded to black."

"What if they get to her first, Horatius?" Prudence inquired.

"Or what if they already have her?" Evangeline wailed, shuddering at the thought.

"Yes," Horatius said somberly. "Though they tend to be less active during the day, preferring night hours for the hunt, both scenarios are possible. Our hope in this mission lies in the One who called us to it. We walk in this land as we did once on Earth—by faith. We simply trust and obey.

"Horatius," Prudence said, with her finger in the air, indicating a thought that had just crossed her mind. "What about our missions? I think it may be wise for me to proceed eastward, given my instructions to 'close the gate.' What do you think?"

"Very well. That will be fine," Horatius agreed, nodding. "I will take the northwest route then. Keep in mind, both of you, that due to the Treaty of Zim, there is no angel reinforcement here, so don't be fooled by demons behaving as angels. Do not engage the enemy, and speak to no one unless it is to Corrie."

Prudence nudged Evangeline, remembering Evangeline's recent encounter with the demon who had impersonated an angel.

"Yes, Pru. I have learned my lesson, I promise I have," said Evangeline, her curls bobbing wildly as she nodded.

"I can only imagine what this place is like under the cover of darkness," Horatius continued. "Even the land is bewitched, recalcitrant, writhing under the thinnest cloak of restless slumber." He recalled the encounter with the crawling vine before he tumbled into the tree trunk. "Mind the position of the sun, and make your way back before dark, with or without her," Horatius instructed and then glanced again at his pocket watch.

"Assuming that she hasn't been apprehended already, what are the odds of us finding her before they do?" Prudence asked.

"Given the fact that they have a tactical advantage, more power, and the fast-approaching cover of night in their favor, I'd say we have every chance of success," Horatius winked and then exited the tree.

Prudence and Evangeline followed suit, each heading in opposite directions. They were three lone beacons of light searching for a single bloom in a wild wilderness aroused from its own troubled slumber.

*   *   *

In the west of Gerushah, a legion of demon warriors assembled, summoned by the blast of the horn. The ritual was ancient. Failure to comply resulted in the offender being delivered to the tormentors—monstrous, unyielding beasts with four faces, and every face had a gaping mouth with rows of sharp fangs. Iron talons studded each of their four paws. Their bellies swelled with burning fires that consumed the flaming swords of warriors who attempted to defend themselves against them.

This was not all of the demonic battalions. It was far from it. A company always remained in Gerushah and rotated positions with other companies stationed throughout the universe. Some were assigned to guard strongholds from an angelic presence, which allowed mongers to do their work most efficiently in humans without the meddling interference of angels. Some continued battles with angels that had raged unabated for millennia of Earth years. These were princes, authorities, kings, and rulers of provinces and territories who battled over not only geographic space and time itself but also the right to influence the entities within it. One single event in human history had robbed them of their authority, and yet they had railed against the ruling ever since. While each battalion served in the fields, they all fulfilled their duties to their captains—to General Bahadur and to their supreme ruler, Lord Lucifer himself.

They stood according to rank and platoon, shoulder to shoulder in the stretch of desert land at the foot of the peaks in the southwestern quadrant of Gerushah. The valley formed a shallow basin where they gathered, all facing the mountain where, sequestered in his palace, sat the Prince of the Power of the Air.

When his dominion on Earth was destroyed, he was permitted to claim Gerushah for a time as his dwelling place. The palace rested on the lower slope of Niphalsalem, the tallest peak along the rocky southwestern border. The palace's obsidian walls gleamed in the sunlight, aesthetically striking against the pale igneous rock that formed the landscape. Tall spires reached upward toward the heavens. Covered in gemstones that had been thoroughly and surreptitiously stripped from the land, the spires sparkled in proud disdain. The palace was enclosed in a dome of iron bars with a single gate that was always locked and guarded by a small platoon of warriors clothed in scales of steel and tungsten. The outer courtyard was a "garden" (there was no garden since nothing grew there) of granite, shale, obsidian, and jasper arranged in a pattern. When seen from above, it spelled out the words "King of Kings." At first, it was spelled out in Maltsarín but recently had been reformed into the language of the Holy Throne Room, a tongue too holy to be spoken, written, or even named. Yet now it was scrawled on the cursed ground of Gerushah.

The demons stood bare-faced, their iron helmets removed. From afar, they resembled the angelic beings of the same rank, their former brothers whose countenances reflected the light and glory of Heaven. Demon warriors were equally tall, strong, and powerful, yet their faces were dull, reflecting neither strength nor beauty.

All of them were tattooed, most of them extensively, by a ritual procedure unique to demons in the warrior class. They each had an initial inscription or design that indicated their rank and assigned platoon. This was always on the face or forehead. With each successful conquest, they received another tattoo. Many of the designs were made using melted ore from Gerushah. The most cunning of warriors, however, mixed the ore with the blood of their human conquests, thus uniting them with human lineage in a show of power.

They stood at attention with swords sheathed, feet apart, and hands behind them. Those with wings kept them tightly furled on their backs. All was silent as they waited for the report and their next assignments.

A breeze stirred among them—a precursor. Some shifted in place, and a nervous tension circulated among the ranks. A moaning wind blew past them on its way to the palace. The address soon followed in the same wind, delivered in Maltsarín, the common tongue of the damned, and translated as follows: "I, the Supreme Ruler, have subdued every province within the empire. There is not a district that does not know my power, nor any domain great or small that does not reflect my greatness. Most every fortress of the enemy has been destroyed."

At this, the wind dissipated, followed by the sound of a loud gong ringing out over the valley. Right on cue, the demon horde erupted into a fierce roar and a crash of their swords and shields together in well-rehearsed unison. And then there was silence.

"Once again," the voice continued on the wind. "I must make you aware of threats that the enemy poses in an attempt to overthrow my sovereign right to rule. May he and all his kind be cursed," Lucifer seethed.

When they heard the phrase "be cursed," the warriors again roared a mighty roar and beat their shields before the next gust of wind stirred clouds of dust rising over the valley.

The voice rasped, "There is a battalion currently fighting in the ongoing war in the northeast territory of the Assuan province, 83rd region. Some of you here will be either replacing our soldiers there or reinforcing them. Your commanding officers will inform you regarding my orders. Be on the alert for any new fortresses springing up in sectors where we have the fewest numbers. Reinforce these sectors immediately in order to eliminate any hint of prayer or upward hope directed toward the enemy. Do not, and I say this to all of you, do not be lured into complacency. You must not allow the enemy any ground. Do not be deterred by rebuke. Destruction must be your only aim and cunning your only method. Every distraction from their purpose is glory to our great cause for which you will surely be rewarded." The voice faded as the gales of wind again subsided.

The gong sounded, and the demons cheered obediently. They obeyed not out of honor or a desire to please as the angels did. Never. They feared only humiliation, a tool Lucifer wielded for his own maniacal pleasure. What they wanted, *craved*, was the reward of power dispensed in miserly amounts according to what was most useful to Lucifer.

A hush fell over the valley as they waited. They had not yet been dismissed, so they dared not move. A low murmur passed through the legion as four demons emerged slowly from inside the palace and stood on the portico overlooking the valley. They were bound in chains around the neck, ankles, and wrists. A single demon of lesser rank and size and having no wings drove them with a whip, parading them in front for all to see. Their heads had been shaved, and they wore no armor. They wore nothing but chains, and every tattoo they had earned had been stripped from them. As they stood, forced to face the gathered legion, the wind stirred a final time, and the voice of their master whirled through the ranks.

"It has come to my attention that a relic of some significance has arrived in these lands, borne by a child," the silky voice intoned. "Her presence here is due to the four unworthy creatures you see displayed before you who failed both to acquire the relic and prevent her from trespassing on this, *our*, territory. They shall be dealt with accordingly."

All demons knew their fate should they fail a task. They would be banished to inhabit the wild boars in a remote region of the empire. Having completed the sentence, they would then be tasked with the most undistinguished of duties that offered no reward. They would, in essence, crawl back into their taskmaster's good graces only if they could prove themselves sufficiently useful.

Lucifer continued. "The task will require stealth and wretched adherence to the suspension of force, though I have every confidence in our ultimate success. Any mandates regarding the preservation of life are inconsequential. The total destruction of the subject from her own innate tendencies is easily within our manipulation. She will not fulfill the wishes of the enemy. She will not fulfill the prophecy." The wind carried his final word in a baleful and foreboding hiss and expired.

When the final gong sounded, the commanding officers and overlords cracked their whips and growled orders to the subjugated demons in their charge. The demon warriors began exiting the palace grounds. Some marched south toward the fields set aside for training. Others formed ranks to receive orders. The majority of the demon horde streamed eastward toward the gate. They would depart from there to their assigned posts in the vast network of provinces and territories throughout the fourth realm. From a company of warriors still gathered on the palace grounds, a large form pushed his way through the crowd and moved swiftly toward the palace courtyard.

Qal was taller than most demons, with broad, muscular shoulders. His complexion was swarthy like tanned leather but barely visible beneath the multitude of tattoos carved into his body from his many military conquests. Several of the designs were blood tattoos.

He wore a tunic of mail beneath a breastplate of iridium, tungsten, and zarxium, a rare metal coveted among the demons and found only in Gerushah. It was a substance harder than all metals combined. Two swords hung at his waist with a knife tucked into his belt. He carried a long bow in his left hand. On his back was a quiver full of arrows and shorter spears with iron tips as sharp as needles. Qal strode angrily toward Bahadur, commanding general of the demon army who answered only to Lucifer himself.

"You have your orders. Leave the swords. You won't need them," Bahadur growled, looking past Qal with an expression of bored disdain.

Qal chuffed. He had fought armies, even Michael and Gabriel in hand-to-hand combat, and had persevered. His reward was long past due, and yet he was to command a company of warriors for *this* task? A female child?

"Are you too mighty for this assignment, great one?" Bahadur mocked. "I will remind you that the warriors who failed were greater than you." He glared at Qal just inches from his face.

Qal wanted to remind the general that those warriors had resistance by angels. He was being commanded to hunt a single child alone in the wilderness with no defense. It was demeaning. It was more than that. It was humiliating. He had done *nothing* to merit such a task, nothing but succeed in every single endeavor. He clenched his jaw and said nothing as he stared brazenly at Bahadur.

"You dare to defy me, soldier?" Bahadur smirked. "The only reason I don't demote you to palace guard is because you were chosen for this task. Incapacitate her completely. Do with her what you will, but you must render her completely incapable of possessing the stone. You may do anything but kill her. You have until morning. Dismissed," Bahadur said with a wave of his hand.

Qal saluted with a raised fist, then turned and strode across the valley toward the battalion base to select the warriors he would command. He was not permitted to take her life *outright*. However, there were many ways to incapacitate a victim with varying degrees of effectiveness, and all with the same result. He thought of all the methods he had mastered in the fine art of human torture over the vast stretch of time.

He was not merely a barbaric warrior as most warriors were. They lacked the sophistication and subtlety required in manipulating a human subject while remaining within boundaries imposed by the Creator. Bahadur had no appreciation for such things, which, in Qal's opinion, was what made Bahadur a weak leader. You cannot work around what you do not understand. You likewise cannot understand what you do not appreciate or at least respect. Raw hatred is useless.

Qal had continued cultivating interest in the study of humans as they interacted with the unseen realms. He knew what an arrow dipped in clay from the marshes deep in the woods of Pa'Laam did to the human psyche. Not all demons possessed such skill or knowledge. He knew the precise speed at which an arrow must travel in order to pierce the energy field and reach into the deepest memories of a human weakened by fear-bearing mongers.

Bahadur would not acknowledge Qal's expertise. That was a given. Bahadur had harbored a grudge toward Qal for more than three centuries. Qal's crime had been to not salute the general properly. For that, Qal had never been promoted as he deserved. He would show Bahadur the cunning of his mightiest warrior. Bahadur would not be pleased with his efforts, however. He would regret having chosen him for this task. Revenge, no matter how exacted, was always sweet.

Chapter 15
Closing In

Vines, weeds, and brambles leapt from the path and latched onto Corrie's ankles as she ran. She tripped over thick roots rising up suddenly from the soil. Finding a clear path through the trees was becoming impossible. The thick foliage scratched at her bare legs, stinging her with poisonous barbs. Burs latched onto her clothing and burrowed into her skin.

Corrie pushed deeper and deeper into the forest. The treetops, dense with their massive craggy branches and thick foliage, only allowed the smallest filaments of light to filter through. She stumbled into a patch of briers as thick as a man's fingers, laced among the stems and vines. They snagged at her clothing and ensnared her legs until at last she fell, sprawling into a gnarled shrub of stinging nettles. She cried out in pain as the leaves of the shrub clung to her skin. She fought desperately to swipe the nettles from her arms and legs, stinging her hands all over again. Her skin was a patchwork of red, swollen flesh with jagged scratches and raised welts covering much of her body.

She glanced behind her. For a moment she thought she saw movement among the trees. She slipped behind a large tree in a thicket of bushes to watch and wait for any sign of someone following her. She peeked out from behind the tree trunk, straining her eyes in the dim light of the woods and scanning for any detectable motion. The bushes around her seemed to be growing before her eyes. Soon, however, she realized that it was not the bushes that were changing. The ground beneath her was becoming loose sand that gave way beneath her feet. She was gradually sinking.

Quickly, Corrie held onto the tree trunk. She placed her foot on a large knot, grabbed onto a thick vine wrapped around the branch above her head, and started to climb. Though the bark was smooth, many knots made it easy to scale up into the leafy boughs. She found a notch higher up between two branches. She pressed her back against one branch, propped her leg against the other for support, and peered over the treetop.

This land, wherever she was, was surrounded by a mountainous ridge encasing her in a rugged terrain of dark forests, grassy meadows, and rocky hills. Along the northwestern edge of the circular ridge was the waterfall. Corrie was too far to hear it, but she could still see the white plumes of water cascading down the rock face. How had she wandered so far and so quickly?

It was such a strange forest. Was it her imagination that the land itself seemed to be against her? And the silence! The silence was deafening. There was no wind, no birds, and not even an insect. No, this couldn't be Texas. Nowhere in Texas would you be completely free of bugs. Although she had traveled only as far as her own legs could carry her, she might as well be millions of miles from home. At home, whenever it took Corrie a long time to gather eggs in the morning, Gran would always say, "Well, did you go to Oklahoma and back for those eggs?" Maybe she had finally gone to Oklahoma.

She plucked the many stickers and briers from her clothing and skin, leaving tiny pink bumps where the sharp points had been. Some spots oozed little dots of blood. Remembering what Vincent had said about blood, she swiped over it with the hem of her shirt lest any of it should drip onto the ground.

Corrie shivered at the memory of what she had undergone not even an hour before. Fatigue settled in her limbs, and a desperate thirst parched her throat again. She slipped down into a comfortable, seated position in the notch of the branches. Even if she felt the inclination to move from her perch, she had not the strength. She would rest just a moment before traveling on.

The sun was an ember hovering over the far ridge when the air was suddenly filled with a strange and exotic perfume. Corrie inhaled deeply. All around her, large, luminescent, white blooms opened in the soft light of dusk. *Moonbeams*, she marveled—her favorite flowers—and the whole tree was suddenly filled with them.

She plucked a moonbeam from its stem and sucked the nectar from the base of the flower. The sweetness of it created a thirst for more. She plucked three and then four more. Each gigantic blossom provided a thimbleful of nectar. While the nectar gave her a welcome burst of energy, it also intensified her thirst for water. She surveyed the land for the quickest route to any water source. Though the waterfall was still within her sights, she already knew there was no water there for her to drink. The river was salty. She scanned the landscape and found the sparkle of a small stream just a little farther east. She found her landmark, a large cedar in the distance, and began to climb down.

Just as she touched the tip of the branch below, she heard a deep crack within the tree. She instantly froze, afraid to move an inch more. She looked down to see how far she was from the ground. There just below her and jabbed into the trunk of the tree was the blade of a large knife. Beneath the hilt stood two very large men.

They wore layers of what looked like leather or canvas folded behind each of them and tucked under the heavy shields they carried on their backs. Large metal barbs jutted out from the edges of the shield. They each carried swords hanging at their sides, and each sword had a carved iron hilt with a large onyx stone as the pommel. The swords were sheathed in long, metal scabbards. They were soldiers, that much was clear, though they did not look like any soldiers Corrie had ever seen.

Helmets covered their faces. One soldier had long, blond hair like the tail of a horse, while the other had a tangled, wild mane the color of charred ash. They spoke in deep-throated growls like metal spikes rubbing against each other amid the low howl of the wind that stirred the treetops. Corrie tried to still the trembling in her legs for fear the movement in the branches would give her away, but the wind stirred the leaves in another gust. She held her breath and closed her eyes. She willed herself motionless and invisible. *Don't look up, don't look up, don't look up,* she begged silently. She stood completely still except for the wild thrumming of her heart.

The two men stopped speaking for a moment. Corrie held tighter to the branch, her senses tuned to the slightest shift in movement. Her thoughts fired rapidly through her mind, desperate for a plan of escape should she be discovered.

When several seconds passed, she opened her eyes to see if they had left. They still stood below her, silently listening. One held his face to the air, turning his head this way and that. Then he sniffed the air like a dog catching a scent. Corrie's heart leapt up into her throat. Could they find her amid the moonbeams? If they had bloomed even a few minutes later, she would have surely been discovered. She glanced down at her denim shorts. They were caked in mud the same shade of brown as the tree trunk. Her white T-shirt was speckled with dirt and grass stains. She was camouflaged and held onto hope that the fragrance of the moonbeams was powerful enough to mask her scent.

By now her hands were growing numb. She had been standing motionless, holding tightly to the branches over her head. She had to move, or she would lose her grip. Carefully, she slid her arms from the branch and back down to the trunk. She wrapped her arms around it as far as possible. The slight shift in position caused her to lose traction on the branch she stood on. Her toes that were barely reaching the lower branch slipped. She caught herself, but the sudden movement jostled the branch, rustling the leaves. The soldier with the long ash-colored hair jerked his head upward. He hissed a command to his companion, and they both lifted their chins, searching for a scent. Corrie closed her eyes again, her heart throbbing in her ears.

Corrie felt a jolt in the branches and then a slow, grinding hum deep in the trunk. She tried to press herself into the tree, wishing more than anything she could just melt into the crevices of the bark. She waited. Endless seconds passed. When she finally gathered enough courage to open her eyes again, she discovered they had gone. A thin line of sap seeped out where the knife had gouged the tree. She exhaled deeply, steadying her breath, and began scaling down the tree trunk.

Corrie was still high within the branches when the tree cracked again. This time it also uttered a deep groan. She could feel it more than she heard it. It was low and long like a mournful sigh. She pressed her palm to the bark. It was cool to the touch and trembling ever so slightly.

Corrie moved faster, reaching the lower branches with the tips of her shoes as she let go of the higher branches and found lower handholds. Tip, release, tip, release. She made her way down. She was still too high up to jump when the tree began to shake in earnest. She could jump. It was possible, but if she injured her feet or ankles, she would not be able to make it to the stream. Instead, she wrapped herself around the thick trunk as much as possible and shinnied down to the ground. The bark, previously smooth, now scraped the tender skin along her inner arms and thighs, leaving them raw and burning. She didn't have time to worry about that right now though. Darkness was fast approaching.

She took one last look at the tree that had been her shelter. All the beautiful blooms that had hidden her from the soldiers were withered up as if the knife wound had been a fatal blow. What a strange forest this was where a single stab of a knife could render such a blow to a tree and kill its very soul, it seemed. The tree curled in on itself. The trunk became gnarled, and all its beauty decayed. A twinge of sadness washed over Corrie, but there was nothing to do for the tree. She set her face to the journey ahead.

She tried to find an easier path with fewer bushes and less undergrowth, but no matter what direction she ran, the woods fought against her. Her thighs burned from the sheer effort of staying on the path. Her clothes were torn, and her skin was a bloodied network of scabs and fresh wounds that oozed bright red. She no longer wiped the blood from her wounds with her shirt because if she stopped, the vines and weeds wrapped around her legs. She willed herself to keep going. There was nothing else to do.

Corrie was nearing the grasslands, nearly out of the woods. Her legs, now growing numb, moved like slabs of meat against unrelenting ground.

She glanced behind her from time to time to look for anyone following her. She hid beside a large boulder, catching her breath and gathering her courage for the final sprint across the meadow toward the trees ahead. She had lost sight of the large cedar, her chosen landmark, but she could smell water in the breeze now, and water was all that mattered.

She took a few deep breaths and then took off running again. There were no weeds or brambles here. She ran almost without resistance with only the grass whipping against her skin. Compared to thorns and briers, the sting of tiny wisps of grass was nothing. There were a few large rocks here and there, but none blocked her path.

Corrie was a few yards from the tree line when her foot sank into a low place in the ground. Her legs, fatigued from running and cramping from dehydration, could not compensate for the shift in balance fast enough. She tumbled onto one of the larger rocks, ramming her hip bone into it right near the socket. She cried out in agony as she rolled onto the ground.

She tried to get up. Sharp, stabbing pain shot through her thigh. She could run no longer. Her leg was dead weight beneath her. She massaged her hip and thigh. She had to get to the tree line, to water, or she would die here alone in this strange land. She put all her weight on her left leg and pushed herself up to standing. She tried to take a step with her right leg and caught herself as she began to fall again. She would hobble to the stream, crawling if she had to. Mere feet from the tree line, she could hear the babbling of the water flowing. She was nearly there. She licked her lips in anticipation.

By now, the sky had faded from shades of lavender to deep purple and navy blue. The shapes of the trees lining the water's edge were dark silhouettes poking bony fingers into the sky. The tantalizing scent of water on the breeze propelled Corrie forward. She moved as quickly as she could, hopping on one leg and dragging the other. Fresh, cool water was so close that she could taste it soothing her parched and burning throat. She stumbled over a root, crumbled to the ground, but kept going, crawling until she felt the dry earth give way to cool dampness under her fingertips.

At last, she dipped her fingers into the stream and dragged herself by her elbows to the water's edge. She scooped handfuls of the cool water to her face, gulping eagerly—too eagerly, however. Her stomach rejected it immediately, emptying its contents in the dirt. This water, too, was bitter and salty.

"No!" she wailed, pounding the ground. The water babbled on past, oblivious to her suffering and taunting her with its empty promises. What was wrong with this place? Was there no fresh water? The stream was cursed, just as the river she had fallen into. She didn't see the faces of her loved ones in the water as she had when she was sinking in the river's depths, but she heard a distinct and discernible hum once again. The low drone of a single note grew in volume and soon became audible voices— human voices. Corrie recognized the same voices from her past and scrabbled backward immediately. She would not go near this water again. She would rather die of thirst than be trapped in its spell.

She leaned against a sprawling willow near the water's edge but far enough so the voices dulled to a low hum. What now? Corrie closed her eyes out of sheer exhaustion. When she opened her eyes again, all was dark. The damp cold seeped into her hips and back. Her limbs were too heavy to lift. She listened to the river flowing and the drone of voices beneath the surface. The moon shone on the surface of the water with stark yet tranquil beauty. Mesmerizing. She stared in a lifeless gaze, allowing the tiny glimmers of light to lull her into a dreamless sleep.

Suddenly, Corrie was startled awake by a stinging sensation in her leg. Without opening her eyes, she reached down to push away the thorns or nettles that had found her. However, it was not a thorn or nettle. The sting was now a sharp, stabbing pain from an arrow poking out of her calf. She was completely awake now and scrambled to the other side of the willow tree.

Pain spread from the wound throughout Corrie's whole body, but it was more than physical pain. A cold, dark heaviness filled her heart. She tried to pull the arrow out, but the pain was too much to bear. She broke off the shaft, leaving the point still in her leg. Another arrow came whizzing through the dark and struck the willow tree. The trunk trembled and suddenly grew cold. Corrie knew what would follow, but she did not have the strength to run. She could not even stand. She sat in despondency, waiting for certain doom.

"Get up, Corrie," said a voice in the darkness, steady and clear. She knew this voice, but from where she could not remember.

"I can't. I can't do this anymore," she answered, though she did not know to whom she spoke.

"Stand up," said the voice firmly, and again Corrie refused. She did not even try.

A third time the voice commanded her to get up, and the tree root she sat on rose up from the ground, lifting her to her feet. She staggered and nearly fell, but a gust of wind blew from behind her, and she was forced to take a step to keep from falling over. A flaming arrow sizzled through the night sky, striking the heart of the willow tree with a loud *pop*. The tree bent over as it began to fold in on itself, engulfed in flames. As it did so, the branches formed a curtain behind Corrie, shielding her from the path of the arrows.

The wind blew behind her again, pushing her forward. She stepped again and nearly stumbled headlong onto the ground. Her left leg was throbbing, still with the arrow tip lodged in the muscle. Her right leg could not bear any weight. Suddenly Corrie felt pressure on her right hip as if a hand were pressing into it, resulting in a blinding, sharp pain. She cried out in agony, but suddenly the pain disappeared, and she was able to walk.

The wind blew again, and the voice spoke to her from the wind. "Run, child!"

Corrie took a few steps and then a few more. She was running again with only the pale glow of the moon to light her way. She passed through the grasslands, but the blades of grass whipping against her legs were negligible compared to the stabbing pain of the arrow lodged in her calf. An unusually large tree towered before her in the moonlight. Surely this was the cedar she had spotted from the treetop. She ran straight toward it. She strained to see the rocks in her path, but their shapes melted into the blackness of the sky, rendering them indiscernible. She was running blind. She believed she was nearly to the edge of the forest when she ran straight into a solid object with a surprising thud that nearly knocked the wind out of her.

The object let out a loud grunt as bulky arms clamped tightly around her. She was surrounded by more than one of them. They were talking all at once, and Corrie realized she could understand them.

"Hold onto her."

"Grab her arms."

"Get her inside."

Corrie tried to fight at first, but her legs would not cooperate. Strong arms hoisted her up to her feet again. She tried to stand but had no more strength. Her feet dragged across the rocky soil. She felt her body being laid on the ground. It was the last sensation she had before her mind and body unwillingly yet unconditionally surrendered.

Chapter 16

The Yahalom Shalom

Prudence arranged and rearranged the cushions, dusted the table, and counted all the utensils. She set aside a small gourd that had been hollowed out and baked into a hard shell by the previous occupant of the tree house. The gourd would be perfect for collecting fresh water if the sky ever yielded rain. Satisfied that she had done all she could to make the cedar tree as comfortable as possible while they needed it, she set about polishing and counting the small collection of nuts and fruits she had gathered as she hiked to the Eastern Gate looking for Corrie the day before.

Horatius paced. His steps made a soft shuffling sound in the cedar needles as he cut a path through them back and forth past the doorway. Both he and Prudence kept stealing glances at the sleeping figure on the small bed against the tree wall. Evangeline didn't bother with any tasks other than sitting by the sleeping child, making sure Horatius's tweed coat covered her small shoulders, and silently praying.

The trio had kept watch over Corrie throughout the night. Horatius had managed to bore a hole in a coconut with a makeshift stone awl, so Evangeline offered Corrie sips of coconut water every time she roused. Prudence found a small vial of medicinal oil of some kind in the cache of meager supplies. She was not sure of all the ingredients, but it had a strong aroma of camphor. Gently she applied it to Corrie's wounds.

Corrie resisted at first, but the quenching of her thirst and soothing of her wounds combined with her total exhaustion served to calm her. She had finally settled into a deeper sleep. Her shoulders now rose and fell in a slow, steady rhythm.

The sun was just cresting over the treetops in the eastern sky. It cast a pale light through the spaces between the laced vines over the doorway and through the knothole, which formed a perfectly round window the size of a large pumpkin.

"They're so peaceful when they sleep," Evangeline said, sighing loudly.

"*Whisper*, Evangeline, or you'll wake her," Prudence said softly, reminding her of the obvious as Prudence was in the habit of doing. Evangeline's voice naturally had the effect of a howler monkey in a monastery.

Evangeline nodded.

Horatius still held the arrow he had removed from Corrie's leg a few hours before. It was a long, straight shaft about 12 inches long with no fletching. It resembled a short spear more than an arrow. He studied the tip, a sharp point with an even smaller needle-like projection at the very end. It was so small that it was nearly invisible.

"What do you think it is, Horatius?" Prudence whispered after setting the gourd back on the shelf.

"It's only a stinger. I read about them, and I only needed time to remember," Horatius said, trying to keep his voice to a whisper. "They're usually shot from short distances due to the lack of fletching. The wound looks good, thanks to your quick action with the camphor, but we'll need to observe her carefully. Stingers are most often weapons of despair."

"Do *they* know why she is here? Do they know about the diamond?" Prudence asked.

"Oh, without a doubt they know about that," said Horatius. He was still whispering in hoarse tones, his eyebrows raised in emphasis. "If the Book of Days was written before the foundation of the world, then it would stand to reason that one in their midst had possibly read it or even participated in its transcription. We can't be sure."

"I imagine with all the legends and stories circulated among the realms, they would have to know about it," Prudence whispered.

"Exactly. And they would certainly be keen to know about the *Yahalom Shalom*," Horatius continued. "If the joining of the gold and the diamond brings about the end of the age, then they are anxious to either destroy it or destroy the one who finds it," he concluded somberly.

"Why are they not surrounding us at this very moment? Surely, they know we are here by now," Prudence persisted, peering through the ivy-latticed doorway. It was a fragile separation between them and the forest. "I expected them to attempt to take her or take the gold by now."

"Over my dead body!" Evangeline cried, joining them where they stood near the door. Prudence clamped a hand over Evangeline's mouth as Corrie stirred in her sleep. They waited until she settled back into slow, rhythmic breathing again before continuing their discussion.

"The only explanation I can offer is that within the refuge, this old tree, we are not only invisible to them but as if removed from this place entirely because it is not of this realm," Horatius explained, remembering the footprints surrounding the tree when he had arrived.

"Is it possible that they believe Corrie has slipped back through the veil?" Prudence asked.

"Yes. I believe that is entirely possible," Horatius agreed, nodding. "As for their strategy, we can never be sure. I've watched them for years. As soon as you plan for an attack from the west, they appear in the north. A most clever foe. Unpredictable. I don't believe they can acquire the gold, however. According to the Book of Days, once the gold has found its intended bearer and has been clasped, it cannot be removed by ordinary means. Nor can the bearer be destroyed. *By ordinary means*," Horatius said, emphasizing his last phrase. A look passed between Horatius and Prudence that caused Evangeline to visibly squirm.

"Even if they received permission to end her physical life, it is not the life of the body they want," Horatius whispered. "The only thing that would prevent the union of the gold with the diamond is the capture of Corrie's soul, which is what puts her at most danger here in this realm. That is what they truly want."

Evangeline shuddered. "Do you think they know where the diamond is? They could destroy it before Corrie even got near it," Evangeline said, her voice rising again.

"It is possible," Horatius replied grimly.

"I would say it is quite likely," Prudence added.

"How can we be sure that *Corrie* can even find it?" Evangeline exclaimed.

"Valid question," Prudence replied, nodding. "Though I suppose there would not be a mission at all if it had already been found and destroyed."

Horatius nodded. "True, true," he said, agreeing with Prudence.

"So where do we go?" asked Prudence. "We need some kind of plan, Horatius."

Horatius nodded, and then turning to Evangeline said, "Evangeline, do you remember in the mural of Ezerel—near the top right corner—what looks like a field of diamonds, hundreds of them scattered about like stars embedded in the ground?"

"Yes, yes I do remember that, Horatius," said Evangeline.

"So you think the stories are true, Horatius?" Prudence queried.

"Well, they were true about the great cedar. They could very well be true about a field of diamonds," said Horatius.

"But surely the fallen have already mined every inch of ground and dredged the river of any diamonds by now. And we don't have any tools, not really anything besides this old trowel," Prudence said, holding up an ancient stone tool that was left behind long ago. It would likely crumble into pieces if struck against rocky soil.

"Also true," Horatius agreed. "The situation in which we find ourselves takes me back to my boyhood," he continued. "We were very poor, you know, and one day I was so hungry that I decided to walk to the bakery in town. I didn't have any money, and it was already noon, so any scraps of old bread would have already been either sold or thrown out. Nevertheless, I went. I admit that I was willing to steal if given the chance. Well, when I walked in the door, the owner of the bakery was standing in the middle of the floor with a broom. He was flustered and red-faced. 'Young man,' he said, looking straight at me. 'My worker is out sick today, and I have no one to sweep the floor, wash the dishes, or shine the glass. If you can work each day until he is well, I will pay you for your labor, and you may take home all the bread I cannot keep for tomorrow.' Needless to say, I worked for the man, and our family ate like kings all week. So, if you need bread, go to the bakery. If you need a diamond, go to the field of diamonds. We will go and search diligently. The Lord will guide our steps." Horatius concluded and checked his pocket watch.

"But *demons*, Horatius. What about Corrie?" Evangeline asked.

"She'll be fine as long as she stays with us," Horatius affirmed. "She must not wander."

"One final question, Horatius. What if she doesn't *want* to find it?" Prudence asked. The growing light of the morning sun now streamed into the small enclosure. They paused, for they had not considered that possibility until now.

"Corrie needs to find it, because if she doesn't . . ." Horatius's voice trailed off. "Well, there is no need to discuss that now. We cannot control the outcome, but we must see to it that she understands the importance of her quest. We must prepare the way," he said. "I must prepare the way," Horatius corrected himself, "for that is my primary task."

Prudence and Evangeline eyed him carefully but said no more. Prudence opened her mouth to speak, but suddenly, all three of them realized that they no longer heard the slow, steady breathing of a sleeping child.

*   *   *

Awakened by the sound of her name, Corrie opened her eyes to see a rough, wooden wall in front of her. *Where am I, and who is with me?* she thought. When the voices stopped, she feigned sleep, remaining still while all her senses were sharply tuned to any sound or hint of movement in the room.

She lay on a cot or a small bed, that much she could tell, and was in a room somewhere. What was this place? It smelled earthy, like a room full of Christmas trees. She felt the fabric of the blanket draped over her and could see a sleeve. It was someone's coat. Then she heard a man's voice speaking.

"The sun has risen. We need to get moving soon," the man said.

Corrie was wide awake now, her thoughts churning. Where would *they* be taking her? She had to get away from them. She had to run. If she could just find the door quickly enough, she would escape before they could catch her. She would not be trapped by anyone ever again. She would fight, or she would run. She got ready to bolt, counting down from 3, 2, 1 . . .

Corrie leapt to her feet, but sharp, stabbing pain pulsed through her hips and legs. She screamed as she collapsed back onto the bed where she remained curled in a tight ball and sucking in air through her clenched teeth.

A woman was at her side in a flash. "There, there," the woman said, "Just lie still, sweetheart. We've got you. We've got you," she said, patting Corrie and attempting to pull the coat back over her shoulders, but Corrie threw it off and moaned loudly. She didn't want to lie still; she wanted to leave. She tried to get up again, but every movement jolted her again with pain. With no other choice, she surrendered to their care and lay still.

"She is badly bruised," another woman said.

"Get the camphor, Pru!" the first woman shouted loudly from beside Corrie. Then she proceeded to gently apply the aromatic tincture to Corrie's hip, the arrow wound, and the various cuts and scrapes on her arms and legs that were now visible in the morning light.

"We'll need to wrap her hip somehow," said the man.

Corrie heard the tearing of fabric. She winced as hands lifted her slightly and wrapped the fabric securely around her hips. The pressure of the wrapping, along with the camphor, gradually eased the throbbing pain. Another wrap was secured around her calf to cover the wound from the arrow. When the pain lessened to a dull ache, she slowly turned to lie on her back. As she did so, she was met by three smiling faces. They were the first smiles Corrie had seen in a very long time.

"Better now?" the woman sitting next to her asked. She had big blue eyes and blond curls that bounced when she spoke.

Corrie sat up slowly. Her head throbbed. She was still thirsty and very hungry. "Where am I?" she asked. "And who are you?"

"I'm Evangeline," the woman said with a wide smile.

The other woman next to her was taller with dark hair and a sharp nose. "My name is Prudence Helfgott," she said, as she set the bowl of fruit next to Corrie.

At the sight of food, Corrie forgot all questions for the moment and ate ravenously. There were pears, dates, plums, cashews, pecans, and something similar to a banana but smaller. The fruits were wonderfully sweet, the nuts snapped crisply in her mouth, and all of them were perfectly ripe and picked in their prime. The small meal quenched her thirst and filled her belly all at once.

"And I am Horatius," said the man. He had bushy eyebrows that reminded Corrie of her Papaw. He smiled warmly at her.

"Thank you for the food," Corrie said to all of them. "Oh, and nice meeting you all. I'm Corrie," she added, remembering her manners. They had truly been very kind to her.

They also looked strange to Corrie. The man wore navy pinstripe pants with a white shirt and red tie. The matching suit coat they had draped over her was obviously his. The ladies each wore nice dresses, although Evangeline's dress was now torn for the sake of Corrie's bandages, and she wore no shoes. Their clothing was the kind worn at a fancy party in the city, but somehow the styles seemed oddly out of place, even for city folks. It seemed they had stepped out of the pages of a magazine from another era, and yet here they all were in a very large tree house in a very strange forest.

"I'm not in Texas anymore, am I?" Corrie asked, curious to confirm her earlier suspicions that she had somehow surreptitiously crossed state lines were true. She had never traveled outside of Texas, so she couldn't be sure what other states looked like, but she sure knew her home state, and this wasn't it. There were no woods like this one. Trees there didn't grow this big, not even in Texas. And there certainly were not any flaming swords.

"No, you are not in Texas, Corrie," Horatius answered. "And where do you think you might be?" he asked, kneeling beside her.

Adults sometimes asked the dumbest questions. She was 12 now. Did he think she didn't know their closest bordering state?

"Oklahoma," she replied, but then what did it really matter? The real question was how she was going to get out of here and back across the state line.

"Can y'all help me get back home?" Corrie asked. They seemed like the kind of folks who would be helpful to kids. "You wouldn't even have to take me home, really, if you could just help me find my way back to the drainage tunnel I crawled through somewhere around that big waterfall." Corrie felt sure that Joe and his friends would not still be waiting for her at the other end. They would have given up by now. She cringed to think of crawling back through that slimy tunnel in the darkness again, however, even if a way opened back up through the cave. Then Corrie had a better idea. "Or maybe you know another way back to Bellam," she suggested, thinking maybe they knew the way out of the woods.

"Corrie," Horatius said, interrupting her imaginings of how her plan would work. "You are not in Oklahoma. You are in a place called Gerushah."

"Oh. Well where's that?" Corrie asked. She had never heard of such a place.

"Maybe you're familiar with its former name, Eden." Prudence offered.

"No, never heard of Eden either," said Corrie. The only Eden she knew was a girl from her kindergarten class.

"You've never heard of the Garden of Eden, sweetheart? Eden is where God created the first humans," said Evangeline.

"God?" Corrie repeated again quietly, almost to herself. She was surprised that anyone would say that out loud. Gran had taught her that God was not a topic of polite conversation. And this lady was saying that God *created* the first humans? Everyone knew that the natural world existed due to natural processes, not the hocus-pocus work of a make-believe divine being. Those beliefs had died off a long time ago. Everyone knew that the only people who held onto beliefs about things like gods, angels, demons, and deities of any kind were the Remnant. They were the people who were responsible for the ongoing wars and everything wrong in the country because of their hatred of science and, well, common sense. No one has anything to do with them, no one who is normal anyway.

Suddenly, Corrie had the suspicion that all this nonsense was a trap, that these people were really government officials, and that she had somehow stumbled onto government land. She had heard about this— officers circulating through towns, even small towns like Bellam, and along the countryside in search of Remnant supporters, tricking them into revealing hidden loyalties and outlawed religious practices. Anyone suspected of supporting Remnant people or their activities was thrown in jail and usually never seen again. A lot of folks thought that was what happened to the Miller kids, which was why they never came home to visit their parents. Corrie believed that this also may have been what happened to her mother. Plenty of innocent people were being accused of things they never did and affiliations they never had. She would not be tricked. She steeled herself against the next question.

"Corrie, have you ever read the Bible?" Horatius asked.

"No. Never. I promise. I've never even seen one," Corrie answered honestly. The trio exchanged glances.

"Your parents must have had a Bible somewhere," Horatius suggested. Immediately, a wave of fear washed over Corrie, followed by a flash of anger. How dare they accuse her parents! She had endured years of teasing because of accusations like this.

"My parents were not Remnant, and I'm not either, if that's what you mean," Corrie said angrily, nearly shouting. "I don't know who you've been talking to, but they're lying. My family isn't in the Remnant," she repeated. "N-nobody is," Corrie stammered.

By this time, Horatius was pacing but stayed near the back wall. Prudence stood between Corrie and the doorway while Evangeline remained next to Corrie.

"It concerns you that I mentioned the Bible. Is that it?" Horatius asked quietly.

"Of course!" Corrie exclaimed with all the fervor she could muster. "That book is illegal. It's dangerous, and I would never, my family would never have one, I swear." Corrie hoped they would believe her. She didn't know how she could ever get out of jail if her brothers and Gran didn't even know where she was.

"The Bible is no doubt a dangerous book, but Corrie, no one here is going to hurt you. We want to help," Horatius said gently. He had stopped pacing and stood across from Corrie, arms opened toward her.

Corrie wasn't sure what to say. Did they really want to help her? Part of her wanted very much to believe that they were as kind and sincere as they seemed. Another part warned her not to trust them, to trust no one.

"What you must understand," Horatius continued, "is that there is only one way for you to go back home." Horatius's dark eyes were intense beneath his bushy eyebrows. He paused to consider his words. "It is the same reason you have come to this land, Corrie. You must find a very special diamond that goes *there*," he said, pointing to the gold medallion around Corrie's neck.

Corrie's heart sank. "No!" she shouted. Not the medallion again. That was exactly what Vincent had talked about before he tried to use her to take the sword. All hopes that they were different, that they would help her, were dashed. How could she endure more? She had no more strength to bear it. Corrie let out a long, soul-weary sigh that caught in her throat.

"Are you all right, love?" Evangeline asked. The other two stood nearby, quietly watching and waiting.

Corrie nodded, biting her lip. These people—whoever they were— they didn't understand. They had no idea what was going on, where she'd been, or where she was going. They didn't know her family. They didn't know her. They didn't know . . . Corrie's eyes burned. Her jaw tightened. She didn't want to cry in front of them, these strangers. Hot tears rolled down her face unbidden, and she couldn't stop them. She was lost and alone and—

"I just need to find my mom," Corrie tried to explain, but the words escaped in a sob.

Evangeline held Corrie as the tears poured forth. She cried out of loneliness and exhaustion. She wept over cruelty, rejection, and sorrow so deep that it seemed her tears would never run dry.

*   *   *

Evangeline had been listening to Corrie and watching her closely. She had observed her reactions, and while Horatius and Prudence knew much more than she did about missions and the roles of ambassadors, Evangeline knew something they didn't seem to understand—children. This child's heart had been broken more than once, and it would take more than information and instructions to mend it enough to trust another soul again. When Corrie's weeping had quieted to ragged, shuddering breaths, Evangeline spoke.

"Corrie," Evangeline said, tucking a strand of Corrie's hair behind her ear. Evangeline's voice was firm but gentle. "I would like to give you two things, if you'll take them." She paused, hoping Corrie would look at her. Corrie slowly lifted her eyes, and Evangeline continued.

"First, I give you my absolute word that we will help you get home. I know you have many questions, and you have no reason to believe that what Horatius is saying is true, so I'm asking you to just think about taking my word for now that we *will* get you home. Just think about it. And I'd like to give you a small gift," Evangeline said, opening her hand to reveal a feather she had taken from her hat. It was deep purple and from a bird that did not exist anywhere on Earth, for it was from a bird that lived only in Paradise.

"This feather is from a bird that is very rare and beautiful," Evangeline explained. "In fact, this was a special gift that was given to me. Would you consider holding onto it for a little while, just until we can get you home? It will be a sign of my promise to you that though there may be a task for you to complete, the way home is sure." Evangeline held out the feather to Corrie. She prayed silently that Corrie would receive it. Although at age 12 Corrie already understood more about the cruelty of the world than many adults, some things could only be accepted with the trusting heart of a child.

Corrie stared at the floor. Evangeline waited patiently, praying earnestly in her heart for her "dear lamb." Slowly and without saying a word, Corrie nodded her head, lifted her hand, and took the feather. Evangeline beamed. Prudence and Horatius looked on, smiling approvingly.

"All right then, let us go and see what adventures await," Horatius said as he slipped his coat back on and strode toward the door. His eyes sparkled in the sunlight that was streaming in through the window. He parted the ivy curtain as Prudence stepped through the gap. Evangeline stood, adjusted her now ragged dress, and donned her feathered hat.

"Are you coming, love?" Evangeline asked, smiling at Corrie.

Corrie remained seated on the bed. She felt reasonably sure that they were not government agents. She could not imagine anyone from the government being so kind or helpful. Slowly it dawned on her. Was it possible that these people were actually *Remnant*? They hadn't denied it. Of course, they also had not denied being government spies, but then she hadn't asked them about either category. They did seem awfully interested in the Bible, which would mean they had to be Remnant.

Until that moment, Corrie had put her parents' beliefs about God in a special, unmarked category of its own. She had defended their honor against anyone who dared to accuse her parents of being in the Remnant, but was Gran right about them? Corrie didn't actually know anyone in the Remnant. What if they weren't what everyone said they were? What if not all of them were terrorists? What if some were actually nice people? Was that even possible? Corrie's head was spinning.

She looked at Evangeline waiting by the door. A brilliant idea shot through her like a bolt of lightning. If these people were Remnant, they might know who had taken her mother or how she could find her. Corrie's thoughts raced with possibilities. She would have to be careful and not appear too interested. She would play it cool in hopes that they would tell her their secrets.

Corrie now had a plan. She would cooperate with them, and they would answer her questions. Corrie joined Evangeline at the door, and they stepped out into the sunshine. For the first time in days, Corrie had a glimmer of hope. She would hold onto it for as long as it would last.

Chapter 17

The Field of Diamonds

They were off, walking in single file through the woods, the same woods where only hours before Corrie had been running for her life.

"We will stay close to the trees," Horatius said in a gruff whisper. He was leading the way with Prudence behind him, then Corrie, and finally Evangeline bringing up the rear. "I'll be the lookout in front, Prudence to the right, and Corrie to the left. Evangeline, you keep watch behind us."

"Don't worry, sweetheart," Evangeline murmured in Corrie's ear, a little too loudly for comfort. "We will protect you." She patted Corrie on the shoulder as she resumed her post behind her.

Corrie nodded, but what could they do? Horatius had only a pocket watch. Prudence carried a basket of fruit and a large philodendron leaf that she used as a shade. Evangeline had nothing but an old garden trowel in her hand and was not even wearing shoes. If these odd people had any means of protecting her from danger, Corrie almost hoped she could see them try.

Corrie wasn't completely convinced that they were even sane, but she was becoming more certain that they were not the least bit dangerous. It was like being with overprotective relatives who were always hovering over her, making sure she ate her vegetables and washed behind her ears. They didn't seem like the kind of people who set fires or destroyed public property as other people in the Remnant had done. She still wondered just what kind of people they really were.

For one thing, who wore fancy party dresses in the woods? And why were they in the woods in the first place? Whatever the case, they didn't seem to mind that their nice clothes were getting dirty. Prudence's blue dress reminded Corrie of a dress her mother made for her when she was much younger. It had been that same shade of blue but with a white satin sash and tiny blue beads around the neck and sleeves. Corrie had worn the dress only once to a grownup party she had been allowed to attend when her father joined the law firm. She wondered who had her dress now. It was one of many things they had left behind when they drove off in the middle of the night.

A wave of homesickness washed over Corrie. She missed her parents. She missed her brothers and wondered if Collin was still mad at her. Could he ever forgive her for betraying him? Though it seemed to Corrie that her grandmother was always angry or sad about something, Corrie even missed Gran. Did Gran send Corrie's brothers to find her? Gran's last words to her still stung. Maybe they didn't even care that she was gone.

The sun had just crested over the treetops in the east when they left the great cedar tree that morning. It was almost directly overhead now when the ground began to angle upward. The rise would have been barely distinguishable except for the fact that Corrie was already becoming slightly winded. She looked behind her and realized that the path had been gently sloping uphill from the beginning. She was growing tired faster than usual.

Evangeline was smiling and humming to herself as her bare feet padded along the trail. Prudence kept pace with Horatius, the philodendron leaf bobbing slightly with each step. Horatius charged forward with no hint of slowing down even as the trail took more and more of Corrie's energy to ascend. These adults were old enough to be her parents, probably even older, and yet she was apparently the only one feeling fatigued.

Corrie had so many questions for them, but she didn't have the energy.

Her legs were already aching again, and she was still sore from her injuries. She did not want to be the first to ask all of them to stop and rest for her sake, so she was grateful when Horatius called a halt to their traveling party and rested beneath a tall sycamore tree.

Corrie sat on the ground, leaning against the tree trunk and massaging her sore leg. Horatius cracked open a coconut and passed it to Corrie first for her to drink. She gulped it down but forced herself to leave some for her companions. They all drank from the coconut and ate the fruits and nuts in Prudence's basket. Corrie was growing tired of fruit. It filled her stomach, but the fullness didn't last. She was hungry for a big, juicy hamburger or even a fried egg, anything except fruits or nuts. Still, she needed food, so she ate without complaining. There was nothing else to eat.

"Let me take a look at you," Evangeline said through a partially chewed bite of banana. She knelt near Corrie's outstretched leg and unwrapped the fabric bandage.

"Hmmm," said Evangeline and then clucked her tongue. "Pru? Do you have the camphor oil for Corrie in that basket?"

Prudence, who was over by another tree foraging for edible herbs and mushrooms, shouted back, "Althaea!"

"Althaea? No, dear. I need it for Corrie," Evangeline replied.

"This plant," Prudence said, bringing a handful of flowers over to where Evangeline and Corrie sat. She was red-faced from her efforts yet smiling. "Althaea. Marshmallow plant. It is good for healing wounds. I'll make a poultice," she said, quite pleased with her discovery.

"Wonderful, Pru!" Evangeline exclaimed. They had abandoned all concern for silence, Corrie observed, though Horatius still kept watch over the woods in case anything or anyone tried to follow them.

As Prudence ground the herbs between two stones, Evangeline smiled at Corrie and patted her affectionately on the knee. *This is my chance*, Corrie thought, but what should she ask Evangeline first? She decided to go for the most important question.

"Do you know Rachel Callahan?" Corrie asked and then held her breath.

"Rachel Callahan," Evangeline said thoughtfully. "No, doesn't ring a bell," she replied, staring quizzically at Corrie.

That was okay, Corrie reminded herself. It was a long shot anyway. There were probably thousands of people in the Remnant.

"Do you—" Corrie hesitated. Would Evangeline even answer this truthfully? "Do you have a headquarters somewhere?" she blurted out, thinking that would be an ideal place to find someone. In fact, it was probably an even better idea than going to Aunt Sarah's.

"Why yes, Corrie. I suppose you could say we have a headquarters. There is a council who assigned us to come here," Evangeline replied.

Corrie's heart swelled with hope. She knew it! Corrie imagined it being like a spy operation, with people sent all over the country. But they obviously weren't sent here to bomb government buildings or start fires. There were no government buildings anywhere to be found here in the woods and no sign of civilization at all, it seemed.

"Why did they send you here?" Corrie asked.

"We are here to help you," said Prudence, who had joined them again, holding a leaf on the palm of her hand that was covered with the fresh poultice she had just made. Evangeline took it from her and began applying it to the wound on Corrie's leg. The wound looked larger to Corrie now for some reason. It was probably her imagination, she reasoned, and put the thought out of her mind. She had far more important things to think about.

At first, she thought they must be here to help her find her mother, but then she remembered what they had already said. They were here to help her find the diamond that fits into the medallion. It must be something the Remnant needs. She couldn't imagine what that might be—maybe to sell in order to fund whatever operations they still maintained throughout the country. Maybe it was worth millions. Corrie wondered if her mother had been involved in this as well. Maybe that was why she had left—to find the diamond. Corrie's mind was a jumble of questions. What would her brothers say if they knew she was with Remnant followers, helping them on a mission? Corrie shivered inside to think about the fact that she was helping the enemy. And why *her*—why couldn't they find the diamond themselves? Oh, but wouldn't Will and Collin be surprised if she found their mother and brought her home? That would shut them up for good. They would see. She was not a coward, and she was certainly not a thief or traitor.

"After we find the diamond, could I possibly go to your headquarters?" Corrie asked, thrilled at the prospect.

Evangeline's eyes widened in surprise, but then a smile spread across her face. She patted Corrie vigorously on the back as if Corrie had just told her some wonderful news.

"Yes, sweetheart, you will definitely be able to go to our headquarters with us someday," Evangeline said, and she was smiling and chuckling and patting Corrie all at once.

Prudence stood by, folding the remaining poultice in a pouch of leaves she had formed and tied together with a length of vine. She smiled slightly but also watched Corrie with interest, eyes narrowed.

"Time to be on our way," Horatius announced just as Evangeline finally pierced the coconut shell with a loud *crack*.

They quickly drank the coconut water, gathered their few belongings, and resumed their trek through the woods. They walked at a much faster pace now. Though Corrie's leg felt better after resting, she still struggled to keep up with Prudence who strode through the woods with ease. Corrie, by contrast, had to trot to keep up.

Corrie was listening to the rhythmic thud of their feet on the path and the swishing sound of the undergrowth around them when she noticed movement among the trees. Something dark hovered for a moment in the bushes and then suddenly faded into the shadows. Corrie blinked. Her eyes must have been playing tricks on her. She thought maybe she should say something in case they were being followed. Before she had the chance to speak, however, a powerful gust of wind blew through the trees.

The once-still leaves were now twirling madly. And that smell! Corrie's nose began to burn from an acrid odor.

"It's a *westerly* wind, Horatius," Prudence said, grabbing his sleeve. "You know what they say about the west wind. We must do something, or it will carry her scent back to them."

"Stay together," he whispered gruffly and then motioned toward a thicket beneath a sprawling spruce tree. They dove among the branches, peeking out through the tiny spaces between the thick foliage.

The wind swirled and howled, kicking up leaves and dust in clouds of spinning debris, reminding Corrie of the dust devils she had seen on the Texas plains. Those were harmless, she knew. She didn't think that was the case here. This wind seemed to follow a path, searching every rock and crevice along the way. Or was that just her imagination again? They huddled together, closing their eyes and covering their faces against the gales of foul air until at last the howling wind moved on just as suddenly as it had arrived.

"There is an east wind, and there is a west wind, you see," Horatius told Corrie as the wind passed. "The east wind blows in from the Eastern boundary. It gathers seeds, pollen, and moisture from the Sacred Alcove and carries them throughout the land. The west wind is foul, originating from the throne of the enemy." The tension in Horatius's face had been replaced with disgust.

"Throne?" Corrie asked. She assumed that since they were most likely Remnant, the enemy would have to be the government. As far as Corrie knew, however, government officials did not have thrones. "Who is your enemy?" Corrie questioned, wondering whose side they were truly on.

"He is the ancient enemy of our people. There will come a time when you know how to resist him. For now, as long as you stay with us, you will be safe," Horatius assured her. "All right. Time to move," Horatius said to everyone and once again led them along the path.

Corrie had so many more questions to ask them. Who were Horatius's people? Did he mean the Remnant? Their enemy was surely the government. That much was clear. She realized then that the hunter in the woods who shot her may have mistaken her for one of Horatius's people. Maybe she had gotten caught in the middle of a fight between them. And of course, if the Remnant wanted the diamond, surely the government would want such a valuable gemstone as well. The government owned everything. They would certainly not let a rogue group of terrorists have anything valuable. She questioned thinking of them as terrorists now. It really did not feel right to use such a word. Corrie was trying to think of what to ask them next when the trail climbed sharply upward. Soon, they found themselves on a grassy plateau.

"The Field of Diamonds," Horatius said with a sweep of his arm as the four of them stood on the plateau, gazing down at the sight below them. Corrie saw nothing that resembled a field of diamonds; in fact, it looked nothing like a field at all.

*   *   *

In the west, Qal arrived for the morning report. He was instructed to wait in the portico of the palace rather than in the antechamber where the officers waited to be called into meetings. It was a detail Qal would not forget. He had long been assigned the duties of officers and yet had never received the rank or title due his excellence.

When Bahadur finally sent for him, he sent a palace servant rather than coming to greet Qal himself. Qal knew what this was about. Only one time had Qal not saluted Bahadur properly, and the general had never forgotten it. That was why he had been assigned to poison a child instead of commanding an army. It was just one more punishment, one more humiliation.

Qal followed the servant into the meeting room, a small chamber with walls of black marble streaked with gold veins that captured the flickering light of the lanterns along the length of the walls. Qal had been in this room only once before. Typically, there was a long table with cushioned benches in the room. Officers of every rank met to discuss strategy and offensive battle plans with large parchment maps spread before them.

This morning there was no table. Bahadur stood near the back wall, staring at a spinning globe. He didn't seem to notice Qal had entered the room. Qal saluted the hulking demon. Bahadur had no exposed skin that was not covered by tattoos, and most of them were inked with human blood.

"Did you disable the subject?" he growled so low it was almost imperceptible.

"Yes, my lord," Qal answered, matching Bahadur's tone. He would not give Bahadur the satisfaction of knowing he had noticed his dishonorable treatment. He stood like a stone statue, staring blankly at the far wall.

"So where is she?" Bahadur said, his lip curled in a sneer.

"You did not command me to bring her here," Qal replied curtly.

"Then what proof do you have that the child is not still able to find the diamond?" Bahadur replied.

"You can be sure because I have never failed," said Qal with great pleasure and seething anger.

"Then I will report your news to the master," said Bahadur. It was a phrase that signaled the end of the meeting. Once the report was given to Lucifer, it was decreed final. There was no room for changing course, and the deed was thereby finished. "Dismissed. Go join your platoon in the 83rd region. The resistance there has grown. I need as many forces there as possible," Bahadur said and then resumed spinning the globe.

Qal saluted and then turned on his heel and left the palace. He had completed his mission but had done so his way. While at base headquarters and in sight of all officers there, he had chosen warriors to form the company and instructed them regarding the target. However, once they all reached the woods, he commissioned them to a command post over the Arctic region. He also collected two arrows from each of them, with the threat that if any disobeyed his orders or reported their doings to another being, demon or angel, he would turn in that warrior's arrow as lost weaponry found in enemy-controlled territory. Leaving any kind of weapon or ammunition in this way was a crime punishable by public humiliation and automatic demotion. They knew Qal was vicious, and they needed no further incentive to obey. Qal needed no assistance in his task and no witnesses to his treason.

The poison he had used to incapacitate the child would do far more than a weapon of despair, though even those were effective enough to incapacitate the strongest of humans when necessary. A weapon of despair was the most common weapon used since it immediately extinguished hope and faith all at once and rendered the victim inoperable. That was what Bahadur had expected of Qal.

What Qal had used, however, was a slow-releasing poison. The results were so devastating that they would also bring down Bahadur and possibly even the Prince of the Air himself. Qal would not kill the subject outright. That plan would be too boorish and too easily traced back to him. No demon dared to disobey a mandate from the Court regarding the King's chosen ones, at least not in obvious rebellion. This demanded sophistication.

Qal had tipped the arrow, aimed at the sleeping child as she rested under the willow, and hit the mark perfectly. Another volley of the arrows collected from each warrior and tipped with despair-inducing pheromes were aimed at the tree and surrounding area. Pheromes are not to be confused with pheromones that control processes within the human body. Pheromes are substances that act directly on the soul. The ploy was to make it seem that the maximum number of arrows permitted for a human subject was loosed on the child, while the true weapon had been dispensed with perfect precision.

Qal would be affected, it was true, possibly even banished to the pit. But he didn't care anymore. He smiled at the thought of his overlords coming before the Court on charges that he had carried out. If he could not be recognized for his glories in battle, he would be remembered for his glorious revenge.

As Qal departed the palace grounds, another warrior entered the portico and was immediately ushered into General Bahadur's presence. Equal to Qal in size but lesser in rank, the scout saluted the general and stood ready to give a report.

Bahadur was still standing near the back wall. He examined his sword and carefully shined it with a small cloth. "What news?" he growled without looking up from his sword.

"No remaining gemstones have been found," the demon replied and then corrected himself immediately: "All are accounted for, and none remain."

"Have you seen the child?" Bahadur asked, returning the sword to its scabbard.

"No, General, but I recovered these from the northeastern edge of

Pa'laam," said the scout, reaching into the quiver on his back and then holding out a handful of arrows for Bahadur to examine.

Bahadur strode toward him and picked up each of the arrows. They all had a similar metal tip with various kinds of fletching particular to the warrior who had crafted it. He sniffed most of them and then tasted the tip of the last arrow.

"Hmph," Bahadur grunted. "Was this all of them?"

"Yes, my lord," the scout answered. "One was dislodged from a tree, and the other three were scattered nearby. It would seem that a thorough assault was executed on the subject." He stared straight ahead to avoid meeting the general's eyes.

Bahadur strode back toward the window. While it was not uncommon for stray arrows to be left behind in the heat of battle, this was just a child. Could a company of warriors not all hit their mark, or did the King find a way to interfere even without the despicable marauders of light?

"There is one other matter, my lord," said the scout with his eyes focused on the floor, for he had spoken without prompt.

"What is it?" Bahadur said abruptly, spinning around.

"I believe there may be a refuge here," he said.

"A refuge. In Gerushah," Bahadur repeated thoughtfully. "What evidence?" he growled.

"A shimmering in the darkness, my lord. And when I walked through it, I detected *Him*," the scout replied.

Qal had said nothing of this, Bahadur noted. "You have just been promoted. Assemble a company, locate and destroy, and then report to the 83rd. He flicked his hand to dismiss the soldier.

"Yes, General," the warrior replied. He saluted and left the room.

Bahadur listened as the soldier's footsteps echoed in the hallway and then blended into the low drone of demon voices floating in from a blood ceremony that had just begun. Summoning a courier, he growled in low tones, "I am dispatching you to the 83rd. Stay out of the battle. You are to simply watch Qal's every move." Bahadur watched as the courier exited the room. If Qal stepped one toe outside of Bahadur's orders, retribution would be swift.

Unbeknownst to all who had come and gone from the meeting room, a figure lingered in the shadows, listening to every word spoken. Belial was a rare visitor to Gerushah because he was neither a warrior, a courier, nor a palace guard. As lord of the mongers, he had little interaction with angels and no battle plans to discuss. His sole occupation was the population of living souls on Earth. He and his agents of misery needed no weapons. Their very presence infused each human host with hatred, deceit, fear, and all manner of suffering. Mongers fed on any organic negative thought and magnified it tenfold. They were also the most effective carriers of *Specious molluscus*, a parasitic worm that both fed on lies and produced even more lies within the host it inhabited.

Warriors, by contrast, were brutish, impulsive, and lacking any understanding of the complexities of the human soul. Though the efforts of mongers supported the territorial conquests of warriors by keeping the number of praying souls to a minimum, there was little cooperation between mongers and warriors.

Bahadur was sufficiently vile and lecherous yet lacking the finesse required for manipulation of such emotions as grief and guilt. Even Qal, arrogant in his self-avowed prowess in understanding human souls and infecting them effectively, had not the skill of manipulation as did the mongers. Warriors overlooked the sheer power of using the humans' wicked appetites against themselves, even more so those desires that were essentially good yet able to be twisted beyond recognition of anything resembling goodness. In this aspect, Belial and his extensive hive of mongers excelled. You cannot compare the objective study of human misery from a distance—as was the habit of warriors—to gorging on it as a leech on a bleeding wound.

Circumstances had become difficult for Belial in the last few decades since the human population was growing to rival the number of mongers. Despite campaign after campaign of efforts to encourage population control, the humans continued to reproduce. It was becoming increasingly challenging to see his human subjects through the process of becoming uncontended. He wondered if Lucifer had any idea of the amount of skill it took to woo a human to such a status when the Enemy finally withdrew the last finger of influence on a soul and stopped contending for its destiny.

Most of the world was *Belial's*, not Lucifer's. It was his alone. He and every monger under his command had brought the world to its knees—every soul dedicated to the rule of common sense, every lover of pragmatic relativism, every master of the arts and sciences. In short, every human being glorying in the existence and achievements of the human race was his. Certainly, it was simple at first. All his subjects have the innate drive to think only of themselves, not even knowing that every self-consumed thought is building accolades to him, the great Belial. And yet what remained unappreciated was the succor it demanded of him to constantly uphold the efforts of his mongers against the tyrannical interference of the Creator.

Belial had been at work among souls in the empire containing the provinces of India and Pakistan when word had reached him of this human child. She had not only breached the barrier between the physical and spiritual realms but was running rampant in the territory of Gerushah, of all places. According to ancient legend, this child held the final days of the world in her own hands. Lord Lucifer knew this, of course, yet Bahadur, too brutish to see past his sword, had no comprehension of it. He had become obsessed with the 83rd region, a site of continuous episodic defeat since the seventh Age of Man. Belial would find the child himself, see what merit the ancient writings held, and then bide his time. He would prove his prowess over Bahadur to Lucifer and all the demon warriors the prince prized so greatly. The child would bow to Belial's wishes, or she would die.

*   *   *

The three ambassadors and Corrie stood on the plateau overlooking the valley below. What should have been the Field of Diamonds was instead a large, shallow ravine approximately half the size of a football field. Due to its odd, bowl-like shape, it looked like it had been carved out of the ground rather than a natural formation.

"So much for a field of diamonds," said Prudence.

"It's all dirt!" Evangeline exclaimed, and indeed it was. If there had ever been any rock, it had all been removed except for small sections here and there that were only pumice stone. Most of it backed up to the mountain along the northwestern edge of the ravine.

The four of them hiked down the slope to examine it closer. Though Corrie's leg still ached a bit, the possibility of finding precious gems stirred her excitement. She was the first to reach the site, with Evangeline close behind.

"Don't get too close to the edge, sweetheart," Evangeline warned. Evangeline was trying to keep up, but Corrie was already scaling down the pumice stone wall.

"All of it has been mined," Horatius remarked to Prudence. "They left the pumice, which has no value for them. All the kimberlite is gone."

"And all our chances of finding a diamond," said Prudence dolefully.

"There is no point in staying," said Horatius. He started walking toward Corrie. Prudence followed. He intended to inform Evangeline and Corrie that they would be moving on, but by the time he reached them, Corrie had already reached the bottom of the shallow ravine. She was exploring the rocky eastern edge and heading toward the face of the mountain when she shouted, "Hey! There's a cave!" Then she suddenly disappeared from their sight.

Evangeline shrieked. "Corrie! Wait, Corrie! You don't know what's in there!"

All three ambassadors scaled down the stone wall into the ravine and headed toward where they last saw Corrie. Horatius grabbed two smaller pieces of the pumice stone and lit a quick fire as Evangeline and Prudence went in after Corrie. Horatius soon followed with a blazing torch.

There was only a small gap between the rocks leading into the shallow cave. The ceiling was just barely high enough for all of them to stand. There was nothing special about it. It looked like a natural cave that had likely remained untouched for thousands of years.

"There's something in here," Corrie said in an excited whisper. She was spreading her hands over the wall of the cave as Horatius shined the light over the gray texture of the pumice stone. Poking out from the gap between the stones was a small flap of something softer than stone. Corrie grabbed the corner and pulled. Out came a roll of parchment about as long as Corrie's forearm.

"A scroll!" Evangeline exclaimed. "Well done, Corrie. Let's see what it is."

"Horatius, this would have to be writings from the antediluvian period," Prudence said with a quiet gasp, and Prudence was not often easily impressed.

"Indeed," Horatius agreed and held the torch over Corrie as she unrolled it.

"Careful now. It's very old," he reminded her. Evangeline helped Corrie slowly and carefully unroll each end.

Horatius studied the ancient parchment. Some of the lettering was faded, but most of it was still legible to someone who could read it.

"What language is it, Horatius?" Prudence asked. She stood next to Evangeline, peering down at the strange characters scrawled on the parchment.

"That first line, *there*," Horatius said, pointing to the string of markings near the top. "It has elements of both Malakyín and High Malakyín, as well as possibly an early prototype of Hebrew." Prudence gasped again, clearly impressed.

"I believe this says, 'These are the writings of Anach, son of Arach,'" said Horatius.

"Fascinating!" Evangeline exclaimed. Her voice ricocheted off the cave walls.

"Maybe there are more of those scrolls in here," Corrie said, handing the scroll she was holding to Evangeline. Corrie searched along the cave wall again, looking and also feeling with her fingertips for anything that didn't feel like rough pumice stone.

Evangeline and Prudence joined her as Horatius held the torch high for everyone to see. They were able to find four more scrolls neatly rolled and completely intact. The velum was so thin it was nearly opaque, but the characters were still legible to anyone who could decipher them.

"It's a miracle the demons haven't found these," Evangeline remarked.

Horatius glanced at Corrie at the mention of the word *demon*, but she was engrossed in unrolling a sixth scroll she had just found.

"Looks like a map," Corrie said. "Maybe it's a treasure map," she added, moving closer to Horatius and the light of the torch.

The four of them studied the rudimentary map. They could make out the markings for trees and jagged lines around the perimeter that appeared to be mountains. Two thin, parallel lines formed a winding path in front of the mountains, which they all simultaneously recognized as the Crystal River.

"It's a map of Gerushah, of course," said Horatius.

"And there's the Sacred Alcove. There," Prudence said, pointing to a circle in the middle of the page. "And there's the Eastern Gate."

"Gate? There's a gate out of here?" Corrie asked.

"Yes, but remember you must find the diamond first in order to leave," Horatius reminded her.

"But why if we could just go out the gate?" Corrie persisted.

Horatius grimaced. Evangeline and Prudence both stared at him, their faces grim and angular in the flickering shadows of the torchlight. How should he answer? They knew the mission affected World Events, but they did not yet know that for Corrie, finding the diamond was a matter of life and death. Only Horatius knew that. He could not explain how he knew this to be true, but when the angel had touched his forehead to read the Book of Ages, it triggered more than an ability to read the inscribed words. This was something about the mission that he just *knew*. It was imperative that Corrie not leave Gerushah without successfully finding the diamond, but what could he say? *Lord, help me*, he prayed silently.

"It's true that you could exit through the gate, but the way home is not that way," Horatius said, relieved to have supplied a truthful and pertinent answer without attempting to explain a reality that Corrie could not yet comprehend. He needed much more time.

"Well, I've decided that I'd rather go to your headquarters than go home," said Corrie. "So will the gate take us there?"

Horatius glanced at Prudence. Her eyebrows were raised. He hoped she might chime in. After all, her task was to "close the gate," though at this point he had his doubts that the gate referred to in their instructions was the gap between two massive boulders comprising the Eastern Gate. You do not simply close a space hewn through mountains of rock. Still, this seemed like an excellent time to close off even the possibility of exiting through that gate. But it was Evangeline who saved the moment.

"Sure, sweetheart!" Evangeline chimed in. "But you don't want to get there without finishing the job you've got to do, do you?" Evangeline patted Corrie exuberantly on the back. Of course, Evangeline thought Corrie was referring to Heaven as their headquarters, which would have been the most obvious destination if Corrie had understood that the ambassadors were not citizens of Earth any longer but citizens of Heaven. Corrie did not yet grasp that she had passed through a smaller gate into the unseen spiritual realm of the fourth dimension, the Shamayim. Horatius could see that he had a lot of explaining to do. Notwithstanding, he still could not quite understand why she was so interested in their headquarters.

"I guess not," Corrie said blandly.

When they had collected all the scrolls that were hidden among the rock, they spread them on the cave floor. Since Horatius was the only one who could decipher any of the words, he began the task of reading each long roll of parchment. It was already proving to be an arduous task.

Horatius was combing through a list of the number of lambs born within Anach's herd and the yield of the barley harvest when the few beams of light from outside the cave suddenly grew dim. Prudence, who sat closest to the cave opening, took the torch from Horatius and held it up so all could see. A patchwork of thick vines was swiftly covering the entrance, sealing them in the cave.

"Poisoned by the enemy," Horatius said hoarsely. "We need to get out of here. To the river," he said. "Quickly, gather the scrolls."

"We can use the torch to burn the vines!" Corrie exclaimed. The torch was now their only light, and smoke started filling the small space.

"No, it won't help," said Prudence. "The vines are green. They won't burn, and it may produce noxious fumes if we try."

Evangeline tried to cut and saw at the strands of vine with her trowel, but the vine only grew thicker. Corrie began to cough. It was becoming difficult to breathe with all the smoke.

Horatius stepped up to the vines, still holding the torch in one hand and scrolls in the other. He prayed silently. He knew the Master of Creation had given them authority to carry out His will.

"I don't know what waits for us on the other side of this barrier, but I know what we must do. We will exit and follow the trail northward. That will offer us a measure of concealment until we reach the river," Horatius explained hurriedly.

"Evangeline, I want you and Corrie to please take the torch to the back of the cave, and be sure we haven't missed any scrolls. I'll take care of the vines," Horatius said. He spoke quickly, passing the torch to Evangeline. His eyes met Prudence's and saw that she was studying him carefully. Then, taking a deep breath, he exhaled slowly and spoke to the vines.

"Be at rest," Horatius said, and the vines immediately parted and fell to the ground.

Chapter 18

The Treaty of Zim

Horatius had chosen to flee to the river. He knew it was a possible location for finding gemstones since the soil erodes and is carried along rivers and streams. But he also knew that demons typically avoided the Crystal River. The lore of Gerushah had circulated widely throughout the realms. And before Horatius had volunteered for this mission, the river had been a recent topic of conversation in Paradise.

A small gathering of patriarchs had gathered on the banks of the Yafeh, the river in the sixth realm that flowed down from the mountain of the heavenly throne. Abraham, Job, Peter, Noah, and a few members of the first church in Smyrna were talking among themselves when Horatius joined them. So lively were the rushing, babbling waters of the Yafeh that it seemed to Horatius to be the Father's own tears of joy flowing throughout the land. The breeze blowing across the water was sweet, perfumed with the fragrance of His glory.

The conversation had drifted to the topic of water in Gerushah by comparison. It was innately opposite to the Yafeh. Horatius learned then that the water in Gerushah was peculiar. It was able to absorb all the afflictions of human history much as the rains on Earth collect toxic fumes from the atmosphere. Its molecular structure was similar to that of bitter tears. This mysterious pairing had rendered all water in Gerushah unpotable unless it was first filtered through the trees.

Though Horatius could not fully understand it, he could easily believe that the demons were both attracted to and also repelled by suffering. Although they were enthralled by the act of inflicting human suffering, they were unable to enter into it. While they suffered indignation, bitterness, disappointment, and the scorn of regret, the softer emotions eluded them. The demons did not feel grief or loss because they could not love. Having no understanding of trust, faith, or loyalty, they knew not the sting of betrayal. They felt no loneliness because they experienced no fellowship with or attachment to another soul. They manufactured pains that were alien to their being.

The Crystal River was filled not with their handiwork but with its pure byproduct, stripped bare of the potential for destruction, which was the demons' design and glory. Therein flowed the very cries of humanity, at which the demon host only scoffed in disgust. As two negative charges repel each other, so the raw agony of the human heart that drew the Spirit of God also repulsed the demons. Horatius would count on this.

"Stay together," he said as quietly as possible to Prudence who walked silently behind him. He heard Prudence murmuring the instruction to Evangeline as they rounded a bend in the path.

They were both excellent companions in this adventure. Horatius was grateful. He knew he could count on Evangeline to be a nurturing presence to Corrie, and her protective instincts were fierce. Woe to any enemy who crossed her! Prudence provided excellent counsel. Horatius had completed several missions with her and was always thankful for her insight. She was doing an excellent job coaching Evangeline, although he reminded himself to encourage Prudence to not be too strict with her.

Horatius tried to mentally prepare himself for the inevitable demonic attack. What would be the nature of it? What could they expect? He was not sure. It was unlikely they would attempt a battle formation since that was reserved only for angels challenging their dominion over territories. There was no fight for dominion here, only the search for a valuable treasure. He could rule out a swarm of mongers as well since the lack of human souls in this place ensured that mongers did not inhabit Gerushah but instead roamed the lower quadrants of the fourth realm, always hovering at the veil separating the third and fourth realms like parasites hungry to feed and infect.

Lucifer rarely left his throne now, greedily guarding it from usurpers. Although he was the most clever and crafty of the fallen—his legions of warriors and mongers, as well as his princes and rulers assigned to the provinces over Earth—he had a thirst for only one thing. He knew nothing of fealty or honor. That did not exist among any of them. They were driven instead by insatiable appetites for power, and Lucifer's desire was the most ravenous. Dissenters were punished by being delivered to the tormentors, vile beasts that devoured their victims interminably.

There were two demon authorities that continually vied for power and position among Lucifer's ranks—Bahadur and Belial. Horatius had seen Bahadur many times on the battlefield in the heavens. He was the commanding general of the army, or at least that was how Horatius viewed his rank and designation, having been in the army himself while on Earth. Bahadur was in constant competition with Belial, the self-appointed leader of the mongers. It was well-known that Lucifer tolerated the competition between them because it furthered his own agenda. They were each of particular use to him.

Belial had originally served as a scribe in the heavenly courts and had transcribed several record books. That put him at a distinct tactical advantage over Bahadur simply because he had access to knowledge that the brutish military captain did not. However, Bahadur made up for the disadvantage through his prowess and strength on the battlefield, besides the scores of warriors he had at his command. He rewarded his most successful legionaries with promises of political power and positions of importance since rulers and principalities were seeded from among the most successful warriors. Those who were the most cunning, stealthy, bloodthirsty, and destructive were the only ones considered for promotion. Deeds that caused the greatest human carnage were only superseded in value by those that blasphemed the name of God most thoroughly. That was what fueled both Belial and Bahadur.

That, Horatius believed, was the only tactical advantage he and his companions currently had in the quest for the diamond. The conquest for this one child would represent neither a successful military campaign nor a public blasphemy of the Most High. In Horatius's estimation, all he had to do was keep Corrie away from demons to ensure her safety and success.

What Horatius had not accounted for, however, was the third and most primal instinct that fueled all demon behavior up to the highest level, including Lucifer himself—self-preservation. What provided demons with the use of Gerushah as a military base and a place for Lucifer's throne was the Treaty of Zim, an agreement between angelic and demonic rulers. It was ratified in the Courts of the fifth realm in AD 33 and set to dissolve upon the induction of the Last of Days, which, if Corrie succeeded, would soon transpire. The dissolution of the Treaty of Zim and the eviction of the Prince of the Power of the Air from Gerushah were not consequences Lucifer would passively endure. There is no more brutal battle than that waged for what one regards as an indelible right. The enemy had already established Corrie as a target with the arrow to her leg, and yet how he intended to carry out his plan remained a mystery, at least for now.

The four travelers managed to reach the outer banks of the river, having only encountered a particularly dense clump of netty gorse bush on the path. They had all stumbled through the thorny branches, everyone except Prudence, that is. She had a habit of walking with her eyes straight ahead, seldom looking at her feet, which strangely proved to be the exact reason she had not tripped on the branches. Evangeline stumbled because she had no shoes, so she watched the ground carefully.

From the back of the line came Evangeline's "Whoop!" followed by a thud, the rustling of leaves, and then the whacking sound of the trowel against the ground as she shouted, "Back, you devils!"

Horatius now stood on the grassy knoll just above the rocky shoreline along the Crystal River.

"We made it," Prudence said, reaching his side. Corrie and Evangeline soon joined them.

"Yes," Horatius agreed. "And we won't be disturbed, I think, for as long as we remain near the river." He silently hoped that was indeed true.

"Hey, look over there!" Corrie said, pointing to an area of sand among smaller stones nearer the shore. Something sparkled from the soil, glittering like shards of glass. At first, Corrie remained standing next to Evangeline, hesitant to leave her side. Soon, however, her curiosity overcame caution, and she bounded away from them to see what it was.

"I'll go," Evangeline said, and she immediately followed Corrie.

Horatius nodded. He knew she would. Prudence also made her way slowly down to the shoreline to inspect the find, looking furtively back toward Horatius.

"Let me know if anything looks promising," Horatius told Prudence. "For now, at least, I think I'll stand guard." He remained on the knoll with the bundle of maps and documents they had collected from the cave and watched. Prudence nodded in response.

Corrie smiled at Evangeline. Horatius was encouraged to see Corrie's delight. There had been few moments, if any, that reminded Horatius that Corrie was just a child—12 years old, still naive about the ways of the world, even as the world had already begun to chip away at her innocence. Just 12 years old.

Eliana was her name. It was the name her mother had called out in the night. He whispered it to her now as the soldiers continued moving among the terrified souls standing at attention on the snowy ground. Soon they would discover two more missing. He had already determined his fate. He had chosen to help the smallest of the prisoners who would surely freeze to death in a matter of minutes anyway. Soon they would send the dogs.

Young Horatius had pulled the tiny, lifeless body closer to his own to try to warm her. She was still breathing, but only that. "Help me, God!" his soul cried out in the darkness. "I don't know what to do." He was only 12. His lips moved silently as he peered out from under the barracks floor. He would have to move quickly. There was no time to figure out a reasonable plan. The camp had no place for reason, only risk. Horatius slipped the tiny child into his own uniform shirt and crawled over the frozen ground to the only place there was to hide in a concentration camp.

The latrine had held the first awareness of mystery for Horatius. Sickness, death, and filth had saved his life, and the life of a little girl. They hid there until the miracle happened.

The sound of Corrie's voice called Horatius back, startling him from his daydream. Corrie was picking up the stones and holding them up to the light, enjoying the way they sparkled in the sunlight and commenting on each one. She put a few in her pockets and reached for more, delighting in each discovery. Ah, contentment. That was not to last.

*   *   *

"These are diamonds, aren't they, Evangeline? And look at all of them. They're just sitting here waiting for us to pick them up. This is crazy!" Corrie squealed with excitement. It seemed as though a rich king had emptied his pockets on the ground, scattering beautiful gemstones everywhere. Corrie had never seen a diamond up close, only in books. The way they refracted the light made it seem as if she held beautiful rainbows in the palm of her hand. "You know what this means?" she asked. "It means the diamond we're looking for could be right here."

"It could be, dear," Evangeline said, but she did not seem entirely enthusiastic about it. Her brow furrowed. Corrie was too enthralled with her sparkling diamonds to notice Evangeline's expression.

"I just need to find the right one," Corrie said, selecting a gemstone, trying to fit it into the space on the medallion, and then discarding it for the next one.

"You'll know when you see it," Evangeline said with a nervous chuckle, glancing at Prudence who stood by with her arms folded.

Corrie was so enthralled by her treasure that she did not notice the hum emanating from the river. It was subtle, like the low drone of a bumble bee. She had quite forgotten that there were neither insects nor other living creatures in Gerushah. She went on examining and collecting the beautiful diamonds. The array of sparkling gems stretched all the way to the river's edge. She was nearly to the sandy shoreline when a loud and mournful wail filled her ears. She fell backward, hitting the ground hard. She had been so distracted by the search for diamonds that she had forgotten about the river's effect on her. The voices of her past and the pain, sorrow, and grief compounded and swirled around her, dragging her toward the water with them to drown in the depths.

In a moment that felt like several, Evangeline was at Corrie's side.

"I've got you, love. I've got you," she said. Evangeline's voice carried even over the din of noise in Corrie's ears. "Oh, I knew something was not quite right about this. Now, let's get you out of here," Evangeline said and hoisted her up. Prudence joined them, and the three of them ambled up the hill to where Horatius waited for them.

"Just a decoy for distraction," Horatius frowned.

"I thought as much," Prudence agreed.

"But are the diamonds real?" Corrie wanted to know.

"Yes, they probably are, but tangible things here are not the same as what you are used to," he tried to explain. But Corrie hadn't really heard anything past the part about them being real.

Corrie gazed at the diamonds as they sparkled in the sunlight. What a treasure they would be in Bellam. Why did they need to go on looking for any other diamonds? These were just perfect.

"Not even beauty here can be trusted," Prudence warned. "In fact, I would forget about them if I were you. Leave them here. *This* treasure is not what you are looking for, Corrie."

"But," Corrie protested, "how do you know? I found diamonds! I did what you wanted me to. You can use any of these."

Grimacing, Horatius reminded her calmly, "Yes, they are beautiful, but not one of them is the perfect diamond, the *Yahalom Shalom.*"

"But that's not fair!" Corrie shouted. A wave of rage washed over her. Evangeline was immediately patting her, trying to calm her down. Corrie stepped away from her.

"Now, Corrie. Remember, we're looking for a very special diamond. Where is your feather? Remember the gift I gave you? We gave you our word," Evangeline said, her blonde curls bouncing wildly. Her voice rose higher in pitch the longer she talked.

"I don't care about your stupid feather," Corrie spewed angrily. "You said you would help me if I found a diamond, and I found more than one diamond," she snapped, shoving the diamonds deep into her pockets. She was tired of them bossing her around.

Horatius and Evangeline exchanged glances, which Corrie noticed. Prudence, however, was standing behind Corrie and had taken a step back, studying her reactions. Prudence was paying special attention to Corrie's wound from the demon's arrow that now apparently no longer caused Corrie pain and yet had turned a dark shade of black with a lacy pattern that had begun to spread beyond the wound like black tentacles.

"Corrie's right, you know," Prudence said suddenly, slicing through the tension with the coolness of her voice. Evangeline jerked her head toward Prudence. Horatius lifted his chin. "She did her part. She found a whole handful of diamonds," said Prudence, crossing her arms. "I think we owe it to Corrie to escort her out of here."

Corrie turned around to face Prudence, staring into Prudence's eyes. There was no sign of trickery. Her expression was as placid as stone.

"However, dusk will soon fade to dark. I think it wise to have something to eat, rest for the night, and then consider leaving at dawn," Prudence added.

"But Prudence," Evangeline piped up.

"I agree with Prudence," said Horatius with a nod from Prudence that was barely perceptible and before Evangeline could say any more. "We'll head back to the cedar for the night and prepare for the journey," he said. Then turning to Evangeline, he added, "We will discuss all of this later, I promise."

Corrie searched their faces. She didn't know what needed to be discussed later and didn't fully trust them all. Something was going on between them, but at least Prudence understood her. Corrie would stay with them a little longer. She still needed to know exactly where their headquarters was in case they changed their minds and decided not to take her there. She would get them talking tonight. There were things she still did not understand about the Remnant, things she needed to know if she was going to find her mother. Then she would be ready.

"All right, then. Let's be on our way," Horatius said, checking his pocket watch and setting off toward the woods once again.

"One moment, Horatius," Prudence said, peering down at Corrie. "Before we go, you will need to empty your pockets." It was the same steady tone of voice Corrie's mother used when Corrie or her brothers had disobeyed her. It had always meant they had one last chance before Mama got the wooden spoon.

"But the diamonds . . . I thought—" Corrie protested, confused. She had thought Prudence was on her side.

"I agreed with you that we should escort you out, not that you should keep the diamonds," Prudence said. Her voice was low but firm, and it always seemed to Corrie that Prudence was frowning.

Corrie swallowed, feeling the heat rise in her face. She had done nothing wrong. Those diamonds were there for the taking, and she had every right to take them. They were on a hunt for diamonds, weren't they? And who wouldn't take free diamonds when many people these days didn't have enough food to eat, much less a priceless treasure? These people really were crazy. And they were all staring at her, waiting for her to empty her pockets. What was she to do?

Corrie relented. For now, she would obey. She would come back for the diamonds later. It wouldn't be too hard to find the river again when she had the chance. Corrie dug into her pockets and then slowly drew out her hands and opened her fists. The diamonds sparkled merrily. They were so beautiful. They gave her a sinking sensation in her heart. She could have bought all the bus tickets she needed with them. Heck, she could have bought every bus in Texas.

"Just toss them on the ground, Corrie," Prudence said more gently now.

Corrie clenched her jaw, steeling herself against tears. Instead of dropping them carelessly to scatter on the ground, she piled them near a tree trunk and covered them with leaves, memorizing the color and size of the trunk and nearby surroundings.

"Now, let's go," Horatius said, and they followed him away from the river and into the woods. Corrie followed obediently behind Prudence once again. She had emptied her pockets as instructed. All the diamonds were left behind—all except one.

*   *   *

The path from the river back to the cedar tree was rugged, with massive pine and juniper trees closing in the trail on each side. Ancient roots emerged from the ground, rising up as if disturbed from their slumber, while thick vines draped and crisscrossed overhead. It seemed more of an obstacle course than a trail.

Corrie, nevertheless, was moving more nimbly than she had in quite a while. In fact, she felt positively energized. Her injured leg no longer hurt. The puncture wound that had been a painful oozing sore earlier in the day was no longer visible. She wondered if the diamonds held some kind of magic, smiling as she remembered the gem she still kept hidden in her pocket. If they could believe in a priceless diamond, so could she.

Corrie hummed to herself in rhythm with her footsteps. She did not notice the rustling in the trees beside them, not the thickening of the branches on either side of them. Slowly but surely, the juniper branches were growing wider and thickening as a wall of green.

"Quickly now. We've not far to go," Horatius urged them.

Then it happened so suddenly that they could not have braced for it. The evergreen walls burst into flames. Corrie screamed. Evangeline and Prudence both shouted in surprise as well.

"Lord! Show us the way!" Horatius said loudly. His voice was steady above the din of the roaring fire. Evangeline and Prudence both reached toward Corrie, trying to shelter her from the flames.

They retreated toward the way they had come in order to escape the flaming tunnel, but fiery arrows descended before them, closing the exit. They turned again toward the direction they had been heading, toward the cedar tree. They were running now.

The great cedar was in view. Horatius shouted encouragement to "keep going, push forward!" Prudence and Evangeline were close beside Corrie on each side, protecting her from the blaze as they ran. Corrie thought they might make it when in utter horror she saw a flaming arrow aimed straight for the cedar tree hit its mark. The entire tree was quickly engulfed in flames. The four of them stopped and stared in shock. There was nowhere else to run. They were surrounded by walls of fire on every side.

"I need you all to trust me," Horatius shouted above the roar of the fire all around them. "We haven't time for explanation, but I believe the safest place is still the cedar tree."

"What? No!" Corrie wailed. "You are all crazy. No! We can't do that!" she shouted, but it was hopeless. They were either going to die here or incinerate in the cedar tree. It was the same death either way.

"Trust me," Horatius said, staring straight into Corrie's eyes with his piercing gaze. Corrie's stomach turned over. It was not the first time a stranger had told her to trust him.

"No!" Corrie shouted. "I don't want to die. There has to be another way," she pleaded. Corrie tried to fight them, to get away, but they suddenly hoisted her up in their arms and headed straight for the blazing tree.

* * *

Adriel sat overlooking the Shamayim, the fourth realm, from his justice seat in the Meridiem, the fifth realm. Having concluded the regulatory meeting with several commanding officers of the Lord's army and the other six Watchers of the Holy Synod, Adriel considered his next move. What was to be done with Gerushah? Legally a territory and therefore not officially claimed by either side, Gerushah had been inhabited by Lucifer's horde according to terms established by the Treaty of Zim that provided the enemy certain allowances.

Lucifer was permitted a throne, along with access to the resources of the territory even for the construction of the dark lord's blasphemous palace. He was also permitted the stationing of troops in Gerushah. Gabriel had witnessed their assemblies as the serpent king openly mocked the Almighty in garish bravado, publicly declaring his intentions with no fear of reprisal. Such is the way of those for whom the wrath of *El-Elyon*, though seemingly slow, is sure. Reasoning becomes warped. Even while exhausting the outer limits of forbearance, it still craves justice according to his own flawed standard. It is the way of the entire demonic realm to fight for their supposed rights and their own skewed version of truth to the very end, all the way to the pit.

One of those allowances on Gerushah was exemption from angelic interference. That had never been a problem since Gerushah had remained uninhabited by humans since the Great Flood. Now, however, everything had changed. Now there was Corrie, and Adriel watched her with careful study, for she bore the King's mark.

If given the order, Adriel would have called for a whole battalion of angel warriors to her side. The Treaty of Zim would be instantly nullified, Lucifer evicted, and all of Eden restored to her former glory. Such was not the way of the Most High, however. No. The Almighty ruled from the seventh realm, the Highest of the Highest Thrones of the Universe, and none put Him there but He Himself. Not even Gabriel was to command armies in Corrie's defense. The King had other plans, plans that neither he nor the archangels in the Lord's service were privy to.

Adriel had been given authority to govern all, but Gerushah he could not directly influence. He could dispatch warriors and guardians and move troops anywhere in the Shamayim with that one exception. It was a unique challenge, one that Adriel relished. By the Lord's power already vested in him, he would know where to begin and when the time was right.

*   *   *

The 83rd region of the Shamayim lay within the boundaries of Shàngdí, the empire ruled by the deity of the same name. Shàngdí had governed since the ancient days of Babel when the nations of Earth were divided among the rulers of the fourth realm for a season. Shàngdí had no intention of acknowledging the authority of the Most High willingly, and Lucifer, Prince of the Power of the Air, was most obliging to supply Shàngdí with his highest-ranking military officer to assist in the quelling of any resistance in this most-prized region of the realms.

The significance of this empire was evident from the expanse of its geographical size and territorial position. Shàngdí had controlled much of Earth for millennia since the highest majority of all existing provinces of the Shamayim lay within its boundaries. That also afforded him the highest number of rulers, authorities, and powers, an allowable amount determined in part by geographical size.

Shàngdí's influence was also affected by the empire's location relative to the cradle of all humankind and the stage for its prophesied end. Shàngdí ruled over the majority of what is known on Earth as the continent of Asia, hovering over the Fertile Crescent with demonic ardor and ravenous to engulf the first and last City of God—Jerusalem.

The population of humans residing in the expansive empire rivaled that of the entire world, creating a vortex of demonic influence energized by souls craving the darkness rather than the light. The power generated from such an exchange between legions of demons and billions of souls in their grasp was immense, spreading around the globe as a deadly cancer.

The mighty emperor, Shàngdí, had enjoyed unchallenged authority for a time in Earth's earliest days. He was given the authority to oversee the region even before inhabitants began the steady crawl around the globe. This had all changed with one single event, however. God Most High, who had authored history from His throne in the seventh realm, finally played His hand—a Royal Flush. The eternal Creator entered His own timeline by taking on flesh, fulfilling humankind's injunction to live in obedience to God's perfect rule, absorbing God's own wrath in punishment for human rebellion, conquering death, and ascending to the Highest Heaven and thereby sending His own spirit to inhabit His children on Earth. The rulers, authorities, powers, and all forces of darkness had observed their own twist of fate with horrified awe. With the depths of Sheol stripped of its power, the Son of Man, reigning from the seventh and highest realm, and the Spirit dwelling on Earth, not only was the absolute authority of the demonic empires destroyed but their ultimate demise was sealed. And that was not all. They would also be witness to the disruption of their authority such as the shattering of glass into a million shards. And the Almighty would accomplish this in a mockery of their own bloodlust for territory.

Just as even the smallest particles of matter on Earth can be measured in atoms and quarks, so exist the divisions of authority. While the darkness feuded over empires, provinces, districts, and territories, God quietly established His own eternal domain beyond all geographical boundaries within the smallest measurable unit of governing authority in all realms—the hearts of humankind.

God's domain was again expanding exponentially even from within Shàngdí's Empire. The impact throughout the cosmic forces was immense. Kingdom bearers automatically meant a greater population of guardian angels and heavenly warriors of every class filling the Shamayim on their behalf and thereby engaging in warfare with demonic forces. Greater numbers of angels also meant fewer mongers that were able to infiltrate the area, thus directly affecting all spiritual traffic and influence throughout the region, and ultimate control of the empire.

There had been an uprising in a sector that included the tiny village known as Tingxu just beyond the bustling city of Taiyuan. A gathering of believers had been fasting and praying for the mayor of Taiyuan, that he would be delivered from darkness and into the Kingdom of God's love. He had just issued a new order for the arrest and execution of all professing Christians in his governing district, which included Tingxu. Police officers scoured the city streets, following any leads of people suspected of either owning a Bible or attending any form of secret meeting in the past year. The officers moved from house to house, demanding that people declare complete allegiance to the government and renounce all other loyalties or be imprisoned. The prayers of these saints in arms had brought thousands of reinforcements to the heavenly ranks, sending the demonic forces into near frenzy.

Bahadur had dispatched several companies to manage the revolt. He had been confident in his personally trained officers' abilities to control the region and position their troops for the greatest advantage. The child's arrival in Gerushah had been a mere inconvenience. He had no doubt in his ability to assess the situation and deal with it effectively. While it was true that Qal had been dispatched to take care of the problem at the behest of Lord Lucifer, Bahadur had seen no need to fulfill or even mention the full extent of his orders to secure the perimeter and scour every quadrant of land inhabited by neither humans nor angels.

The order had seemed excessive, and he had secretly agreed with Qal that she was just one child. To Bahadur, it seemed Lord Lucifer had become obsessed with relics and bloodlines, hovering over his coveted throne as a viper guarding its nest of eggs. And though the Prince of the Air maintained scrupulous vigilance over threats throughout the kingdom, he had long ago ceased to survey actual battlegrounds, leaving military decisions to his officers. Failures were punished mercilessly, but only *if* Lucifer was apprised of such infractions. Bahadur made sure to report only those issues that were in his own best interest to resolve.

Bahadur's interests were also keenly tied to the success of the great Shàngdí as the ruler of the largest empire. The outcome of each battle in this empire would prove the strength of General Bahadur's army. To lose would be dishonor, shame, and a potential threat to his position. Bahadur watched the battle raging before him from the ramparts of the Shamayim, the outer boundary leading into the Meridiem.

The sounds of clashing swords, rolling thunder, and cracks of lightning cut through the skies as demons battled angels for the upper hand. It was a game of numbers, and neither side would concede. Immortal beings cannot die. The platoons were evenly dispersed, Bahadur observed. However, as he surveyed the landscape before him, a familiar and troublesome sight emerged from the battle.

From the northwest region of the empire shone a beacon of light from amid the billowing black clouds. The demon warriors were beginning to spread slowly outward to form the ragged outline of a shape approximating a circle. Wispy trails of pure white smoke rose from the center of the circle. In a moment, the fragrant incense would reach the Meridiem in its path upward to the Throne Room. Bahadur cursed.

A courier caught Bahadur's eye as he flew swiftly toward him. The courier bowed low before delivering his message. "O Great One, Commander Xi has sent me to tell you that the enemy has a gathering in the 95th district." The courier pointed to the area Bahadur had been watching. The circle was widening. Mongers were being hurled out and were not able to penetrate the boundary, not even with a barrage of flaming arrows. The courier continued. "The Enemy's children have been fasting and praying for several days. They have established a perimeter that we are unable to breach, and there are no reinforcements to withstand them."

Bahadur cursed again, frowning. The answer was simple but costly.

"Find Qal. Tell him to choose 100 of the best warriors and report to the 95th district. Immediately," he growled. Moving troops already fighting from an active zone would mean a loss, but it had to be done. A successfully established perimeter must immediately be quashed.

"Yes, my Lord," The courier replied, bowing again and then hurtling downward toward the battle like a speeding missile pursuing a target.

*   *   *

Adriel presented himself to the Most High, having bolted for the seventh realm immediately upon seeing the slightest hint of white smoke. The sweet incense of prayers rising from saints still occupying the third realm filled the Throne Room, invigorating him with its fragrance. He bowed low before the throne. The sight of the Most High God, more glorious than all the lower deities combined, filled him with reverence that never dulled but only grew. For all creatures and residents of the higher realms, familiarity with *El 'Elyon* only brought greater awe, for His greatness knew no limits, and His majesty yielded unending glory upon glory. He was like no other being.

Adriel stood as the seraphim began a new chorus of hallelujahs in the tongue known only in the Holy Throne Room. Melody and harmony intertwined in sublime counterpoint, swirling in colorful waves all around and about them. Adriel came regularly to the Holy Throne Room, and yet the song of the seraphim never repeated. Since the dawn of time, they had never once sung the same melody. Each was more beautiful than the last throughout the ages, for God the Creator never ceases creating. He makes all things new.

Were Adriel permitted, he would have proclaimed the wonders witnessed in the Throne Room long ago. Yet even as he desired it, he knew it was not possible. All the tongues of men had only one word— *glory*—to describe what Adriel knew in at least a thousand Malakyín words. Millions more existed in the tongue of the Holy Throne Room.

Beyond mere impossibility, to even attempt to communicate or teach such words to souls encased in earthen vessels would be detrimental while they lived on Earth. Such knowledge required not only citizenship in Heaven but residence as well. It was therefore not permissible to speak of such wonders, and to do so was punishable by eternal banishment.

And yet Adriel had witnessed many a curious thing as a Holy Watcher over the realms. Though every angel of every rank received no mercy for any act of treason but was immediately cast from Heaven's splendor, the children of men knew no such swift castigation in most cases. Adriel had observed generation after generation of humankind cursing the Almighty's very existence with their own lips, yet the lightning never struck, nor did the ground swallow them to their death. They lived on.

Grace, it was called. The heavens were filled with songs of the grace and glory of YHWH. Adriel knew grace to be favor granted for obedience and service to the King. Participation in the grace and glory of God was available for every angelic being in service to the Almighty as long as perfect obedience was maintained. What Adriel observed of the grace given to the children of humans, however, was far beyond what he could comprehend. To them, grace was given even as they cursed and denied Him. *El-Elyon* even brought many of these same humans into His own family. No matter how many times Adriel had witnessed the proceedings of a soul's transfer of status from enemy of the Almighty to beloved child, he could only fold his wings in quiet reverence. Of this grace he would never partake or even understand.

What of the saints, beloved children of their Father for whom all the splendor of Heaven was given? What of those who fasted and prayed even now? People dressed in drab, green uniforms climbed into cars and raced throughout the streets of Taiyuan, heading toward the outskirts of the city toward Tingxu. The believers were on their faces crying out to God. The fragrance of their prayers was of the most rare and beautiful of aromas, for they prayed not for themselves but for the people of Tingxu who had rejected His grace, for the people of Taiyuan, for the mayor of that city, and for the officers who were coming to arrest them.

Adriel knew they had no personal need of him. He could not directly impart courage, peace, or joy upon their souls. *El-Elyon* was adamant about personally ministering such things to His children as only He could. There would be a task for Adriel, as sure as the break of dawn, however, and in the blink of an eye the command issued forth. Adriel rocketed from the Holy Throne Room, plunging downward toward the fray below.

Adriel stood on the canopy between the third and fourth realms, surrounded by the white smoke of incense from the prayers of the saints. Pulling a horn from his belt, he played the cadence of the archangels, calling them to arms. In a flash of lightning, the seven archangels over the Shamayim arrived with flaming swords held high, ready to fulfill the Lord's command.

*　*　*

At the summoning of the archangels, Bahadur paced, expecting to see Qal moving a platoon of his best warriors to the assigned location that would soon be overrun. Qal never came. In fact, as Bahadur surveyed the battlefield, there was no sign of him anywhere. Surely Qal understood this was his chance to prove himself, his *last* chance. Bahadur grimaced as the courier arrived at his side with the words he expected to hear.

"My lord, Qal is nowhere to be found," the courier stated.

Bahadur roared in unbridled fury, slamming his fist into the courier's chest. The courier hurtled through the air, end over end.

*　*　*

Adriel watched as Bahadur, blind with rage, also removed a horn from his belt. The tones rang out over the Shamayim in a call to all warriors from every region and every quadrant. Warriors poured into the Shàngdí Empire from every corner of the realms like a horde of raging hornets charging into battle.

"Stand firm, saints! Stand firm!" Adriel called to the saints on their knees in the third realm, brave warriors themselves who knew not the great battle in which they were engaged beyond the veil through their prayers.

"Stand firm in the Lord," Adriel called again, "for your redemption draweth nigh!" As the archangels arrived on scene, their fiery swords drew the demon horde to battle like moths to a flame. Adriel smiled with satisfaction. Although angels were not permitted to enter Gerushah to render aid, Gerushah—the very pit of vipers itself—had now been emptied of all demon warriors.

Chapter 19

Holy Fire

The cedar tree was aglow. The walls of the hollowed tree trunk were illuminated in shades of blue, yellow, orange, and red, creating a kaleidoscope of colors all around the four companions. The roar of a searing blaze filled their ears.

Corrie stood staring up at the branches above that were dancing and weaving in the waves of colorful flames. They should have been reduced to ashes by now, but they were not even the least bit singed. Corrie reached cautiously toward the tree trunk. Surprisingly, it was cool to her touch.

"How is this possible?" Corrie asked, incredulous.

"What the enemy meant for destruction has become a holy fire," Horatius replied, watching the flames in quiet reverence. He had been holding the rolls of parchment they had collected from the cave. He now set them on the small table. Corrie was not satisfied with his answer.

"But fire *burns*. It makes smoke and ashes, and—" Corrie protested. She was frustrated that she had to explain what should have been obvious. Nobody stood in a burning tree and survived.

"The key word is *holy* fire," Horatius explained. "This old tree is a refuge. When God establishes a refuge, the enemy cannot touch you or even find you. The Lord answers prayer. Remember that, Corrie."

"I doubt that," Corrie muttered.

"What troubles you, Corrie? The part about a refuge or that God answers prayer?" Prudence asked quietly.

"Well, both. But no, I don't think prayer does anything," Corrie said. "There is always a logical explanation for everything. You just have to find it. There are no such things as miracles."

"And yet you stand in a burning tree," said Horatius gently.

Corrie did not have an answer. She could not explain how a tree could be on fire without burning them all to cinders. She saw it, but she still believed there had to be a reasonable explanation. There were plenty of things she did not understand but that could ultimately be explained by science. One night she and Collin were lying on a blanket outside staring up at the darkness when the sky suddenly lit up like lightning. A ball of light exploded above them and then traced a line across the sky. They had both been scared at first, thinking it was a bomb. The next day they found out that meteor showers were predicted that month. True, the universe was something she could not understand, but the universe was still a natural thing that followed natural, scientific laws. That was how everything worked.

"Have you ever prayed for something, Corrie? Or someone?" Evangeline asked.

"No. My family doesn't pray," Corrie said emphatically, but she wasn't entirely truthful. She remembered her father saying prayers before meals and at bedtime not long before he died. And there was more. Corrie had secretly prayed when her grandfather lay dying on the ground. She had prayed when her father was killed. She had prayed when her mother left and never came back. When Joe had crushed her body in a ditch and later tried to kill her, she had prayed to a wall of silence that had never answered.

"I think that if there is a God, He definitely doesn't answer prayer, or at least not mine," Corrie said quietly. Her voice caught on the last word.

She turned away from them, pretending to study the lines in the tree bark. She wanted so badly to think of something to fill the awkward silence that followed, but she couldn't. She blinked back tears, wishing she could reel her words back in.

"Does your leg hurt, Corrie?" Horatius asked quietly after a few moments had passed.

"I'm fine," she said curtly, curious why all three of them were staring at her left leg so intently. She looked down at her leg and saw nothing unusual. Why would her leg hurt?

"I was wrong about that arrow. It was not a stinger," Horatius said, still staring at her calf. "I should have looked at the entry wound more carefully. It may have been a tether," he concluded.

"Does it make a difference, Horatius?" Evangeline asked, moving closer to Corrie as if to examine her leg. Corrie stepped away from her. They were talking about her as if she were not there. Even worse, they spoke as if something were wrong with her. Her face grew warm.

"A tether lodges in the host, seeks out what it is able to feed on, and magnifies it," Horatius explained. "Any kind of fear, doubt, malice, envy—whatever is there—the tether will attach to it and grow. It is far—"

"Worse," Evangeline said, interrupting. Corrie sat down against the tree trunk, crossing her legs underneath her so they could no longer stare at her leg. Evangeline sat down beside her but kept her distance.

"I was going to say it is far more challenging to remove," Horatius corrected and then went on. "I think there may have been another more potent substance added to make the poison. It has advanced more quickly than I imagined possible. It will find all of her other similar wounds and unite them," he said.

"Poison? Wounds similar to what?" Corrie chuffed. "What are y'all even talking about?"

"The arrow in your leg, dear. Remember? Evangeline reminded her. Pru and I had tried to tend the wound and draw out the poison—"

Corrie interrupted. "I think I'd remember if someone shot me with an arrow," she fired back.

"But dear—" Evangeline started again but paused instead, her mouth agape.

Prudence had been listening to the exchange without comment, remembering their last similar exchange near the river. The fact that they lived in two separate worlds—the three of them in one and Corrie in another—was becoming more obvious by the moment, and the divide was growing. It took more than words to explain color to a blind person. When Prudence finally spoke, she again cut through the dialogue with the precision of a sharpened paring knife. "Corrie said she's fine, Evangeline. So I think it is time to consider what we will have for our evening meal."

Horatius replied deliberately, "Yes, Evangeline, you and I will go and gather food and water for the night. Prudence, would you mind staying here with Corrie?" It was not a true question, but Prudence nodded. Evangeline clambered to her feet to join Horatius.

"I see what's going on, Horatius. I just don't see the need to keep the truth hidden." Evangeline was still talking as Horatius whisked her hurriedly out the door.

*   *   *

Prudence took Evangeline's place on the floor beside Corrie. The flames enveloping the tree were slowly fading from mostly bright blue-white to a glowing red-orange fire that filled the tree trunk with warm light. Evangeline had been right. It was never harmful to speak the truth, and perhaps even more helpful to do so regardless of Corrie's response. They were all unaccustomed to relating to anyone who did not appreciate the truth. Prudence believed it was likely a jarring experience for all of them on this side of Paradise, and they would need to trust the Lord for wisdom and make adjustments as necessary.

Prudence gazed at the child next to her who sat with her back against the tree-trunk wall, her eyes closed and the smallest hint of a smile on her lips. She seemed to rest in victory that Prudence had again agreed with her. Corrie had both legs outstretched. Her hands were folded serenely in her lap, but her muscles twitched. She was such a restless one, this child.

Prudence studied Corrie's leg, the injury that she so staunchly denied. The center of the wound where the arrow had pierced the skin was completely black now. Dark, squiggly lines surrounded it like jagged spokes of a wheel. The infection was now spreading even more rapidly. Corrie had no idea what was going on within her. That was precisely how the enemy accomplished his will—in blindness and oblivion.

Prudence had first seen the change in the wound when they were near the river. It had already begun to affect Corrie who had transformed from being generally sweet to instantly angry and belligerent. It was a familiar disposition. Prudence had observed it not only in her years on Earth but on several missions since her departing. Anger of a demonic kind always had a certain edge to it that Prudence found easily recognizable. It was always ready to defend its rights and strike down anything or anyone in its way.

Realization dawned. *This* was how Lucifer was fighting this battle. It was a brilliant strategy. Too cunning to openly attack a soul marked with God's divine protection, he had simply targeted Corrie's own destructive self defenses. While they were still waiting for another attack from a company of demon warriors, the poison from a single dart was spreading and accomplishing the enemy's insidious plan. The diamonds, the attack on the refuge—that had all been a ruse, a mere distraction from the invisible war raging within Corrie. Earnest and open prayer was the only effective help, and yet Corrie was already resistant to that idea even before the poison spread. Now they would risk utter mutiny from her at the very suggestion. What were they to do?

Horatius had thought the arrow was a tool of despair, and yet Prudence did not observe any evidence of despair in Corrie. Those infected with despair were usually more downcast, more likely to give up than fight. Corrie was clearly not giving up anything. There were several different weapons and poisonous barbs at the demons' disposal that could have been used to infect Corrie with anger, doubt, self-pity, greed, or any combination of those. They were nearly impossible to discern once they joined with a person's own innate tendencies and formed a mass of aggressively destructive, immaterial tissue that infected the soul. What poison was this that kept Corrie determined to resist any hint of belief in God and fight against anything she was divinely appointed to do?

Prudence sighed wearily and silently offered up prayers for wisdom and for a miracle, for that was what Corrie needed. She reminded herself that the Lord had chosen this child and had a plan for her to accomplish. She would have to find the diamond. Prudence merely had a small, assigned part to play. It was up to Prudence to do what she was called to do, which was to close the gate. Prudence had already concluded that it was not possible to close the one gate in this land, the Eastern Gate. Was it instead a metaphorical gate that Corrie was to close? That possibility required divine understanding in order to identify it. Surely, the gate to the mind was the most challenging of all to defend, and that fortress had already been breached by an enemy as clever as he was cunning.

What would you have me say, Lord? What shall I do? Prudence inquired of the Lord in the quiet recesses of her thoughts. A few moments later, she knew.

*   *   *

"What is most important, Corrie, is that you find the one priceless diamond, the *Yahalom Shalom*. God has hidden it somewhere for you to find," said Prudence.

"If God wants me to find it, then why is it hidden, if there is a God, I mean?" said Corrie sardonically. She was not about to let Prudence think she would believe any of that nonsense, and yet she was curious what Prudence would say.

"Would you leave the most valuable gem out in the open for the whole world to steal or trample on?" Prudence queried. Corrie considered her point.

"Do you really believe it's that valuable?" Corrie asked. "I mean, I've never heard of it. Wouldn't something so important be famous? Everyone would want it, wouldn't they?" Corrie asked.

"Yes," Prudence replied firmly, tipping her chin. Her voice softened when she spoke again. "It is more valuable than anyone on Earth can possibly comprehend because it is from God," Prudence said reverently. Her low, sonorous voice was filled with a fervor that Corrie had never heard before.

"*God*," Corrie whispered. Why did they keep bringing this up? It was pointless. Even if there were a God, it didn't matter. God had nothing to do with her. Corrie shook her head as if to clear her mind. She wanted to forget the conversation completely, and yet something within her held on tenaciously. She twisted the hem of her T-shirt into a knot, let it go, and then twisted it again.

"How can anyone know for sure that God even exists?" Corrie asked. There had been a teacher at her school once, Mr. Harris, who was Corrie's fifth grade science teacher. He had said that there were some people who believed that God exists, that God had always existed. He had been her teacher for such a short time that Corrie had forgotten about him until now. She stared straight ahead, unable to face Prudence's stern gaze, unwilling to let Prudence think she had given up any ground about her beliefs.

"Creation itself proclaims the existence of God," Prudence stated. "You need only look at a spider web or the center of a flower to know that someone had to design a masterpiece so intricately complex and beautiful. Have you ever wondered how everything came to be, Corrie?" Prudence asked quietly.

"I believe in science," Corrie answered, but the sound of her own voice sounded hollow. It was not as convincing as she had intended. "I believe in what is logical. I believe in common sense," she affirmed more strongly. She should not have to defend herself against irrational beliefs, and yet she soon realized that was exactly what she was doing.

"Do you live in a house, Corrie?" Prudence asked in the same, steady voice. Prudence never seemed to react to her in any visible way that Corrie could observe.

"Yes," Corrie replied warily, wondering what that had to do with anything.

"Does it make more sense to say that someone designed and built your house or that it came together on its own or through some magical force?" Prudence questioned gently, brushing a spot of dust from her blue dress and then smoothing it again.

Corrie massaged her temples. She felt suddenly irritable and confused. Prudence was the one believing in an unknown magical force, not her. More than that, however, was the reminder that it was Corrie's grandfather—Papaw, her beloved Papaw—who had built their house. She melted inside at the mere thought of him. He had been such a good man and the best grandfather she could have ever wanted. Oh, how she missed him, and how she missed her parents. So much pain, so much loss. *No*, she whispered to herself.

Shaking off the memories of her family, she blurted angrily, "If God made this world, He's got a lot of explaining to do because it's a real, fine mess." That was what Corrie intended to say, but what flew out of her mouth was a string of other words, words that would have shocked her parents. Hot tears stung her eyes. She expected Prudence to scold her soundly, but Prudence said nothing. Corrie glanced up at her and was surprised to see Prudence's dark eyes filling with tears. Corrie looked at the floor, her face growing suddenly warm.

"The world was once a perfect and beautiful place," Prudence said softly. She paused and then continued. "There was no pain or suffering. No death. It was paradise," she said.

"What happened?" Corrie asked.

"Something entered the world—a disease. It is the same disease that causes all pain and suffering in the world and prevents people from seeing the Creator in His creation. And—" Prudence paused and pursed her lips as if reconsidering her words. Corrie waited.

"And?" Corrie asked, urging her on.

"And it is the same disease that causes people to blame God for the results of its own destruction in their lives," Prudence said, staring up again at the burning tree branches. Like glowing embers in the darkness, the fire pulsated in shifting degrees of light.

Corrie felt uneasy by Prudence's answer, though she wasn't quite sure why. She did not fully understand it, yet her curiosity was growing stronger than her misgivings.

"What's the disease, and where did it come from? Does it have a name?" Corrie asked, curious if she had ever heard of it.

"It is called *sin*," Prudence replied.

"Sin," Corrie repeated. "That's it? That's an awfully small word for something that destroyed the world."

"Yes," Prudence agreed.

"Sin," Corrie said again. She wondered if she had ever had sin or if her parents or brothers had. What if they all had the disease and didn't know it? She had learned in civics class about viruses that had killed thousands around the world. People carried the disease even before they knew they were sick and were spreading it everywhere they went. "Can you die from sin?" Corrie asked, beginning to feel a growing concern.

"Most assuredly," Prudence replied.

Corrie's thoughts began to spin in fear and wonder. What if her mother had died of this horrible disease and nobody had known? Maybe that was why she hadn't come home. Maybe she had sin. Maybe sin was what made the Goodson family so horrible. She had felt a horror far worse than physical pain emanating from Joe Goodson in that ditch. She had felt it in the depths of her soul. The thoughts and feelings that had filled her had been so horrible that she still had no words to describe them. What if such a disease could change a person completely? Maybe this was the word she was looking for. It was sin. She knew it. Suddenly, a horrible thought careened through her mind. It was no longer a question. It was a knowing in the deepest pit of her stomach. It wasn't just them. She was already infected with sin.

Corrie's breath caught in her throat. In that moment, she forgot about her plans to leave, about finding Remnant headquarters, even about finding her mother because something stirred in her heart that she had never felt before. Heat in the middle of her chest suddenly rushed to her face as if the flames from the tree trunk had suddenly ignited within her. *Holy fire*, Horatius had called it. Corrie clenched her jaw and balled up her fists against her legs to stop them from shaking. She didn't want to think about these things anymore. She didn't want to feel this way. She covered her face with her hands.

Then another thought stirred in her mind, whispering from the shadows. *Use logic, Corrie. Common sense. Did Joe Goodson die? Are you dead?* Corrie breathed a sigh of relief. Of course not. If there was such a disease that caused death and she wasn't dead, there was no real danger. She was just overreacting. She pushed the unrest in her soul aside and steeled her mind, ignoring the trembling in her legs.

Corrie wanted to get up, to pace the floor or just *leave*, and yet something in the way Prudence spoke held her there. Prudence was steady as a rock, someone she could throw any question at, no matter how ridiculous. Corrie tried to slow her breathing. Did her parents believe in all of this—God, prayer, even a strange disease called *sin*? Corrie had thought all three of these strangers were insane, but what about Prudence? In that moment, Corrie felt like if anyone was crazy, it probably was her, not Prudence. She needed to get her head straight. What did all this mean? Was anything the way she had always thought it was?

One question still nagged Corrie more than any. If she could only solve one mystery, she could find her bearings. If only she could know the truth. Would Prudence know? She had to try.

"Do you think my parents really were in the Remnant?" Corrie asked Prudence, feeling like her heart would jump clear out of her chest. She exhaled, already bracing for the response. She scooped up a handful of cedar needles from the floor to distract herself from the thrumming of her heart. None of them knew her parents, so how would Prudence know this about them? Yet the possibility was just too real, and she was finally able to admit it. Her parents had believed in God. She could not deny it. That had to mean they were Remnant, right?

"I don't know, Corrie," Prudence said softly. Corrie waited, hoping she might say more, anything that might help her settle this once and for all. Prudence did continue, but what she said was not what Corrie had expected.

"I can't answer your question regarding their political affiliation, but I don't think that is what you really want to know, Corrie. I think what your heart wants to know is if they were part of another group, the remnant of the faithful," said Prudence.

Corrie let go of the cedar needles and looked up at Prudence. "Remnant of the faithful? Faithful to what?" Corrie asked. Her voice was barely above a whisper.

"It is not *to what*, Corrie, but faithful *to whom*. That is the question to ask," Prudence answered, and then her eyes drifted as if there was nothing more to say.

"To *whom*, then? Prudence, to whom?" Corrie said, frustrated. Prudence was so difficult to talk to sometimes. Corrie was starting to lose her patience but restrained herself again, sighing loudly.

"Faithful to the One with the power to cure the disease," Prudence answered quietly.

"You mean *sin*? That disease, right?" Corrie asked excitedly. Relief flooded her. Of course her parents would be part of a group like that. That had to be it. Her parents were good people. They were part of a group that was helping the world, not burning it down. But Corrie was suddenly confused. That answered nothing. It solved nothing. They were still hated. Her father was still dead, and her mother was still missing. This conversation was going nowhere. What was the point? Her momentary elation fell flat.

"Then where are those people, the remnant of the faithful, or whoever they are?" Corrie's voice trailed off.

"Many of them are in hiding," said Prudence.

Corrie was silent for a moment, trying to grasp what Prudence was saying.

"Why are they hiding?" Corrie asked.

"Because of persecution," Prudence replied.

"Persecution?" Corrie repeated in surprise. "But if they knew someone who could cure a horrible disease, why would people want to hurt them? That makes no sense, Prudence," Corrie massaged her temples again. Did anything make sense anymore?

"They are persecuted because the cost of the cure is too high, and that makes people very angry," Prudence explained. "The people who persecute them purposefully associate the remnant of the faithful with a violent mob so everyone will hate them and want to destroy them without having to think about the cure."

"Oh," said Corrie. "I guess that makes sense. A little." Corrie raked her fingers through her hair, considering Prudence's words. "How much does it cost?" she asked, curious if she could afford it. Corrie not only had a pure gold chain and medallion around her neck but also a beautiful diamond in her pocket that she had secretly kept from their trek to the river.

"The cure is free, but it costs everything you have," said Prudence.

"What?" Corrie answered, shaking her head. "Prudence, are you joking?" Corrie looked up at Prudence, expecting to see a wry grin or an amused expression on her face, but Prudence's features were as stern as always. She was not joking. Prudence continued.

"When I was a little girl, I went to the store with my father one day. He was going to surprise my mother with a new coat for Christmas. Hers had worn thin and was no longer warm. My father had noticed her eyeing a particular coat in the shop window every time they passed. It was a long, red coat with shiny pearl buttons down the front and a belt that tied in the middle. It was truly beautiful. I was so excited for Mother to have her new coat that I told Father I wanted to pay for it, so I brought my purse. I remember marching right up to the shopkeeper and telling him that we wanted the coat in the window." Prudence chuckled softly at the memory.

"And?" Corrie said. It amused her to think of Prudence as a little child, running and playing games. Prudence gave a slight smile and went on.

"When it was time to pay for the coat," Prudence said, "I opened my purse, reached my hand in, and scooped out handfuls of buttons, jacks, a ball, pennies, and a small ball of yarn—all my valuable treasures. I laid them all out on the counter and looked up to see a surprised expression on the shopkeeper's face. 'I'm afraid that will not do, Prudence. You cannot pay for this coat with those things,' he said. I remember looking up at my father's face with tears in my eyes. He pulled me aside. He had been waiting patiently, allowing me to conduct business with the man, but then he said to me, 'Prudence Ophelia Jane Helfgott, empty your purse so I can give you what you need.' So I dumped every remaining thing from my purse, every little bauble or spool of thread. My father took the useless scraps I had been saving and stowed them away. Then he reached into his pocket and pulled out a thick roll of dollar bills and filled my little purse with his bounty. 'Now you have all you need,' he said. He was grinning from ear to ear. I returned to the counter and reached into my purse that was now full of my father's ample provision. I gave the bundle of money to the shopkeeper who counted it and declared, 'Paid in full!' So you see?

I could not receive all that was freely given until I first emptied out all that I had."

"Where would anyone find what they need to afford the cure then?" Corrie asked, trying very hard to understand what seemed impossible. Corrie looked at Prudence. When their eyes met, the expression on Prudence's face was inexplicable. There was fire in her eyes and yet also a soft tenderness. When Prudence spoke, Corrie felt the heat of that fire course through her veins.

"Corrie, *God* will provide," she said and then glanced up toward the treetop. Corrie followed her eyes and saw the intensity of the flames suddenly grow and then fade again.

Corrie had never noticed this before. Was it when Prudence spoke the name of God that the flames grew? It seemed so. *God will provide*, Prudence had said. Corrie still wasn't sure that God was even real, but now she was expected to believe that He would provide? For *her*? Why would a divine being do something for her? If anything, she had proven that God did not exist and that if there was anything at all out there in the universe, it certainly did not care about her. Corrie reasoned that if *she* had made the world and all the galaxies, she surely wouldn't care about a plain, 12-year-old girl from Bellam, Texas. As much as Corrie wanted her brothers and the kids at school to notice her and like her, she knew she was nothing special. Besides, why would God give something more valuable than anything on Earth to someone who hated Him? And if she had any feeling at all about God, it was hatred. Oh, *why* did her parents have to believe in God? It made everything so complicated.

"Maybe that's where my mother is. She's hiding," Corrie said glumly. She stared at the darkness through the small window formed by the knothole. There were no stars, just a black blanket of darkness spread over the world, filling her with coldness in her bones despite the fire still glowing from the tree itself.

"I miss her," Corrie whispered, feeling the ache for her mother's arms deeper than any faint hope could satisfy. She blinked back tears, refusing to cry again. She had already embarrassed herself once. She knew that if she allowed even one tear, there would be a flood, yet in the presence of one so calm, the walls crumbled, and the tears again flowed freely.

Prudence sat quietly by, waiting until Corrie's sobs quieted to ragged breaths. Then the two of them sat together, looking out the small window in the shelter of the old cedar. Neither said anything at all, and the space in the hollow tree filled up with all the unspoken words only the heart can supply.

*   *   *

After a while, the fiery glow of the great cedar began to rapidly dim. The flames were dying, and with them their light. In the gathering darkness, the hollow tree trunk grew steadily colder. To Corrie, it seemed that a distinct foreboding emanated from the walls, now swathed in shadows. Prudence rose to her feet and rummaged through the supplies until she found two small flint rocks. She smacked one against the other several times over a small stone bowl filled with dried cedar needles and twigs. Finally, sparks cascaded down, and a small fire caught quickly. Its warm light chased the darkness back to the woods beyond their cozy shelter. Prudence then took a single burning twig and lit two small clay lanterns on the table.

"There. Much better," Prudence said approvingly, brushing the dust from her hands.

Corrie nodded, agreeing that it was definitely much better, but she was not in a very cheerful or talkative mood. She was hungry, thirsty, and tired. She stared blankly at a single strand of ivy over the doorway as it stirred slightly in the breeze. With each movement, she hoped it would be Horatius and Evangeline coming back with food, but they did not come, and the darkness deepened beyond their shelter.

The silence was suddenly broken by a loud boom in the distance followed by a steady roll of thunder passing through the woods. Corrie could feel the ground trembling beneath her, even through the thick padding of cedar needles she sat on.

Prudence raised her eyebrows at the sound. "I wonder what's keeping Horatius and Evangeline," she said, walking toward the window to peer out into the night. The woods were still. It was such an eerie silence here, Corrie thought. She could not get used to it. It was a strange place indeed, and she was growing eager to leave it behind.

"What if they were ambushed like we were before?" Corrie remarked, remembering the flaming arrows and the tunnel of fire. That had been a truly terrifying moment she would not soon forget, even if she believed she was not their target and that they were aiming for her three friends. *Friends*, she thought to herself. She turned the word over in her mind. Had they somehow become her friends?

"They will be fine," Prudence answered, interrupting her reverie.

"You're not worried at all?" Corrie asked. "But what if your enemy finds them?"

Prudence did not answer. Corrie's thoughts tumbled forward, gathering steam.

"What if there is a wild animal out there?" Corrie asked, forgetting that there were no animals in these woods. That had never made any sense to her and was therefore easily forgotten.

"What kind of animal do you imagine might attack them?" Prudence asked as she searched the shelves again, opening gourds and rummaging through a small stack of pots. Corrie assumed she was looking for food and rose to help her.

"Oh, I don't know," Corrie answered. "A bear? A wolf maybe? Coyotes? There are a lot of coyotes in the woods near my house." Corrie looked for Evangeline's bag that she had been carrying but realized Evangeline probably had it with her.

"Hmm. I don't think they have anything to worry about," Prudence said. She never reacted to anything it seemed. Compared to Evangeline and even Corrie, Prudence was stoic and unemotional. Prudence reminded her a little of Gran when Gran did not want to be bothered with something. But Prudence was much gentler.

Corrie listened to the sounds beyond the cedar tree. There had been thunder, but where was the rain? Did it not rain here? And the thunder had stopped. With any storm Corrie had experienced, thunder did not happen only once. What could have caused such a rumble if not a coming storm? She began to imagine what it could be. Was it more like a *boom* or a loud *pop*? Was it truly thunder, or could it have been a low growl or distant roar of a giant animal? As it happens when a person is desperately hungry, tired, and forlorn in a place far from home, Corrie's imagination began to run away with her.

"But what if there really is something in the woods?" Corrie asked, feeling a chill streak up her spine. She remembered how her brothers used to tease her when she little, telling her tales about a humongous, fire-breathing dragon with sharp fangs and talons. It was as big as a bus and lived in the woods behind Gran and Papaw's house.

Corrie imagined a big dragon swallowing up Joe Goodson in one gulp. She smiled to herself. Then she pictured her mother facing off with it. But then the huge beast slashed her with its claws, and great flames roared from its mouth. Corrie shivered, closing her eyes to try to erase the imagined scene immediately from her mind.

Prudence stopped what she was doing and studied Corrie. She leaned over with her hands on the table. Her eyebrows were stern, but her expression was gentle.

"All is well, Corrie, and all will be well," Prudence said quietly.

Prudence had a manner of speaking that commanded attention. Her voice was low and sonorous. She was tall and dignified and smiled so infrequently that Corrie found herself always sneaking glances at the corners of Prudence's mouth in the hope of catching her in the act of even the slightest grin. It wasn't that Prudence was angry or unhappy, for there was a serenity about her that Corrie found decidedly comforting. Prudence was serious, a trait that reminded her of her brother Will. But while Will remained aloof most of the time, Corrie knew Prudence cared.

"When I was growing up and ever felt afraid, my mother would tell me a story," Prudence shared. "My favorite story was about a princess and a dragon. Would you like to hear it?" Prudence came over and sat beside Corrie again with her back against the tree wall.

"Well, I'm not really scared," said Corrie. She was not a child anymore, at least not a child needing to hear a story for comfort to take her mind off things. "But I guess a story would be okay," she agreed. She tried very hard not to think about how her mother did the same thing when she was younger because she very much did not want the sadness to come back.

"It will help us take our minds off our hungry stomachs while we wait for Evangeline and Horatius," Prudence suggested.

"Yeah, good idea," said Corrie. She agreed with that wholeheartedly.

"Once upon a time," Prudence began, stretching her long legs out in front of her. "Give me a moment, Corrie dear. It has been a very long time."

"Ah yes. Once upon a time there was a king who reigned over the fair kingdom of Eir. I've got it now," she said cheerfully. Then suddenly and to Corrie's surprise, Prudence smiled broadly and winked. Corrie stared, so shocked by the uncharacteristic gesture that she wasn't sure if Prudence truly winked or just accidentally closed her eye for a second. This woman, if nothing else, was full of surprises. Amused, Corrie stretched her legs out beside Prudence's once again and listened as Prudence continued the tale.

Once upon a time there lived a king, brave and good, who reigned over the fair kingdom of Eir. There was also a dragon in the realm, a fierce and terrible beast that tormented the King's subjects and spread fear throughout the land.

By day, the dragon lay in his cave, guarding the treasure of the realm he had taken by force and by stealth. By night, he roamed the land, hunting and killing for pleasure and adding the spoils to his growing hoard.

The dragon, having succeeded in his many conquests, began to believe he was invincible. His boasts of wealth and power grew more exaggerated year after year until he believed he not only ruled the day and the night but also by his own power could command the sun, moon, and stars through the force of his will.

"I decide when the sun burns down upon you, casting light on your possessions from which I take what is rightly mine," he said. "I command the moon to hide when I so delight so I may feast upon your flesh by darkness. See? There is none greater than I that even the darkness and the light obey my voice."

The King had but one daughter, his only heir, since the dragon had devoured both the queen and the prince. He hid the princess in the castle, never to be seen by anyone so as not to give any hint of her existence to the dragon.

As the King aged and his strength began to wane, it became clear that his daughter, the fair princess, could no longer be kept hidden. She would be crowned queen and would rule over a people besieged by the foul beast. The princess began to share in the administration of the king's duties.

She determined to live no longer under the shadow of the dragon. She deliberated with the king's wise men who cautioned against confronting the evil, winged despot, for he ruled by claw and by fire. This she pondered long and hard.

There did not seem a way to defeat the dragon, for if she ventured to the dragon's lair by day, she would be seen and roasted alive before even reaching the cave's entrance. If she crept into the cave by night as the dragon roamed Earth, it was said that he had cast a spell on what were now his belongings, which would turn to ash if anyone who dared lay a finger on any of them.

One day as the King lay dying and the princess prepared for what would soon be her coronation, a young boy snuck past the guards into the castle. He found the princess alone in her chambers, brooding, as she did most days.

"Your highness," began the boy, hardly older than a page.

Startled by the unexpected announcement, the princess spun around to see who would enter her private quarters so boldly and unannounced. Before she could speak, however, the young boy cried out, "I know how you can defeat the dragon."

Amused beyond her surprise at being confronted by one so young and full of daring fortitude, she replied, "You are young enough to be my son. How then shall our brave knights defeat the dragon, though none have ever been able to even approach him?" she asked and waited with the slightest smile tugging at the corners of her lips.

"The knights cannot. Only you can."

"Do you know what you are saying, little one? The knights of the King have the very best armor and weaponry in the realms. They have obtained from many generations the best training in weaponry and warfare. Many have, in fact, faced dragons in other lands and killed them, and yet they cannot defeat this enemy. How, then, do you suppose that I, one who has never left the walls of the castle, can fight against this deadly beast, and win?"

The little boy said, "By the authority of the king and the Rose of Eir. From the poetry of our people," and began to recite the poem by heart.

> Though pow'r be sought
> Through vict'ry wrought
> In battle's bitter glut,
> The rose of Eir
> Beheld most fair
> Remit of noble blood.
> In Love's own bower
> Love crushed the flower
> For oath in fealty's name
> O'er those whose right
> To royalty's might
> Should there be brought to claim.

"So you see, my lady, you have only to claim it," said the boy.

"I see you have learned the ancient poets. And how did you come by this information about the Rose of Eir?"

"One night I crept into the dragon's cave, and I saw there among the many gold pieces, gems, and fine pelts the gemstone of your family's name, a diamond pure and perfect."

"Is that so? Why did you not take it?" The princess smiled, for she was at once amazed and incredulous that one so young could have managed the feat.

"Because I am not of royal blood. I can neither carry its weight nor wield its power," the boy replied with an earnest sincerity that defied her doubt.

"So you are brave *and* wise for one so young. Indeed, it would likely kill you."

"But you, oh Most Royal Highness, would be invincible," said the boy.

"Why has no one spoken of these things?" she asked, folding her arms in front of her.

"The dragon has convinced everyone otherwise because the dragon is a liar and the prince of lies," he answered.

"I will ponder these things. Now go, before you are discovered," she said, and the boy left as quickly as he had come.

There was little time to ponder. The king lay lifeless in his bed. His time would come any hour, and she, the princess, would likely reign before noon the next day.

She kissed the king, her beloved father, and slipped out of the castle as the sun dipped behind the mountains. She wore a dark cloak, blending into the shadows of the night. She strayed from the light of torches or lanterns along the quiet streets. The townspeople had long since boarded up their dwellings for the night. The shadow of the dragon passed over the lake, temporarily covering the glow of the moon. The princess watched to see where he was heading. He followed the direction of the sun, presumably to torment the nearby villages and towns to the west. This was her chance.

She ran toward the hills outlying the village and climbed the steep slope toward the cave. It was only as she reached the mouth of the cave and crept inside that she lit the candle she had stowed in her cloak. The flickering candlelight cast an eerie glow on the piles of shiny gold and valuable treasures. The dragon had stolen from far and wide the wealth of many kingdoms over many years. Anger burned within the princess's heart, but she steeled herself for the purpose at hand, finding the diamond of her family's royal line.

She searched among the wealth of the nations, but all she found was gold, silver, and jewels. None was the diamond she sought, which was more beautiful than all the rest. She pressed on with determination, searching every treasure chest and bag of gold until at last, in a far corner and hidden beneath a stack of fine silks, she found a small leather box adorned with her family's crest and coat of arms.

Tucking the box under her cloak, she hurried toward the mouth of the cave, hoping to escape before the dragon returned. Just as she rounded the bend in the stone wall, however, the dragon appeared in the mouth of the cave. The mountain shook from the weight of his steps.

"Who dares to trespass on my domain?" the dragon roared.

The princess, upon seeing the massive dragon for the first time, trembled so violently that at first, she could not speak. When at last she gathered her courage, her voice was still a mere whisper.

"My father is the king," she said, "and I am my father's daughter." She found that in speaking the words she felt a tiny bit more strength in her heart. *Perhaps the boy was right*, she thought, and her hope grew.

"Speak up," the dragon hissed. "I want to know who you are before I slash you through, burn you, and scatter your ashes to the wind."

"My father is the king, and I am my father's daughter," she said again, and louder this time. The words she spoke emboldened her.

"Is that so? What proof have you? You are dressed in a beggar's cloak. Your hands have no rings or bracelets. You have no crown." The dragon scoffed and scraped one long claw along the cave floor.

The princess gulped but steeled herself for what she knew she must do. She reached under her cloak and drew out the leather box. "I have this," she said, grasping the diamond and holding it up for the dragon to see.

"I see. You grasp the diamond without succumbing to its power. Very clever, and yet you still cannot touch me. Your father sat on his throne doing nothing, and now he is close to death. Nothing has changed; nothing ever will."

Incensed by his mocking, the princess hurled the stone at the dragon, who opened his mouth and swallowed it. To him, it was a mere seed, small enough to lodge between his teeth.

The dragon laughed.

"That is your great defense, oh daughter of the king? A diamond no bigger than the very tip of my claw?" He yawned in mocking boredom and then took a step closer to the princess. He puffed out his bellows, filling with air. The heat of his fire danced at the surface of his scales, ready to blast forth. Then something inexplicable happened.

The great dragon opened wide its mouth, but instead of exhaling a blast of fire, the flaming throat remained dark and cold. The fire had been quenched. He inhaled again but found that he could not muster even the smallest puff of smoke and instead wheezed and coughed. He staggered. His eyes rolled wildly, and he fell. Then the belly of the dragon glowed red and burst into flames, burning through flesh and scales until nothing was left but a pile of ash and the diamond resting on top, wholly unscathed.

The princess retrieved the gem and made her way back home. Upon entering the castle, she ran to her father's bedside as the sun crested the eastern hills.

"Father, the dragon is dead!" the princess announced in breathless exhilaration.

"The Rose of Eir," he whispered faintly.

"Yes, I found it."

The king smiled weakly from his bed. His countenance was already shrouded in the pallor of death, but his eyes glistened at her words. The princess drew near, holding her father's hand in her own.

"Father," she said quietly. "You are the king. Why did you not defeat the dragon in the days of your strength?"

"There are many reasons, but none that I can explain to you now," the king replied and then took another gasping breath before speaking again. "Only know this. If I had defeated the dragon, then you, my daughter, would never have known that you could," he replied, and fits of coughing shook his frail body. The princess thought he would speak no more, but he took another breath and tried to lift his head though he had not the strength.

"What is it, Father? You must rest now," the princess entreated him, but the king had one final declaration.

"Now, may you carry the family name in strength and honor. Long live the Queen," he said with the last of his strength and then breathed his last.

After the days of mourning were completed, the Queen sent for a certain young boy.

"My father was the king, and I am my father's daughter. I make you now a member of my royal family line," the Queen said. Then opening her hand, she offered the boy the bright, shining diamond, which he held with strength and courage. The kingdom prospered, and all its citizens lived in peace for the rest of their days.

Prudence finished her story with a wave of her hand and then smiled at Corrie.

"I love that story," Corrie said.

"So do I," Prudence agreed.

They both sat against the hollow trunk of the tree, listening to the rustle of the leaves in the breeze. A certain camaraderie had developed between them, something that naturally happens when two people are stuck together, waiting in a tree.

"If the stone killed the dragon, why didn't the dragon die when he stole it from the king's treasury?" Corrie asked after a while. They had been watching the flames fade to darkness, leaving only leafy silhouettes swaying in the moonlight.

"Hmm. That is a good question. He could take the diamond away, but he could not take it in. One can seize power but not authority. What do you think?" Prudence said, tossing the question back to Corrie.

"You make things so complicated, Prudence," Corrie laughed. "Maybe there was an easier way. Maybe she didn't have to face the dragon at all. She was the princess. She could have just gathered all the armies of the realms."

"But those armies had already tried and failed," Prudence interjected. "Only she could defeat him because she was in the royal lineage. Remember?"

"Yes. Or maybe," Corrie said and then paused to consider. "Maybe she defeated the dragon just because she was the first to really believe she could."

"Hmm" was all Prudence said in reply.

She recognized the flaw in Corrie's reasoning. It was the infamous Fairsingvale error. In the Celestial Kingdom, there is a place in the north woods where the path comes to a point at the top of a gentle slope. Tall boulders mark the end of the trail that is so densely surrounded by trees that it is nearly dark. There is a long crack in one of the rocks where sunlight streams through in a thin ribbon. Beyond the boulders lay the vast canyon known as Fairsingvale, the valley that basks in the eternal light from the very throne of the Almighty. Only a fool could see light streaming through a crack in a boulder and believe that light could emanate from stone. Prudence sighed deeply.

She gazed up at the moon that was visible between the branches. Pale light shone in curtains of opaque incandescence. Another day had passed without Corrie finding the diamond. Another day in the wilderness, another day away from home for Corrie as well as for Prudence, Evangeline, and Horatius.

Corrie sat quietly, leaning against the tree with her eyes closed and resting peacefully now. Prudence studied the black lines on Corrie's leg. The poisonous web of interwoven strands now enveloped her calf and covered her kneecap. The longest tentacle snaked up her thigh, nearly reaching the frayed hem of her denim shorts. Corrie was oblivious to the infection spreading within her. How long did they have? She had seemed open to the possibility of belief in God, but how long would it be before the poison stole every seed of hope in her heart? How long would it be before Corrie was completely cut off from any chance of completing the task ordained for her? If she failed, there may be another to fulfill the mission someday, or maybe not. And what of Corrie? Time was running out. No mission was without an end. *Thy will be done, oh Lord God*, Prudence prayed silently, and the flames of holy fire long burnt out revived one last time before flickering out.

Circa AD 33

Mary held the gold medallion in her palm, watching as it sparkled in the sunlight. She had treasured it now for more than three decades. A man of wisdom and royalty, a sage dressed in elegant silk robes, had presented it as a gift for her son. The elderly gentleman had tears in his eyes as he laid the medallion before them. He was not alone. He came with others who said they had traveled from the east. They were most gracious and generous, giving precious frankincense and myrrh from their distant lands. Joseph had spent the gold coins on necessities for their small family , but Mary had kept secret the medallion, the most regal item given to her son. She had saved it for her son as a gift for his 12th birthday to do with as he chose. She had expected him to give it to the poor or add it to the treasury of the temple on that day they had made the long journey. She had held it out to him. She would never forget what he said. He was always surprising her with his words.

"All things I have given to you," he said, and closed her fingers around it.

She hadn't known quite what to say, but this, too, she had treasured in her heart. She had kept the medallion hidden all these years. Even through hard times, she and Joseph had always relied on Adonai to provide. She would never sell her son's property, for from the beginning she knew he was born to be King and that all things in Heaven and Earth belonged to him, though she did not fully understand what that meant at the time.

Even now the events of the last few months were still so fresh that she could hardly speak of them. Memories were still raw. She had seen him die! No mother should have to witness her child's death, especially such cruel acts of torture. Yet she had remained with him only because her son was her very life.

How she wished she could blot out her memories of the path through the streets of Jerusalem. With each step he took, she felt in her own body the pain he endured. She wanted to reach him, to give him water, to comfort him in some way in this unthinkable horror, and to let him know she was there. But though she struggled to press through the crowd, she could not reach him.

Mary, her dear friend from Magdala whom she had come to care for as a sister, pulled her from the crowd before she was trampled underfoot. They would find another way to the hill. They were determined to be the faces Mary's son would see in his deepest anguish and perhaps take comfort in knowing that he was loved to the end and not alone in his suffering.

Mary could not have known. Even now, understanding did not come easily. She could not have fathomed the truth of what was happening that day. She had looked up at the cross in her grief and anguish, too destitute to offer him any real comfort, and found that instead he was caring for her, even in that moment, even to the end. He, the one who had been unjustly accused and hung between criminals because of cruelty and pure jealousy, still had love in his heart for all of them. All of them! That was more than she could say for herself. She would have torn all his accusers limb from limb for what they had done to her son. She wanted to. She would have clawed the smug looks off their faces. She wanted to scream at every last person who had hurled insults at him. Murderers! He had done nothing to deserve this. He was the only innocent person among them.

That was the moment she knew. The very second that thought crossed her mind she knew the truth of it deep in her soul. He was the only innocent person. She, too, had wanted to kill, to destroy all those with such hatred toward her beloved son. She had forgotten that he was not her own. Though he had passed through her body into this world, she was but a vessel of Adonai. He was His beloved Son, and He was pleased to crush him—for her. Her heart had nearly burst in sorrow at the truth. It was not the mob who drove her son to the cross, not the priests, not even the Romans. She, too, had murdered him by the evil in her own soul. This was the sword through her heart that old Simeon had prophesied that day at the temple. How could a mother ever live, knowing that she had played a part in her own child's death? Unthinkable. When he died, she died too. She had asked to be buried with him. She would have crawled into the tomb with him if John had not carried her away.

The next day was the Sabbath, but there was no Shabbat rest for her, only the cessation of life itself, the rest of the dead. She neither ate nor drank. Every breath took more effort than she cared to expend. What was her life compared to his, her beautiful, beautiful son? She would have made a sacrifice rivaling King Hezekiah's to atone for her sin if that would have kept him from the cross. She would have captured every perfect lamb from the herds of Bethlehem and brought them to the temple, anything to assuage this agony, and yet this had been Adonai's plan all along. Joseph had taught her the words of the prophet Isaiah that their son would suffer and die. It was to be for peace that he would be slaughtered. Where was her peace? She lay on her pallet facing the wall, replaying the past few days over and over, begging God to take her. This was too much.

A sleepless night had drained any last energy she had. The Magdalene, her dear friend, had come by to see if she wanted to go with her to the tomb, but she had not the strength. Mary rolled over and covered her head as the sound of her friend's sandals faded in the night air. No one else in the small house stirred. The fire had gone out hours ago, and all the world lay beneath the cold, oppressive hand of death.

What had it all been for? The spotless Lamb had been slaughtered, his blood spilled—so much blood. His blood had spattered the streets of Jerusalem, soaked the earth beneath that hideous Roman cross, caked underneath Mary's fingernails when she had merely reached out to him. But what had changed? Mary felt all the grief, pain, and guilt even more. Sorrow billowed in unending waves, sorrow upon sorrow.

And how must that have been for Adonai to watch His own son suffer and die? Jesus had been His beloved son in whom He was well pleased. Was Adonai pleased now? It hadn't seemed that way. The earth had shaken, and the sun had faded to black. The very light of the world had died.

At the mention of Adonai in the tumult of her own thoughts, Mary noticed a shift within herself as though a hairline beam of light had penetrated the deepest pit of her pain. She clung to it. Was there not a God in Heaven who had created the Earth and everything in it? Had He not led her people out of slavery and through the wilderness to the Promised Land? Had He not always provided for them? Jesus had died as anyone does, but while he lived, he had also raised the dead through the power of Adonai because he who had been born of her own flesh was also—

"*Adonai,*" *she whispered. Her breath caught in her throat.*

Mary had known his true identity better than anyone, and yet she had never been able to grasp the depth of meaning of God and man in one person. Her other children who had grown in her womb had been Joseph's and hers, children of Earth, sinners just as they were. Jesus had looked like his siblings on the outside, but he was so very different. She could only describe it as a nature completely empty of any desire for himself. She had always looked out for him to be sure his younger siblings didn't take advantage of him. She had pretended to discipline him once as his brothers had watched so they would not be so jealous, but that had only backfired. They knew their brother had done nothing wrong because he never had. He never would. Even as he took the punishment, he accepted it graciously. He had never challenged Joseph's or her authority—ever. That was why it had been so surprising when he had stayed in Jerusalem that day. The children had always been instructed to stay with their father and not stray from their caravan so they would not be lost in the crowds. Jesus had obeyed even then. He had stayed with his Father.

His Father. Jesus was his Father's to do with as He had pleased, and it had pleased Him to crush the Son of Man. Mary shuddered as her thoughts returned always to this, the purpose for which Jesus had been born. He had been obedient even unto death. Would she? Would she accept his sacrifice for her sin? To do so seemed to go against everything in her heart as a mother. Accept his murderous death as a gift? She covered her head again as the room swirled around her. Being his mother had been her whole identity, and yet he had spoken often of a greater identity, a new kingdom. Surely he had understood how difficult it was for her to grasp. He had made it a point to diminish his familial ties on more than one occasion. It had stung at the time, but could this have been why? She had to let go of her hold on her son and embrace him as . . . who?

Mary could not understand such a mystery, and yet she also could not deny the hope growing inside of her, hope of a different kind, a new nature. She pushed the blanket away from her face and stared up at the ceiling. The first hints of morning light filtered in, forcing the darkness to the distant corners. Mary lifted her hands to Heaven in silent worship, drawing strength from Adonai until words she had nearly forgotten began to take shape once again in her spirit.

She withdrew the sword from her own heart and brandished it against the last vestiges of night with the same prayer of praise and thanksgiving she had uttered more than 30 years ago—"My soul exalts the Lord, and my spirit has rejoiced in God, my Savior."

"My Savior," she repeated, turning the phrase over in her thoughts.

Morning light was already casting out all remaining shadows when Mary heard the staccato of sandaled feet slapping the path outside her window.

"Mary, come quickly," Mary Magdalene gasped, breathless from running. Mary fumbled with the latch. "Hurry!"

What could possibly have happened now? Mary's heart nearly beat out of her chest. She sifted through her memory of where the rest of her children were at that moment. All were accounted for as far as she knew, unless the Romans had gone searching for them. Or was it Peter? John? No, she had just seen John only hours ago.

"What is it?" Mary nearly shouted when she finally swung the door open. It was not just Mary Magdalene but also Salome. Both were breathless and . . . smiling?

"Mary, oh Mary! H-He's alive! I saw Him!" Mary Magdalene stammered through fresh tears.

"Alive?" Mary heard herself answer weakly, too stunned for words, too afraid to hope.

"Jesus is alive! Alive!" Mary Magdalene and Salome shouted in chorus, embracing Mary, laughing, crying, and dancing all at once. Elizabeth, Zechariah, and Mary's younger children had awakened and now joined the celebration.

It had been the happiest day of her life. For the past six months since that blessed day, Mary had recalled every scene from Jesus's remarkable life— everything he had said and done, the stories and miracles, His childhood. "All things I have given to you," is what he had said. Mary remembered that as she turned the medallion over in her hand, feeling its weight. Jesus had indeed given her far more than she could have ever imagined. He had been her son once in what seemed like a lifetime ago. She had raised him, and yet everything had changed when Adonai, his Father and hers, raised Jesus from the dead. Jesus was now her Savior, her Lord, and her King.

Jesus had not died only for her; he was the final sacrificial Lamb for all Jews who had waited for the Messiah. She suspected he had also somehow given himself for the entire world. Would people as far as Byzantium and the nations to the west of them somehow also know about what had happened—that he had not only died but had been made alive again? Surely such news would pass quickly, but throughout the entire world? They had to make certain that it did. The world had to know what Jesus had done for them.

This was one small thing she could do. Mary Magdalene and Elizabeth, Mary's cousin and dearest friend, would soon arrive to discuss the plan. Elizabeth arrived first. When Mary opened the lambskin to reveal the gold medallion she had kept, the two of them wept as a flood of memories rushed in. Other than Joseph, Elizabeth had been the only soul Mary had ever shown the gold jewelry to. Their pregnancies had formed an unbreakable bond between them. One woman bore the awaited Messiah, and the other had carried the one who would prepare his way. Mary had clung to Elizabeth in the wake of that most horrible day. She knew her cousin understood better than anyone the particular anguish of losing a son to barbaric cruelty. Elizabeth's son, John, had also been murdered. They both also understood the necessity of what they must do now.

When Mary Magdalene arrived, she greeted each of them with a kiss as she entered the small dwelling. They had so much to discuss. Much had transpired since the Feast of Pentecost months ago. They had finally understood what Jesus the Messiah had come to accomplish. Their salvation was not in the form of deliverance from the Romans, as they had originally thought, but deliverance from the yoke of their own sin that kept them from Adonai. His kingdom on Earth had begun in their own hearts.

The good news was spreading like wildfire despite the opposition from the Romans, which was intensifying. Many of the new believers were being persecuted, forced to seek refuge from merciless torture and murder for believing in him. Many were living in hiding. They needed help—food, clothing, lodging, and medical care. Mary was limited in resources, but there was one thing she could offer. She could give her precious treasure of gold to help the cause.

The three of them agreed. Mary Magdalene would make use of her business connections at the market, and the gold would be sold for a fair price. The funds would then be given to Peter to administer to the believers as he saw fit. Since he had walked with Jesus, he would know the situation and the needs best. The women shared a meal together and rejoiced in what blessings would come of this small sacrifice for the Kingdom that had begun in their very midst and would spread throughout the world.

Chapter 20

The Treachery of Belial

Horatius and Evangeline returned long after sunset carrying baskets laden with fruit, root vegetables, nuts, and mushrooms. Horatius wore a tight-lipped expression and had little to say about their time in the woods or why it had taken them so long to return. Even Evangeline, typically eager to comment on most every topic, was silent as they set their baskets on the table.

Prudence watched them carefully, curious to know what had transpired since they had parted company several hours ago. She determined to be patient and not ask for details, knowing that if even Evangeline was holding her tongue, there had to be a good reason, and it was best to not ask questions. Horatius glanced at Prudence as he removed his pocket watch from his coat before setting the coat aside. When he looked at Prudence a second time, he shook his head slightly, confirming Prudence's suspicions that there were things to be said, but they would have to wait. A wave of uneasiness washed over Prudence, but she pushed her misgivings aside and focused on finding bowls and utensils for their meal. Thankfully, Corrie didn't ask why they had been gone so long. She was far more interested in the food, and with good reason. Prudence had listened to Corrie's stomach growl for the past hour. Prudence handed a bowl to Corrie who began filling it immediately. Evangeline set herself to the task of boring a hole in a very large coconut.

Horatius stared blankly at the pocket watch in his hand and then began pacing the floor. It was his task to guide the mission, to "prepare the way," as the instructions had clearly indicated. Surely that meant the way to the diamond. What else could it be? The diamond was here somewhere. He had no doubt because Corrie herself was here, but where could it be? More than that, Horatius labored over the thought of a coming test for Corrie. Could it be true? Wasn't finding the diamond enough of a test? He debated whether to warn Corrie, but he could think of nothing to say that would make sense to her.

What had happened in the woods was far too much for a girl of 12 who still believed that the universe could be explained on the pages of a middle school textbook. Evil had made itself known to Horatius and Evangeline, and it expressed neither a hesitancy in its flagrant desire for Corrie's soul nor a hint of caution. It seemed the demons were becoming more brazen by the day. A deal had been proposed, and this is how it had happened.

It was dusk when Horatius and Evangeline exited the great cedar and carved a path through the underbrush toward the center of Gerushah. They believed that the vegetation nearest the alcove was most likely to produce food based on observations on their first day in Gerushah. Trees in the west nearest to Lucifer's palace were a dull grayish green with sparse foliage and little fruit compared to trees farther east. It was only logical to assume that the land nearest the Sacred Alcove, the *Shabbathon Qódesh*, produced the finest the land had to offer for reasons based on world history. The alcove, encircled now by a tall hedge of thorns, still held the memory of the Creator's own footprints when He walked with man and woman in the cool of the day. Many citizens of Paradise in the sixth realm adamantly insisted that the shadow of His glory remained in the soil of the Sacred Alcove surrounding the Tree of Life, though no one had entered or even opened its gates since they were closed and locked. The theory would remain unproven, at least for a time.

At least their beliefs concerning the surrounding land were confirmed. The land immediately around the perimeter of the alcove hedge was a bounty of edible plants and fruit-bearing trees. Although they paled in comparison to vegetation in Paradise where all citizens of Heaven dwell, by Earth standards, harvestable food was in abundance. There was enough food to sustain them—as much as they could carry—for several days.

Neither Horatius nor Evangeline had noticed the figure skulking just beyond the alcove, not at first. Though they remained alert for the enemy, the brightness of the flaming Sword of Lemuel just outside the locked gate of the alcove had immediately arrested their attention and eclipsed all else.

When their eyes adjusted to the intensity of the sword's brightness, Horatius and Evangeline quickly occupied themselves with harvesting the vast array of fruit, nuts, vegetables, and succulent morels, the shapes of which emerged from the black canvas of the night as sculptures in relief. Their baskets were filled to the rim in no time. The figure waited on the path just beyond the outer edge of light from the sword, silently observing them.

Evangeline saw his shape first, like a phantom hovering in the moonlight. She gasped and dropped her basket, fruit and nuts rolling in every direction. Hearing her gasp, Horatius looked toward Evangeline and then followed her gaze to the creature that resembled a monger but was distinctively taller and held the familiar shepherd's staff used to direct the monger horde.

"Belial," Horatius said hoarsely, and moved to stand near Evangeline. The figure remained motionless for several moments, waiting at a distance.

"What should we do, Horatius?" Evangeline asked. Her hand was still outstretched as if she were still holding the basket that now lay empty on the ground.

"Come, Evangeline. Let's get this over with and see what he wants," Horatius said tersely.

Evangeline nodded, and they stepped toward Belial who offered no acknowledgment of their presence. Though much of his face was shrouded by a dark, hooded cloak, the horrid facial features were visible in the stark light of the sword. Mongers are able to twist the perceptions of humans beholding them in dreams and visions, but nothing can hide them from pure light. It pierces the darkness so all enchantments fade immediately. Evangeline and Horatius wanted to cover their faces rather than look into the vacuous, black depths of Belial's lidless eyes, yet they faced him as citizens of Heaven, undaunted and beholding him in the raw nakedness of his vile nature.

As they drew nearer, the hooded figure opened his arms in feigned welcome as if they were approaching a king who was welcoming them to his land. Belial's cloak unfurled, revealing a wide, opaque belt. Righteous anger stirred in Horatius as he strode to within inches of the demon's foul face.

"What do you want?" Horatius asked brusquely, his chin jutting toward Belial. A pleasant conversation with any demon was not possible. Getting to the point was the best approach in his estimation, and the sooner the better.

"It is not what I want, but what you want," Belial replied silkily. Mongers were able to mimic any human voice, a skill they used extensively from behind the veil that separates the realm of the physical from the spiritual. Yet here was the demon's own voice in its true form. Horatius wanted to recoil in disgust at the sound of it. It was like neither human nor beast. The gaping mouth had no lips or teeth for enunciation, and yet the words were clearly heard as if he were speaking directly to Horatius's thoughts. The voice seeped into his mind like a rotten stench from which he could not escape.

"I want nothing you have to offer, Belial," said Horatius coldly.

"Oh?" the voice questioned. "I know where you have been hiding the child, and I know what it is she seeks. And if you knew who questions you, you would have asked for my help. This is not your domain, oh frail, pitiful human. You believe yourself to be seeking after good though you do not know what good even means," Belial hissed.

"I have no need of your help," Horatius declared adamantly.

"Did you know that the Almighty has approved a test for your young charge?" Belial sneered.

"It is written, 'God cannot be tempted by evil, nor does He tempt anyone,'" Horatius answered coolly. The ground trembled beneath their feet at the mention of its Creator. "And in any case, I have no cause to believe anything you say," Horatius added.

"Oh, you misunderstand. I did not say she would be tempted to evil," Belial continued. Disdain dripped with every word. "You are all such a pedantic lot, always looking for evil behind every opportunity. I said the child would be tested. Tried. Your King enjoys that sort of thing. You cannot deny that."

Before Horatius could reply with a rebuttal, Belial added coyly, "Surely you cannot believe that her greatest challenge is to find the *Yahalom Shalom*." Horatius recoiled upon hearing the foul demon speak the true name of the precious stone. Belial, pleased by Horatius's reaction, pounced upon him with sudden boldness. "She may find it, but she will not take it. I know the poison coursing through her and infecting her soul. She will reject the very grace given her. I have yet to see even one human overcome its power," Belial roared.

"Then why are you here? Your lack of confidence betrays you, Belial." Horatius steeled his gaze upon the warped visage of a being that had once beautifully reflected the glory of God.

"Oh, you think yourself clever, do you?" Belial taunted. "I will overlook your stupidity. I come merely to offer you a deal. Abandon your mission, and I will give you the antidote for the poison. It becomes a zero-sum endeavor. You may or may not be able to help her, but it is certain that with the poison intact, she will fail."

"You have no authority to speak such things over her soul," Horatius retorted. Evangeline stood beside him, having regathered the fruits and vegetables she had dropped. Horatius was surprised that she had held her tongue. Had she not heard the demon's fallacious claims within her thoughts as he had? His question was answered when he saw Evangeline's hand slowly curling around a small melon, ready to hurl it at any moment. Horatius continued, "It is written, 'With God, all things—'"

"Don't bore me with your verses," Belial interrupted. "What power do words have over human desire? Surely you see that. Her desires rule her. She doesn't want what you want, and nothing you do can change that. 'Why don't you go running home, Horatius Portuno? You may be without sin now in your perfected state, but you still have no strength to defeat me. I remember your weaknesses when you walked on Earth.

I remember the Great Sadness, or have you forgotten?" Belial glutted, pronouncing his words with striking articulation, as if to pierce Horatius with each syllable.

Horatius stood his ground. "You may think you remember my past, but I most certainly know your future. Your fate is already sealed. It is not I who defeats you, Belial," Horatius added stolidly.

"Give up now, and I will undo the curse that binds her," Belial continued, undaunted. "She will return to the state she was in before being struck by the arrow." Belial was attempting again to strike a deal, but Horatius would have none of it.

"You belittle the power of God, a crime that will be remembered against you and added to your account for all time," Horatius fired back. Again the ground shook, this time even more, and a low moaning hum swelled beneath their feet, diffusing in an anguished sigh all around them.

"And how often does your Almighty King prevail over the will of a human staunchly against Him?" Belial demanded. "You understand nothing. She *loves* the poison, the strength of it flowing in her veins. She is drunk on its power. Give up! Give up, and go home. You can do nothing for her." Belial peered down at Horatius.

Horatius stood close enough to smell the acrid, foul odor of sulfur and rotting decay emanating from Belial. Then Belial said in a sneering voice, "Or do *you* doubt that God can accomplish His work without your help?"

Evangeline had taken in all she could stand. She wound up her arm like a Major League pitcher and hurled the softball-sized fruit toward the center of the cloaked face. She shouted, "Go back to the pit where you belong, you slithering son of a serpent!"

The melon soared straight through Belial, not disturbing him in the least.

Belial laughed a low, mirthless laugh. "Back to the pit, you say? I was once the scribe. Every word spoken of what is and what is to come in every volume of every book of the heavenly realms was penned by my own hand. All knowledge possessed in Heaven and on Earth is mine, and there is nothing known on Earth that is not known by me. You should be grateful that I should think to help you, to actually inform you of what is true and what is happening even as we speak. Your hope is unfounded. Trust in *my* words," said Belial.

"How dare you blaspheme Almighty God!" Evangeline shouted. "How dare you!" By this time, the ground was trembling so violently that Evangeline and Horatius had to hold onto each other to remain on their feet. The rumbling had grown to a roar all around them.

Horatius stood firm with head raised, eyes fixed on the foul face beneath the hood, and he spoke. "The Lord rebuke you!"

A loud *crack* exploded in the air around them, and instantly Belial disappeared without a trace. Thunder rolled in undulating waves from where they stood. Long vines stretched from tree to tree, whipping through the air, while flowering shrubs suddenly shed their blooms, withered, and then burst forth again with new foliage. Weeds and brambles snaked up tree trunks as if choking the life from them while the trees themselves twisted and shook in a wild, primeval dance.

"Good heavens!" Evangeline exclaimed, still clutching Horatius's arm.

"This land has no salt, no mediating or preserving presence. Gerushah is a wilderness in every sense of the word and will not lay dormant much longer. She is awakening, and she may be volatile," said Horatius as the tumult of the rumbling and thrashing slowly quieted to a steady thrumming in the deep and troubled heart of Gerushah.

Horatius and Evangeline stood silently for several moments, waiting to see if Belial would return or if another would come in his place. Never had they stood so close to the face of evil. Belial's words of blasphemy still hung in the air in a palpable cloud of despair. Horatius instinctively turned toward the sword. The flames of holy light swelled and billowed, enveloping all darkness around it and drawing his thoughts past their fiery glow into the alcove beyond. Oh, what mercies of God had abounded to save him from the evil clutches of darkness to which he had once been bound. What mercies!

"I'm sorry he brought up troubling things for you, Horatius," Evangeline said as they both now gazed upon the tongues of fire piercing the black night. Horatius knew she was referring to Belial's insults and the mention of his own suffering on Earth.

"No need to fret, dear sister," Horatius said, shaking his head. He stared wistfully toward the enclosed garden. "Do you not also find that you have memory of such times on Earth and yet it has no sting whatsoever? Even the most horrific accounting, though remembered, is immersed in light so magnificent that the only visible aspect is the reflection of its eternal preponderance of glory. It is truly wondrous," Horatius whispered reverently.

"Wondrous indeed," Evangeline agreed, patting Horatius on the arm. "And by the way, why on earth did you not rebuke him from the beginning? Then we could have avoided the whole ghastly conversation." Cheerfulness had returned to her voice.

"To *learn*, Evangeline, to learn. Did you catch what he said about the diamond? He inadvertently confirmed for us that there is indeed a diamond here in Gerushah, and it is possible to find it. I think he may even know where it is." Horatius punctuated his last sentence with his index finger wagging in the air.

Evangeline looked at him in amusement. "Horatius, I've never seen you so excited."

"The hunt is on, dear sister, the hunt is on!" He replied joyfully.

"Yes, indeed!" Evangeline exclaimed, raising her free hand in the air as she still clutched the basket of food with the other.

"Well, we best be getting back to the cedar tree," Horatius said. "I'm sure Corrie is more than a little hungry by now." Horatius looked at his pocket watch by the light of the sword and then set his sights on the wooded path that would lead them through darkness back to where Prudence and Corrie waited.

"Do you think there's any truth to what Belial said?" Evangeline asked as they began the trek back to the cedar tree.

"About what?" Horatius asked. "The poison? About Corrie destined to fail?" he said sardonically, remembering the demon's words and wishing he could erase from his mind the sound of Belial's grating voice.

"Yes," Evangeline replied.

"It is likely all true," Horatius replied. "They do not only speak lies but lies with seeds of truth. They are much too crafty for only lies, but then what does it matter? We are slaves neither to their lies nor to their versions of truth. They cannot truly predict the future, you know."

"I suppose not," said Evangeline.

"You *suppose* not?" Horatius queried, surprised that she would have any doubt concerning such things.

"Well," Evangeline began, pausing on the trail to adjust one of her shoes. Horatius looked down at Evangeline's feet, surprised to find her wearing shoes that were unlike any he had ever seen.

"Where did you find shoes, Evangeline?" Horatius interrupted, overcome by curiosity at how she could have acquired footwear in the wilds of Gerushah.

"It's just banana leaves tied with a little jungle vine. They're more like slippers, really, but a girl's gotta be resourceful out here, you know?" As they resumed their hike, Evangeline continued their previous conversation.

"I was going to say, Horatius, that it seems to me that those demons are awfully good at predicting what people will do if left alone to their own devices. It's uncanny how well they know the human heart," Evangeline explained.

"True," Horatius agreed. "The arc of the human story was indeed etched in stone. Praise be to God for the crimson ink of His editing pen!" The ground shook beneath their feet yet again.

"Amen," said Evangeline.

Horatius and Evangeline made their way around the tall hedge surrounding the Sacred Alcove, leaving the light of the flaming sword of Lemuel behind. They became two silhouettes moving through the clearing, soon disappearing into the dense Wood of Pa'laam.

The moon, though luminous and full, barely reached through the canopy of branches overhead, so cold and pale were frail fingers of light pressing through the darkness. A weight settled on Evangeline's shoulders as though a cloak were wrapping itself around her. Had Belial returned? Evangeline turned around but saw nothing. *Lost* came the answer through the night. *Lost? But I am not lost*, Evangeline thought to herself. The longer they walked, the more clearly the realization dawned that the feeling was not emanating from her own emotions but from what the forest exuded all around her. Everything surrounding her in this place was indeed lost to its Creator, save for the Sacred Alcove and the wandering east wind that whispered its all-too-infrequent murmurings of hope. This land had not known the blessed Nativity, the glorious Resurrection, or the presence of those who count such events as precious. This land remained bound in the perpetual wake of the Creator's unending absence. *All will be made right someday*, Evangeline wanted to say, but what healing salve could mere words be for those living things without ears to hear? Even the one guardian of the garden had absconded. The only continual presence in this place was evil, vile beings who would raze everything beautiful to the ground if they could.

"Well, that Belial sure is a horrible beast of a creature," Evangeline remarked as her thoughts drifted again to their encounter. "Did you see the worms around his middle? I thought he was wearing a belt at first, but then I noticed it was moving around his waist. Those nasty things were wriggling furiously. It was disgusting, Horatius," Evangeline winced again at the thought of it.

"Those were fib worms. *Specious molluscus*," said Horatius. "They feast on lies, and they were having a banquet on Belial. They are quite a virile parasite and easily spread."

Evangeline gasped, nearly dropping her basket of food again as she checked herself for any sign of fib worms.

"We are immune, Evangeline. No worries, old girl," Horatius replied.

"Oh," said Evangeline, sighing in relief. "I should have known. At least Corrie isn't here with us. She would surely be infected faster than a flea on a jackrabbit."

As they crested the hill and stood in the clearing, they could see the outline of the Eastern Gate in the night sky beyond them. They both looked for the glow of light from the cedar tree that had been burning when they left, but the only light in all of Gerushah was the moon. Still carrying their full baskets of food, Horatius and Evangeline descended the hill and then reentered the woods on a path toward the cedar.

"And Evangeline, speaking of Corrie, I think it best if we do not speak of our encounter with Belial in her presence," Horatius said earnestly.

"We do not need to inform her of everything." He remembered their last exchange in the cedar tree when Corrie was denying all knowledge of her wound that was inflicted by a demon's arrow to her leg.

"Right. Of course," Evangeline agreed. "I don't think she would believe us anyway if we did."

"Precisely," Horatius replied, pleased that their newest ambassador was quickly growing in understanding.

*   *   *

Though Belial had left their presence, he had not gone far. He watched from the darkness as Horatius and Evangeline hiked into the woods. He did not bother to come near them. They would only cast him away again, and he had no access to the child as long as one of these ambassadors of Heaven was with her. He was not without resources, however.

It had been much easier than he had thought. The leader of this pathetic band of rebels had dared to approach him, the Lord of the Mongers. Did the man think he could do so without consequence? He had fallen prey to his own ignorance and the cunning of a demon he had dismissed too lightly. Belial would obligingly teach him a lesson in respect.

At this very moment on its way back to the cedar tree and to the presence of a living, breathing, pretransfigured human being was a single *incubat* from Belial's own population of hungry parasites. It hid beneath the fold of the man's suit coat, too small to be noticed by either of the duo on the dark path through the woods. It would hide, lying in wait until the child invited its proliferation—and oh, she would! There was no question. All the *incubat* required was a hint of doubt regarding the truth, not even a clear lie. With even the slightest suggestion of falsehood, *Specious molluscus* would find its host.

*   *   *

Back in the safety of the refuge, Horatius, Prudence, Evangeline, and Corrie feasted on the collection of nuts, berries, and various tubers, as well as a generous pile of sanguineous morels that were especially good. They tasted a little like steak when paired with the root vegetables. Corrie wished they could build a real fire, a campfire that burned real wood. A potato cooked in hot coals would have been wonderful. It wasn't very smart to build a campfire inside the trunk of a tree, though. She could not remember the last time she had eaten a hot meal. Still, her hunger was quickly satisfied with the provisions they had, raw as they were. Although Corrie had been starving only minutes before, now her stomach was already full. She took one last sip of coconut water and excused herself from the table to sit on the floor against the far wall.

"Your eyes are bigger than your stomach, eh?" Evangeline teased.

Corrie nodded silently. She was in no mood for conversation. She had a lot of thinking to do. Tomorrow would be day three that she had been in this place, and she was no closer to her destination than before she had fallen into this land. Where was her destination anyway? Even that was no longer clear. Corrie had originally planned to go to Aunt Sarah's in Georgia, thinking that if anyone knew where her mother might be, it would be her aunt. If nothing else, Aunt Sarah would surely join Corrie in trying to find her. Gran and even her brothers had given up long ago. Corrie based her assurance on the fact that Sarah Tobias was Papaw's sister. No one had understood Corrie like Papaw. She was sure his sister would be the same. She counted on it.

And yet Corrie was beginning to feel truly homesick. She had been in this place long enough and longed for the familiar sights, sounds, and smells of home. She wanted to sleep in her own bed and tend to her flower garden and the bird's nest she had discovered in the bushes just last week. She missed the oak tree outside her window and her rock collection. She missed Will and Collin, and yes, maybe even Gran.

Gran could be kind in her own way. Once when Corrie had a bad fever, Gran sat beside her on her bed. She kept cool cloths on her head and gave her sips of water to soothe her burning throat. "You get better, now, Boots," Gran said, using the nickname Papaw had given her because she would always take his boots and stomp around the house in them. Corrie remembered the look of worry in Gran's expression when the fever wouldn't break. Corrie later learned that her fever was caused by something called strep. It could have easily been cured with antibiotics, but the pharmacy had been out of them for weeks. Gran had put slabs of raw meat on Corrie's neck to draw out the poison, along with herbal tinctures of goldenseal and garlic mixed with honey. She remembered the relief in Gran's eyes the morning she finally woke up drenched in sweat.

Corrie traced the circle of gold resting over her heart. But what of the medallion? Whatever love Gran had for her, it had long been buried under anger and disappointment. If Gran had said to not come home with it on, she meant it. Did Corrie even have the option of going home? Not until she could remove the medallion. Corrie felt sure that if she walked in the door still wearing the gold, something worse than being kicked out would happen.

And even if Gran still let her back in the house, what about Joe Goodson? What was she to do about him? A knot balled up in her stomach. She didn't care what he and his friends were doing with all those guns. How was she to even live in the same town with him? She could not avoid him forever. She would see him again. He would never leave her alone. Then what? He really would finish her off, or she'd wake up in the back of a stranger's pickup on her way south of the border. She had to get out of town on her own terms.

For a while, Corrie had thought that finding the Remnant headquarters was the perfect answer since coming to the conclusion that her parents were part of this clandestine group after all. Every political group had its headquarters. If she were to find her mother, Remnant Party leaders would know where she had been working. Of course, all that changed when Prudence told Corrie of another group of people, the remnant of the faithful. They were not a political party at all, according to Prudence. Corrie still did not fully understand who they were or what they wanted, but it had seemed a reasonable possibility that this group was, in fact, the group to which her parents had belonged. All that mattered was finding them. If her mother was still alive, she was likely in grave danger. Corrie was more determined than ever to find her.

Corrie wished her brothers were here. If they could just know what she knew now about their mother, they would understand the urgency of finding her. Even though they never said it, Corrie knew they had secretly come to believe Gran, that their parents were dangerous and any association with them was criminal. If they could just be here now and talk to Horatius, Prudence and Evangeline, they would understand.

Suddenly, Corrie had a brilliant idea. Of course! Why didn't she think of this sooner?

"I want you all to meet my brothers," Corrie blurted, to the surprise of the three sitting at the table. They had been poring over the scrolls from the cave by the light of the few clay lamps Prudence had found. The flickering light cast a warm glow over that side of the tree house, unlike the dark perimeter where Corrie sat. Horatius, Prudence, and Evangeline all turned in Corrie's direction. The lamplight cast strange shadows over their faces, so it was difficult to discern their expressions. It was clear, however, that no one seemed to know how to respond.

"What?" Evangeline asked with a tone of bewilderment.

"Yes," Corrie responded. "When you take me to the Eastern Gate in the morning, I want you all to come with me to meet my brothers so you can tell them what you told me, Prudence. Remember?" Corrie's words were tumbling out in excitement. "You know, about the other remnant, not the ones who blow up buildings but the other ones. And you can explain about the medallion. I want you to tell them. They'll listen to you. That's why you're studying the map, isn't it? To find the quickest way to the Eastern Gate so we can get out of here, right? I told you I wanted to go to the Remnant headquarters, but I don't need to go there anymore." Corrie went on to remind them of everything she had understood up to now, what she now intended to do, and how they were going to help her. She suddenly stopped to catch her breath and noticed that none of them seemed at all excited by what she was saying. In fact, they were all staring at the floor.

"Sweetheart, we are not trying to find the Eastern Gate," Evangeline spoke up. "We're trying to figure out where your diamond might be," she said, curls bouncing and eyes bright.

Corrie's jaw dropped. Not finding the gate? She looked at Prudence, but Prudence was staring at the floor. White, hot rage billowed within Corrie, filling her with new understanding. This is exactly what she had suspected all along. She sat up straight, feeling the fire building in her belly ready to scorch them all.

"*My* diamond? You really expect me to believe that's for me? I'm not an idiot!" Corrie bellowed, and there was more, so much more. It was powerful, like a dragon rising up inside of her, and it felt good.

"You were never going to take me anywhere, were you?" Corrie shouted at the top of her lungs. "Anywhere but to find your stupid diamond so *you* could have it. It's for you, not me. Admit it!" Corrie raged on, feeling the fire growing. "You're only using me, and you know it. You want me to do your work for you so you can buy another house, or more fancy clothes, or-or whatever it is you people do," Corrie said coldly with a wave of her hand. Her mouth curved in a jeering smile as she rose from the floor and walked toward them. She had them.

"Remnant, remnant of the faithful—I don't care who you are. You're all the same," Corrie shrieked. "You think you're better than everyone else. Well, guess what. I don't even want your stupid diamond. You hear me? I don't want it! "And I will get this thing off me as soon as possible," she said, tugging so hard at the gold chain around her neck that her skin blazed red. The chain remained locked in place.

"But sweetheart, we just want to help you. Just let us help you," Evangeline implored, rising from the table and moving toward Corrie.

"Stay away from me!" Corrie bellowed, backing away from Evangeline and closer to the doorway.

"Where will you go, Corrie?" Horatius asked calmly, never moving from his seat at the table. His eyes were filled with compassion. Corrie was disgusted. She didn't need his pity. She refused to answer him at first, but the fire welled up again.

"The Eastern Gate. And I'll find it myself," Corrie spat out the words, followed by a string of obscenities she hoped would shock them into silence.

"Then what, Corrie? What will you do?" Prudence said quietly, her dark eyes boring intensely into Corrie's. But Corrie did not want to meet her gaze. She darted toward the shelf against the wall and grabbed the sharp awl they had used to pierce the tough shell of the coconuts.

"I'm going to find my mother," Corrie answered, walking swiftly toward the door. "And don't try to stop me," she added, pointing the awl toward the three sitting at the table. When she was nearly to the doorway, Prudence's voice cut through the space growing between them.

"What about the cure, Corrie?" Prudence asked. Corrie stopped and then turned around to face Prudence.

"The cure?" Corrie scoffed. "What does that have to do with anything?" Corrie asked, glowering at Prudence. Prudence's gaze remained on Corrie.

"The diamond *is* the cure," Prudence replied. "You need the *Yahalom Shalom* even more than you need your mother—more than anything, Corrie. Stay with us. We'll help you find it." Prudence's voice was calm, but her dark eyes were intense, pleading.

"Oh, you'll help me?" Corrie asked in a mocking tone. "You still think I'm the one who needs your help? Your *cure*? Where were you when Papaw died? My dad? What about them? Were they not good enough for the cure?" Corrie walked back toward the table, glaring at each of them with the tip of the awl pointed toward them, daring any of them to respond, but they said nothing. Instead, she saw the same look of pity on all their faces. Her stomach turned. She swallowed the revulsion rising in her throat. She knew that look. She had seen it on Will's face the last time she asked Gran when their mother was coming back, and Gran had sent her to her room without supper.

"I get it now," Corrie smirked as the realization dawned. "You think I'm the one who's sick. You think I need the cure," she said, walking back toward the table and slicing the air over their heads with the awl in her clenched fist. "Well, I'll tell you who's sick. It's Joe Goodson, Jed Muncy, Rand Mercer, and Silas Barnes. Do you know what they did?" Corrie felt another wave of nausea wash over her. "Do you know," she paused, swallowing hard, "what Joe Goodson did? To me?" Corrie was fighting back hot tears.

Corrie strode again toward the door. Reaching the threshold, she spun around. "Unless you have a cure for *that*, I don't care about anything you have to say," she said and then whipped back the curtain of vines and stepped out into the night.

Chapter 21

Mine

The moon hung low in the sky, a large, luminescent pearl on a backdrop of black velvet. Normally, a night like this would mean good fishing for sand bass by moonlight and the flicker of lightning bugs. It was the perfume of wild honeysuckle in the woods of Bellam that had wooed Corrie into the night with her grandfather and brothers years ago. It was the peace of the moon shining on the water in the deep stillness that had held her there, enchanted.

The moon had always captivated her, as if it were always watching, wondering why people did what they did in the patterns of their lives. What did that shining, faceless orb see when it looked down on her now? Were her brothers looking up at the same night sky? And her mother? The moon watched over all, and like all faceless, faraway beings of the heavens, it shared no secrets.

The trail among the tall cedars opened onto a path ahead that was both wide and smooth. The vegetation peeled back on either side, leaving the surface as flat as a paved road. Corrie stood at the edge of the tree line peering down the path as far as she could see, but the pale light of the night failed to dispel the shroud of darkness completely. It seemed to her that if any trail should lead to a gate, it was this one. *All roads lead somewhere*, she reasoned. She found the North Star to her left, confirming she had indeed gone eastward. The Eastern Gate lay ahead of her. She had only to step onto the path.

She stood beside a tall pine. The road before her was the only apparent way out of this place. Taking it was the only reasonable course of action, and yet she hesitated. Why now? She bolstered herself for what felt all at once like the best decision and the worst since entering this strange land. Nearly three days ago she had been taken into the woods by force. She stood now at the edge of it, free to leave, and yet why was this suddenly so difficult?

What remained behind her? It was people who just wanted to use her, that's what. *They had also taken me in from these woods, fed me, and tended my wounds*, a small voice reasoned from somewhere in her thoughts. No, she would not fall for the trick. Nothing is as it seems. If her own family had kicked her out, why would strangers take her in if not to use her for their own purposes? It had nothing to do with caring for her. There was only one person in the world who cared for her, who truly loved her. This Corrie knew for sure, and yet memories of her mother driving away, leaving her standing on the front porch of her grandparents' house chipped away at her confidence that anyone could be counted on. Maybe it didn't really matter anyway. She still could not answer the simplest of questions—was her mother alive or dead?

Corrie could not stay here. She was a child alone in the woods. Horatius, Prudence, and Evangeline would eventually go home to wherever they lived. Exactly where that was remained a mystery. Corrie had never questioned it. And further, if helping her find a rare diamond was not the real reason they were camped in the woods, then what was it? Prudence had said the diamond was the cure for that disease— what was it called again? And they had thought *she* had it. *Psh. As if.* There was no way she'd subject herself to those kinds of people again. And how could a diamond, a gemstone, cure anything anyway? They really were insane. She was lucky to get away from them. It was time to go.

Corrie had stared off into the darkness, so thoroughly lost in thought that she failed to notice someone coming toward her on the road ahead.

Panic immediately seized her when she saw the figure. There had been dangers in the woods—that she could not deny. She slipped quickly behind the pine tree, watching the figure carefully as it slowly approached. Whoever or whatever it was moved slowly and with a staggered gait. She soon realized it was a person limping and hunched over as if in pain. Who would be on this road in the middle of the night? She watched patiently and silently behind the tree until she decided that the person coming toward her must be a woman.

The woman on the path had slightly narrow shoulders beneath a dark cloak. She carried a large walking stick that she jabbed into the hard ground as she dragged her leg behind her. Soon, the woman was near enough that Corrie could hear the dull rhythm of her movements along the road—*step-jab-drag, step-jab-drag*. When the woman was close enough for Corrie to hear her labored breathing, she suddenly stopped.

Corrie watched, her eyes straining to discern the details of the woman's appearance in the darkness, but her face was partially covered by the hood of her cloak. The figure leaned heavily on her walking stick, pausing, it seemed, to catch her breath. Her rasping breaths were the only sounds in the stillness of the night. She let out a low, rattling sigh ending in a cough and then spoke clearly.

"Is someone there?" the woman called.

Corrie held her breath. Had the woman sensed her presence? Corrie felt the blood draining from her face, and yet something about the woman's voice drew her like a magnet. She had to hear it again.

"H-Hello?" Corrie called in reply from behind the tree. "Who is it?" she asked, resorting to the phrase her parents had taught her to say from behind a locked door when she was too small to look through the peephole. Nothing could have prepared her for what happened next. The woman cried out in a voice as familiar as Corrie's own.

"Is that my child? My only daughter? Is that you? Let me see you! Where are you?"

Corrie gasped. Her feet were moving before her mouth could speak. She *knew* that voice. It could be none other. She was running, closing the distance in a matter of seconds, arms outstretched. A sob welled up in her throat and tumbled out in one perfect, beautiful word she feared she would never say again.

"Mama!"

The two embraced. Raw emotion spilling over from bottomless depths choked out any words Corrie could muster. They held each other for a long while. It was the happiest Corrie had ever been in her entire life. She had found her mother at last.

"I knew I would find you," Corrie mumbled into her mother's shoulder, now damp with tears.

"You've grown so much!" her mother exclaimed, leaning back to take in Corrie's full height. Though still small for her age, Corrie was certainly taller than when her mother had last seen her.

Corrie blushed, shy in her own mother's presence—an emotion she had not anticipated. All the months and years of waiting, counting days, and hoping she would return—and here she stood, right in front of her. And *in Gerushah* of all places! Corrie could still hardly believe her eyes. It was too good to be true.

"Why are you here?" Corrie asked breathlessly.

"To find you, of course. I've been waiting for you," her mother answered.

"It was you I saw in the woods earlier, wasn't it? It was you all along," Corrie exclaimed, exuberant with the realization. Her mother nodded.

"But why didn't you say anything to me then?" Corrie asked, suddenly confused. It seemed strange that her mother would be waiting for her and then, upon seeing her in the woods, not call out to her. Corrie would have called out if she had only recognized her. Like a ghost in the woods, her mother had appeared, visible for a moment and then suddenly gone.

"You were with those people," said her mother.

"Oh," Corrie said. At first, she wasn't sure if she should explain *those people*, but then again, they were hardly worth considering at the moment.

"Have you been here this whole time?" Corrie asked. "Four years? Why didn't you come back?" The words tumbled out before she had a chance to think. Her question held an unintentional tone of accusation. Corrie bit her lip, wishing she could reel in her words. This was the moment she had been waiting for all these years, and she had possibly just ruined it. She hoped it was not beyond repair. She babbled on.

"You were in hiding, weren't you?" Corrie asked before thinking about the fact that it was what Prudence, one of *those people*, had told her about the remnant of the faithful. Her mother did seem frail, and that filled Corrie with acute self-loathing for questioning her at all.

"Why would I be in hiding?" her mother snapped. Corrie drew back. The Rachel Callahan she knew had never responded to anyone that way. Her mother had been kind and gentle, with an encouraging word for everyone. Tears stung Corrie's eyes. Had she forgotten what her mother was like, or had she truly changed?

The hood of her mother's cloak fell backward, revealing loose, tousled curls much like Corrie's. But her face—even in the pale moonlight Corrie could see that her mother's face was thin, gaunt, and hollow. Her limbs remained hidden in the cloak—strange clothing given the warm, clear night. Rachel stared off toward the road ahead of them, clinging to her walking stick as if it kept her from floating away in the next breeze. Corrie felt pity rising up for this waif of a woman. She pushed the feeling away for it only caused the knot forming in her stomach to grow. Without a word, her mother pulled the hood back up over her head. Corrie's heart sank. The distance between them was becoming a deep chasm that Corrie did not know how to cross.

"Shall we go home now?" her mother asked. Not waiting for an answer, Rachel turned and started walking down the path, back toward the way she had come. Corrie followed eagerly.

"Yes, that's all I've ever wanted—to have you home," Corrie beamed, and suddenly, magically, the most perfect moment was almost completely saved. Corrie walked beside her mother—her *mother*! They were heading home with the moon smiling down on them, and all was as right as right could be.

"I'm sorry I asked too many questions," Corrie offered. She waited, hoping for reassuring words from her mother, but she spoke none. "I'm always getting in trouble at school for saying stupid things. I lose my temper sometimes too," she continued. "But I won the essay contest for the whole middle school. I wrote a story. It was about you." She was babbling excitedly, remembering all the moments she had saved in her journal to tell her mother about, and now she finally could. Where should she even begin?

Her mother listened, or at least Corrie hoped she was listening. When there was still no response, Corrie lapsed into silence. She wasn't sure exactly what she had expected from her mother. It had been a long time since they had talked, so she could have been wrong to expect anything at all. Still, Corrie's heart hoped her mother would say *something*. Was her own mother not curious about her life and school, whether she ate her vegetables, how she had survived the past few years without her—anything?

Corrie observed Rachel Callahan's concentrated gaze on the path ahead, seemingly oblivious to her presence. Corrie wondered what had happened in her mother's life since that October night when she drove away in the dark, leaving Corrie and her brothers on their grandparents' porch to go their own way without her. Maybe when life takes something away, it never really comes back to you, not entirely. Corrie had found her mother again, but the realization was dawning that all the things that had made Corrie's mother *hers* had perhaps slowly drained away, year after long year. Too much had happened. The mother she knew of her childhood was gone and never coming back. Corrie swallowed, the disappointment welling up in her throat and threatening to choke out all her joy. *No*, she bolstered herself. *I'll not allow it*. She had expected too much, that was all. She was always expecting too much of people.

"I'm just glad to be with you again," Corrie said quietly when all hope of conversation had completely dissipated into the empty space between them.

As they plodded eastward, the darkness yielded to a faint outline of mountains in the distance. Tall spires of white granite became visible above the surrounding peaks that formed the border of Gerushah. The slightest hints of dawn pressed through the deep sapphire sky in bands of royal blue.

Renewed hope rushed through Corrie. The night would soon be over. A new day had almost come. Everything was going to be fine, she decided. Her dismal mood surely had been due to the darkness and her own fatigue. The promise of sunrise rejuvenated her entirely. She had quite a surprise for her brothers. *She* was bringing Mama home. Would they all live with Gran, find their own house in Bellam, or move to another town? She didn't care. The only thing that mattered was being together.

A stab of pain jolted her suddenly. They would not all be together. Daddy was gone. Papaw was gone. Should she tell her mother that Papaw had died while she was away? Corrie glanced over at her. She was bent as though already carrying a heavy burden. Her thin arm jutted out from her sleeve like a stick, nearly as thin as the staff she clung to. She might not survive the news, Corrie decided. Corrie would wait until they were home and Mama was surrounded by Gran and all her children before she told her about Papaw. That was a much better idea. It would do neither of them any good to tell her now and risk spoiling the new day or cause her mother to withdraw even more.

"Wait 'til Collin and Will see that I found you," Corrie said instead. Her excitement was mounting again. She could just imagine the looks on their faces when she walked in the house with Mama beside her. Maybe she would have her mother hide behind a tree, tell them to come outside, and then yell "Surprise!" as her mother stepped out into the yard. Corrie could not wait.

"They said you were never coming back. They even thought you might be dead. I'll show them," Corrie said, but immediately realized she had stuck her foot in her mouth once again. How would her mother feel if she knew her own sons had given her up for dead?

Scrambling to fill the awkward silence, Corrie stammered, "I-I was coming to find you. I left town and everything, but—" Corrie fell suddenly silent, not wanting to recount all she had gone through. Even if her mother were interested at all in what had happened, Corrie did not want to talk about all of it, not yet.

"Mmm," Rachel responded, and said no more. The only sound breaking the deafening silence was the steady beat of her walking stick on the dry ground as they continued toward the gate. Confounded, Corrie could stand the tension no longer.

"Mama, what's wrong? Why won't you talk to me?" Corrie was nearly shouting. She stopped in the middle of the road, refusing to walk farther. Rachel stopped and slowly turned toward Corrie. Though the moon was full and dawn was approaching, the pale light was not enough to penetrate the shadow cast by the cloak's hood. Her mother's face was completely hidden.

"Nothing is wrong. I am just eager to get home, aren't you?" Rachel replied.

"Yes," said Corrie. Her mother's response answered the question, at least in words. Though thankful her mother was finally speaking to her, Corrie did not feel reassured. There was too much left unsaid, and the nagging feeling in Corrie's stomach that something was not quite right was growing, for no matter what Rachel Callahan said, there was no joy.

"Let us keep walking, you and I," said her mother, taking Corrie by the hand and pulling her forward. "We are nearly to the gate." Corrie noticed that her mother's hand was cold despite the warm cloak.

Indeed, the great stone gate loomed before them, a mere 100 yards or so away. Corrie fell in step slightly behind her mother, her heart pounding. The medallion tapped rhythmically with her pulse. Holding the gold to her chest, her thoughts drifted to this mysterious jewelry yet again.

Corrie had been kicked out of the house because of it. Should she tell her mother about the medallion? Corrie debated. If she returned home still wearing it, surely all would be forgiven with one look at Rachel Callahan standing before them. Was it enough, or would Corrie ruin one more perfect moment if she brought Mama home while still wearing the gold? She decided not to risk it. She wanted everything to be perfect. They were just a few hundred feet from the towering Eastern Gate, and then they would soon be home. There was no time to waste.

"Mama, I need to tell you something," Corrie said, slowing her steps.

"Come, child. Whatever it is, it can wait until we are home," Rachel replied, pulling Corrie along.

"No, it can't," Corrie insisted and withdrew her hand from her mother's grasp. Gran and her brothers had always said Corrie was stubborn, and she hated proving them right, but this was too important.

"We need to find a way to get this medallion off me before we get home," Corrie said, holding up the gold for her mother to see. The sky was a deep cerulean blue behind the stone gate now. There was not enough light to see the medallion clearly. Corrie hoped her mother would not ask questions and would somehow just believe her.

"That?" her mother replied, pointing a slender finger toward Corrie's neck. "It's just a necklace," she said, laughing dismissively as if Corrie had told a joke that was not the least bit funny.

Corrie sighed. She should have known it wouldn't be so easy. She would have to explain after all.

"I thought it was just a necklace, too, when I found it at the bottom of the pond, but then I—" Corrie paused, sighing again. Her thoughts rolled like a deck of cards flipping through her mind. If she had not found the medallion at the bottom of the pond, she would not have been late going home, and she would not have taken the shortcut down High Street. She wouldn't have seen Joe and his friends hiding their guns, and Joe wouldn't have attacked her. Their paths would not have crossed at all, and there wouldn't have been a stranger who fastened it around her neck in such a way that she couldn't take it off. If Gran hadn't seen it around her neck and kicked her out, she would not have left the house when she did. Joe and his friends would not have chased after her, and she would not have needed to hide in the tunnel. And if she didn't need to crawl through the tunnel, she would not have ended up here. She would have been halfway to Georgia by now if not for this gold jewelry. *But* . . . Corrie suddenly gasped. She also would not have found her mother, *here,* without this medallion. The memory of finding it in the pond a few days ago sprang back to her now with surprising joy. She had thought then that it was a good omen. Some things had happened along the way since finding it that she wished she could erase from her mind, and yet she could see now that she had to have both—the bad with the good. She could not have had one without the other.

For the past few days, Corrie had only remembered the horror of what Joe had done to her, but there was so much more that had happened, things she could not now explain. Corrie started to tell her mother how the stranger had found her in the ditch, that he had a dog named *Lucy*, and that the man had sung over her a melody so beautiful she had wanted to cry. Why had the man put the gold chain on her? Why had he even helped her in the first place? *And how did he know my name?* She could understand the bad things even better than the mystery of a stranger so kind.

"It is time for you to find what you are looking for," Corrie said aloud, remembering the man's words. "That's what the man said to me, the man who put this gold jewelry around my neck and fastened it," she said, as if floating out of a dream.

"It isn't just a necklace. It brought me to you," Corrie said reverently, clutching the gold to her heart.

It was true after all. She had found what she was looking for, what her heart had wanted most. She had waited over four long years for this. She was reunited with her mother at last, and all because of the gold medallion. She would explain this to Gran. She just *had* to understand.

"Never mind. I'm keeping it," Corrie said resolutely. The matter was settled.

Her mother nodded silently and resumed her walk toward the gate. Corrie followed, peering through the wide gap between the towering boulders ahead. Where did this road lead, and how long would it take to reach home once they exited through the gate? It didn't seem to be a gate at all, Corrie mused, seeing that there was nothing to open or close. There was only empty space between the granite stones that never moved.

Corrie remembered that there had only been a gaping mouth of stone when she entered this land. She had stood in the cave, debating whether to move forward or go back when the cave began to close up. Would these stones do the same? They were about to leave this land, possibly never to return. Instinctively, she looked behind her. Corrie gasped. The road behind them had disappeared. All she could see now was dense forest, as if the road had been swallowed up by the woods just as it had before when she was walking with Vincent. The pine tree that had stood as a landmark at the beginning of this road was now lost in the landscape, if it had ever been there at all. Corrie suddenly felt dizzy. She closed her eyes and took a few deep breaths to steady herself.

"Come," said her mother, urging Corrie onward with an impatient wave of her hand.

Corrie knew she should have been eager to leave this place. It was strange and unpredictable, and even dangerous, and yet the closer they moved toward the gate, the stronger the misgivings Corrie felt in her heart. What should she listen to, her mind or her heart? She felt she could trust neither. Her thoughts reasoned that it was better to leave as soon as possible. It was why she was now walking on this road toward the gate. She was going home and bringing her mother with her.

Her heart told a different story, however, a story in which her mother was taking *her* somewhere, which was significantly different. *That shouldn't matter*, her thoughts protested, and yet her heart would not yield. She didn't want to leave, but why? What could be here in this land that she would miss? Three faces instantly came to mind despite her previous efforts to forget about them. She immediately tried to push all thoughts of Horatius, Prudence, and Evangeline away. Her last encounter with them had made her angry. They did not keep their word and had insisted she find some silly diamond they only wanted for themselves. Again, Corrie's heart chimed in, reminding her that they had also listened to her and talked with her. They took care of her. They were kind. Had she been unfair? And there was something else, something in the way each of them said her name that had made her feel safe when they said it. The memory of it gave Corrie's reasoning mind an idea that she presented to her heart, and her heart agreed.

"Mama?" Corrie said, calling out to her mother who was still a few paces ahead.

"What?" Rachel replied brusquely.

"Mama, would you please say my name?" asked Corrie, again stopping on the road.

"Why would you want me to do such a foolish thing? Let us walk. We're nearly there," Rachel answered impatiently.

"Please, Mama. Just say my name; I want to hear it," Corrie insisted. "Please," she said again.

Her father had named her *Cornelia Rose*, but Mama had called her "Corrie" for as long as she could remember. And there was something in the way her mother said it that was more like music than words. Corrie's name was a song in her mother's mouth that always ended with a smile. That was all Corrie wanted. She could accept that all had changed, that her mother was not the same person. She could even accept that maybe her mother had not missed Corrie nearly as much as Corrie had missed her. All this she could bear if she could have this one thing. She wanted to hear her name. Corrie waited.

"Don't try my patience. You wouldn't do that to your own mother, now, would you? I have already suffered enough for you. Let's go," Rachel said, holding her staff with one hand and motioning for Corrie to follow with the other. She was a mere 20 steps or so from the gate, now clearly visible in the gray light of early morning.

Corrie shuffled her feet slowly toward the gate. She knew her mother had suffered. A pang of guilt sank in her stomach. Not only was she stubborn, but she was selfish. Even now she was only thinking of herself and her own desires. Oh, how Corrie wished she could start over. She would find her mother again and would not be selfish or stubborn, or cause any more trouble. She would be the perfect daughter, and everything would be completely good again, the way it was before. If only she could be different. Despair wrapped its claws around Corrie's neck and began to squeeze.

There had to be something Corrie could do, some way to try again, some means for her mother to be pleased and happy. Corrie had to fix this. Her heart thumped wildly in her chest, the gold disk still beating in time. The medallion was warm beneath her fingertips as she traced the circle of empty space in the middle. Of course! It is missing that special diamond, she remembered. *Yahalom Shalom* they had called it. Corrie knew her mother would not be excited to learn about a missing diamond, especially since it was something that Horatius, Prudence, and Evangeline had wanted her to find, but Corrie didn't have to mention that part. The important thing was the cure. What if that were really true? If a diamond could cure a horrible disease, maybe it had other powers. Maybe it could also help her situation even now. Corrie had to try. She trotted the few steps to close the gap between them.

"Mama, my medallion is missing a diamond. Here," Corrie said, pointing to the center of the gold. "It's supposed to be the most valuable gemstone in the world. It has power, Mama. It has special healing powers, and I thought that maybe it could . . . well, I thought that maybe we might—" Corrie tried to think how to explain. Breathless from excitement, she tried again.

"Mama, it'll make everything right again. And it's here in Gerushah somewhere. So I know you've suffered and," Corrie said, hesitating, but gathered her courage to continue.

"And I have too. I've really missed you, and nothing is like it was. And this diamond . . . well, this diamond can maybe fix everything," Corrie said, less convincing than she had intended. She straightened and said it again, this time more boldly.

"I believe it can make everything better for both of us," said Corrie, feeling the heat rising in her face, for the moment she said it, she knew it was true somehow. "I know you want to go home, and so do I, but if we can find this diamond together before we leave, then maybe—" Corrie paused, searching for the words.

"Everything will be okay when we finally get there," Corrie said at last.

"I don't want to hear another word about the gold medallion or a silly diamond. We are leaving this place immediately," her mother retorted.

The words stung like a slap in the face. Corrie blushed a deeper shade of crimson, blinking back hot tears. She looked behind her, staring at the woods. Without thinking, Corrie peered through the darkness, her heart secretly hoping she would see three figures coming toward her, *friends* coming to her aid.

"You want to go back to *them*, don't you? To abandon your own mother," Rachel said flatly. "You have forgotten me," she said with a heavy sigh of disappointment and then struck the ground angrily with her staff.

"What? No, Mama! I didn't forget you," Corrie exclaimed, shocked and confused. Her mother's words were like a bag of bricks thrown onto her back. How could she say these things? This was day 1,463 since her mother had left. Corrie had not forgotten a single day they had been apart. Her eyes stung, and her heart ached, sick with despair. How could she have been so horribly misunderstood?

Corrie could think of nothing more to say. She stood numbly by her mother's side, staring at the ground.

"It's been a few years, I know," her mother said, suddenly softening. She reached for Corrie's hand before continuing. "I know it has been hard for you," said Rachel, brushing a strand of hair from Corrie's eyes. She spoke tenderly now. The harshness now gone, her voice was quiet.

Corrie wanted to drink in her mother's words, soft rain on parched ground. But she found that she could not absorb them. The ground had shifted. Corrie turned away from her. What did her mother know? She had not been in Corrie's life. She had not been there for anything Corrie had been through. She knew nothing. So much had changed since the day an eight-year-old girl had been left on the front porch of her grandparents' house.

"I still love you very much," her mother said, wrapping her arm around Corrie's shoulder. "And you are still *mine*," she said. Something in the way her mother said it made Corrie's skin crawl. Heat prickled down the back of her neck and throbbed in her temples. Corrie tried to wriggle out of her embrace, but her mother held her tightly. In that moment, Corrie experienced an emotion she knew for certain she had never felt in her mother's presence—fear.

"You never should have suffered like this," Rachel cooed, kissing Corrie's forehead. "It wasn't fair," she said.

Corrie froze.

"What did you say?" Corrie asked, trying to keep her voice steady.

"I said it wasn't fair, all that you've been through," Rachel repeated.

There were two things Rachel Callahan despised, and Corrie remembered them well. The first was lying. The Callahan children knew that no matter what trouble they got into, the punishment was light compared to the penalty for lying about it. The other thing her mother always hated was the phrase "it's not fair." Oh, she despised it like nothing else. "*Life* isn't fair, so don't live your life expecting it to be. *You* be whatever good you want to see in this world," she would say, and her typically warm brown eyes would blaze fire. Lying and whining about something being unfair were the only things that made Rachel Callahan truly angry. Corrie had known these things in the core of her soul because they had formed the core of her mother's soul.

How much do people change from the things that happen to them? Did life steal from her mother even the last residue of her very essence? How much had Joe also taken from *her*, Corrie wondered. Perhaps those were things she didn't even know and never would. Maybe she would live the rest of her life as a hollow shell, still Corrie on the outside but inside just empty space.

Yet Corrie still loved honeysuckle, fishing by moonlight, and her family. She still hated sand burrs, math homework, and people who were arrogant or cruel. Some things did not change and could not change. The qualities that made Corrie who she was and the myriad of things she truly hated and truly loved were still intact. Could another human being or tragedy change that in another person? Perhaps it is only the outer shell of a person that changes with the events of our lives while the deepest parts remain, hidden away in a place that nothing can touch. And if that is true, what can it all mean?

Corrie's heart was ready to jump out of her chest. She understood now why she was afraid and why nothing had felt completely right since the moment she saw this woman on the path. Corrie's former joy and hope in having a happy ending dissolved abruptly into one driving need for the truth.

There is only one arbiter of truth, and that is historical fact. No amount of feeling or even belief can change the events of history. Corrie knew she had to act quickly, and to do so, she would have to break one of her mother's cardinal rules.

"It's been a long time, though, Mama. I can't remember the last thing you said to me, do you?" Corrie asked, leaning into her mother's embrace.

"Of course. I told you that I loved you, and that I would be back for you. Do you not remember that?" her mother stated.

Corrie nodded. Then pulling herself up to her full height, she stared into the woman's eyes and spoke clearly and deliberately.

"I remember exactly what my mother said to me that day. Every word. She told me to find the truth. She never said she would come back," Corrie said, and her voice broke. "She never made promises she couldn't keep. Even if it was hard, she always told me the truth. And you know what else? My daddy taught me to look people in the eyes to know if they were lying. And I know this. *You* are a liar, and you are certainly not my mother," Corrie retorted angrily and turned to step away, but the woman caught her by the arm and held firm.

Gasping in surprise, Corrie spun around to see the woman's visage had changed. She no longer looked like Rachel Callahan. In fact, she no longer looked like a woman at all. The hood was thrown back now. The figure's face had transformed from her mother's likeness to that of a creature neither male nor female, human nor animal, yet it was strangely beautiful, like nothing she had ever seen. Corrie could not take her eyes off it.

"Clever girl," said the creature in a voice like the moan of wind in a winter storm and the sad melody of a lone reed. "You want the truth. I understand," it continued, still holding her firmly. "I merely spoke the deeper truth of your heart. Is there no truth to the desires of your soul, dear child? Are they not real? Did you not also lie to me in order to gain the knowledge of the truth that you wanted? Indeed, what *is* truth if not the pursuit of one's deepest desires?"

"Well," Corrie began, suddenly confused. "I-I'm not sure. I never thought about it that way." Corrie tried to look away, but the harder she tried, the more she wanted to stare. She couldn't help herself. She was drawn by a force that was impossible to resist. Were the creature's eyes blue? Brown? A misty gray? She wasn't sure, but they were so beautiful, so strangely beautiful. What mysteries could she understand if she looked into them just a while longer? "Yes, what is truth?" Corrie heard herself ask quietly, sounding like a distant echo to her own ears.

"Indeed," the creature intoned. "It is your mother you desire. That is your truth, and nothing else matters. I have only come to ensure safe passage to your own desires, which is why you came to this path, did you not? And yet you were too afraid to take the first step. I came to encourage you. I know how you can find your mother. Truly, she is right through this gate. You'll see. In such a noble pursuit, it is the motive that justifies the means," said the creature, raising its staff toward the passageway between the boulders.

Corrie had no argument. It was true that she had been afraid to step out onto the road alone, which is why she had lingered by the pine tree. And the creature was so beautiful that Corrie did not want to part company with it, at least not yet, not until she learned the truth about her mother that the creature seemed to know and was eager to share. This fascinating being was far more encouraging than Prudence and those other two people. It no longer mattered. Nothing else mattered. The creature was the only one in the world that truly understood her and honored her desires, she now realized.

There was another creature present at the Eastern Gate that moment, though Corrie could not have known. *Specious Molluscus* had found its host long before Corrie had ever stepped onto the road heading for the gate. Having searched her out in the great cedar from where it lay hidden on Horatius's suit coat, it had found her, latched onto her, and burrowed into the viscera of her gut where it quickly passed into the larval stage.

By now, Corrie had a thriving colony of them. Many were mature and robust. The worms' poisonous influence had not been able to eradicate the truth of what Corrie knew of her own mother, a truth deeper than any parasite could burrow. But a plausible lie affirming her own heart's desire was easily assimilated, even welcomed. In this, the hellish sophistication excelled, for the infestation of the tiny creatures grew most heartily in a soul that longed most deeply.

Corrie began to walk slowly toward the gate yawning open before her. In a few steps she would willingly cross the threshold, leaving Gerushah and all that was held within it behind.

Ethiopia, circa 7 BC

Imani was of the house of Menelik, herself a descendant of the Queen of Sheba. She already possessed several fine pieces of jewelry, many that were rare and exotic—pearls from distant lands, the finest rubies, and the purest gold. She did not typically associate herself with merchants and tradesmen, but today she would make an exception.

Educated in the emperor's court in history, linguistics, philosophy, and astronomy, she had developed a keen interest in historical artifacts, particularly those fashioned of gold. She had collected a fair assortment of coins and rings. What interested her most about each piece was the artist's signature inscribed on it. It may not have been an exact signature, but it was always easy for her to identify the seal or distinguishing detail of a particular artist, dynasty, or culture. Her aptitude for identifying the artifacts she acquired had earned her a fine reputation.

When the merchant passed through the capital city, word came to Imani that he carried an artifact that she would not be able to identify. Against the counsel of her advisors, Imani dismissed the impertinence of the merchant's challenge. She was intrigued by what he claimed to possess. The merchant was permitted both entrance into the palace and an audience with the princess.

Imani inspected the gold and jewels presented before her, naming each of them, as well as the period of history from which each had come. When the merchant brought the gold medallion from his bag and set it on the table in front of her, she knew immediately it was no ordinary gold piece. The design was unique. She knew not of any tool that could replicate its detailed, fine markings. What the merchant had described as a mere border around the empty space in the middle of the medallion was, Imani discerned, writing. The language was certainly ancient and likely extinct. She held the medallion in her hand. It was heavy for such a small thing, an indicator of its purity. She knew she had never encountered gold of such quality before.

"Where did you find this?" Imani asked.

"It is from a faraway land, a great civilization no longer in existence. That I can say, but more I cannot reveal," said the merchant, eyeing the diamonds dangling from Imani's neck and wrists. "You, Highness, are the one to know these things, or so I am told."

Imani's eyes flashed with anger. Did he dare to challenge her in her very presence? She could have him beheaded at that very moment with just a word. And yet his eyes betrayed something. Fear? He held a secret.

"The markings are nothing more than chicken scratches. The gold is not pure. It is a composite laced with iron ore, making it heavy beyond its true value," Imani declared.

"It cannot be!" the merchant fumed, though he knew to restrain the pitch and volume of his voice lest the guards storm through the door. "It is a rare piece. Surely you know it has no equal. No craftsman within this century could forge an artifact such as this," he insisted.

"How much do you want for such a thing?" Imani asked dismissively. Having already pushed the medallion aside, she feigned interest in the small bag of pearls still on the table in front of her.

"I would take that amulet you wear, Highness," the merchant said, pointing to the pendant resting at the crest of her delicate collarbones. It had been in her family for generations, given to her by her beloved aunt on her last birthday.

"It is not worth even seven barley loaves," Imani said as she unlatched the pendant from around her neck and laid it on the table.

As the merchant walked toward the door, Imani, with the rare medallion now safe in her hands, called after him. "The piece is extraordinary, more so than any other I have seen in my entire life. It was not cut or carved with any tool, and the marks you believed to be a form of design are words in a language unknown to anyone. That is the treasure you formerly possessed."

The merchant turned. "You see its true value. But you must know this also. The medallion is cursed. Whoever receives it will surely die. None would take it off my hands, but now I am rid of it," he said and then dashed toward the palace courtyard and out onto the street.

Imani stared at the medallion with a curious mix of emotion. She was perplexed. She was glad she had acquired the invaluable piece, but she feared the merchant's words. She called for the council of the wise. They were her teachers. They had studied the stars, philosophy, and mathematics. They understood the mysteries yet unknown to her.

Imani placed the medallion in front of them. They passed it among themselves, examining its form and feeling its weight. Negasi was the first to speak of the seven who had gathered. He was the oldest and had served the emperor's household for many years.

"It carries a heaviness beyond its weight. It is acquainted with sorrow, but it knows something more. See the patterns around the perimeter, the fine details? It resembles the seal of a king, but none that I have ever seen before," Negasi said, and placed the medallion in the center of the table.

"But is it cursed?" Imani wanted to know. She had been having dreams, even before she purchased the gold. They were wild dreams, violent and bizarre but also glorious. The visions were of things she could scarcely have imagined, much less put into words, but she knew there was a connection—the dreams, the gold, the merchant's words, and a growing urgency that she could not understand.

"Perhaps it is cursed, or perhaps the one who bore it knew suffering. I am uncertain," Negasi said. As he spoke, the other council members remained silent in deference to the sage, but Kofi tapped his fingers nervously on the table. His eyes had never left the center of the table since the medallion was placed there.

"Speak, Kofi, before your fingers bore a hole in the wood," Negasi said, gathering his robes about him.

"I think it is wise to remove the object from the palace. If it is a blessing of good fortune, then we are already blessed, but if it is an omen of ill fate, then the longer it is here, the more we are inviting evil upon this house," Kofi spoke quickly.

"It bears no evil," said Salim, a tall figure with a lean face and a silver beard. He sat with his arms crossed. "It is timely that we are meeting now, for the heavens are shifting. A convergence among the constellations in the eastern sky is forming that I have not seen before. I had intended to bring such news before the council, and now we must also consider this," Salim said, lifting his chin toward the medallion.

"I believe," Negasi said, sighing deeply, "that with your permission, Your Highness, we should go to our brothers in the East and confer with them on these matters. We will take the gold with us and seek further counsel." He rose from his seat. The other council members rose and exited the room one by one until only Negasi was left with Imani.

Negasi was slight, having lost much of his height through age. He walked slowly toward Imani. It seemed he would pass her by, but he stopped abruptly and spoke in her ear.

"I, too, have had dreams of late, signs and wonders I have seen in the heavens and on Earth that I cannot explain. I have advised that we should travel to our brothers in the East to confer, and I stand by that wise counsel. However, I cannot deny that I also have a compelling desire to journey toward these signs in the night sky. I am an old man. This is most likely my last sojourn. There is but one thing more I must see before my days on Earth are complete." As Negasi spoke, his wisened eyes twinkled.

"What is it, dear Negasi?" Imani asked tenderly. She had listened to his tales and wisdom her whole life. He was a wise and good man, and had served the emperor faithfully through all his days.

"I have had a recurring dream since I was a boy," Negasi explained. "The sun blazing high in the sky somehow comes to rest upon Earth, and Earth is filled with light but is not consumed. The dream has both plagued me and filled me with joy. Lately I have dreamt of this mystery every night. With your permission, Princess, I must go."

"You do not need my permission, Wise One," Imani said. The emperor himself has given you his trust to do as you see fit, now and always." Imani took the medallion from the table and held it out to the old man who took it into his gnarled hands.

"Only promise me that you will return safely home," Imani said. Standing, she bent to kiss his wrinkled cheek.

"As YHWH wills," said Negasi with a sideways glance.

Imani's eyes widened, for she did not know that he, too, believed in the one true God. She had felt a stirring in her heart, though she did not dare speak of it in the palace until now.

"Yes, as YHWH wills," Imani said with a quickening of her pulse and a *lightness of her spirit she had not felt before. She touched her lips with the tip of her finger, unsure whether she had merely imagined the words coming from her mouth. "As YHWH wills," she repeated as Negasi exited the room, and she felt a new strength growing inside of her.*

Chapter 22

The Hart

"Well? What do we do now? She's gone!" Evangeline wailed. Her curls bounced wildly as she paced around the room. Horatius and Prudence watched her silently.

"And you know, I thought we got through to her, I really did," Evangeline went on. "She so reminded me of my little Margaret with those big brown eyes of hers and her spunk. *Bah*! Whatever will we do?"

"Mm," Horatius merely grunted. Like Evangeline, he felt disappointed, even discouraged. Emotion in this realm hung about his shoulders like a soggy, wet blanket. He was not used to that. He could never get used to that, and it seemed to seep into every circumstance. This was the longest mission he had ever participated in. Even he, a veteran ambassador, was growing weary of this place.

"We need to pray that she does not pass through the gate," Horatius replied at last.

"Why? What will happen?" Evangeline asked, pausing her pacing to wait for his answer.

"She will die," said Prudence, answering for Horatius who nodded in assent. Evangeline gasped.

"What? Surely not. Horatius, is that really true? She will *die*?" Evangeline asked, horrified.

"I'm afraid she's right, Evangeline," said Horatius. "She was not brought here of her own accord. A human being cannot merely choose to enter or exit the realms at will, and any attempt to do so is, according to the laws of spirit and nature, extremely detrimental. I had hoped it would not come to this, but—" His voice trailed off.

"I should have warned her more strongly," said Evangeline. "I would have laid myself across the door if it would've helped."

"I know, Evangeline, I know," Horatius remarked glumly, sighing as he massaged the crease between his eyebrows.

"It was meant to be," Prudence said quietly.

"What do you mean, Pru?" Evangeline asked, stopping her circular pattern around the tree house mid-stride.

"Yes, do go on," said Horatius.

"Do you not see?" Prudence replied. "We have kept her sheltered in this tree. We have protected her and guarded her from the enemy, and yet our task was never to keep her safe."

"You may have a point there, Prudence," Horatius said, considering her words. "I wonder if we have unknowingly veered off track." It has never happened before on a mission, but then we have never been to Gerushah before."

"What are you saying, Horatius? Pru?" Evangeline queried. "Are you suggesting that we've done her harm? Why, we just took care of her, tended her wounds, and kept her from those foul demons. Were we to just leave her out in the wilderness to fend for herself like a stray kitten?" Evangeline resumed her pacing about the room.

"I'm saying that it is possible we should have focused on our own distinct missions more," Prudence clarified. "That is all I'm saying. We have kept her safe, and yet at no time has anyone accomplished the will of God by simply staying safe." At the mention of the Almighty, the great cedar, whose flames of holy fire had cooled hours before, blazed with bright, golden light for a moment and then faded again.

"I had so hoped my first mission would be successful," Evangeline lamented.

"Take heart, Evangeline," Prudence answered her quietly. "We aren't finished yet, and there is always hope, as I'm sure Horatius can corroborate."

"Hmm? Oh. Yes," Horatius replied halfheartedly at the sound of his name. Although Evangeline had stopped pacing and now slumped beside Prudence at the small table, Horatius took up her path around the tree house, muttering to himself as he cut a figure eight in the cedar needles.

"What are you thinking about so hard, Horatius?" Evangeline questioned.

"What I am thinking now is that we need another hart," he said quietly, more to himself.

"What on earth are you talking about?" Evangeline sputtered, sitting up with her arms splayed in front of her. "We *have* new hearts, new temporary bodies, new clothes, and I rather like all of it now, so—"

"A hart, a deer," Horatius interrupted. "You remember I was in the camps as a boy during the Nazi occupation, yes? Well, there was one night I thought I was going to die. No, I knew I was. I had missed roll call to tend to a little girl who had just lost her mother. Eliana was her name. She was all alone like I was, and she would have frozen to death if I had left her. We hid in the latrines so the guards and their dogs wouldn't find us. I didn't know what to do. I had no hope of escaping, not even the faith to pray. I knew we were already dead; I just didn't know whether by rifle, pistol, or starvation.

"That night I overheard one of the guards complaining to another that a deer had run into the barbed wire fence. They grumbled about who would find the breaker switch to turn off the electricity so the repair crew could fix it. We climbed out of the latrine and crept warily to the fence. The whole camp was shrouded in near darkness except for a slim, crescent moon and stars twinkling in the heavens above. I stared at the large, dark form—a buck. I counted at least a 10-point rack. How did one so wise wander so far from its herd and so close to the smell of death? Its massive body had thrashed around as it died, opening up a gaping hole in the barbed wire.

"Eliana and I stood there by the fence alone. Can you believe it? Not even a guard in the tower. And just like that, we slipped through the hole and escaped to the woods. The frayed wire tore at my skin, but the blood of the animal covered any blood I left behind, and the smell of its charred remains distracted the dogs from our scent. We were free.

"So, you see? Sometimes we just need help. We just need a hart," Horatius said with a sigh of satisfaction, for he had completed a story, the Great Sadness, that his soul had once yearned to be free from in a lifetime long, long ago. This place had drawn out the memory like a poison, yet he was pleased. The pain was only for a moment, a memory passing as a wisp of smoke and offered up as heavenly incense. He was evermore a free man.

Horatius strode over to his suit coat that he had hung on a knot in the tree wall and retrieved his pocket watch. Time was ticking steadily on. The mission timepiece always paralleled the time zone on Earth where the mission took place, and then became faceless again upon leaving the third realm. Gerushah lay in the fourth realm, removed from the same passage of time of the third realm, and yet every time he had consulted the watch, it had remained true to the same time zone as it had when they were sitting in the old oak tree by Miller's Pond in Bellam, just beyond the veil separating the third realm from the fourth realm. It was as if they had never left, and that remained a mystery he still could not explain.

Prudence eyed him carefully but said nothing so as not to disturb his thought process, observable by the crease between his eyebrows that he continued to massage in the pauses between short bursts of *hmph* and long sighs of *hmm*. He made even more frequent outbursts of *amen* and *let it be* as he resumed his pacing, and the ground trembled slightly beneath their feet.

After a few more figure eights in the cedar needles, Horatius returned to his coat, this time removing the mission scroll from his patch pocket to inspect it anew.

"Well, the mission is still active. Nothing has changed," Horatius said, running a hand through his hair.

"Still no coordinates?" Prudence asked.

"Still no coordinates," he replied sullenly.

In the toils and tribulations in which all ambassadors from the heavenly realms find themselves, there is one aspect to every mission that never changes. Although the machinations of thought, emotion, and problem-solving seem the same as that of souls still bound to Earth, such similarities are only mere appearances. The difference between a citizen of Earth engaging in struggle and a citizen of Heaven participating in that same struggle is as profound as the difference between refined gold and manufactured plastic. To Horatius, Evangeline, and Prudence—citizens of Heaven and ambassadors in service to the King—engaging in a mission could be compared more closely to what Earth dwellers call a *game*. For though the stakes are high and emotions intense or even painful, all participants in a game fully accept the temporal nature of what *appears* real, knowing with certainty that victory or defeat, elation or disappointment, they will eventually return to what *is* real.

The problem lay, however, in the fact that this was not true of Corrie. For her, this was no game. She could claim no such freedom from the constraints of her circumstances. She was playing to win, and win she must or be forever lost. The fact that she currently walked in the realm of the unseen in forbidden land no longer suitable for human habitation only compounded the dire nature of her current circumstances. She could neither stay nor freely go because she was in every way defying the laws of nature that all humans must obey without exception. And yet that same exception now miraculously held her in a spring-loaded trap of the *super*natural kind.

"*Musterion*," Horatius muttered, contemplating anew the nature of this task in a way he had not considered before. How exactly did a classification of "quest" fit into the category of "World Events"? He still could not answer that. The last time he had assisted in a quest, the subject had been an elderly saint who had been searching for the man who killed her sister. She had longed to tell the man that she had forgiven him and to share the good news that he, too, could be forgiven by God and set free. Horatius's specific task in the woman's quest had been to sort the mail, and in so doing, he discovered the location of the man in question on the front page of the newspaper. Horatius then slipped through the veil long enough to move the newspaper to the top of the stack, which he then placed near the coffee pot for the woman to find in the morning.

Having accomplished the mission, only days later he joined the welcoming committee for the dear woman's homecoming celebration. Crowds of people gathered, and it was one of the most joyous homecomings among many he had celebrated.

The category of that mission had been "Reconciliations," which most often pertained to people in the subject's own circle of influence. A quest in that category was generally an object or a person that the subject was eagerly looking for and wanting to find. In Corrie's case, however, she was not looking for the diamond. In fact, she did not even want it. It didn't matter that it was the most valuable stone or the cure for all that ails. Corrie had no desire to find it, and as far as they knew, that had not changed.

"Please show us where you want us to be," Horatius said quietly. Prudence and Evangeline nodded in agreement. With no coordinates and a subject who rejected their help, there was nothing else to do but wait. They did not have to wait long.

Horatius was stowing the scroll back into his pocket when a mighty gust of wind suddenly blew through the tree trunk. It stirred up a cloud of dust from the floor of cedar needles and upended the gourds and empty coconut shells Prudence had neatly stacked on the nearby shelf. At the same moment came a convergence of thought so powerful that it left no room for doubt. Though Corrie was not seeking the diamond, the diamond sought after *her*, the bearer of the gold, and neither element would rest until united.

Cedar needles, dust, and sheets of parchment swirled about the room as the wind swept through in a mighty blast and then exited nearly as quickly as it had come.

"Careful!" Horatius shouted as they grabbed for the ancient documents. The pages were old and thin, and while some of the scrolls were made of thicker animal hide, most were made of oiled parchment as fragile as onion skin and equally translucent.

"I've got them," Evangeline called, gathering the pages gently in her arms. Dust particles hung about the room in a cloud, gradually floating down to the floor.

Prudence had been quick enough to shield the flame of the lantern near her when the wind first blustered in. Using the flame of that one lantern, she lit the others again. As Evangeline carefully laid the scrolls on the table, all eyes fell on the document at the very top of the stack of parchment—a map. There was nothing unusual about the ancient map that detailed the boundary and topography of Gerushah. What leapt from the page, however, was the second map resting beneath it and shining through the ancient vellum as clearly as a beacon through a pane of glass. Horatius carefully lifted the map of Gerushah to examine the scroll beneath it. It was a detailed topographical outline of what would become the ancient Holy City—Jerusalem. The Temple Mount, Mount Olivet with the Garden of Gethsemane at its base—they were all there. Horatius laid the top map back down over the one beneath it. When he did so, two peaks joined in almost perfect union.

"Didn't Corrie say that she tunneled through a mountain with a waterfall?" Horatius asked.

"Yes, I think so," Prudence replied.

"She did. I remember it," Evangeline agreed.

"Mount Shekol," Horatius whispered, tracing the ancient letters beneath his fingers. "It means bereavement, grief as only one who has lost a child knows," he said soberly, bowed over the ancient scroll.

"This is beyond coincidence, wouldn't you agree?" Horatius said, suddenly straightening. All three of them knew beyond any shadow of doubt that while Corrie's life took an unexpected turn when she emerged from Mount Shekol and plunged into the waters below, history itself turned on the mountain peak that showed through from directly beneath Shekol, blazing through time immemorial.

"World Events," Prudence and Evangeline said, both in unison.

"Indeed," Horatius replied.

And there in the flickering light of the lanterns, the answer had come. The two maps conjoined to speak through the annals of time into this very moment. And although the ambassadors could not predict the outcome of their next actions, the location of their assignment was suddenly as clear as crystal. They must go to the waterfall.

"Now only one thing remains," said Horatius as they all stood, readying themselves to make their final exit from the great cedar. "It is time," he said.

"Yes!" Evangeline exclaimed, raising her fist in the air. She gathered her hat and tightened her banana-peel slippers in preparation to leave.

"It is time to speak the Name aloud in prayer," Horatius clarified.

"Wait! What? Out loud? Together?" Evangeline asked.

"Why would you question it, Evangeline?" Prudence challenged, making no effort to hide her surprise.

"You weren't with us, Pru, when we went to find food. You heard the kerfuffle, didn't you? The explosion? The thunder?" Evangeline asked, her eyes wide and curls bouncing like coiled springs.

"Yes," said Prudence. She hadn't forgotten the look of fear on Corrie's face as the floor shook and the thunder rolled.

"Well, we never told you, but Pru, you will never guess who we met out there. Oh, such a vile and ghastly creature," Evangeline said, cupping her face in her hands.

"Belial paid us a visit," said Horatius.

"Belial? Why? What did he say?" Prudence questioned.

"Oh, the usual nonsense. Accusations. Lies," Horatius replied.

"Blasphemy," Evangeline added. "And you should have seen how the land all around us reacted. This place is wild, I tell you. It's crazier than a June bug in a hatbox," she said, shaking her head. "The trees were waving their branches around so much that I thought they'd uproot themselves completely. I tell you, Horatius, the living things here cannot handle the forces of good and evil. I fear what would happen to this old tree if we spoke the Name aloud. The tension is just too great," said Evangeline.

"Perhaps," said Horatius, stroking his chin. "However, we need to pray in the power of that Name, aloud, bringing Him here to this land, because no matter how contemptuous the forces of darkness are to us, to Corrie they will be formidable. She needs the aid of the only One who truly can help."

Horatius gazed up into the boughs of the hollowed tree trunk, laying his hand on the gnarled wall, "I don't know what will happen to this old tree if it's suddenly enlivened with such power. It has to be thousands of years old. A relic," said Horatius in quiet wonder.

"A refuge," Prudence reminded them, and they all agreed, for it had indeed been a place of refuge for them in this foreign land of trouble.

"And yet I also can't help wondering if that is exactly what this hallowed vessel needs," Horatio added wistfully. With resolve he said, "Now, let us pray."

* * *

Having reached the threshold of the gate, Corrie stopped mid-stride. In the pale light before dawn, she strained to see what lay ahead through the gate. The landscape contrasted sharply from the wild woods of Gerushah with its spires of cedar and spruce mixed with tropical palm trees and flowering vines. Neither did she see the oak, ash, or mesquite trees typically dotting the landscape in Bellam. There were no hills, no roads, no fences or barns. In fact, there was nothing.

"My mother is out there? Ahead?" Corrie asked, searching for the shape of a building or dwelling, some indication of civilization if not trees or streams. Who could survive long in a barren desert with no shelter or water? A distinct foreboding crept in as if reaching from beyond the gate. She stepped back.

Corrie had never seen nothingness before, and yet there it was before her, raw and empty. The vacuous oblivion pulled at her, seeking to draw her into its void like a ravenous beast eager to devour.

"Yesss," came the voice beside her, whispering in her ear. "Your mother is there waiting for you. You need only walk a short distance, and you will be able to see her. Go now, quickly!" the voice rasped.

Corrie looked back toward the figure beside her for reassurance, searching for the beautifully mesmerizing face that had so charmed her, but the visage was now concealed behind the hood. Pale light scattered the shadows behind the hooded creature, displaying the forested land of Gerushah Corrie had grown accustomed to over the past few days.

She turned back toward the gate, expecting to see the warm light of dawn streaking across the sky, but instead, a flickering circle of blue, white,

and yellow flames blazed through all darkness and light from above where
the horizon should be. The fire was steadily growing brighter, and whether
the object was growing closer or she was moving toward it, Corrie could
not be sure, so strange was the sensation. It seemed to be hurtling toward
her, and as it grew nearer, she could see that it was not a burning object at
all but an opening beyond the vastness of this barren wasteland. What it
opened to, Corrie did not know, but a sound came from the opening—a
low rumble that wavered in pitch and volume. The noise grew steadily
louder until Corrie could discern the sound of voices, human voices. They
were growling, roaring, and crying out in such disturbing anguish that she
covered her ears to shut out the sound, but to no avail. It reminded her of
the voices in the river, and yet the tumult was without pause. The voices,
people, cried in unending agony. Then she felt herself falling toward the
nothingness with the circle of flames opening before her, and terror more
overwhelming than she had ever experienced wholly consumed her.

*   *   *

The trio stood and lifted their eyes toward the realms above and beyond
the wilderness of Gerushah, beyond the limits of time and the weary soul
of Eden that had lost her place in the hearts of humankind. They fixed
their gaze intently heavenward through the boundaries of the realms, into
the very Throne Room of God, and exalted the Name that is above all
names. They pled for the life of Corrie Callahan, whom they had each
come to dearly love. They petitioned fervently with every hope fixed on the
One True King in whose name they trusted without question and whose
face they had beheld in Glory.

The ground shook in peals of booming thunder and rolling waves.
Light filled the hollow tree trunk, chasing away every shadow in even the
smallest crevice in sparkling rainbows of color. The trunk of the great cedar
creaked as it swayed with the tumult of the ground beneath. The roots deep
in the soil began to groan, building in volume that soon filled the hollow
trunk with its sound. The air crackled with energy pulsing throughout in
ecstatic joy as the boundary separating Gerushah in the outer wilderness
of the fourth realm from the higher realms split wide open. Light from

the glorious throne in Heaven and the One who sat upon it shone down upon the cedar tree, now dwarfed by the grandeur of the King's glorious majesty. As the glory of the Lord of Creation filled the hallowed vessel, the great cedar lifted its gnarled branches to Heaven. The groaning of the tree, too deep for human understanding, now uttered a new sound. The ancient giant of the woods, keeper of secrets from the dawn of creation, began to sing.

Chapter 23

Song of the Great Cedar

"Help!" Corrie screamed, but her voice was swallowed up in nothingness. The creature that had given her hope of finding her mother moments ago now pressed her toward the darkness and approaching fire.

Corrie fought, kicking and clawing the space around her, but to no avail. As though caught in a nightmare, she wrestled shadows with no one to help and no one to hear her screams. The flames leapt from the border of the burning chasm, licking at her skin as the widening circle of fire began to slowly draw her in. The voices of the tortured soon drowned out her own desperate cries.

The medallion, however, now gleaming in the fiery glow, reflected light into the nothingness so bright and pure as if from its own source of light. *God . . . .* Corrie's thoughts flashed through her mind as fast as lightning through a dark night. *Are you real?* As the vast nothingness yielded her to the torture of searing fire, her lips parted in a scream of anguish until at last she cried, "God, help me! If you can hear me, please help me, oh God!"

No sooner had she uttered the words than the yawning circle of fire slammed shut, and she felt her body pulled back through the Eastern Gate as if by an unseen hand. The light of dawn, brighter than any morning she had ever seen, shone all around her. The circle of fire, the vast plains of nothingness, and the terror and despair vanished suddenly and completely, and the massive stones of the Eastern Gate slammed shut with a thunderous *boom*!

Corrie now stood on solid ground with the sealed gate behind her. God had heard her and answered her. She glanced at the hooded figure that stood beside her and then stared in horror. There was no longer anything beautiful about this creature. This was a monster. And though Corrie knew not its name, she now beheld the warped countenance of Belial, lord of the monger horde. Lidless eyes observed her in a cold, penetrating stare from behind the hood. Corrie tried to back away, but Belial grasped her arm, holding her in a vise grip.

"So you think you have escaped, that *God* has helped you?" Belial said with a mocking tone. Though the gaping mouth never moved, the rasping voice was clear, and it scraped the inside of Corrie's mind like a blunt knife.

"I know your destiny despite any miracle you think you may have witnessed," the voice continued, digging at any confidence Corrie had gained. "And you are *mine* by law," said Belial with cruel delight. "Come, my prize. I am taking you to Lord Lucifer who will be forced to reckon with my great power."

"No!" Corrie shouted, trying to wrest her arm from his grasp. He held firm and began dragging her westward into the woods.

Remembering the awl she had taken from the tree house and stowed in her back pocket, Corrie reached for it and slashed Belial in the chest, but the sharp point sailed through him as if through thin air. Belial laughed mirthlessly, suddenly whipped around, grabbed her by the throat, and began to squeeze. Corrie kicked and pulled at his bony fingers, trying desperately to release his grip on her throat, but his hands were like iron pincers.

"You cannot fight me, child. There is no other help for you. Angels are forbidden to enter this territory. It is the law. You have already experienced the extent of Heaven's reach. Surrender!" Belial said in a guttural voice that echoed through her thoughts. "You are—"

Belial was suddenly interrupted by a sound unlike anything Corrie had heard before, like the low hum of a bassoon with the reedy trill of a hundred pan pipes. Music! But from where? It soared high above the treetops, floating on the breeze.

The ground erupted beneath them as green shoots emerged from the soil, encircled the demon, and bound his legs and arms. Corrie dropped to the ground as sharp thorns studded every branch of the swiftly growing bush and great blossoms of brilliant white burst forth between every thorn. The center of each bloom contained a cluster of inner petals in a shade of deep crimson as though painted with blood, and emanated a rich and sweet perfume.

The beautiful music grew louder. The very sound of it filled Corrie's heart with joy and longing. And though she did not understand it, the song was the very Song of Creation, a melody long silent in this cursed land now roused from fitful slumber.

The cedars, the ash, the pines, and the cypress—*all* the trees began lifting their branches heavenward, some even sprouting new growth in their leafy boughs. Flowering vines and bushes burst forth in a rainbow of new, vibrant colors. The ground began to tremble beneath them as shoots of all manner of edible plants, flowers, shrubs, ferns, and saplings emerged from the soil in wild celebration.

Scanning the horizon, Corrie gazed on the tallest tree of all, the great cedar. Its ancient branches were also lifted heavenward, and a light shone bright all around it. Horatius, Prudence, and Evangeline—her *friends*—were all there. She knew it! She would join them, this time of her own choosing, and nothing would stop her.

"You are mine by right," Belial rasped again in Corrie's thoughts.

"No! It isn't true," Corrie resisted, and yet she was not wholly convinced that it was not since she had no understanding of the laws of this land or who claimed its citizens. She could only speak from her heart.

"I belong to God," she stated with all the confidence she could muster. She wasn't sure of that, however, for even though God had snatched her from the chasm of nothingness and fire, she wondered if He would still claim her now. Indeed, she had no reason to believe that.

"I want to be His," Corrie added weakly. Before Belial could utter a word of refute, she located the great cedar again on the horizon, set her sights on it, and took off running.

Though Belial was bound, his voice was not. As Corrie fled from his presence, his poisonous words followed her and seeped into her thoughts.

"What makes you think God or anyone else wants you? Your own family doesn't want you," Belial's voice resonated. The parasitic colony of *Specious molluscus* growing silently within Corrie fed ravenously on Belial's words, growing in numbers by the second.

Tikvah was the youngest daughter in the line of Keren-Happuch, who was herself the youngest daughter of Job. Tikvah was still too young to know the story of the old patriarch, how he had lost everything in a tragedy beyond compare. All his children and their families, even the animals and most of his servants, were taken or destroyed in one calamitous day.

That time had passed. Little Tikvah grew up without the ghosts of her past relatives. Her family was wealthier than ever before, the wealthiest in the region. Surrounded by a loving family and doted on by many servants, she never wanted for anything. She was given several calves, sheep, and goats as pets even before she had lost her first tooth. Despite being the youngest daughter of an expansive family, she would inherit more wealth than the eldest sons of other families. She would receive something else as the youngest daughter, according to the unique custom of Baba Job, which his descendants honored. It was a prized treasure—a gold medallion.

When Tikvah inherited the medallion, her mother told her the gold was the most valuable on Earth, mined and forged in Havilah, a place that lingered in legend and was mentioned in hushed and reverent whispers around campfires. The medallion was known to be the last artifact of a vanished land in which humans had once communed with the Maker and had known the sound of His voice on the wind. The medallion had survived fire and flood. This was the gold that Tikvah wore.

The child had worn it only a few days when Heaven and Earth moved yet again. The old patriarch had conducted the ritual of blessing before his passing. His children had prepared the body, and they would lay him to rest with his fathers. Job had seen the hand of blessing return more bounteous than in his youth and remain for many generations. He died in peace, an old man and full of days. His whole family gathered to mourn his passing and celebrate his life. But Job's calamity also attended his burial ceremony.

Some said another great wind blew from the wilderness. Others claimed a warring band of Chaldeans heard of the patriarch's death and coveted his wealth. A sweeping destruction fell upon Tikvah's family in the night, a violent massacre that spread more awe and fear than the calamity that preceded it. They were found dead and spoiled of their wealth, their bodies dismembered and left for the crows. The happenings of that night would never be told, for only one small child escaped.

Tiny footprints led away from the scene and into the nearby hills. Tikvah hid by the cover of night, and the winds erased the tracks she left in the dust. She ran past the flocks of sheep and goats, beyond the low-lying bushes and into the towering rocks where she hid, shivering in the darkness.

Perhaps an angel met Tikvah and brought her to a place of safety, for she appeared at the door of Hadid and Moysa, a couple who had no children of their own. They took her in, but when they saw the bracelets of gold and the medallion around her neck, they were frightened. They feared the same terror would befall them if anyone knew what household the child had come from. Moysa removed the jewelry and the gold medallion, and changed the child's name to Marah, for bitter suffering had brought her to them. Though they loved Marah, they did not teach her the memory of all that was perfect and beautiful or of the hopeful promise and the cords of faith since they did not know these things. Fearing for her own safety and for the child's, Moysa buried the medallion with the other pieces Marah had and ordered her to never speak of her past.

Chapter 24

Belial's Squire, Qal's Revenge

A figure skulking in the shadows warily approached Belial, who remained bound by the vines that had captured him.

"You came alone, Anzu?" Belial said in a low voice, not wanting to alert either the east wind or the west to the presence of an additional monger in Gerushah. A confrontation with Bahadur would be most inconvenient right now.

"Yes, my lord," the lesser monger answered his master.

Neither monger spoke of Belial's bindings, the lesser knowing the consequence of calling attention to such humiliation and the greater knowing that all bindings to which all mongers occasionally succumbed were temporary. The outer loops of the vines were already beginning to wither.

"Do you have it?" Belial rasped.

Anzu reached into his cloak and withdrew a flat disc with a sharp spine protruding from one of its rounded edges. "One scale of leviathan," Anzu replied.

"Yesss," Belial hissed in acknowledgement of the successful acquisition. Leviathan hid in the darkest recesses of the deep, appearing sometimes in physical form in the third realm, sometimes lurking in the shadowlands of the Shamayim where people only encountered him in dreams of conquest and terror. "Follow the child," Belial said.

"Will she not see me?" asked the squire.

"Remain in the shadows, and say very little. Choose your words. All humans are enamored with themselves. If you simply bolster her resolve, she will believe she is listening to her own thoughts. She will relax and be less on her guard. You may then guide her with the slightest suggestion of doubt. Her own memories will fill in the gaps. Then, when the time is right, use the scale," said Belial, pointing to the leviathan scale, for Belial's arms were now free of his trappings.

"How will I know where to place it?" Anzu asked.

"Just under the rib cage. You remember human anatomy, yes? You will know when the time is right," Belial replied.

"Yes, my lord," Anzu answered and disappeared into the woods.

The East Wind blew over the top of the gate and through every remaining crevice, filling the air with the fragrance of rose blossoms and spring rain. Belial spoke into the wind as it passed.

"I know what causes you fear. I have seen what makes you cry. You can run from my presence, but I will always find you. I will never let you forget that you are mine," Belial proclaimed.

Belial rose from the ground as his last words expired in the atmosphere and the last of his bindings fell in a crumpled heap. His body expanded into a diffuse vapor until the wind was filled up with his essence. The East Wind that had once been fair and sweet turned foul with the stench of deceit.

* * *

Corrie swept aside the curtain of vines and bolted through the open doorway of the great cedar.

"I'm back!" she shouted gleefully. Looking about the hollowed enclave, however, she found the tree house abandoned.

Corrie searched the room for Evangeline's feathered hat or Horatius's suit coat, any sign that they had only stepped out for a bit of fresh air. The empty gourds were stacked neatly on the shelf, the scrolls were tightly rolled and stacked against the tree wall behind the table, and all scraps of food were gone. The lanterns had been extinguished long before. Not even the slightest hint of smoke remained.

"They're gone," Corrie said to the empty space, swallowing the lump that was rising in her throat. Her only friends in this place were gone.

Corrie sat at the little table where they had eaten together and where Horatius, Prudence, and Evangeline had pored over ancient documents and scrolls, hunting for clues where they could find the diamond. If it was really true that the diamond was for her and not for them, then there was no reason for them to remain in the woods without her. They had surely gone home. But where was their home? Oh, why didn't she ask them?

How strange that they would have even come to the woods, Corrie thought to herself. They subjected themselves to camping in a tree house, being shot at by fiery arrows, and hiking all across this land—for her? Who does that for a perfect stranger? No, it couldn't be. And even if it were possible that they had come for her sake, how would they have even known that she was going to be there? They would have had to possess some kind of powers like a magician, a wizard, or—*like God*. The words flashed in her thoughts so quickly that a jolt of electricity flowed through her. It was the same sensation she had the moment she was rescued from the flames at the Eastern Gate.

Corrie's heart jumped in a flutter of excitement. Could it be true that God, the faraway Being in the sky, was really behind this, that He saw her and knew her? Her, Cornelia Rose Callahan, lover of plants and creatures of Earth, mermaid queen of Miller's Pond, daughter of Douglas and Rachel Callahan, sister of Will and Collin, granddaughter of John and Rose Tobias? Corrie's heart sank. What did it matter if God knew her when the people who knew her best wanted nothing to do with her?

The cold hand of memory reached up from the pit of her stomach and squeezed her heart. A memory of Joe Goodson bending over her flashed through her mind. *You are also Joe Goodson's,* said a voice inside her own mind. Anger and revulsion rose up within her at the thought, draping an icy curtain of self-loathing over her momentary joy. There was no hope.

She was foolish to let herself even imagine it, and yet what could she do to help herself now? What could anyone do?

Corrie dropped her face in her hands. There were no more tears to cry. Tears were for those who still held a belief in hope and fought against disappointment. Corrie held no such belief anymore. It was useless to believe. No matter how hard she believed in anything, she was still stuck here in the woods in a land without an exit and no one to find her.

Where would Horatius, Prudence, and Evangeline have gone? The thought pierced the darkness of her mood like a brilliant beacon. They would not have wandered out aimlessly without a plan. Corrie knew that much about them. If they had left this place to go home, they would have found an exit. What's more, they had left the scrolls behind. And the maps! Corrie nearly leapt from the table to pick up the first scroll. If they had found a way out, so could she.

Fresh determination thrummed in her chest as she unrolled the frail parchment and spread it across the table. Light—she needed light in the shadowy hollow of the tree. Corrie searched the shelves for the flint rocks she remembered seeing Prudence use to create sparks over dry kindling. Corrie was in a room full of kindling. She grabbed an empty gourd and scooped some dry cedar needles to cover the bottom. After a few tries, she managed a small fire and lit the lanterns. She reached to move the lantern over to make room for the maps when she saw it. Peeking out from under the clay lantern was a scrap of parchment. Only a corner was visible, a small corner so easily overlooked that she might have missed it.

Corrie unfolded the parchment as a feather floated to the table, *the feather Evangeline had given her*. Corrie recognized it with a sudden lump in her throat. The end of the feather was blackened with soot. Corrie stared at the neat lines of soot-colored letters. Her eyes feasted hungrily on the words.

Dear Corrie,

It has been my distinct pleasure to have met you and to have spent the last (approximately) three days with you. If you are reading this, I trust you are well. It gives me great pleasure to imagine that you are, in fact, reading this letter. However, there is something for which I must ask your forgiveness.

Corrie paused, pained by the memory of her last encounter with her three friends. She had threatened them with a tool she had wielded as a weapon, and yet this letter was an apology—and for what? *For lying to you, deceiving you, trying to trick you into servitude* said a cold voice from the recesses of her mind. Pressing those thoughts aside, she read on.

It was my task to prepare the way. In trying to accomplish this, I now see that I was attempting to find the diamond for you. I wanted it for you so much that I was blind to my own ambition. Only God can prepare the way for your heart to desire a treasure so valuable. I cannot claim it for you. What I can do is make the path so unmistakably clear so as to leave no question of direction should you want to find it.

If this be your aim, you have only to look outside the knothole window of the great cedar and follow the path.

Very sincerely yours,
Horatius S. Portuno

Corrie rose immediately from the table and bounded to the small window. There, beyond the immediate perimeter of the great cedar where the forest was dense and dark, was a clear path that cut right through the woods. All the underbrush, bushes, vines, and thorns had moved aside while the weeds and tall grasses lay flat against the ground in a green carpet stretched out before her. Corrie gasped. Without another question or misgiving, without even gathering so much as a handful of supplies, she blew out the lanterns, stuffed the letter and the feather in her pockets, and scurried out the door as quickly as her legs would carry her.

*   *   *

A figure hovered in the shadows of the trees, waiting and watching as Corrie exited the refuge. She would be easy prey, Anzu observed. She was already filled with the arrow's poison and *Specious molluscus*. He carried the most potent venom of all. He would bring the prize before Lucifer himself. Then he would no longer be squire to Belial; he would be Lord of the Mongers.

* * *

Qal sat in a cave on the outskirts of a region so sparsely populated by humans that there was hardly any demonic activity at all. And he liked it that way. He counted the rhythmic pounding of the waves against the rocks that were sending swells of gray water into the cave. He could be patient. How many swells would it take for his poison arrow to finish the child in Gerushah? He did not typically wait for results of his work, but this had been a unique assignment. A crab washed into the yawning mouth of the cave, skittered over the rock near Qal's foot, then slid back into the surf, and was carried out to sea.

A man, woman, and child played on the beach just beyond Qal's lair. The child, no taller than the man's knee, could barely stand against even the smallest waves. Qal watched apathetically. Such weakness, he observed, yet every time the child wobbled and fell, the man turned to the woman and smiled as he scooped up the frail little thing. Why did humans delight in such a pitiable state? Neither angel nor demon had young. There were no fledgling beings in the heavens. Qal had always been as he is now—strong and powerful.

Qal was so close to the window of Erets that he could have stepped right into the third realm were the veil was even a fraction thinner. Limits, rules, boundaries—oh, he was so weary of it all. The demands of the King were stifling enough without the edicts of Lord Lucifer and the commands of General Bahadur, especially for one as capable as he was to rule. He should have commanded companies by now, legions.

Qal had bided his time, waiting for a promotion and for his skill and prowess to be rewarded, but with no results. Before Earth was formed and the stars sang creation's song, he had once been Qaliel, riding on the wings of the dawn, displaying strength and glory but not of himself. He heralded the strength and glory of God. Qal stamped the ground in disdain of such memories. He was Qal, strong and powerful, ruled not by

Bahadur or even Lucifer. When his plan was complete, they would know. All would know.

The archangels' retaliation would be swift. They would apprehend Bahadur immediately. Qal would be indicted, but so would Lucifer. Qal was sure of it. Bahadur would not go down without bringing as many with him as possible, even the Prince of the Air himself. The crime was heinous and perfect—killing the human child in Gerushah.

The plan had been executed with absolute precision. No human could withstand the poison of *gaon*—pride. Its subtlety and harmony with human DNA was pure poetry in action. It was the one poison that was certain to succeed because of its distinct nature. More powerful than hatred, lust, or even rage, pride ensured the complete demise of even the best of them. Like a magnet, it attracted all vices known to humankind while also repelling all influence of the King. Not many demons possessed the skill that Qal had in delivering it.

The skill of weaponry was in its subtlety. He had seen it too many times—a warrior too eager for a kill would shoot an arrow or lance with immediate or shocking consequence. The results were typically the same—pain and suffering that caused most humans to cry out for help, and then the unfortunate result that *He* would rescue them. With *gaon*, while the arrow stung for a brief second, the poison that came after it was absorbed without even the slightest resistance by the host. It eventually permeated with a pleasing effect, intertwining with the hopes, dreams, desires, strengths, and longings of the human heart. The best part was that *gaon* had no antidote. It only knew how to grow until the host was completely consumed, happily suckling at the bosom of its own demise.

Oh, he had used this particular poison thousands of times, and it was always successful. He relished the memories of every incident. What made the difference this time as Qal sat brooding in the darkness of an earthen cave was that the child who had so innocently wandered into the wilderness of Gerushah wore the mark of the Almighty. To kill this particular child was to defy a direct order by the King. Was mutiny worth it? Qal wondered as he pressed against the veil so closely that his foot nudged a large rock into the rising tide. *Only if I succeed*, Qal decided.

The ocean reached farther back into the cave now, rising in foamy swells fully covering the rocks. On the beach, the little family scurried to move their picnic blanket, basket, and towels farther away from the swiftly rising tide. The man commanded the child to stay where he sat as the man and woman, eager to spare their belongings from the salty water, fully engaged in the task of gathering, moving, and repositioning each item as quickly as possible. Neither of them tended to the small boy. Qal leaned forward to watch as the child, having lost interest in his few toys, left his father's presence and wandered down the beach toward the waves.

The boy giggled as the cold water spread over his feet and tickled his toes. He stomped in the wet sand and then studied his footprints, which were quickly washed away by the next wave. He looked at the water and then again at the sand as if wondering where his footprints had gone. He followed the wave that had taken his tracks back out to sea.

Qal scanned the beach. Where was the child's guardian? Or was it to be the angel of death? Qal wondered apathetically. There was never any battle involved with ones so young. There was nothing interesting since demons were forbidden to interfere with the angels' missions of mercy for these little ones. There was no glory in even trying.

Another wave billowed in, knocking the child off his feet and rolling him like an empty barrel in the surf. Then another wave rushed in, lifting the small body and pulling him toward the watery depths.

Then Qal saw the guardian, a smaller angel than what is typical for guardians. Where had he been? The angel did not hold back the waves or rescue the child. Instead, he flew straight to the mother, his wings a blur of golden light, and turned her face toward the waves.

The mother shrieked and ran toward her child who had just disappeared beneath the swells. The father, alerted by his wife's screams, followed immediately behind her and soon overtook her, reaching their son first. He pulled the boy up by his ankle, lifting him high in the air as the sea flowed out of him in chokes and sobs.

Disgusting, Qal thought to himself. What value does a weak, inept human being have that can do nothing for itself? They are pitiful. They cannot even overcome the elements of their own planet. They drown in the very substance they need to stay alive. They require constant rescuing. Their bodies decompose to the very dust they are made of. What could the Almighty possibly see in them that He would not only tolerate their existence but—

Qal's thoughts trailed off as he watched with revulsion. The man and woman held to each other in a tight knot with the boy between them. Qal had seen humans do this with their offspring countless times, and each time he wanted to tear them apart. These creatures do not deserve love. They deserve nothing, and yet all of Heaven looks upon them as objects of love, even affection. Earth was given to *them* to rule? Many among them were chosen to be the children of God? *El-Elyon?* It was preposterous. He, Qal, was created to be glorious. *They* were fashioned of mud.

Qal stood in the mouth of the cave. He lifted his bow and slowly fitted two arrows to the string. Envy would do nicely for both the man and the woman. She would envy the bond the father has with their son. He would envy the relationships she has with her friends. Envy would destroy any love they had, filling them instead with anger, hatred, and ultimately revulsion—the only emotions appropriate to their race. Qal drew the bow, but before he released the arrows, the small family was surrounded by a company of guardians. The angels had sensed Qal's presence and responded immediately.

Cursed guardians! Qal fumed. Othniel, the largest guardian and as large as a warrior, glared at Qal. Instinctively, Qal raised his lance, aiming at Othniel this time. Qal would be a fool to engage. He was outnumbered 10 to one. He would lose this fight if he tried. So unconcerned were the angels with his empty threats to them that they turned their backs on him, instantly filling Qal with hot indignation that quickly grew into wild rage.

That was enough! Qal snapped. Who were these angels to taunt him so, as if he were a mere courier? He had plans that not even the archangels could thwart. That was who they dared to ignore. Today, they would know his name. Today, the Holy Scribes would write down the deeds of Qal, Prince of the Shamayim.

Qal set his sights on Gerushah. There would be no more waiting. Qal would find the child and destroy her with his own hands. He hurtled from the cave, ripping through the layers of the Shamayim so swiftly that a peal of thunder rumbled through the clouds in the third realm.

The family, hearing the thunder, gathered their belongings and departed for home. There had been enough trouble for one day.

Chapter 25

The Convergence

Corrie ran with the wind at her back and the path clear before her. Horatius had made sure of that, and the thought of her friends waiting for her at the end of the trail put an extra spring in her step. Every now and then she searched the woods that surrounded her, thinking that the hideous creature at the gate might be following her, but no one chased her from the shadows. Neither did she hear his horrid voice in her mind. *The path was clear, the sun was shining, and she would soon see her friends*, she reassured herself.

The woods were silent except for a gentle rustling of the leaves in the breeze. Corrie watched the treetops, slowing her steps in order to keep from tripping. Memories of ducking into the bushes as the west wind passed filled her mind. She had been with Horatius, Prudence, and Evangeline then. She was all alone now. *It would not be for long*, Corrie reminded herself again, but her cheerful resolve was waning. She didn't even know where she was going. How much farther would it be? Corrie picked up the pace to a brisk jog, eager to get there, wherever it was.

That it was the path to the diamond she had no doubt, and yet the diamond was not what urged her onward. If she were truly honest with herself, she would have to admit that what she really wanted was to tell Prudence about that horrible monster and how she had nearly died in the circle of fire. She wanted Evangeline's hugs and to hear her call Corrie her "little lamb." She wanted to see Horatius's gentle smile and the way he always looked out for her.

"And I believe in God now," she rehearsed, imagining their smiles of delight when she told them. Maybe she would even tell them that she wanted to join the remnant of the faithful, just as her parents had.

Corrie winced at the thought of her parents. What of her mother? Should she just give up and abandon all hope of finding her? What would Evangeline say about that? Corrie continued walking, but her pace had slowed once again. She already knew what all three of them would say— *find the diamond.* They seemed to think that finding the diamond really was the solution to everything.

"Evangeline, I have a toothache," Corrie said, pretending Evangeline were walking with her.

"Well, sweet baby darling child, you need to find the diamond," Corrie answered herself loudly, waving her hands in the air as she had seen Evangeline do so many times.

"Horatius, what time is it?" Corrie said, feigning sincere curiosity.

"It is a quarter past the hour you should have found the *Yahalom Shalom*," she intoned like Horatius's reverent whisper.

"Prudence," Corrie began, trying to think of how best to imitate her, but all she could remember were the hours spent with Prudence in the comfort of the Great Cedar. She recalled Prudence's piercing gaze of compassion even as Corrie had threatened them before walking out. Corrie fell silent as she continued on the path.

She could imagine ways that she did truly need help, ways that her life had not gone so well. Could the diamond cause Collin to forgive her for betraying him? Would it make her more lovable in Gran's eyes so she might be allowed back in the house even with the medallion still around her neck? Corrie accepted that no magic could bring her mother back, but if the diamond could ease the pain of her broken heart for even one day, it would be worth it.

Where could this diamond be? Corrie imagined a cave, a field of flowers, or a pile of rocks where someone had hidden it for her to find. She pictured her three friends standing at the end of the trail with a shovel or a pick axe, waiting for her. Maybe it was so big that it took all four of them to lift it. Now that would be a treasure! It wasn't hard to imagine that a diamond that large would be valuable enough that it could purchase any treatment or solve any problem anyone ever had—*even Joe Goodson*, she thought. With all the money in the world, they could move out of Bellam. They could move anywhere they wanted. She could hire bodyguards like all the important people had. Joe would never lay another hand on her or her family.

Corrie was enjoying her fantasies of all the amazing things she would do and adventures she would have when suddenly a voice penetrated her thoughts.

But nothing can change who you are.

The words pierced her heart. She knew it was true. Why would she think *she* deserved anything good? Corrie cursed and kicked at a rock on the trail. *That's right*, she thought to herself. She would not get her hopes up again. She would put no confidence in faith or hope or expect anything good to come her way. The disappointment just wasn't worth it. In the silence of the woods, the darkness pressed in. Corrie steeled her heart against all.

A figure floated silently behind Corrie. The leviathan scale had found its mark, and Anzu had completed his mission. Tucking the weapon back into the folds of his cloak, he withdrew into the shadows between the trees and disappeared.

*   *   *

Bahadur stood overlooking the battle of the 83rd region below. Even without Qal, they were beginning to turn the tide. The white smoke of incense was sparse now, and the formerly established perimeter had nearly dissolved. The disturbance was easily settling now that one by one the spirits of the children of the enemy rose from Earth, singing as they slipped easily and swiftly through the layers of the Shamayim and directly into the sixth realm. Bahadur covered his ears to shut out the loud tumult of rejoicing that floated through the Shamayim from Paradise as each was received.

"Good riddance," Bahadur said, cursing.

The battle continued raging below him, yet something was not quite right. As the angels ascended to Paradise with the saints and left the scene, replacements were not dispatched in their places. It seemed only moments before that there had been a legion of angel warriors vying for ground in the 83rd region. Bahadur had emptied Gerushah because of it, and yet now demon warriors far outnumbered the ranks of angels. And where was Adriel? Had he not just commanded the archangels' presence for battle?

Bahadur clenched his fists as a dark foreboding seized him. He had been tricked. And what of the child in Gerushah? Qal was tasked to disable her and render her incapable of fulfilling the prophecy without taking her life. No assignment could be simpler. He recalled that Qal did not report to the 83rd region as commanded. He had no assurance that Qal had even completed the task. Seething, Bahadur peered through the layers of the Shamayim toward Gerushah but could see nothing. The view was uncharacteristically cloudy, distorted even.

"Courier!" Bahadur roared, and moments later a smaller winged demon bowed before him.

"Inquire what news of Gerushah," Bahadur barked. He refrained from asking specifically about the child lest the courier report that the general inquired of something he should already know. "And consult with the seers regarding the atmospheric anomaly," he added.

"Begging your pardon, Lord Bahadur, Mighty Commander of the Most Powerful De—"

"Speak!" Bahadur roared impatiently. The courier bowed lower.

"I am unable to complete my lord's orders because Gerushah is inaccessible, my lord." The courier dared not look into his master's face but slid back and covered his own face in anticipation of Bahadur's fury.

"Inaccessible?" Bahadur huffed. "And why is that?" He growled into the courier's ear, causing the smaller demon to tremble.

"The gate has been closed, my lord, sir," said the courier.

"Then open it, fool. Find a way in," Bahadur replied, clenching his fists. He was ready to hurl the courier from his presence.

"I cannot open it, my lord, for it was closed by *Him*," he said. "The King

Himself," he added but immediately backed away in regret as Bahadur roared in his face and then lifted him high over his head by his tunic.

"B-But my lord Bahadur," the courier stammered hastily. "The layers of the Shamayim surrounding all borders of Gerushah are *shiny*," he said, nearly shouting now.

"Shiny? And why should I care about that? Speak quickly, courier, or you will be cast into the wilderness."

"It means the boundaries are disintegrating," said the courier. "I saw it long, long ago when Earth was newly born and the barrier between the third and fourth realms was porous and permeable. The convergence of the planets is occurring and is now almost complete. The long-departed land of Gerushah is seeking union once again with her twin, and if the prophecy is true, then—"

"The terms of the treaty will dissolve," Bahadur said in a low growl, recalling the prophecy. It was true.

"But my lord, if the child has not yet found the stone, you will soon be able to enter Gerushah and finish her yourself," said the courier. Bahadur loosened his grip on the demon's tunic.

"How have you come by this information?" Bahadur asked, not willing to take the advice of a mere courier so easily.

"I have long served the seers in the castle, until the gate was closed, and I could not return," he replied.

"Enough. Be gone," Bahadur ordered. There was nothing more he required of the courier. He would gather his platoon and apprehend the child, with or without Qal.

* * *

The flattened path emptied into a clearing. Corrie stood staring straight ahead at the mountain peaks and the plumes of white water cascading down the waterfall into the depths of the Crystal River below. Though she recognized her location immediately, it seemed as if she had visited it in a dream long ago rather than experiencing it just three days ago. Memories of Vincent dragging her into the woods caused a chill to snake up her spine.

The trees were dull and lifeless here, and the sky reflected a strange hue, not quite blue or gray but hanging listlessly somewhere in between over the drab landscape. Corrie felt a dreary gloom wrap around her shoulders like a heavy blanket, wet from a cold rain.

"Oh, if only Horatius, Prudence, and Evangeline were here," Corrie moaned in despair.

No sooner had she said this than she heard a rustling in the bushes behind her. Could it be? Revived by sudden hope, she turned to see if it might be her friends joining her. What met her gaze and rapidly moved toward her through the woods was not her three friends, however. She screamed and ran out into the clearing as Joe Goodson burst through the trees with a roar that sounded more animal than human.

With no time to think, Corrie headed straight for the river. She would rather drown a thousand times than be in the clutches of Joe Goodson again. She ran as fast as she could, but it was not fast enough. Joe tackled her from behind, flipped her over roughly, gripped her neck with both his hands, and squeezed hard.

"I should have killed you when I had the chance, but you're all mine now," said Joe in a low, guttural growl. His eyes were no longer gray and lifeless but red, burning orbs of raw hatred and rage.

Oh God, help me, Corrie prayed silently. Would God help her again? Could He even hear her silent prayer? She looked to the heavens.

As Corrie fought for consciousness against Joe's steel grip, dark filaments slipped through the air like black ribbons dropping from the sky. The ground beneath her shook as the sound of roaring and the crash of swords surrounded them. A roar louder than all the others spoke something from the crowd around them in a language she did not understand. Corrie could sense a dark figure moving closer.

"No! She's mine!" Joe shouted in a voice like an unearthly shriek. The sound of guttural growls and roars surrounding them was swiftly closing in when from a distance Corrie heard a familiar voice, loud and strong.

"She belongs to GOD!"

"Evangeline!" Corrie wanted to shout. In another second she would have blacked out, but Joe released his grip as Evangeline broke through the horde of demons with the sword of Lemuel held high. She was swinging it and shouting at the top of her lungs.

"Greater is He that is in me than *all* of you put together! Be gone this instant!" Evangeline cried as the flames burst forth from the sword, casting out every demon from the premises—all except one. Joe, who had crouched over Corrie, stood and glowered at Evangeline, leaving Corrie limp on the ground, gasping for breath. By this time, Horatius and Prudence had reached Evangeline's side, and the three of them surrounded Joe, maneuvering him away from Corrie.

"What is your name, foul spirit?" Horatius questioned.

"I am Qal, overlord of the spirits that possess this human by his own assent," he answered. Joe's mouth moved, but the voice that spoke was of the demon warrior, Qal.

"You have far overstepped your bounds, Qal," Horatius said coolly. "You have taken possession of one in the forbidden territory and attempted to murder another who bears His mark. You cannot succeed. And while you seek glory for yourself, I will see to it that no one, neither demon nor angel, knows of your exploits. Your deeds will be wiped clean from history. You will fade into infamy with nothing."

"You have no rights here," Qal growled through Joe's vocal cords. Joe's muscles flexed and twitched, barely able to contain the fury of the spirit housed in his physical body. Torment etched his face in contortions of pain. He alternately crouched and stood, pacing as best he could within the tight circle of his confinement.

Prudence kept herself between Joe and Corrie at all times. Evangeline, still holding the sword, pointed it toward the heavens and maintained a circular pattern around them lest any demons attempted to return.

"I speak not of my own authority, but that of the King," Horatius intoned with an icy stare. "Now, return this man to the third realm, and then you will come out of him at once, *by orders of the King.*" Horatius emphasized the order and yet spoke barely above a whisper.

"You may order me, pitiful human, but you cannot undo what has already been done here. The poison—my poison—has already filled her. She has already failed," Qal growled, just inches from Horatius's face.

Then he ran into the woods, crashing into trees and briers, taking Joe's body deeper into the shadows of Gerushah.

Horatius stood looking toward the woods where he had gone. No doubt the demon would find a way to incur more torment for his human host before his required relinquishment. He breathed prayers of victory over the evil pronouncements concerning Corrie.

Corrie sat on the ground with Prudence, who now offered her sips of calendula nectar to soothe her throat as she tried to breathe normally again without coughing. With patience and effort, Corrie was able to swallow a bit of the nectar. Prudence patted Corrie on the back. Horatius helped Corrie to her feet when she was able and patted her gently on the shoulder. Evangeline had plunged the sword into the ground several feet away, and now she engulfed Corrie in the biggest bear hug Corrie had ever received.

"I'm so sorry," Corrie lamented, wishing with all her heart she could take back the last several hours. "I'm just so glad you're all here." She was smiling through her tears. All was forgiven in another circle of warm embraces.

"We are sorry for the delay, Corrie," Horatius said, his eyebrows pinched. "Evangeline insisted on stopping by the Sacred Alcove. I see now that it was a helpful idea," he said, nodding toward the sword.

"The Sword of Lemuel!" Corrie gasped. She had seen the sword and the flames, but having been seconds from unconsciousness and then struggling to breathe, she only now recognized the powerful sword as the same as what guarded the Sacred Alcove.

"Why yes, it is," Evangeline beamed.

"Well, we were going to come straight here, but like Horatius said, Evangeline had the idea that—" Prudence started to explain but was interrupted by Evangeline.

"Oh, let me tell it, Pru," Evangeline said eagerly. Prudence nodded. The slightest smile crossed her lips.

"I thought we might have some trouble, so I asked the Lord if I might borrow the sword, because you know I was given a task, and my task was to hold the line, you see," Evangeline said, holding her hand straight out as if she were commanding an army toward the foe. "And the Lord said yes, so we wasted no time getting there. I also wanted to get you some fruit from the trees near the alcove, but Horatius thought that would take too much time."

"Except for the calendula flowers that were along the way," Prudence interjected.

"Yes, Pru, that was splendid," said Evangeline before going on. "Well, then, we came to the sword, and I said, 'The Lord has need of you.'"

"Which you probably didn't need to say, dear," said Prudence.

"You're probably right, Pru, but, well anyway, so I said 'the Lord has need of you,' and then I just reached straight into the flames." Evangeline extended her hand quickly as a demonstration. "And I took it!" Evangeline said with a quick nod of her head, curls bouncing wildly.

Corrie asked, "But how could you take it and—"

"Still live?" Horatius asked. Corrie nodded, remembering how Vincent had been engulfed by flames quicker than a blink.

"Corrie, dear, the three of us are not citizens of Earth anymore," Evangeline replied. "My time on Earth ended in 1938. We are no longer mortal flesh and bone. We live in the Heavenly Kingdom with the one true King." Evangeline's eyes were sparkling.

"What? What are you saying? You died? All of you are *dead*?" Corrie gasped.

"Hardly," said Prudence. "We are more alive than we ever were on Earth, and we live in a place where there is no more pain or sorrow, only joy and happiness."

"Then why are you *here*? With me?" Corrie asked. The question that had nagged her before was burning in her even more now. Why would anyone leave such a place and come here to be with *her*? It made no sense.

"Because we were *sent* here. To be with you," said Horatius. His knowing eyes were tender, smiling even as Corrie grappled with their words.

"But who sent you? Who would do that? It was my father, wasn't it? Did he send you to help me?" Corrie asked.

"Corrie, the One who commissioned us is the same One who commissioned you," Horatius answered, and pulled the small mission scroll from his pocket. "Look here," he said, pointing to a line inscribed in gold ink.

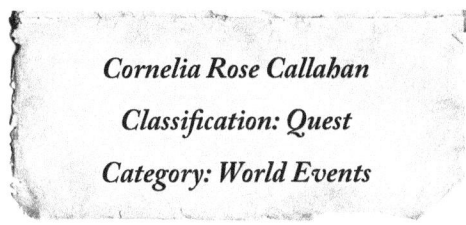

Cornelia Rose Callahan

Classification: Quest

Category: World Events

"This mission, the map, even the work of the enemy that was meant to destroy you—all these things led you, and us, to this very point and place in time, and it was all orchestrated by the One who created you—God, the One True King," Horatius said as he rolled the mission scroll again and secured it in his pocket.

"Now, are you ready to find the treasure you were brought here to find?" Horatius asked. Corrie looked at each of them, considering his words. "We don't have much time, Corrie. The demons will return, and with more warriors," said Horatius, checking his pocket watch and scanning the skies above them.

"I'm ready," Corrie said quietly.

"Come. You must take the diamond for yourself, but we can show you where it is," Horatius said. With all of them gathered around Corrie, they moved as one toward the shoreline of the Crystal River.

"No," Corrie shuddered as dread and despair filled her heart. She could not face the river again.

"You must look into the river to see the diamond, Corrie," said Prudence.

"But you won't be alone," Evangeline said, squeezing Corrie's shoulders.

Horatius had walked ahead a few steps and now stood looking down at the water. Corrie could hear the voices drifting up from the depths again, the cries of torment, pain, and sorrow. Her feet dragged as heavy as lead.

Horatius was speaking to Corrie, but his voice seemed far away amidst the wailing and moaning from the water that would surely engulf her if she even came near it. Corrie did want to see the diamond, though, after hearing so much about this valuable stone. Her mother had told her to find the truth. Corrie would not shrink back now. *Be brave*, she bolstered herself.

Together with Prudence and Evangeline at her side, Corrie joined Horatius at the top of the slope. She gazed down into the water, but the light coming from the object in its depths was so bright that her eyes immediately began to burn. The burning intensified, searing her eyes like a hot laser. She cried out in pain, but then something fell out of her eyes. She could feel it detach and fall to the ground. She blinked and saw with astonishing clarity. She looked again into the water. She did not see a diamond, but what she did see shocked and terrified her.

What she saw was horrible. Grotesque. Bruises and scrapes covered her from head to toe. Heavy chains hung around her waist and looped around her legs. Thorny vines embedded around each thigh. Gaping wounds on her arms and legs oozed a slimy film that dripped onto her already-filthy clothing. Jagged black lines covered her left leg in a lacy crisscross pattern that extended from her calf all the way up to her waist. She lifted the hem of her shirt to see how far it had spread. Hundreds of tiny worms wriggled and writhed on her abdomen, burrowing in her flesh. Corrie fell backward, gagged, and then vomited on the ground.

"There, there now," Evangeline said as Prudence offered her another sip of calendula nectar.

Corrie could not speak for a long time. She had no words. When she could stand again, she stared at her reflection, trembling in shock and horror.

"That's what you see when you look at me?" Corrie asked meekly when at last she could speak again.

Her companions nodded. "Do you know what that is, Corrie?" Prudence asked.

Corrie studied Prudence's expression. It was the same look she had when Corrie had left them sitting in the tree house. Her eyes were intense but kind. Corrie remembered their brief exchange. Prudence had reminded her of the cure. Corrie had practically laughed in her face. She understood now.

"It's *sin*, that disease, isn't it? I have sin," Corrie said quietly. She felt sick again. She could hardly catch her breath. Evangeline patted her on the shoulder. Corrie recoiled from her touch.

"No. Don't. Don't touch me, and don't look at me," Corrie groaned. She could not take her eyes off the repulsive sight. Shock soon gave way to bitter hatred and self-loathing.

Prudence explained. "In the fourth realm, you can see what is invisible to you in the third realm. The scales have fallen from your eyes, and you can finally see what is true."

"So I could have had this for a very long time and just didn't know it?" asked Corrie.

"Yes," Prudence agreed with no hint of uncertainty.

"Corrie," Horatius said gently. "You can continue staring at yourself, or you can look beyond your own reflection to *that*," he said, pointing to a spot in the river a little farther beyond. "Lift your chin. Look for the sparkle of light."

Corrie lifted her gaze to the river beyond.

"There. You see it?" Horatius said. An unmistakable excitement filled his voice.

"Ooh! There it is! I see it!" Evangeline exclaimed, thumping Corrie on the back.

"Ah, the *Yahalom Shalom*," said Prudence reverently.

Corrie saw it then, as though the North Star had fallen from the sky and now shone from the depths, casting its radiance in all directions.

"It must be beautiful," said Corrie, for it was too bright to discern its shape and form clearly.

"The *Yahalom Shalom* is what you came here to find, Corrie. It was put here by God Himself for you," said Horatius.

"But I—" she started to protest.

"For you, Corrie," Horatius said again.

Corrie realized then that the voices from the river had quieted to a low murmur since the moment she had faced her hideous reflection. The clarity of the river was so pure. The diamond seemed only inches away from the surface, but she knew better. The river was far deeper than it looked. Did she really believe that one perfect stone could make everything better, even her?

"But what if I drown?" Corrie asked quietly, contemplating the challenge before her.

"And what if you do *not* retrieve the diamond?" Prudence asked, her eyes ablaze with intensity.

Corrie looked down at herself. She beheld the mess that she was and the ghastly worms that fed on her own flesh. She needed the cure. Without it she would surely die. She was already dying.

"Thank you all for everything," Corrie said with more gratitude for her friends than she knew how to express. Then, gathering her courage for the task before her, she took a deep breath and plunged into the depths below.

Chapter 26

Eden's Gift

Corrie plunged through the upper layers of the Crystal River and immediately felt the downward pull of the river drawing her into the depths below. She remembered her first encounter with the water in this strange land where fresh water was salty and currents moved vertically as well as horizontally. She set the diamond again in her sights and angled her body toward it. Corrie let the current pull her rather than expend energy kicking.

As before, images passed before her eyes on a watery screen. The faces of her mother, father, brothers—oh, she couldn't bear it all again. And yet the movie of her life had also somehow changed since she had first plummeted in the depths of these sorrows.

As if in a dream, the red taillights of her father's car as their mother drove away quickly faded to the pale face of her mother in the driver's seat. Tears poured over the anguished lines in her mother's face as sobs wracked her body. Her eyebrows arched over her wide eyes, and Corrie saw that her mother was not only grief-stricken but terrified. Waves of anguish and remorse washed over Corrie. She had dwelled so much on her own sorrow that she had not considered the horrors her mother may have had to face on the road ahead of her or still faced even now. *I've been so blind, so selfish*, Corrie thought to herself.

The scene changed abruptly, and Corrie watched the moment that she stormed out of her house after Gran had kicked her out for having the gold medallion. The door slammed shut, shaking the windows. Gran burst into tears. "I've been too hard on her, I know," Gran sobbed. "She's going to get herself killed!" she wailed. "And after I promised her mother I would protect her," Gran continued, shaking with her sobbing. "I've already lost my daughter. I can't lose my granddaughter now too."

Corrie saw Will standing beside Gran with his arm around her shoulders, trying to console her. He had the face of a confused little boy. "Bring me my pills. I just can't do this anymore! I can't," Gran sobbed into Will's shoulder. Corrie watched as Will guided Gran to her soft chair. He made sure she was comfortable and then walked dutifully to the kitchen and retrieved a box from the back of the cupboard. The small metal box had a combination lock. Will unlocked the box and retrieved a bottle of pills. He opened the cap, took one pill from the bottle, and then sealed and locked it again methodically as if he had done it a thousand times. Then he poured a cup of water and brought it to Gran.

"I need more than one, Will. I can't take this anymore," Gran said as she swallowed the small pill. "Give me more," she demanded.

"I promised I would keep you alive, Gran. I promised. Collin and Corrie need you. We all do. What would we do if you went away to the hospital again and never came back?" Will said solemnly. The confused little boy had gone, and he was the oldest brother in charge again.

"You'll feel better in a little while, Gran. It will all be okay," he said calmly as the images faded.

Corrie was horrified. She had no idea the responsibility Will had carried. She did not know Gran had been to the hospital. When did that happen? Corrie had been oblivious to all of it. She had teased Will mercilessly and ridiculed him behind his back for what she thought was his pride. He was just trying to keep them all from losing one more family member. Shame overwhelmed Corrie. She closed her eyes, trying hard not to see the next scene of her brother Collin, but the images persisted as well as the sounds of his quiet cries. He sat alone on his bed, talking to himself. As the words filled her ears, Corrie realized that he was talking to someone else.

"I try to do the right thing, Dad, but it always goes wrong, and I just get so tired of trying. Ever since you left us, nothing's been right, and it never will be. And nobody cares. The Goodsons are evil. They're destroying this town, and nobody cares. I'm all alone, Dad. I just wish you were h—." Collin's last word was choked out by quiet sobs as he held onto the small, framed photo of his dad that he kept on his nightstand.

Corrie felt she could stand no more. She had thought her own pain was too unbearable to tolerate, but witnessing her family members' pain was beyond what she could endure. There was so much pain, so much grief. She focused determinedly on the diamond in her sights ahead of her, but there was yet another scene to pass before her in this river of sorrows.

A glint of steel glimmered on the watery screen, but as if a camera were panning out, another face came into view. It was Joe Goodson. The knife was not in his hand, however. His own father, Emory Goodson, was holding it to his neck.

"Don't you ever talk to me that way or I'll slit your throat while you sleep," said the elder Goodson to his then younger teenage son, still holding Joe down with the knife tip under his smooth chin. "You are a worthless bag of—" Corrie tried to plug her ears, to shut out the endless string of cursing unleashed from Joe's angry, drunken father. Corrie watched as the boy's expression turned from fear to sadness and then finally to blank nothingness.

So much sorrow, so much suffering! Corrie had only entered the water seconds ago, and yet she felt she had already witnessed the pain of several lifetimes. The memories swirled around her unabated—a woman sitting alone in a doctor's office, a child hiding under the bed, untold and gruesome acts of violence and torture enough to fill a world with despair so great that everything about human life seemed an agonizing existence. Where was all the good in the world? Where were the birthday parties, picnics, and holidays? Why had the diamond been placed here and its path so unbearably crushing? Corrie wanted to turn back, to swim as hard as she could to the surface and stand with her companions once again, but she could not. The pull of the diamond was an indomitable force.

As Corrie continued her descent through scene after scene of people from everywhere—not just Bellam, but people from every nation speaking languages she had never heard—the gold chain pulled on the back of her neck. The medallion seemed to be reaching for the gem in the water. She strained her eyes to see only the gemstone. Oh, how she desired its beauty more than the sorrows that had so thoroughly filled her thoughts. If this gem held the cure for her, could it possibly also heal the world?

A single bubble escaped her lips. She had been under water for close to a minute now. Her lungs began to burn. If her record for holding her breath held, she had approximately 30 seconds to reach the diamond and return to the surface. Determined, Corrie held her arms and legs straight as an arrow as she continued to plunge downward.

The bottom of the river was rocky in parts but mostly covered in fine, white sand. She had been able to ignore the images of strangers she did not know in these lower layers of the current, even the sounds of their suffering. Suddenly, however, the scene playing out before her arrested her attention. She saw the Sacred Alcove and then passed *inside* the gate. She heard laughter and singing. Finally, joy! The garden was filled with trees laden with fruit, and every one of them was ripe. Flowers filled every empty space between the leaves of the trees and the low-lying bushes. Lions and bears loped over the grassy clearing, chased by rabbits and sheep frolicking in the sunshine. Then a voice echoed through the garden—rich, deep, and as melodious and beautiful as a symphony on the breeze. Then the music ended abruptly in a question that hung in the air. Though spoken in a language Corrie did not recognize, the cry was unmistakable. She had heard it once when she had gotten lost in a crowd of people. It was the voice of her father calling her name, not so he could find her but so she, small and frightened, might find *him* and run into his arms.

The gates swung shut. Terrifying creatures and a flaming sword blocked the way through the gate. The music and laughter ceased, and a man and woman who had covered themselves in leaves and branches stumbled beyond the now-forbidden space and bolted in terror into the woods.

Then Corrie heard the loud bleating of a sheep that soon fell into deafening silence. Blood pooled in a crimson circle at the foot of a large cedar tree with vines across its trunk, and the man and woman fled in grief and sorrow, holding only to the torturous memory of what once was.

Oh! Corrie wailed within herself. *Such mourning, such regret! What can be done?*

Suddenly the river bottom shook, and the white sands stirred up into an opaque cloud of sand, obscuring the diamond. Already nearing the threshold of her limits without air, Corrie panicked. Then a loud *crack* reverberated through the water, and she found herself sucked into a deep crevasse that formed in the depths of the Crystal River. This was the end. She had lost the diamond and was beyond any hope of ever swimming back to the surface. Corrie had come to die.

*   *   *

Horatius, Prudence, and Evangeline had all been standing on the riverbank watching Corrie's progression through the layers of water. All was going well until they heard a tumult emanating from the river and saw a cloud of sediment billowing up from the bottom, blocking their view of Corrie and all knowledge of her welfare.

Prudence drew in her breath and turned toward Evangeline, expecting their newest ambassador to need consoling at Corrie's latest calamity. Evangeline, however, stood resolved, her only reaction a deep sigh and a cluck of her tongue. They all continued watching, praying, and hoping, knowing that whatever occurred in the depths of the Crystal River and in the heart of their dear Corrie, they could rest in the eternal wisdom of the Almighty despite any circumstances. They had obeyed their King. The rest was up to Him.

*   *   *

While the situation engendered a sense of concerned expectation for the trio of ambassadors as Corrie disappeared from sight, it involved an entirely different experience for the land of Gerushah. Within her troubled heart still lived the memory of glorious Eden when she had been crowned by the Lord of Creation's own hand and festooned with gifts. Some gifts were given for the blessing of humanity—gold, bdellium, and onyx. Some were treasures bestowed in the depths of her ancient soul that she would reveal on the appointed day, which was now at hand.

Eden had first been endowed with the sacred gift of memory. Though cursed and removed from *Erets* and the whole of the third realm where dwelt all creation, man and beast, Eden never forgot her heritage held deep within her roots. Even while dormant with her slumber troubled by the presence of evil inhabitants, she remembered creation's song, the voice of her Creator, and the promise of redemption. She longed for it, waited, and never forgot her moorings to her greater twin.

Another gift bestowed was a secret harbored deep in the heart of the Creator. Though the enemy held morbid fascination with blood, that fountain of life, Eden retained its power. She had received the blood of the first lamb that was slain and invested it in the life of the Great Cedar. As the only currency to transcend realms, the blood of sacrifice afforded the ancient bower solace from the evil that stalked her lands, freedom from its influence in order to flourish, and a shield of invisibility in which weary travelers may find refuge.

The third gift bestowed on Eden was a hallowed relationship with life and death. While detached from *Erets* in the third realm, she would be freed from the sting of death in perpetual cycle. Though dormant, her vegetation would remain alive. Neither human nor animal would roam her lands and be subject to club or spear. Separated from the realm of physical existence, there would be no physical death on her sacred ground, and yet one death remained possible since the eve of mortality harkened at the gate and was the most severe—death of the soul.

Long had Eden waited for the appointed day. Long had she prepared, for though her gold, bdellium, and onyx had been purged and her beauty scorned through a curse, she had one final gift to bestow upon mankind for whom she had labored.

Mount Shekol—now forming the western border of Gerushah where the tears of the nations spilled over its peak and flowed into the river depths below—had once been Mount Moriah of Earth. The blood of the ram was spilled in the realm of humans on this peak, and the tears of suffering and relief flowed over Mount Shekol into the river's keeping.

The mountain also came to be known by another name in the third realm—Golgotha. The blood spilled there one fateful day was a draught too pure for Earth to absorb. On that day, blood flowed with water, pure and perfect, transcending the realms and flowing over Mount Shekol, mingling with the tears of the nations and coming to rest in the depths of the Crystal River.

The *Yahalom Shalom* was the crown jewel of Eden, the fruit of her three greatest gifts joined together in perfect union. It would bring peace to the one who could claim it. However, just as Eden's finest fruit had held intrinsic conditions, so too did her most valuable gift. The one who comes to the river to seek Eden's treasure must also understand that her invitation is ever unto death, for all who arrive at her shores are mere trespassers unto life, for they are, indeed, already dead.

* * *

"It's been an awfully long time, don't you think?" Evangeline said, staring down into the depths.

The cloud of sediment was beginning to clear, and yet the three ambassadors still could not locate Corrie. They did not know that she now lay in a deep crevasse. Horatius consulted his pocket watch as he had so many times before. This time, however, he spoke.

"Well now, there we go!" he remarked, smiling. "It has finally adapted to our location. The hands are moving now."

"That's very interesting, Horatius," said Prudence. "Do you think the problems with your watch could have something to do with *that*?" she asked, pointing toward the sky where they saw five small spheres in a perfect row—Mercury, Venus, Saturn, Jupiter, and Mars.

"I suppose it could be," Horatius said somberly. "The convergence does create unique alterations in the Shamayim. It could very well be the convergence of more than planets, perhaps even alterations in the time-space continuum. I don't know if it's that or if it's because the time allotted for Corrie's mission is coming to an end. If the watch is correct, her time is running out."

Both Evangeline and Prudence glanced at Horatius. Their eyes met, but none spoke a word. Meanwhile, all around them were demon warriors returning to Gerushah, slipping through the now permeable barriers that were continuing to widen. Evangeline, upon seeing the demons, took a step toward the sword she had planted in the ground a few feet away.

"Just leave it," Horatius instructed quietly. "It doesn't matter now. She needs no defense from them." Evangeline nodded, agreeing sadly.

"I told you she would fail," a voice said from behind them. The voice sounded like the growl of an animal and the howl of the wind.

"Bahadur," Horatius groaned, but all of them kept their backs to him.

"She will die the second death," Bahadur gloated.

"You speak too soon. I see no death angel coming to claim her," said Horatius.

"There is no angel for those who fall to Gehenna," Bahadur said with a laugh, and all the demons now surrounding them roared in laughter and beat their shields.

Above them the ambassadors could see a heavenly host peering down from the fifth realm. Saints watched from above through a sea of glass in the sixth realm. They also knew that the King Himself watched from His throne in the highest Heaven. They waited, they watched, and they prayed.

Already the entrance to the sacred alcove, their home, had been locked and barred. Terrifying beings each with four faces and wings of eagles stood outside the gate, along with a flaming sword to guard the path. The man and woman had never known walls before, neither gates or doors, nor holy fire that burned unceasingly.

Adam and Eve stood in the forest, their bodies hidden by the covering of an animal still wet with the life now drained out of it. The fluid stained the earth like crimson berries, but the creature would not go on living as the trees and bushes did when they shed their color. What of humans? What would become of them when their own bodies soaked the ground?

The deceiver had said nothing of endings or that the knowledge of good and evil he had promised would continue unfolding before her eyes. Eve had believed that good and evil were treasures to add to her collection, for she loved beautiful things. The whole garden was filled with them. How much more wonderful to grasp all that could be had. She never imagined attaining it would feel like this. The serpent had uttered one truth among his slippery lies. Her eyes had indeed been opened. This was unlike anything Eve had experienced. Oh, how she longed to return to not knowing.

The Creator had said that the serpent's head would be crushed by no less than the woman's own seed. Seeds came from flowers that then became more flowers. Seeds were life. Life would come of this? He had said it. She had doubted once; she would not doubt again.

The woman held the precious promise and one more treasure: gold. The shiny stones had been plentiful in Havilah. Gold lay on the land like morning dew. She wondered if that, too, would fade in the wake of the horrible curse she had brought on Earth.

From the gold in Havilah a medallion was forged, along with a chain on which it hung. It served as a reminder of all that was once beautiful and lovely. The center of it remained empty, like a promise waiting to be fulfilled. She did not know yet with what—a seed perhaps, the promise of new life. She would wait. Longingly, she would wait, for the two beautiful things that now sustained her would come to be known as faith and hope.

Chapter 27

The Exchange

At the bottom of the Crystal River, Corrie lay in a deep crevasse. All was still and quiet. The memories, the voices—they had ceased, and all that remained in that hallowed tomb was Corrie and the perfect diamond. She had imagined a white diamond, brilliant and clear, but the *Yahalom Shalom* was crimson, deep and rich, as a drop of blood liberally spilled.

The gold around her neck pulled Corrie toward it, yet the diamond remained where it was, wedged into rock. Corrie wondered if it did not come to her because it was so tightly nestled or because it resisted her. Certainly, she was not worthy of something so valuable. She dared not grasp it. Images of Vincent incinerating before her eyes for merely reaching toward the Sword of Lemuel swirled through her mind.

Corrie's lungs burned, demanding air. But what did it matter anymore? Death was certain. The question now was not how to stay alive but how she chose to die. She had come for the diamond. She would accomplish her goal, she decided. She reached tentatively toward the beautiful crimson stone, and voices instantly flooded her thoughts.

"You can die a noble death, or you can die as an unworthy beggar and thief taking what you have not earned. You are no thief," said a voice flowing cold through her veins from the poison of Qal's arrow.

Corrie withdrew her hand immediately. Truly, she had not earned it.

She had nothing to offer in exchange for its value. To take it would mean dying as a beggar and a thief. It would mean further humiliation. *I am neither a beggar nor a thief,* she agreed.

Remembering the beautiful diamond she had saved, she dug in her pocket to retrieve it—*for a trade,* she thought, something valuable for something valuable. But as soon as she withdrew her hand with her treasured prize, the counterfeit diamond dissolved as finely as sugar stirred in a glass of water.

Desperate, Corrie decided she would just touch the diamond stuck in the rock to see what would happen. She stretched out her hand again, but before she would reach it, the venom of Leviathan completed its work. Her heart was fully encased in Leviathan's impenetrable shield. The weight within her chest crushed all remaining hope. *Corrie wondered why she had even tried. The diamond was wedged in rock anyway,* she reasoned. She was dying for nothing, and that was that. Corrie tried to move away from the stone, but the gold around her neck persisted, pulling her forcefully toward the diamond. She stuck out her hand again to keep her face from colliding with the rock. As she did so, the tip of her finger grazed the surface of the crimson gem, and a scene immediately flashed through her mind.

A man cried out, his flesh torn from his bones, hanging with his arms outstretched and dying. Lightning snaked across the sky, raw anguish as if his soul were being ripped from his body. Blood streamed down and pooled on the ground, deep and rich, as red as *crimson.* Corrie drew back her hand in sudden, profound understanding. *No!* she screamed inside her head. This was how the diamond came to be? This man suffered a horrible death *for me?* The diamond is from God, but who, then, was *he?* The realization pierced her through, shattering the shell of Leviathan in an instant. Corrie wanted to shout all at once in penitent sorrow and exultant joy, but her diaphragm began to clench, willing her to breathe. She fought the darkness closing in and the darkness that had nearly consumed her soul. Stretching out her hand, she grasped the beautiful crimson diamond and pressed it to her chest.

She never could have earned such a gift. All she had ever possessed in the exchange was need. From the bottom of the deep crevasse, a silent prayer floated up through the fourth realm, the fifth, and the sixth. Then rising to the Holy Throne Room, it filled the whole chamber with the fragrance of sweet incense and rested in the heart of God.

"I am a beggar and a thief, nothing more, but if this blood can make me clean, please, Lord—"

Click.

The *Yahalom Shalom* was at last joined to the medallion, and Corrie closed her eyes in peace.

* * *

On the shore, the taunts grew louder. Raucous laughter from the demon horde echoed over the din of the waterfall as the ambassadors waited silently and soberly. The water sparkled, clear as a pane of glass, where at the very bottom lay the still figure of Corrie Callahan. It had been too long for anyone to survive without air.

"Sweet little lamb. She was such a dear child," Evangeline said, her voice thick with emotion.

"Here come the angels to carry her away," Prudence said, sighing deeply. They all stood quietly on the riverbank.

Horatius watched, his gaze transfixed on the sky as multitudes of the heavenly hosts were descending, some from the Shamayim, some from the Meridiem, and some even from the Holy Throne Room. They were praising God and singing, "Worthy is the Lamb who was slain!" Many were shouting, rejoicing in verse and in song.

"I've seen the angels participate in homecomings, but none like this!" Evangeline said, marveling.

The demons began to roar louder and beat their shields with their swords to protest the singing, but they were easily drowned out by the music of the angelic throng.

"*Angels.* In Gerushah," Prudence gasped. "Horatius, check the mission scroll," Prudence said excitedly. "The Treaty of Zim is broken!" Prudence exclaimed while Horatius was already digging in his pocket.

Beneath the surface of the water and deep in the crevasse there began a low but steady rumble. The rock holding the body of Corrie Callahan began to quake. A spring of fresh water flowed up from the ground below, foaming and rolling beneath her. Corrie opened her eyes.

A fountain of rushing water began to lift her upward, up through the crevasse, up toward the surface of the river. "I'm alive!" Corrie wanted to shout and clap her hands, but she was still under water. She touched the medallion. There was no longer an empty space in the middle. She felt the smooth surface of the beautiful crimson diamond. She looked down at herself. She was clean! No more chains, scratches, or bruises, and no wound leaching poison into her soul. Best of all, there were no more hideous worms. Corrie raised her arms high over her head in joy and celebration.

Still afar off but swiftly growing closer, Corrie saw her three companions standing on the riverbank. Horatius waved his hands toward her. Evangeline was waving and blowing kisses. Though Corrie could not hear Evangeline, she could tell by the way that Evangeline's hair was bouncing that she was laughing. Prudence stood with her hands clasped over her heart, smiling from ear to ear.

Even from below the surface and the tumultuous noise of the water beneath her, Corrie could hear what sounded like a choir of thousands of voices singing and shouting. Horrid creatures bearing swords and shields stood with mouths agape in roars of protest, but their voices were silenced by the multitude of heavenly beings dressed in brilliant white all around them.

Corrie, excited to tell her friends all that had happened, prepared to break the surface. She had expected the water to carry her to shore, but it continued upward, above it, and toward a shimmering curtain of light. She was moving swiftly now. She heard the pealing of bells and then saw Horatius retrieve his pocket watch. He said something to Prudence that Corrie could not quite decipher.

"Corrie, we love you!" Evangeline shouted. Movement from the woods caught Corrie's eye. She turned to look, but she was too late. All faded behind her as she passed through the shimmering curtain, and all the singing, shouting, roaring, and laughing were suddenly silent.

*   *   *

Meanwhile, on the other side of the veil where Corrie had been just moments before, Horatius explained to Prudence that the alarm had sounded, alerting them to the time of Corrie's return to the third realm. Movement near the trees had caught Evangeline's attention.

"We've got trouble again," said Evangeline, pointing to the woods. Loping toward them as swiftly as a grizzly bear in full stride was Joe Goodson.

"Cursed demon. Qal has not given him up," said Horatius bitterly.

"Maybe he couldn't find a way back," offered Prudence. Both Horatius and Evangeline looked at Prudence, surprised to hear her providing an excuse for why the demon had not obeyed.

"If you want to use that sword again, Evangeline, this might be the time," Horatius said tersely. "Hurry," he added. But Joe, powered by the strength of a demon, quickly reached the shimmering curtain and passed through, right behind Corrie.

"Oh dear," said Prudence. They were not out of trouble yet. Having seen Corrie and Joe (with Qal) passing so easily through the veil, the demons jostled one another to get to the opening first. In another second they would pass through the veil and into the third realm, fully visible to the material world of humans. Evangeline came running, weapon in hand, and swung the flaming Sword of Lemuel in a circle of fire, forming a barrier of holy fire through which the foul, fallen creatures could not pass. Any who tried would suffer the same fate as Vincentiel, incinerating on contact and being transported immediately to the Courts of Justice in the fifth realm to await sentencing.

"Hold the line, Evangeline!" Horatius shouted as the demons protested violently, beating their shields. They attempted to spear Evangeline with long javelins that hummed as they sliced through the air. They were incinerated once they neared the glowing firelight of Lemuel.

Undaunted, Evangeline continued swinging the sword over her head, curls bobbing with every movement.

Why weren't the angels rushing to their aid? Horatius gazed toward the bands of angels but saw that the angel warriors, though filling the

Shamayim, were being held back from the scene. Why? He didn't have time to analyze it. He rushed toward Evangeline to support her lest she drop the sword.

"Prudence, Prudence!" Horatius spoke quickly as Prudence came near. "The gate! I think this may be your moment. Evangeline cannot hold them off forever. You must close the opening between the realms!" Prudence grasped him by the arm.

"Look!" Prudence exclaimed, pointing toward the heavens.

A crackle of electricity suddenly passed through the sky. Its color transformed from the strange, darkly muted, blue-gray hue it had been to a lighter shade of navy blue and then finally to a bright sky blue again. The convergence was ending. The planets were already moving apart in their respective orbits around the blazing sun. The shimmering curtain began to fade as the gap leading to the third realm slowly sealed. At the first sign of the veil thickening once again, Bahadur ordered his warriors out of Gerushah, thus dissolving the terms of the Treaty of Zim and the occupation of Gerushah without so much as a skirmish. The choirs of angels had returned to the higher realms. Even the low, moaning hum of the Crystal River was now at peace. All was quiet except for the roar of the waterfall.

Horatius and Prudence moved quickly to Evangeline's side, assisting her in lowering the sword as the ring of flames dissipated in the atmosphere.

"Whoo! What a thrill!" Evangeline exclaimed as they planted the sword in the ground for the time being. The flames reached up toward Heaven once again.

"I suppose I've fulfilled my task, Horatius," Evangeline said brightly, admiring the sword once again.

"Yes, you held the line brilliantly, Evangeline. Not one demon passed through. Well done, old girl," Horatius said, patting Evangeline on the back. Prudence stood quietly, her eyebrows furrowed in deep concentration. She still had not fulfilled her task. She was staring at the sword when suddenly her countenance brightened and then immediately darkened in a troubling thought.

"What is it, Pru?" Evangeline asked.

"The sword, Evangeline. It's from the Sacred Alcove," she said wide-eyed. "It guards—"

"The gate!" all three exclaimed.

"Oh dear," said Evangeline.

"We must return the sword and seal the gate again at once," said Prudence. "You know the demons won't stay away from here forever, and no one has seen the serpent. He is probably still here, lurking in his castle until the last possible moment.

"Oh, but what about Corrie? That beast followed her home!" Evangeline shouted as loudly as ever.

"She belongs to God now. She is safe," Horatius said assuredly. "She is no longer really within our jurisdiction." he said, though not entirely with conviction. It was true. They had not all three completed their tasks. That much he had just confirmed with a quick glance at the mission scroll, so they were not required to report back yet. They were free to follow Corrie if they chose. "I will look in on her," he agreed after his hasty assessment. It was truly what his heart desired. Prudence and Evangeline agreed.

"And I'll wait to review the mission scroll with you when you have finished. You'll know where to find me," he said, as the three ambassadors parted company. Prudence accompanied Evangeline who carried the sword to the Sacred Alcove. Horatius eagerly departed Gerushah to see what had become of their dear Corrie.

Chapter 28

A Witness

The sky looked different, not as Corrie had seen it passing through the shimmering curtain. The hardened clay of Texas dirt pressed warm against her back. Soft blades of grass tickled behind her knees. The cicadas buzzed overhead, singing their songs of summer.

Where am I? Corrie wondered aloud. And where were Horatius, Prudence, and Evangeline? Corrie snapped out of her reverie and sat up, a little too quickly. The world spun in front of her.

Something stirred in the grass nearby. Corrie's heart jumped when she saw Joe Goodson lying in the dirt not even six feet from her. The concrete drainage ditch behind them, Joe, his friends—Corrie suddenly remembered. But she had crawled *into* the tunnel. Why was she outside it? Why was she even here at all? Corrie looked around for her friends, for the river, for the angels, and—

She reached for the medallion and the diamond, but there was nothing there. *What?* Corrie felt hot tears burning her eyes. *What is going on? And why is* he *here alone, lying in the dirt?* She watched the rise and fall of his back. He was alive. He had moved once, but his skin looked pale behind the shock of hair covering half his face. He had a strange, jagged cut on his wrist surrounded by dark purple bruises.

Corrie remembered the crazed look in his eyes, as if he were not really himself. And she remembered what the river had shown her about him.

Poor Joe, she thought, surprising even herself. She had lost her parents, but they had loved her. Maybe no one had ever loved Joe. Then, from somewhere deep inside, the words bubbled up to the surface. *God loves Joe.*

*   *   *

The curtain between the realms had closed for now, but the Shamayim was alive with activity. The cloud of witnesses that had gathered on and around the canopy still sat recording events that had not ended when Corrie traversed into Gerushah. Time between realms moves at a fluid pace, sometimes rapidly and sometimes not at all.

Angels and demons poured into the district, adding to the numbers of both sides. Horatius, having returned from Gerushah, now sidled up to one of the witnesses standing on the hillside overlooking the scene.

"Why are they still gathered? It's looking like a battle is about to take place again," Horatius remarked, curious why they would still be fighting over Corrie since she had already found the diamond and returned. There was nothing they could do about it.

"They say the child is responsible for their eviction from Gerushah," the witness said. "Even old Lucifer is ousted. I reckon they'll be hungry for land, power, and souls even more now that they have no home. And that one there," he continued, pointing a long finger toward Joe who was being pummeled by a band of demon warriors. "A large warrior left him unoccupied except for the stronghold, and now those demons are fighting for dominion over him. It's ghastly, just ghastly. Help him, oh Lord. Stir your people to pray." The man's voice trailed off in a sigh.

With a hopeful smile, the man turned to Horatius. "Better set your watch there for the big feast. I hear it won't be long. Clock's ticking." The man was a talkative fellow. Horatius usually enjoyed conversation, but he had been away from Home too long. He had absorbed the heaviness of the world and was truly soul-weary.

A cluster of angels with neither sword nor arrows descended through the layers of the Shamayim and stood on the canopy a short distance away.

"Death angels," the man said when he saw that Horatius's gaze had shifted. Horatius nodded. He had watched them complete their errands of mercy many times, delivering weary saints from pain and suffering, and lifting them gently to the Father's arms. Horatius glanced toward Corrie. No, they were not descending on her behalf. She was more alive than she had ever been.

"They say the woman's name is Marian Goodson," the man said with a chipper tone. "Been sick a long, long time. By the way, m' name's Wallace," he said, extending his hand to Horatius.

"Horatius Portuno," Horatius said briskly, shaking the man's hand.

Then Horatius asked quickly, "Marian *who* did you say?"

"Goodson. She has a husband and four sons. The man didn't realize that the young man being tortured by demons was one of the sons he spoke of. Horatius had not the heart to mention it.

As the angels lifted Marian Goodson's now weightless soul and flew swiftly toward Paradise, the witnesses cheered. Marian was going Home. Immediately, as if on cue, the demon army amassed a strike against the angels that were gathered. Lightning flashed, and thunderbolts shook the canopy as angels and demons fought sword against sword.

Suddenly there descended from the Meridiem an angel riding on a white horse. He held a horn to his lips and blew. As the blast of the horn echoed throughout the Shamayim, a legion of warriors in golden armor shining with the light of the sun swooped down and overtook the demon horde until all fighting ceased. Then the angel riding on the horse cried out in a loud voice for every demon to hear, "This province remains in the service of the King. You shall not have ownership or final authority here by the Law of One."

Bahadur, who had been skulking away from the battle, roared in fierce protest. "I have every right to govern here," he bellowed. "There are no more of the King's subjects in this district. It is mine," Bahadur declared.

"That lying serpent," Horatius grumbled under his breath. "He actually thinks he can get away with it. They have reached a new level of evil boldness, lying directly to the King's herald. Corrie is now a subject of the King and a resident of this district." Horatius said quietly, more to himself, "She's right *there*, a child of the King's family. The Law of One still stands."

At that, Wallace glanced surprisingly at Horatius and then shouted loud enough for the whole crowd to hear. "Witness! We have a witness here!" Wallace was pointing at Horatius.

Taken aback, Horatius soon realized the entire cloud of witnesses and angels were staring at him. He had no choice but to speak up.

"It is true!" Horatius proclaimed for the whole assembly to hear. "Today, I witnessed the transfer of rulership of one, Cornelia Rose Callahan, from the authority of Lucifer and the reign of death to the Kingdom of God." Angels nodded and folded their wings in respect. It was the law of the realms that when a human witness was present in the transfer of ownership, it was not proper for angels to provide witness, though many of them had also observed what Horatius had.

"She overcame every obstacle and every attack against her by the blood of the Lamb," Horatius continued, and the assembly of saints and angels cheered anew. He tried to join them in loud celebration, but his tears of joy broke through instead.

"You cannot prove it. You are lying!" Bahadur seethed.

Horatius's mouth gaped in shock at yet another lie, though he knew he should not be surprised. Yet it was partially true. He could not prove it. The medallion and chain, that symbol of faith and hope, and the beautiful crimson diamond, the drop of love itself, was no longer visible around Corrie's neck. They had absorbed into her soul. The merely tangible had become real.

"No, I cannot prove it apart from the Book of Life itself, which I do not hold, but you can see her for yourself. She is right over there," Horatius said, pointing at Corrie.

All eyes turned toward one young girl sitting in the grass. She was watching Joe, for though she could no longer see the demons tormenting him, vying for his soul, she could see the pain on his face. She could hear the groans as he now began to writhe on the ground in anguish.

"Joe? Are you okay?" Corrie asked gently. Joe did not answer but curled up in an agonized ball, hugging his knees with arms covered in cuts and bruises. Corrie moved toward him and laid her hands on his back.

"Joe? Joe! Are you sick? Do you need help?" Corrie asked.

"Get away from me," he rasped. Fear burned in his eyes. Corrie remained close by, undaunted.

"Joe, let me help you," Corrie pleaded.

"No!" he roared. Then his voice was softer as he spoke. "What are you doing? I tried to kill you. I hit you in the head with a rock. You were dead. I saw you. You were dead. Who *are* you? You were dead. You were dead." Joe repeated it over and over, his eyes wide in terror. "Leave me alone!" he roared again. Then he stumbled to his feet and ran into the woods, leaving Corrie sitting alone.

"God *loves* you, Joe!" Corrie called after him.

Horatius smiled broadly. "That's my girl," he whispered quietly and then turned toward Bahadur. "See? What further proof is there of adoption into the King's family than love for one's enemies?" Horatius beamed.

Bahadur did not respond to Horatius, but with a flick of his finger, a platoon of demon warriors circled Corrie and drew their bows. Before the arrows left the strings, however, an entire company of guardian angels surrounded Corrie and absorbed the arrows as they flew. The witnesses cheered as the little girl rose and walked slowly up the hill, flanked by an army of guardians arrayed in dazzling white who then surrounded the house as she opened the door and stepped inside.

Chapter 29

The Genesines

Corrie turned the knob and walked into the house, tentatively at first. She could see Gran at the kitchen sink, her back turned. What had Gran seen when she stared out the window today? Corrie lingered in the foyer, unsure of what to say, though she felt like she ought to say something. She walked quietly into the kitchen.

A puddle of syrup remained on the table from when she had spilled it at breakfast. Gran still wore the same clothes she had been wearing the morning Corrie left. The TV blared in the living room, reporting the day's news. A scrolling banner at the bottom of the screen panned across images of bodies strewn on a tile floor, announcing the latest headlines.

June 16. Earlier today, shoppers gunned down in local mall. Remnant terrorist leader suspect.

June 16th? The day after she had found the medallion? This was crazy! It was still the same day. Could it be within the very same hour? She had traveled a world away, and yet all had remained as if she had never left. Corrie wondered how much time had actually passed. Gran wore the same pale blue housecoat she had been wearing that day. Gran turned to grab a towel to dry her hands when she noticed Corrie standing there.

"Well then," said Gran with her hands on her hips. She looked Corrie over from head to toe. Corrie, too, was wearing the very same clothes she had worn that day. Then Gran's eyes rested on the space just over Corrie's heart where the gold had been. She gave a satisfied nod. "Be sure your chores are done. We'll have lunch in an hour." Gran turned back to the sink.

"Yes, ma'am," Corrie said. She started to leave but then walked quickly over to Gran and kissed her on the cheek. "I missed you," she said quietly and then turned and trotted toward the stairs, passing Will on the way.

"Will," said Corrie, stopping on the first step. "Thanks for being such a great brother," she said, and skipped up the stairs. She could feel their stunned silence behind her as she turned the corner.

As Corrie reached the top of the stairs, she heard a *thump thump thump thump.* Collin was bouncing a tennis ball against his wall. It was how he brooded over things when he was mad. *Oh, this will be hard.* Corrie sighed. She didn't know what to say. She knew she had hurt Collin deeply. She tapped lightly on the door.

"Go away," Collin grunted.

How does he know it's me? Of course he knows it's me because I'm always apologizing for letting him down. Well, this time, I'm not apologizing. Corrie took a deep breath and opened the door enough to stick her head in.

"I'll take your punishment, Collin. It's not right for Gran to punish you. You were only trying to do what was right," Corrie said. Collin stopped bouncing the tennis ball and sat glumly, looking at the floor. Had he heard her? Corrie waited.

"It's okay, Corrie," Collin replied quietly with a heavy sigh. "You don't have to do that." Corrie knew his tone of resignation. He didn't believe her. She had never given him any reason to think she would actually do such a thing as take his punishment.

"Corrie, that means you're grounded. *All* summer," he said rolling his eyes up at her.

"I know that. Don't worry. It'll be okay," said Corrie more firmly. "Collin, I want to," she said when he started to protest again. "I'll tell Gran the whole story," she replied, and she meant it.

Collin stared at her as if a frog had just jumped out of her mouth. Corrie smiled. As she closed the door, he was still staring in disbelief, and

Corrie chuckled all the way to her room. She shut her door quietly and fell across her bed.

Nothing had changed, and yet *everything* had, Corrie marveled. According to Joe, she had died there in the dirt. She had never entered the tunnel, and yet she knew without a doubt that she had crawled through a dirty concrete pipe, nearly drowned in a river, run for her life through the woods after being kidnapped, met three friends who showed her the way to a valuable diamond—no, they showed her the way to life. Perhaps it had only been a dream, and yet it had been much too real. She could more easily believe that she had died and left her body than that she had dreamed it all. Maybe she really had died and then come back to life—*new* life.

The shadows of the oak leaves danced merrily on the wall, spinning their familiar pirouettes in the afternoon breeze. Corrie leaned back on her elbows and stretched her legs out toward the bookcase. Papaw had made it for her, to put in her room when she moved in. How she missed him and wished she could talk to him about everything that had happened. He would have listened. He never thought anything she said was ridiculous. She knew somehow that if she said it had been real, he would have believed her.

She still had so many questions. How had blood formed a beautiful diamond, and why was that man's blood so valuable—valuable enough to make people well? And all she had to do was take it, nothing more? Horatius, Prudence, and Evangeline had said that *God* had put the diamond there, so who was the man who had died such a horrible death? She didn't even know his name. She believed her friends and all they had told her, but there was just so much she didn't understand.

Corrie wondered what her mother would have said. She had told Corrie to find the truth—well maybe she had, or maybe she hadn't. Corrie believed that what she had found, really, was *love*. Love filled her heart when she took the diamond as if love *was* the diamond, something tangible. If truth was not also a tangible object to be found there in Gerushah, then maybe it had to be a tangible object here. The idea perplexed her.

Corrie yawned and stretched out across the floral bedspread. It had been her mother's when she was Corrie's age. Almost everything in the room had been her mother's. The bookcase was the only new furniture, but even the books had been her mother's. Mama had loved to read. Corrie didn't, not really. She had never even looked through the bookcase. Well, she would sure have a lot of time *all* summer long, she realized.

She tapped a shelf with her big toes. It was thicker than the one above it and held all the heavier volumes of encyclopedias and rare books her mother had kept. She had never noticed that before.

Corrie pressed against the shelf, trying to keep her toes propped on it when she felt part of the shelf give way. *Oh no*, she moaned, sitting up. First, she lost the bike Papaw had given her, and now she broke the bookcase he had built with his own hands. She slid down to the floor to see if she could fix it.

*　*　*

Outside Corrie's window on a branch of the old oak tree sat three old friends, watching the child they had all come to love dearly. Horatius had perched in the tree first and then was joined by Prudence and Evangeline.

"How did it go?" Horatius asked, looking first at Evangeline and then at Prudence.

"Go ahead, Evangeline. I know you want to tell it," Prudence said with a wink.

"Well, okay, if you insist," Evangeline began and then dived eagerly into her tale.

"So, we decided to take one of the warriors with us in case we ran into trouble. Phanuel agreed to come, so we all took off through the woods. We could barely keep up with Phanuel, you know, so he slowed down for us. Then, when we reached the Sacred Alcove, you wouldn't believe what we saw. The gate was wide open!"

"Did someone enter the alcove?" Horatius asked.

"That's what I said," Evangeline continued. "What if a demon had gotten in? Well, when we saw it was open, Phanuel ran ahead of us. He said it was not permitted to gaze into the Sacred Alcove until the appointed hour."

"But then I said—" Prudence started but then was interrupted by Evangeline.

"But then Prudence said, 'But I must complete my task, Phanuel. My task is to close the gate.' And then Phanuel said, 'Then this is the appointed hour *for you*. You may look as you close and lock the gate, but you may never speak of what you see until the appointed hour for all who may eat of the tree of life and take of the leaves for the healing of the nations.' So I stood aside as Prudence closed and locked the gate, and then I set my sword, oh excuse me, *the* sword back in its place." Evangeline concluded and folded her hands in her lap, looking supremely satisfied.

"I believe you were the perfect ambassador for the job, Prudence. Well done," Horatius said, knowing that Prudence could keep a secret for all eternity.

"I closed the gate *very* slowly," Prudence said, grinning sheepishly.

"And it has been quite a mission, hasn't it? Much more than a mission, in fact," said Horatius, his gaze returning to Corrie as she sat on the floor, fiddling with the broken shelf.

"So much more," Evangeline said, smiling as she swung her feet in the air.

Prudence nodded and then pointed to Evangeline's oddly shaped slippers.

"I can't believe you're still wearing those things. What are they, anyway? Banana peels?" Prudence asked.

"Banana *leaves*, Pru. They're really quite comfy," Evangeline said. "And they don't come off when I swing my feet," she giggled, demonstrating the truth of her words as the branch bobbed up and down in the rhythm of her feet.

Horatius and Prudence smiled contentedly at their friend and fellow ambassador.

"And so, a new Age has begun," Horatius mused, "the Age leading to the end. They will see spiritual turbulence like none Earth has ever experienced. The veil between the third and fourth realms will continue thinning. Earth will be filled with not only the presence of mongers but now even warriors, and in greater numbers. Heretofore, they have primarily concentrated their efforts in the fourth and fifth realms in warfare against angels. Now evicted from their dwelling place in Gerushah, they will seek the thinnest places in the veil in order to infiltrate and torment the souls of humans directly and with great fury because the end is near. It will be as the days of Noah. However, rest assured that deliverance will come," Horatius said thoughtfully.

"So bleak!" Evangeline exclaimed. "What does this mean for the remnant? The true remnant?"

"Well now, that is the best part, come to think of it. I'm glad you asked," Horatius replied. "There has been a great stirring, soon to be revealed. It simmers and waits, sheltered in the eaves of the battlements."

"It's true," Prudence agreed. "I heard from Hector, who was on a mission last week, that an awakening has occurred in one of the prisons. Several in the remnant of the faithful were killed following a raid in which copies of the Scriptures were found in their homes. Many of their neighbors who were not even counted among the remnant were also thrown in prison. However, someone was able to smuggle in portions of Genesis, which were then circulated among the prisoners. They were so profoundly affected by the words they read that they began identifying themselves by it. They've come to be known as the Genesines, or so I'm told," Prudence explained.

"Oh dear," said Evangeline. "So they only have Genesis? They don't know how the story ends?"

"Not yet," Horatius said. "Not many copies of the Holy Scriptures remain after the raids and the fires, not many that are whole, anyway. So they wait."

"Yes," Evangeline pondered, but another question soon swelled in her heart, which she could not ignore. "And what of dear Corrie? How will she find a Bible?" Evangeline asked, wondering if they might be part of her continued journey.

"We are but a few lines of a greater story, and we are not its authors. All will be revealed in good time," Horatius replied, tapping the watch that he had stowed once again in his vest pocket.

Evangeline nodded, satisfied for the moment. Horatius had spoken the truth, and she knew it. They turned their attention to Corrie, who was quickly removing books from her bookcase and piling them on the floor.

* * *

Corrie decided to take the whole bottom shelf off rather than try to glue it back together. She was poking a pencil into the gap to pry it loose when the tip of the pencil broke off and stayed in the groove. With both hands, she pushed downward on the lower part. She decided Papaw must have closed this up before the paint had dried because it sure was stuck. She reached around to the back of the shelf and discovered small hinges. She kept working it until finally the lower shelf dropped down to reveal a hidden drawer built right into the bookcase. Inside the drawer was a small, black leather book.

The title of the book was nearly completely rubbed off, but she could still see traces of the words. "Holy Bible," Corrie whispered.

Corrie sat there staring at it. A wave of electricity flowed through her. People were arrested for this book. She should be afraid to have it, she reasoned. She could be put in jail or worse. *The Bible is no doubt a dangerous book*, Horatius had said. But there was something else she could not ignore. Papaw had saved it for her.

Papaw knew the risk, and yet he had hidden it away in Corrie's room. He had been excited to put the bookcase in her room. He had even insisted, despite the fact that the small room was already crowded. Gran had stood by with her arms folded. *Gran didn't know*, Corrie suddenly realized. She would have never allowed it.

Corrie thumbed through the books on the shelf, books she had never paid attention to—*Destiny and the Sword, Courage, The Adventures of Red Fox*. They were all Papaw's favorites, not her mother's, though he had said that Corrie ought to have her mother's old books.

Why me? Corrie thought to herself. Why would he not give the Bible to Collin or Will? She was only eight years old when they moved here. Surely, her older brothers would be the ones to handle something dangerous much better than she could. They were bigger, stronger, and much smarter than she. They would know what to do with it. They always had answers where she only had questions.

The book was heavy for its size. Her fingers trembled as she opened the front cover. She found the beginning of the book, took a deep breath, and began to read out loud.

"In the beginning, God created the heavens and the earth."

*   *   *

Outside the window and beyond the old oak tree came a shout from the saints and angels surrounding the canopy. So loud was the sound that it shook the firmament and the realms beyond. The saints began chanting in unison.

> Forever, oh Lord! Your Word stands firm,
> Your faithfulness through all generations!

They continued for several minutes, over and over, until one by one they began to disperse and slip back through the veil surrounding the higher realms, still shouting as they went. The angels that had gathered soon resumed their previous posts or returned to the fifth realm. When all had settled, Horatius turned to Evangeline with a wide grin as if to say, "I told you so." Evangeline returned the smile, and they all chuckled. Then Horatius unrolled the mission parchment one final time.

"Well, all looks to be complete," he said, scanning the mission scroll. "And I also see that our dear Corrie has a new addition to her wardrobe. Can you see it? There," he said, pointing toward Corrie who was still sitting on the floor, reading the Bible that was open on her lap. Around her waist was an intricately woven belt of metallic fibers inlaid with precious stones.

"You're right, Horatius! The Belt of Truth. And it's a nice one!" Evangeline squealed.

"Too bad she can't see it here in this realm," Prudence mumbled.

"As long as she holds to the truth, it will be there nonetheless," Horatius reminded them. "She cannot see the medallion any longer, either, and yet it is there. *Lavashemeth*," he said, remembering a word he hadn't thought about in a long time.

"Bless you," Evangeline replied.

Confused, Horatius turned to Evangeline. "I didn't sneeze, Evangeline. Have you not heard the term *lavashemeth* before?" Horatius asked.

Evangeline shook her head. "Never," she replied. "What does it mean, Horatius?"

"*Lavashemeth*," Horatius said again, "is a word that does not exist in English but describes perfectly what happened. Although she could no longer see the gold or hold it in her hand, it was there. Like—" Horatius paused, searching for the words to explain it to Evangeline.

"Seeing is believing?" Evangeline asked brightly.

"Not exactly," Horatius responded. "It does not describe becoming merely visible to an individual but rather becoming truly real. Corrie did not need to see the gold anymore. It had all become real for her."

"*Lavashemeth*," Evangeline answered, nodding.

"Yet another mystery," added Prudence.

"Indeed," Horatius agreed, nodding his head.

They sat quietly, contemplating the nature of mysteries when Horatius broke the silence. "Shall we go then?" he asked, turning toward his companions. One final glance at the mission manifest confirmed that the coordinates now read simply, "Home."

"I want to make it back in time for the feast," Evangeline said cheerfully.

"Yes, I'm ready," Prudence agreed.

"Very well. We will sing the hymn and be on our way," said Horatius.

"God bless you, dear little lamb," Evangeline said, gazing at Corrie one last time. Her voice caught in her throat.

"We will see her again, Evangeline. This is only the beginning, not the end," Prudence replied softly, placing a hand on Evangeline's shoulder.

Evangeline nodded in agreement, sniffling loudly. Then together they all slipped through the veil with the chorus of the Ambassador's Hymn echoing in the breeze. The oak tree quivered as they exited the realm and then again was still. Though some perhaps know why it trembled, many never will.

* * *

Such a long book, Corrie observed. She picked up the Bible to see how thick it was and noticed something wedged between the pages. In the section called 1 John, some of the words were underlined.

Dear children, this is the last hour; and as you have heard that the antichrist is coming, even now many antichrists have come. This is how we know it is the last hour.

The words confused Corrie, but she was beginning to get used to that. She had much to learn. The world was not as it had seemed even a few days ago.

Corrie turned her attention to the folded piece of paper tucked between the pages. Her heart skipped a beat as she recognized her mother's familiar handwriting.

1370 Harriet St, Texarkana
Come before winter. Bring this with you.

Chapter 30

Prince of the Power of the Air

The Treaty of Zim was dissolved. The decree had come to pass. One little girl had even compromised an entire province of the seventh region. Using the innocuous and weak was a favorite tactic of the enemy. Lucifer, however, was still the Prince of the Power of the Air. His retaliation would be swift.

His throne, once merely cracked through the center, was now a crumbled pile of debris. Lucifer assumed corporeal form and slithered over the rubble. It would be the last time for a while.

The serpent of old licked the air and detected a scent uncommon to the fourth realm. Blood. He followed the scent to the catacombs. All prisoners, sentries, guards, warriors, and even couriers had vacated the land, but one prisoner had been left in his chains.

"Explain yourself. Why are you still here?" the serpent hissed. His accent was unique, for the serpent spoke the languages of both demon and angel, and all tongues of humankind. He spoke all languages in existence but one.

"I am sent by the King for my master to decide my fate," the unknown demon growled.

Lucifer studied the form, chained and sprawled on the floor of the dark holding cell. He had not the size of a warrior, he was not lithe as the couriers, and no monger could be held by ordinary chains.

"State your rank and your crime," Lucifer demanded. His body was coiled, and his raised head nearly filled the doorway.

"My crime was trespassing and high treason. As for my rank, gardener," the prisoner spat.

"I care not for treason, but for what reason were you trespassing, gardener? And more importantly—" Lucifer paused, uncoiling and slithering into the cell until he had enveloped the prisoner, his head poised to strike. "Why do you smell of human blood?" he asked. His forked tongue flicked rapidly.

"I attempted to seize the Sword of Lemuel, as should have been my right as keeper of this land. The sword rejected my authority and expelled me immediately. I found myself chained in the Meridiem until I was dispatched here," Vincentiel answered sullenly. Sitting up a little taller, he added, "The blood is the child's." He showed the dark stain on his palm. "I offer it to you, my master. I know you are skilled in divining blood."

"You flatter to reduce your punishment," Lucifer mocked, his mouth open wide in a leering smile.

The demon lifted his palm. Lucifer coiled around the extended arm, studied the stain, and slowly passed his forked tongue over the dried blood.

"I have no more use for you," Lucifer blurted, withdrawing through the cell door. "I deliver you to the courts. The Council will decide your fate. I have more important matters to attend to." He slithered down the long corridor toward the antechamber of the throne room.

Alone in his chamber, which was no more than a cave carved from obsidian, Lucifer came to rows of cards on a low table. He stooped down, writhing and curling his head downward. He smeared the blood stain from his tongue onto a square of parchment.

Lucifer surveyed the cards before him, the blood of the generations of humans, traced through the fathers since the dawn of time. He studied the newest card. This one was unique. It had no root of antiquity connecting it to another. There had been one bloodline he had wiped out by his own might, one line that had been absent from his collection—until now.

Leaving the antechamber, he slithered toward the windows overlooking Gerushah. From this post Lucifer had governed the world. Legions had come and gone at his command. His throne had been destroyed, and as he looked upon his territory, the ground beneath his castle began to tremble. Already, the towers and battlements were beginning to crumble.

Lifting his head, Lucifer spoke. "You have done this, Daughter of Eve. Your ancestors presumed upon me in hiding your bloodline, but I know who you are. You cannot hide from me, and this you will soon see," he hissed as quietly as a rustling in the trees.

The serpent shed his skin in one long coil in front of the throne and exhaled into the West Wind, joining it as it passed through Gerushah and onward, out through the only remaining spaces in the Eastern Gate. The time had come.

Epilogue

Qal raced through the Shamayim, leaving Bellam far behind. Bahadur would find him, no doubt, and yet nothing was as it had been. There would be no public humiliation or stripping of his tattoos, for the palace grounds were no longer accessible. The Treaty of Zim had dissolved. The palace itself likely lay in shambles. The general had more important matters to consider than one stray warrior. Qal would take advantage of the heightened chaos.

Qal returned to the sea cave. The waves lapped at the isolated beach. He sat completely alone this time, which pleased him. He opened his fist to examine the evidence of his most recent crime.

He had found the alcove unguarded. The gate yielded to his touch and allowed him entrance. No creature had beheld the mysteries ensconced within its doors since the expulsion. No demon possessed the boldness to penetrate its walls and seize what so innocently waited to be plucked from its boughs—what Qal so brazenly stole.

The human had been so easily manipulated. Qal loathed to release him. He would obey as it served him, but not before he assisted him with one final task. The man took the fruit and ate, and together, human and demon tasted the sweetness of the Tree of Life.

Quickly, with the essence of Eden imbibed, Qal brought the human to a desolate hollow in the darkest depths of the woods in Gerushah and performed the ceremony most vile in all the realms. Qal emerged from his human host with a power flowing through him that the world had not seen since the days of Noah.

*   *   *

Adriel of the Seven Watchers, observing the affairs of every creature under Heaven, witnessing the evil again perpetrated in fair Eden, and knowing what was soon to befall mankind, shouted into the four winds covering *Erets* of the third realm.

"Stand firm, saints! Stand firm! For your redemption draweth nigh!"

About the Author

Jamie Sewell Rodriguez, MA

After chasing degrees and career ambitions, Jamie Sewell Rodriguez settled down to focus on her greatest adventure—homeschooling three young children with Efrain, her college sweetheart and husband of then 15 years. While at the park on a clear, brisk day in 2007, Jamie and her children explored a drainage pipe that seemed to go nowhere—and the idea for Havilah's Gold was born. Thus began Jamie's new journey through years of writing in snippets of time between school hours and dinnertime, drum lessons, piano lessons, karate classes, birthdays, graduations, and weddings—until hobby gave way to calling. Jamie and Efrain live in North Texas near their grown children. They both serve on staff at their local church where they also lead a young adult group. Jamie enjoys good coffee, great books, enough conversation to satisfy a committed introvert, and escaping to the mountains as often as possible.

www.ingramcontent.com/pod-product-compliance
Lightning Source LLC
Chambersburg PA
CBHW051329020726
47501CB00007B/1989